What Should Be Wild

What Should Be Wild

A Novel

JULIA FINE

HARPER

An Imprint of HarperCollins*Publishers*

HarperCollins books may be purchased for educational, business, or sales promotional use. For information, please email the Special Markets Department at SPsales@harpercollins.com.

FIRST EDITION

Designed by Leah Carlson-Stanisic

Illustration by cla78/Shutterstock, Inc.

Library of Congress Cataloging-in-Publication Data has been applied for.

ISBN 978-0-06-268413-4

18 19 20 21 22   LSC   10 9 8 7 6 5 4 3 2 1

Mrs. Lattimore let out a deep rich sigh, laughed her weak indulgent laugh, and said: "My God, I wouldn't be a girl again for a million pounds. My God, to go through all that again, not for a million million."

—Doris Lessing, *The Golden Notebook*

The Blakely Family

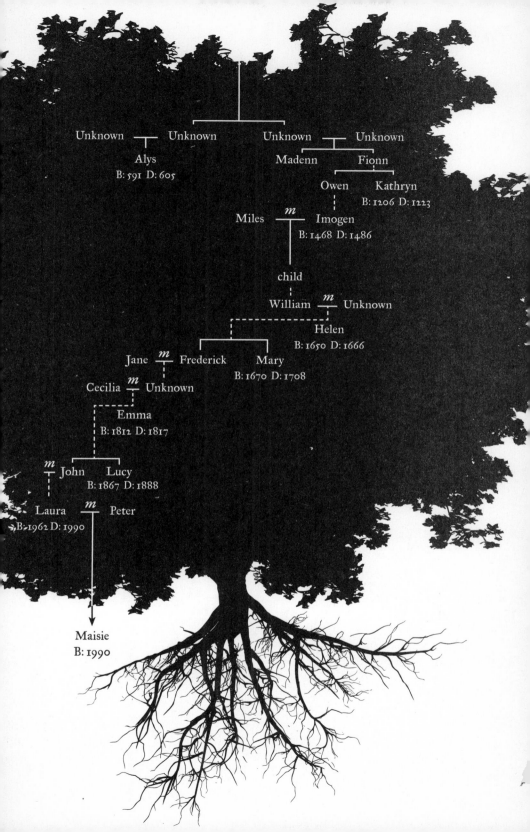

The Weight of Those Who Made Me

Deep in the wood there is a dappled clearing, a quiet, carved space between two hills heavy with trees. A prickling bower joins the fists of land, letting through a single shaft of dusty light. Muffled birdsong can be heard, if you are quiet, carried on the whispering breeze. Old oaks cast heart-deep shadows. Alders bow their branches low.

Naked, but not cold, a young girl lies in a crude wooden casket at the center of the glade. Her eyes are black and blinking. Her glossy hair is wreathed with bone, her small fingers heavy with rings: a wedding band, a tarnished emerald, a dirtied family crest. A promise ring, scratched with the letters *H* and *S*. A brooch of hammered iron. On her wrist, she wears a bit of braided wire. At her throat, a silver necklace, marked with *E*.

She cannot move her slender arms, her legs, cannot twist her neck to see all of the women gathered around her, the women in whose jewels she's been adorned. She senses them, but all she sees is Lucy, bending over her, stroking her hair with sharp fingernails, blue lips forming a kiss.

"Do not be afraid," coos Lucy.

As if the black-eyed girl could know fear.

Part

I

1

They grew me inside of my mother, which was unusual, because she was dead. I developed in a darkness that was not the eager swaddle of her enveloping organs, a heat that was not the heat of her heart-pumped blood. My mother's life burst like a fruit in its fecundity and it was only after, once she was rotted and hollow and still, that I was born.

SHE HAD BEEN keeping me a secret, so you can imagine my father's response when the doctor approached him to discuss the viability of the fetus.

"The fetus?" I can picture Peter in this moment, face rendered expressionless by shock and grief, socks likely sagging and mismatched under his pant legs. He had been jolted out of an idyllic and coddled existence by the sudden collapse of my mother, and it would be years before he truly grasped that fact. "There must be—I'm afraid I don't—"

"It seems strange to even be discussing, given the recentness of your wife's pregnancy, but in this case the circumstances do appear to be . . . miraculous."

"Miraculous," I am told Peter repeated, swaying slightly in the saccharine light of the emergency waiting room. He was steadied by a kindly, gray-haired woman who had witnessed the scene and risen from her hard-backed chair to help him. This was Mrs. Blott. Within thirty-two hours her own husband, one Harold T. Blott, aged sixty-seven, would be pronounced dead from cardiac arrest. Mrs. Blott did not yet know this.

She patted Peter's back and said, "There, there, my dear, it seems you've had a shock," and led him to a vacant chair before turning to address the doctor. "Please continue."

The doctor scratched his temple. Behind him, the hospital doors continued to swing as his colleagues rushed from one patient to the next. Peter could hear the high-pitched beeps of the medical machines and smell the iodine.

"Yes," said the doctor. "Right. Remarkably, the fetus seems so far to be unharmed, despite the cessation of your wife's vital activities. With your approval, we would like to continue to monitor its growth. There is a small chance we can provide the proper nutrients and simulate the role of the mother until the fetus becomes viable outside of the womb."

"Well," said Mrs. Blott, squeezing Peter's shoulder. "Well, isn't that the sun just now coming through the clouds?"

PETER DID NOT know how to be a father to a little girl. He showed up every day of those thirteen months in hospital once I was freed from the corpse of his wife, but when they took me from the incubators, bundled me and placed me in his arms to bring home, he was at a loss. We were lucky to have Mrs. Blott, who by the end of their first meeting had taken a vested interest in our plight, and who would check in on my father to be sure that first he, and then the two of us, were fed and cleaned and rested. Peter was not conventionally handsome, but there was something charming about his unkempt hair, the way his cheeks colored when he was excited. He had a way of blinking his hazel eyes and adjusting his glasses that inspired the women around him to take pity.

I had, for lack of a better term, been born prematurely, and as such there existed an impenetrable medical bubble around me during my first few months of life. The nurses had worn gloves at all times; even the small kisses Peter planted had been through layers of first incubator glass and then waffle-patterned blankets. Afraid their interventions might endanger my fledgling immune system, the doctors took no chances with their miracle, would not have me infected or exposed to human germs. Consequently luck and science conspired to hide my true affliction until I was safely at home. Not until Mrs. Blott laid me on my back to show Peter how to refasten my diaper did it happen: she'd unpinned the one side and was starting on the second when her bare fingers brushed against my thigh. She froze, suddenly, and swayed to the side. I continued gurgling and kicking.

Peter, eager pupil that he was, blinked at us both for a moment before stepping in to catch her. Ignoring the mess I was making as I wiggled my way out of my soiled diaper, he turned Mrs. Blott one way, then the other, pinched her arm, searched for a pulse. When she did not react, he propped her stiffened body against the changing table. A housefly buzzed over me. My father stood, smacked it between his hands, and watched it fall onto my changing pad. My foot brushed against its body. The buzzing resumed.

The nursery was painted pale pink, with little stenciled flowers on the trim up by the ceiling, and must have been a strange place for Peter's first supernatural encounter. This did not faze him. He brought my fluffy teddy, the cream-colored one with the giant red bow that had been a birthday present from the nurses, and touched it lightly against the bare skin of my stomach. Nothing happened. He touched his hand against my layette. He watched the flattened housefly veer across the nursery, searching for a window through which to escape. I could not yet smile, but Peter swore that if I could, I would have beamed at him.

Standing directly behind Mrs. Blott, Peter took hold of her arm at the elbow and stretched it out until the fingers grazed my leg. Immediately she coughed and stepped back, almost tripping over his feet in their fawn-colored slippers.

"Ah," he said.

"What is it?" asked Mrs. Blott, expelling bits of afterlife from her recently roused lungs.

"We'll just be careful not to touch her, then, I think."

And so they were.

*   *   *

STILL, I KILLED my father three times before the age of eight, and caused the demise of over a dozen small animals. We lived at my mother's old family home in the country, far from our nearest human neighbor, but the forest around us was filled with wild beasts. I generally managed to avoid the larger—squirrels, rabbits, deer—yet found no way to spare gnats, midges, or houseflies.

Even the plants could not resist me. This I learned early on, toddling barefooted outside our house, leaving a comet tail of crackling, yellowed grasses where there once had been lush green. Peter, in his odd, dreamy way, simply placed his gloved hand in my chubby one and led me to retrace my steps, watching the color seep back into the landscape.

"It's just that we don't know its full effects, you see," he would say sorrowfully. "In an ideal world, Maisie, my girl, I would encourage you to have your fill of touching. Touch everyone and everything. The skin is a marvelous organ, marvelous indeed. Yet unfortunately, with your condition, I must insist that you refrain. From touching. We just don't know enough, you see."

To his credit, Peter endeavored to know more. He set me up with homeschooling once I'd turned five, and steered me on my own course of studies while continuing with his. I was an early, avid reader. Though I learned little about social interaction, I studied philosophy and history, poetry and science, learned mathematics and the phases of the moon. I especially loved mythology and literature—stories of adventure, tests of fate. From the kitchen where I sat turning pages, I dreamed of one day embarking on an adventure of my own.

While I was immersed in my studies, Peter would write letters and journals and books about my case, none of which led us any closer to my own diagnosis, but did earn him some prestige among his colleagues. He developed a devoted following of those who were hungry to believe—men and women who'd grown tired of the tedium of peer review and soulless academia, who themselves studied parapsychology and extraterrestrials and uncertain religious phenomena. Peter omitted my name in his recountings, referring to me only as "the Child," and rerouted our mail so that the curious could not find us. Yet for one who figured so prominently in such a large branch of Peter's studies, I took a distinctly small role in their direction. It was unheard of to voice my own suggestions, anathema to strike out on my own. He published his ongoing case study under the nom de guerre the Toymaker, a reference to an old fairy tale. I belonged to my father. We were family. All that was mine was also his.

"Are you ready to play?" Peter would ask me, and I, knowing no other sort of group play, would drop my occupation and race up to the old nursery, which since I'd grown out of my cradle had served us as lab. I was to sit very still, to be silent, while Peter took note of our conditions: the hour, the weather, how much I'd slept and what I'd had that day to eat. In his notebook he would draw whatever object was to be that morning's focus, some liminal thing, neither thoroughly alive nor clearly dead: a carved wood figure, a bit of cotton, a glass of juice.

"Very good," he would say with a smile once done with his sketch.

I'd beam back at him, pleased as any other child would be to receive candy, or a gift. Because I was deprived of physical affection, words meant much to me. I could live on a "Well done" from my father for weeks, siphoning the fatty bits of it like a camel drawing food from its hump.

I did not want to sit still, to be studied. I was a little girl constricted, and I wanted to touch everything in sight. There were moments when I thought the utter force of need within me would burst, that my quivering little body would explode, unless I gave in to temptation. Still, I contained myself. I knew that Peter's rules would make me safer. I recognized—from the panic Peter could not conceal when I asked about my history, from the absence of my mother since my birth—that my natural dispositions were dangerous. If I were to indulge myself and run my bare hands over unvarnished hardwood, to sneak up behind my father with my fingers made a mask to hide his eyes, to give a full examination (as Mrs. Blott had once caught me attempting and curtailed) to the warm lips of my pelvis, any number of awful things might happen. There was a badness in my body that had cursed me.

As such, I did not trust my instincts. It was safer to heed Peter. I thought that if I tried very hard to do exactly what he asked of me, my father would forgive me all my failings. I forced myself to sit and smile, and each time I felt an impulse I would fold it in my mind, a sheet of paper that creased easily at first, and then required more muscle as desire took on thicker, complex layers.

THE EXPERIMENTS THEMSELVES were methodical, practical, and conducted only after weeks of theoretical research. Good, scientific experiments, Peter assured me, though I was not the one who needed convincing: despite his best efforts, my father never garnered the respect of the established scientific community. Say our subject was a glass of juice. While I watched, Peter might slice an orange, squeeze it into a cup he had sterilized with alcohol once taken from the kitchen, cover it quickly with a cheesecloth or wax paper so the subject remained pure. A drop of juice might travel into the crook between his thumb and forefinger, and reflexively he would bring the sticky hand to his tongue. He would look at me with a troubled expression, embarrassed at having interfered with our results.

After licking his fingers or coughing (or whatever other action he'd performed that day that could dilute his findings), my father would become very serious, atoning for his lapse in judgment, his misplacement of mind, by being even more exacting.

"Not yet, not yet," he would warn me if I scooted to the edge of my plastic folding chair. "Let me set my watch and then precisely on the hour . . ."

Tempted by the bracing scent of orange, the softness of fleece, my small body would tremble as I resisted the urge to indulge. I'd hold my breath, squeeze my eyes shut.

"Patience," said Peter, "and temperance are a lady's most valuable assets. And you do want to be a lady, Maisie, I know."

He had me there. I very much wanted to be a lady. To be a lady, I imagined, meant welcoming visitors, making trips into the nearby village of Coeurs Crossing, perhaps being courted by gentlemen.

"Now Maisie," Peter would say, finally, "come forward. Dip the tip of your littlest left finger . . . no, my dear, your other left, into the very top of the . . . shallow, very shallow, just a . . . no, no, a lighter touch, a light one, and pull up, up, quickly up, and come and blot against this . . . no, darling, not the paper but the . . . there you are, the towel. Yes. Good."

I'd close the rest of my hand to a fist and stretch out that little finger, inhaling citrus that would not be wiped away. My tongue might dart out, I might lean forward, and Peter would make the sort of sound one makes to a young child, not a true word but an escalating, disapproving vowel. I'd sit back.

"Has the color of the sample changed, my dear?"

Most often it had not.

"Do you feel a slight sensation in your fingertip?"

Never.

"The rest of your body feels well?"

Very well, although once I had the hiccups and Peter spent a long while speculating on their cause.

These experiments were never ambitious. We could have tried to cure diseases, prevent species extinction, combat the injustice of the world. Instead, we practiced small, controlled behaviors, tests whose most unpleasant outcomes had little effect on all parties involved. Occasionally we would see something unexpected: a bit of polished wood would writhe, a seed would shake, try to take root. Peter would watch with wide eyes for a moment, then instruct me: "Be a good girl, now, Maisie. Correct it." And I wanted to be a good girl, so I would.

THERE WAS NO way to correct what I'd done to my mother. This Peter had recognized at once. Beyond the matter of her body's deterioration, which prevented any practical resurrection, her death had been public, headlining the news, putting our small county on the map. Reporters swarmed the hospital after my birth, stalking the doctor who'd delivered me. Religious fanatics declared a second coming, of precisely what they were not certain, but they knew I was divine. Candlelight vigils were held. Sainthood proposed. My admirers wrote numerous notes, all intercepted by Peter. As the years passed, my story would appear in public life in passing, a question of how the baby born from death had fared with chicken pox, how her math skills were progressing, whether she could speak in tongues. They did not know where I'd gone off to, but most respected the decision to hide me. They did not connect the pseudonymous researcher's bizarre account of his young case study's skin condition to that sweet, blanketed babe.

FORTUNATELY, NONE OF the uproar surrounding my nativity was known to me. Despite the demands of the doctors, my father spirited me away as quickly as he could, hiding me from gossip at my mother's family home, a large country estate called Urizon.

The house was set back nicely from the main road, necklaced by a wide front stretch of lawn that led to two cracked red brick pillars flanking a sturdy iron gate, appended by a three-tiered formal garden. Tall hedges grew across the perimeters of the property and presumably at one point they'd been pruned, but as I knew them they were wild, overgrown and prickly, a veritable sleeping beauty's bower. Ivy curled, unfettered, over everything—the stern face of the house, the brick chimneys, the gate.

By the time my parents were married, my mother, Laura, was the last in the family line of once-abundant Blakelys who had made their home at the lip of the wood. Once filled with servants, houseguests, extended relations, in my time it housed only my father and me. We had very few visitors, which I was told had been the case even before I was born.

Urizon's facade was severe—rough stone, spindly turrets, heavy doors, and shut windows—and it had a reputation for tragedy. The estate was over three hundred years old, built at the height of the Blakely fortunes, an attempt to launch the clan into the upper stratum of elite society. Some minor feat of engineering in the mid-seventeenth century, dull to discuss but apparently vital to the direction of the empire, had landed the first in a subsequent series of William Blakelys a windfall. It had to do with waterwheels, ushering in industrialization, the dawn of a new age. I confess I never studied his advances—far more interesting to me was the drama of the domestic: this founding William had failed to cement an important alliance for his daughter, the result of which, it was said, condemned the family to centuries of misfortune and malice.

According to the villagers, ours was a bedeviled family line. Better to be dirt poor and hideously ugly than a Blakely. The house was full of ghosts, claimed some. Cursed, said others. So as not to attract its bad luck, you were best to stay clear. Through the generations Blakelys had supposedly gone missing, suffered falls from great heights, been born with scaly tails or extra fingers. Though none could confirm the veracity of these rumors, which had long plagued Urizon's previous occupants, their existence served Peter and me well, granting the privacy Peter desired.

The main house was large, so we'd closed off all but the areas used regularly, covered furniture with dust sheets, and sealed certain doors. Of Urizon's fifty rooms, we occupied just ten: two bedrooms, the kitchen, a study for Peter, the library, sitting room, nursery turned lab, two full baths and one half. This single wing was easier to maintain, both for Mrs. Blott, who kept the house, and Peter, who protected it from me.

I required a particular environment. To avoid constant disruption, all visible wood had been heavily varnished, plaster applied, carpets laid, tapestries hung. The project of rearranging and inoculating had taken Peter months, but served its purpose. As a child I was little threat to our upkept bit of manor.

Generally I stayed within my boundaries. As a small child I thought these rules would not last very long; initially I thought all children like me. I believed that together we would grow out of the phase in which physical contact was fatal, and into the examples of adulthood all around me. I'd seen Peter shake the hand of our solicitor, Tom Pepper; I'd seen Mrs. Blott check for fever against Peter's flushed cheek. Prior to the awakening that proved my theory false, I obeyed with a sense that mine were common restrictions, a phase to sigh and smile through, my path to human touch. Once I learned that this was not so, that I was alone in my destruction, my obedience was born of my fear.

When the weather was fine, I was usually content to spend my mornings in the kitchen or the library, take lunch out on the terrace, busy myself in the backyard. But on dreary days, or maddeningly hot ones, I grew restless. Then, I did like to explore. Careful to cover myself fully, I would venture into far parts of the house, my anthropologist's eye ready, my historian's hat tied tight. To me, the unadulterated rooms throughout Urizon were a mystery, a menacing, silent shipwreck preserved in the deep. Ancient carvings begged subtle interpretation. Locked chests longed to be picked, stuck drawers shimmied open.

The hallway that circled our dust-laden ballroom was lined with Blakely portraits: very distant relations, their faces very grim. Peter had walked me through the few who he knew: Founding William, of course, taller in paint than he could ever be in life. His wife, pinch-faced, much smaller. The portrait nearest to the east entrance was my great-grandfather's sister, a pretty thing, though very slim and pale, so much that I imagined her tubercular or struck by other illness. She hung next to her brother, my great-grandfather, a bulbous man who seemed much older than she, though it may have been simply that he'd sat down for his portrait some years later. She was Lucy Blakely; he was John. Their lineage was easiest to trace to mine, their images most recent, and they seemed realer to me for it. I sensed a look of longing in Lucy's dark eyes, a dash of devilry in her brother's, that contrasted with the rigidity of their postures.

With them hung Frederick Blakely; several Marys; a man called only General who sat atop his horse; golden-haired Helen, eyes cast downward toward the single white lily in her equally white hands;

Marian, with the name of a woman but the stern stance of a man; a Katherine and an Alice and three other Williams, all rather boring; a little girl called Emma drawn in silhouette; a ragged black dog. Compared to the works of the old masters whose lives I read in our library's art books, and whose images seemed ready to lift off the page and offer a taste of their capon, a feel of their furs, these painted relatives rang hollow. There was a pettiness about them that unnerved me—I could not imagine myself thinking it worthwhile to stand still in these poses for hours for the sake of such hack-handed preservation. I saw these Blakelys all to be inscrutable, whispering about me, judging my behavior as the last of their line.

WHISPERING LOUDER, IF more difficult to understand, was the neighboring forest: a mass of black poplars and conifers and wise old English oaks, yews with trunks like waists of giants, tangles of tree root that twisted together like veins. Trees that to the saplings in the cities were like tigers to a house cat, their breed older, deeper, blessed.

Peter did not like the forest. When I was small he'd had built a shoddy wooden fence to divide the trees from our backyard, fearing I might wander off into the old growth and be lost. That fence stood proudly just a season before weather took its toll, but Peter never did remove it, instead letting the splintered, rotting wood disintegrate back into the line of trees. I could slip through or over it in several places, and though I'd often been told not to leave the yard, I did grow restless. At times I could have sworn the trees were beckoning me. I caught glimpses of a den that had once belonged to foxes, a young tree split by lightning down its center, a poplar overcome by a colony of nests. An entire world, begging to be explored. Were it not for the old stories of villagers gone missing in that forest, stories that magnified the darkness of its depths—were it not for my own darkness, so carefully avoided—I surely would have succumbed sooner.

But I did know the stories. They were part of me. They scared me. This was one:

Many years ago, a woodcutter lived in Coeurs Crossing, the village near Urizon, with his wife, who was pregnant, and their very small son. They were happy together, this family, or so the tale goes—the woodcutter would wake early and kiss his wife goodbye, go off into the forest with his axe and work hard chopping wood through the morning, then return to dine with his family before making his rounds for delivery. People liked him. The family did well. Until one day, having gone off to the forest at his usual time, the woodcutter did not return.

His wife was worried, and when by evening he still had not come, she set off into the wood to go and find him. Someone in Coeurs Crossing reported seeing her tromping through a layer of thin snow, the child toddling behind. A farmer said he called to her from the inside of his barn, as he was brushing down his horses, but she must not have heard him.

She was not seen again.

Her husband, the woodcutter, emerged from the wood before dawn. The same farmer who had watched the wife depart played witness to the husband's return. The woodcutter's face was haggard, all his clothing ripped to shreds, and in his arms he held his little child, whose face was chapped and blue from a night spent in the cold.

The next day, the woodcutter could be found in the village center, babbling on about the trees, swearing that the forest had kept shifting shape around him. No matter how he tried, he said, he could not find his way home; night poured in and icy winds blew, and yet the wood that he had known so well just hours before, the wood he had grown up in, made his livelihood, had changed.

The woodcutter fought valiantly, then at last sank to despair. He gave up all hope of escaping. He lay down on the cold floor of the forest, and he closed his eyes and cried. When he opened them, he said, a path appeared as if from nowhere. He'd followed and it led him to his son, seated shivering in the snow, all alone.

The villagers thought that he was crazy. Some said perhaps the madness had been in him all along, that he'd lured his wife away and then he'd killed her. Others swore that the grief of his loss drove him wild, the disappearance of his lover and with her his unborn child had simply been too much for him to take, his mind had cracked under the pressure. No one could explain where the wife had gone. They never saw a trace of her, nor did the woodcutter recover from this episode. He spent the rest of his days in a garbled, milk-eyed trance, wandering Coeurs Crossing, his beard grown long, his feet unshod, warning its other residents of the terrors of the forest.

I heard this story many times from old Mother Farrow, who lived by the river. I was also told a version by Tom Pepper, our solicitor, and even once a very brief account by Mrs. Blott. I thought it was a wonderful story, mysterious and dark, a good tale to tell when huddled by the fire or when snow fell unexpected late at night. It frightened me, although I did not know if I believed it. The story was too old and deeply rooted to demand my belief; it existed outside acknowledgment, needed no credence, asked for no faith. Its proof was the height and the breadth of that clandestine, hulking forest, lying just beyond my reach.

The Tarnished Emerald

Lucy, 1888

At twenty-one, Lucy Blakely climbed out of her bedroom window, slipped down the siding of that choking house, Urizon, and ran barefoot through the wet grass to the wood.

She had been a sickly child. When she was born—during a late winter snow in the year 1867, her blue veins visible through thin, pale skin—a cousin muttered something to her father about his misfortune at having sired first a veritable demon, then a ghost. Thomas Blakely chuckled, watching through the frosted library window as the governess attempted to prevent his young son John, the demon in discussion, from heaving hard-packed clumps of ice at the gardener.

"She'll be a hale one, old boy, you wait and see," said Thomas.

"She'll have to be," murmured the cousin.

When the doctor was called a week later to examine the newborn, who despite a hearty appetite would not put on weight, he noted that her skin tasted of salt, her bowels moved strangely. He told the Blakelys that they would be lucky to see Lucy through the next six months, at which Lucy's mother, having lost four prior infants, collapsed onto the giltwood settee. Her husband offered a rote hand on her trembling back, whispering a word or two of vague consolation, and then went to confer privately with the doctor. The servants tried to ply the grieving mother with teacakes and clotted cream while young Lucy, oblivious to her declared deficiencies, cooed up at them from her cradle.

Hovering in the doorway, John Blakely saw his sister curl her little fingers, flex her tiny feet. John was seven years Lucy's elder and already pinching servants and smashing priceless antiques. He watched the specialists gather around his sister and heard his mother bemoaning yet another child lost, his father's unfounded reassurances that this one would be different. Eyes slit with envy, John dragged his rocking horse out of the nursery to where the new baby was sleeping, riding the toy animal hard against the floorboards. Later he would plunge the poker into the sitting room fire until it shone orange with heat, reveling in the glow it cast on Lucy, contemplating its power. He waited for his sister's death, the necessary mourning, the attention that would then be redirected to his every whim, as he, the firstborn son, felt he was warranted. But the years stretched on and the little girl grew, each wheeze and cough a call to action, each shiver stymied by a slammed window, new blankets, each breath defying the doctors' expectations, necessitating care.

A queen among her china dolls and pillows, little Lucy lay under the thick canopy of quilts in her vast featherbed, her bedroom fire never quite fulfilling its threat to cross the boundary of the cantilevered hearth. Her semipermanent prostration allowed a view of the wide lawns, the ornate gardens, her brother and his playmates running wild on their holidays from school.

When the weather was just right, when her breathing was stable, Lucy was allowed to leave her bedroom—to socialize in the ballroom or parlor with family or guests, to take in sunshine on the terrace. But if a storm cloud marred the sky, if the sun shone too brightly, if Lucy sniffed or coughed or scratched, she was whisked back up to the bedroom and instructed to be very still, and silent.

Her mother practiced the doctor's early warnings as religion: Lucy was not to overexert herself, not to sit too close to the windows, not to call too loudly for the servants, not to interact with children her own age.

"It's for your health," her mother cautioned. Lucy would smile and nod: *Of course it is, yes, Mother.* And yet what good, she wondered privately, was health, a life extended, if that life was spent beholden to a body that betrayed her? Her mother deemed the library too dusty for her phlegmy lungs, the servants' hands too dirty, even bouquets of flowers too heavy for Lucy's weak limbs to sustain. By the time she'd lived eleven years, Lucy felt she had lived seventy confined to her bedroom, unable to influence even the squeeze of lemon in her tea, the closing of the lush brocade curtains.

WHEN BOTH PARENTS died unexpectedly in a carriage accident the year she turned twelve, it was John, then just twenty, who was named Lucy's guardian. He explicitly forbade Lucy to leave Urizon, a restriction she'd hoped would be lifted at the loss of her mother, who had at least meant well with her insistence on confinement. John's decree was not well meaning. Lucy had contracted a terrible fever the last time she'd ventured into Urizon's garden, and John cited this as impetus for keeping her indoors. The twist of his mouth told her differently. John taught Lucy to be spiteful.

"What would you have me do?" Lucy asked her brother, and in answer she was given books on household management and rules of entertaining, poor substitutes for poetry, cruel in their suggestion that prepubescent Lucy, not the long-tenured, capable housekeeper, would fill her mother's role. Lucy had never been instructed in the usual comportment of young ladies—her mother said such activities were too taxing. And unspoken, but always understood: Lucy would likely never reach the age at which such education would prove useful.

How many years did John expect to be his sister's warden? How long did he think Lucy had to live? She was not sure, but tried her best to please him, as she'd tried to please her parents, the doctors, all who visited the house. John was not impressed with her mastery of table settings, her research on the peerage. Lucy spent more and more of her time in Urizon's library, seeking the knowledge that might justify her middling existence, might prove to her brother her worth.

She sorted through her father's private collection, a varied assortment befitting his lifelong dilettantism, the diversions of a man who had never needed work. Beside the scraped skull of a rodent, Lucy found the work of one Charles Darwin, a manuscript subtitled "The

Preservation of Favoured Races in the Struggle for Life." She took the text out into the front parlor, where John chided her for reading it.

"That book is not meant for women," he said, laughing. "Hard to say who it was meant for, really. Certainly not churchgoers, certainly not anyone who trusts natural theology. Regardless, you won't understand a word."

But Lucy took John's dismissal as a challenge. Lucy read the whole thing through. From the lengthy tracts she came to two firm conclusions. The first: that she herself was an anomaly—if each generation of life was somehow better than the one that came before it, her body must hold some hidden key. She was not pitiful in her long staving-off of sickness but rather the beginning of a new and better breed. A favored race of woman.

The second certainty, a natural extension of the first: whatever child Lucy bore would be magnificent. She imagined a little girl with her own impossible resilience, trapped not in a feeble body but supported by a strong one. She imagined a little girl who'd tell John off, who would not only grasp the complications of new science but propose more of her own. A miracle child, who'd preserve Lucy's legacy far better than the middling portrait that now hung outside the ballroom. The doctors told her that a child was inconceivable—yet they had also claimed she'd never reach age ten. Having conquered one such dire impossibility, surely Lucy could manage to overcome another. There would be a daughter, Lucy was certain. But how, without that first marker of womanhood, menstruation, without access to the world outside Urizon, was Lucy to make her?

AT EIGHTEEN, SHE found her answer in the library, hidden in a far more ancient book. The text was pressed so close against the shelf that a bit of its cover clung to the wood, ripping when Lucy removed it, scarring both book and bastille. At first she understood little of its enigmatic content, a strange series of symbols: a tree drawn out of lines much like Darwin's, with what seemed to be a child emerging from its trunk; an odd series of overlapping arrows; a melting shield; a cross. But Lucy recognized the image of the spiral—a maze to death and back again—and one small, crested bird. Both had been carved crudely onto a stair rail deep within the house. Symbols, the house-maids whispered, of old powers and resurrection. The remnants of the Blakely family curse.

The road to death seemed obvious to Lucy, a constant if meandering journey already begun. But back again . . . For a cloistered young woman long past her predicted expiration, "back again" was a raft to cling to on a sea that threatened to drown her more each day. Understanding the book became Lucy's obsession.

JOHN WATCHED HIS sister study the manuscript, pore over charts and runes, whisper incantations. Lucy had a particular red chaise longue she'd curl up on, accompanied by her favorite of the family hounds. The library fire cast her face in flickering shadow; all was quiet but for its popping, the heavy wheezing of her chest. She had always, John sensed, been angry, but her frustrations had simmered below the surface, directed at her failing body, only an occasional flash of fury in the eyes that suggested her displeasure was with him. Now Lucy seemed finished with hiding, with obedience. More than any new scientific paradigm, this book had changed her.

Imperious, Lucy informed John that she'd no longer be joining him for dinner. She would not perform at the piano, or help the cook map out the menus, would not even change from her thin nightdress into the proper attire in which to greet his guests. She had other matters to attend to, exercises more important than arpeggios, plans more imminent than meals. At first these refusals escaped from Lucy's lips like belches, her eyes wide with her own impertinence, her hand flown up after to cover her mouth. Her brother laughed at her, belittling. When his scorn failed to persuade her, John swore mightily, and threatened to lock Lucy in her room, refuse her dinner. Still, she continued. She would not return to the girl she had been. As Lucy studied her new text, she grew more sure of each decision, more attuned to what she wanted, what she knew. There was a promise in the pages of this ancient tome; a promise, and a secret.

Eventually Lucy opened the French doors that surrounded the ballroom, disregarding the wind's bellow and bite. She knelt amid lit votive candles, arranged in a triangle. Muttered and wailed. Scratched her arms until they bled. Lucy preserved a tooth she'd lost as a child in a small sphere of amber, and held it to the light, humming a low-throated tune.

The servants whispered about her. The postmaster spread gossip. When John hosted a hunting party at the house, the guests remarked upon Lucy, her flights of fancy, her rituals, demands. It was humiliating. They asked John what, in good conscience, he planned to do about his sister. Suggested an institution in the city that was known for resolving just such hysteria, run by revered men of science.

It was the fashion, then, to declare one's woman hysterical. John liked to appear fashionable. He announced his decision once his final guests had left, told Lucy very brusquely over cold sausage and tea that she had one hour to ready her things and settle minor household matters. He went out to smoke a cigar on the back terrace.

Lucy heard the doctors approaching, the horses' whinnies, the patter of the carriage wheels on the drive. She ran upstairs, bolted her bedroom door from the inside, and stepped out onto the roof. Once there she crept across the cupola, the turret a tightrope, shingles scratching her palms. When she jumped she landed strangely on her ankle. From the lawn Lucy could hear the men yelling and pounding, the angry demands that she stop all this silliness and let John and the doctors in at once.

It was quiet for a moment, before they realized she was missing. Then it was chaos. The servants were enlisted to spread out and search the grounds. Lucy remembers John's voice bellowing, the doctors', disguised, calling in deceptive treacle tones. She'd been so young then, cold with fear, struggling to catch her breath. She'd limped through the forest, looking for the proper place to pause in supplication, praying the old stories and her own interpretations of the book's symbols were true. Skittish at the shrill cry of an owl. Shivering.

The last light drained from the low autumn sky.

Now, Lucy pleaded, *now. Now it must happen.*

She heard the heavy steps of one of the city doctors lumbering toward her, wrestling through a thicket. One hundred steps away, then only fifty, twenty-five. Her ankle throbbed. There was nothing else to do. *Now!* Lucy squeezed her eyes shut, and held very still.

The doctor walked past her.

She could smell the whiskey on him, feel the ripple of his body in the air. His overcoat snagged. He swore, turned in place. And as he wandered back in the direction of the house, cursing a wasted evening, Lucy opened her eyes on an entirely different wood. Trees seemed taller. The breeze she felt was warm. Even the birdsong had changed keys into a sharper legato. Lucy raised her arms skyward, letting out a yelp of joy—and found six women, watching her.

For a time, my father, my books, and Mrs. Blott were my only companions. I supposed that other children existed in situations much like mine, and assumed that at a certain age, once we'd all been sufficiently tested and deemed ready, I would meet them. I imagined a kind of cotillion, prepubescents in taffeta dresses and miniature tuxedos parading about the ballroom of a castle, attempting awkward pas de deux. We might discuss the weather, how regal and foolish we felt in our costumes, how thrilling it was to take another child's hand, as the children in the fairy tales we read did so easily. Their hands, I thought, would feel soft, like my bed sheets, the fingernails cold and smooth as metal. Or else we would burn one another with blistering early touches, before our skin cooled to a more comfortable temperature. Perhaps we'd fuse together momentarily, flesh melding into flesh, and come away with peeled pink palms. Then, sufficiently welcomed into the tactile adult world, I believed we'd return to our homes, where the boys would grow up to be Peters, the girls Mrs. Blotts. And so on, forever, as new children blossomed with springtime, as old Mrs. Blotts and Peters returned to the earth with the fall.

The logistics of such ritual did not trouble me. I was eager to be grown, too young to understand much of the world—and by the time I was six the fantasy had shattered. I realized that I was to wear no ball gown; that there would be no ball.

IT HAPPENED LIKE this: I was wandering Urizon's front lawn, dressed in long pants and sleeves, an old pair of gardening gloves fastened at the wrists with twine and a large sun hat tied under my chin. I would have been a sight to anyone unfamiliar with my affliction, and in the mid-May heat I was sweating terribly. Mrs. Blott's initial treatment of my condition involved much what you would expect for someone with extreme sun sensitivity: she'd make me lather myself in lotion and shade all visible parts. Peter would laugh when he saw me done up for the outdoors, but I paid him little mind. I liked to be outside. I enjoyed the vast, untraveled landscape and the lushness of our grasses and the sky's strange sometimes-blue. The sun's caress was warmer than my father's, more direct. The wind was a truer companion than the girls I met in books, who I loved dearly but I knew would never know me. I felt larger out of doors, where my life seemed wider and more meaningful, as if any minute I'd be called upon to fulfill some great destiny, if only I was patient and could learn to bide my time.

On this particular day I had decided to take action against a worrisome patch of ivy that was smothering two great oaks at the front of our property. I was not sure if ivy choking really could kill oak trees, but it troubled me to watch the plant devouring the trunks. I felt that I could not stand idly by and watch them suffer, and thus attempted to remove the climbing vines by attacking each singular root. The work was frustratingly slow. A family of rats had nested in the ground cover, and as I struggled to yank ivy down off one of the oak's branches, I could hear them twittering.

"Quiet, you," I muttered.

The gloves I wore were bulky and prohibitive. I longed to take them off; Mrs. Blott had told me I mustn't.

As I paused to lick a bit of sweat from my upper lip, the squeak of the rats was overwhelmed by a different sort of chatter: high-pitched voices like my own, giggling and singing and calling. I straightened my shoulders, shook a string of ivy off me, and went across the yard to peer around a hedge that hid the main road from my view. We did not have many travelers in our parts, just cars speeding by on their way to the city (a full day's drive away), or the university and its accompanying town (approximately thirty minutes), and the occasional wayward tourist drawn in by the local fables.

It was unusual, then, to see a group I later learned to be the village schoolchildren walk by me, fifteen of them, a teacher as their lead. Peter would not like it. I was about to run back to the house to alert him when I noticed a small, troubling detail: though barely older than I was, the children were all holding hands.

They walked in a line, bodies not quite facing straight, for their arms were stretched forward and back, like elephant's tails clasped by trunks. Little freckly hands touching pale ones, dirtied hands touching clean. I shook off my hat so as to get a better view, and my forehead hit topiary, killing a clump of leaves.

The group was passing so close that were I to reach out, I might touch them. I saw patent leather shoes replaced by sandals, a yellow dress become a tartan skirt, a plain earlobe follow a pierced one. I watched as the owner of the last lobe, the final child in the caravan, let go of his classmate's hand. He turned and looked right at me, gray eyes meeting mine through the shrubbery. He blinked. He was taller than me, and towheaded, his hair curling up around his ears.

"Hello," he said solemnly.

A girl's voice called out, "Mattie!" The little boy was wanted. He nodded at me and ran off to join the rest of his class. I watched him disappear down the road. I bit the twine off my gardening gloves and let them fall from my hands. Returning to the ivy that had given me such trouble, I touched it with a finger and watched dead gray eat its way across the green.

THAT WAS THE last time I wore the gardening gloves. I told Mrs. Blott and Peter that they hurt me, itched my fingers, and made me feel odd. Unsure of how I felt, unable to predict their reactions, I said nothing of the children in the road. Peter took each change in my condition as data, and because I did not generally complain, he and Mrs. Blott let me dispense with the gloves and the hat, sometimes even with the pants, if I preferred tights and was careful. I was still forbidden to fuss with the plant life, but Peter turned a patch of garden at the side of the house into a simple plot of sand where I could sit, barehanded or barefooted, and play without obvious effect.

This act was little consolation. To be given a glimpse of a youth that was not mine had unmoored me; a crack had formed in my formerly smooth world. I grew moody, picked at my food, refused to smile. Having seen myself as one of many, temporarily alone, I'd been excited by my body. That my father was impressed by me—enough to engage in an intense, longitudinal study that mapped my relationship to everything from wooden toys to blueberries—that others were impressed enough to read of what he found, had always been a point of pride. I thought it meant that I was special, better somehow than the other children, who might only be able to sap a flower of its color or curtail a dead tree branch's decay. Now I saw that I was judged not for having risen above the usual mediocre crowd but for having fallen so magnificently short of them. My guardians hid me away not because I was so very clever but because I was tainted, my existence inherently wrong.

Unpacking the logic that had made up my world took me weeks, but once I'd dismantled the old ideas and re-formed them, I was left with a terrible truth: not every child possessed my powers, therefore not all children had sapped their mother's lives while in the womb. Childhood touch was not the silly stuff of fairy tales. I was alone in my deformities, a murderer, a monster.

Peter, pleased with himself for the sandbox, was oblivious to my change in disposition, but Mrs. Blott was not. "Maisie," she said brusquely, "stop this moping about. You've a roof overhead, you have food on your plate. There are those out in the world who have much worse troubles than you."

I nodded, solemn-faced, but made no attempt to move from my place at the kitchen table, where I'd been sitting for hours, staring out the window at our empty, silent drive. I looked down at my hands—the dirt beneath my fingernails, my cuticles chewed pink and pulsing—

and I wished myself outside of them. For the thousandth time that week I shut my eyes and hoped I'd open them inside another body: one that was prettier, cleaner, better.

"She needs company," said Mrs. Blott to Peter that evening. They were in the library without me but had left the door open. If I stood in a particular spot on the main stairs, I could hear everything they said.

"Too dangerous," muttered Peter, "company would not know what to do with her. Nor she with it, I think."

"I understand your worries, I agree, but you cannot raise a child in isolation. As the girl gets older . . ."

Mrs. Blott's voice lowered, and I pressed against the wall to try to make out the rest of her words. A loud floorboard creaked. The library door closed.

As a result of this conversation, it was decided I might go with Mrs. Blott to visit old Mother Farrow, an invalid who lived by the river. With no family to care for the old woman, Mrs. Blott brought her food and company whenever she could. I would be allowed to join her on these visits, so long as I followed Peter's instructions. If ever I did not obey, I'd lose the privilege at once, with no chance of parole.

The instructions were these, typed and printed and hung in a frame in my bedroom:

1. *Under no circumstances will you deliberately touch a living thing.*
2. *Under no circumstances will you deliberately touch a dead thing.*
3. *If a living or a dead thing is touched, you will immediately return it to its natural state.*

"But number three is a circumstance, which means I'd have to break rule number—"

"Maisie," said Peter, "I appreciate your logic. Someday you'll have a fine career in court. But for now, let's keep this simple. Do you understand and agree to these conditions?"

I did.

*   *   *

AND SO AT age seven I met Mother Farrow, who would live to be one hundred, but was then just ninety-six and almost blind. She sat always in her bed, propped up by pillows, so gaunt she looked already like a skeleton, her remaining hair wispy as a child's. She had seven real teeth, and was proud to show them to me, refusing Mrs. Blott's offer to call in the dentist for a new, false set. In place of real feet under her bed sheet, Mother Farrow told me she was rumored to have horse hooves. Mrs. Blott denied the gossip, but I looked once, while she tended to the garden and Mother Farrow dozed, lifting up the heavy blankets at the foot of Mother Farrow's bed to reveal a pair of yellow knit slippers. They seemed the usual shape, but who was to say what was hidden underneath them? I lay the blanket back carefully, content to let the mystery survive.

The very old are like the very sick, the very strange, in how they move about the world, how the world treats them. I sensed in Mother Farrow the same disconnect that I knew in myself, a similar longing to be part of a world that had no place for me, and refused to change its pace to accommodate my particular needs. She'd had a long life, and it seemed that in those final years she feared not death itself but the loss of her accumulated decades of knowledge, which, if unspoken, would wither on the vine. While Mrs. Blott made soup or casserole, swept out the kitchen, changed linens, I'd sit at Mother Farrow's side and listen to her speak.

She told wonderful stories of princesses, and witches, and monsters in the wood. Coeurs Crossing, the village near Urizon, was a haven for stories, and in her girlhood, before the thrills of modern entertainment, there had been little else for Mother Farrow to do once the chores were finished but listen and tell. All her tales were set in our surrounding hills—a young woman lived in our village, a little girl lived in my house. They were the antithesis of Peter's more practical assignments, the dark to logic's light, the remnants, he told me, of a less civilized world. People told stories, he said, to explain natural reactions—the waxing of the moon, an unusual harvest, bizarre psychological behaviors that they witnessed in their peers. These tales, he said, were from an age when people had no understanding of why nature acted in accordance to physical laws. They were pretty explanations, but disproven. They were no longer vital.

A wood witch stole a baby from her cradle, left a changeling in her place.

A young woman magicked herself out of a locked prison and disappeared.

A naughty little girl hurt her mother and was banished to the forest; now her spirit caused mischief through both village and wood.

A mother sacrificed herself for her daughter.

"YOUR MOTHER WAITS for you," Mother Farrow told me once.

Mrs. Blott stood by, holding a cold compress to Mother Farrow's forehead. She looked at me, seated on a stool in the corner, with the expression she used often when we ventured out to care for the old woman. An expression that very clearly told me: *Mind your fantasies.*

"Your mother has been watching you turn into such a pretty little girl," Mother Farrow said. She held her hand out to me, and I stood, ready to go to her, before I was stilled by another telling look from Mrs. Blott. "Mothers are always watching."

Even at eight I had questioned how Mother Farrow, childless for almost a century, might be expert on this topic. Yet since I'd met her she had been a source of wisdom, so I listened. A mother, said old Mother Farrow, at least a mother from Coeurs Crossing, was given ways to watch her children. All because there once had been a troublesome young girl.

This particular girl was especially naughty, eventually jailed for crimes on which, Mrs. Blott interrupted brusquely, they could not elaborate. Her poor mother sat outside her underground cell, without food, without drink, for days on end. She'd hold her hand up to the old stone wall and cry for her child. She'd try to sneak notes to her daughter under the roughly hewn door. The people of the village tried to displace her, for soon her daughter would die, and she should not be afoot when the guards dragged the girl to the pyre. Knowing this, the mother remained at her vigil.

When the men who would burn the foolish child came down to the prison cell, they saw the mother sitting. She faced the wall behind which lay her daughter, forehead pressed to the stones as if in prayer. They unlocked the heavy door.

The girl was gone.

There was no sign of tampering, no way the door could have been forced. The mother, for her part, was too weak to even stand, and it was deemed impossible that she could have stolen the key from the jailers. The only explanation, it was said, was an old sort of magic, the kind that passed between a mother and her child. The mother's longing, her sacrifice, her love, had let the girl escape. From that day on, said Mother Farrow, the women of the village, those who sympathized and all their descendants, possessed a special power over their children. Could watch them through barriers as hefty as stone or as far away as death, and could protect them.

Which meant, of course, my mother might be looking after me.

"Don't believe a word she says," Mrs. Blott told me as we made our way back home. "Don't let her scare you, lead you on. You are doing a kindness to a lonely old woman, and I know you have enough sense to let that be all."

But with Mother Farrow's stories the seed had been planted: an underground hope. Perhaps I was not a strictly Darwinian divergence; perhaps I too was under a spell. Perhaps my mother was not dead, only waiting. Perhaps one day she might come to me and cure me. The possibility of my mother's protection spread its roots in my subconscious, ready for the day it would thrust up above the soil.

TELL A CHILD a tale is not true, give her reason to believe.

No handsome prince awaits you. No godmother hides in the hawthorn. Those stirrings you hear in the forest are foxes and birds, nothing more.

Tell her that after death comes heaven, harpists, bare-bottomed babes with sprouted wings. Show her where her mother has been eaten by the earth, where her ancestors lie buried. Tell her that souls float up around her, as she watches rigor mortis of her own pathetic making cover the body of a loved one with its frost.

Nothing begs question of permanence, of sin, like the power to kill and revive.

Nothing promises revival like a fairy tale.

Very Distant Relations,
Their Faces Very Grim

Across hundreds of years and hundreds of Blakelys, there have been six other women like Lucy, in need of the liminal love of the wood. Lucy looks at the others, that first day. They blink back at her. The usual sounds of the forest—plaintive owls, scuttling wood mice, the papery screech and flutter of young bats—have been usurped by the lullaby of ancient temperate trees, a sentient quiet, a deep and subtle whisper. The gray evening has vanished, replaced by a pale sunlight that gilds each of Lucy's companions. She watches these women, suspicious as they make their salutations—

Mary is the first to step forward. (MARY ELIZABETH BLAKELY, 1670–1708; "Now she rests with the Lord," said her brother, though no body graced the grave.) Over one hundred years before Lucy was born, Mary came to this wood, undesired. Here her hatred has calcified, and the sight of this new, younger sister sends fissures through bone. Mary spits out her name in introduction. Lucy's curling top lip betrays her distaste.

Next, Helen dips an automatic curtsy, her golden hair tangled, her head cocked to one side, eyes bright and bulging as if even in the wood she still must wear the hangman's collar. (HELEN MARIA, 1650–1666, immortalized in oil paint; a memorial to a desecrated daughter.) Lucy nods at her, picturing a particular painted profile hung just outside Urizon's ballroom, the otherworldly whiteness of a clavicle in contrast with the dark frame of the wood. If Lucy's suspicions are correct, if this is truly that same Helen, she is slipperier in person, her cheekbones less prominent, snub nose less deliberate. Her throat is not white, rather puckered pink and rippling, forever displaying fresh scars.

Little Emma toddles over, thumb jammed into her mouth. (EMMA CORDELIA, 1812–1817, "What an odd looking child," "What an ugly little girl.") The large birthmark that mars her left cheek flares even redder when she's frightened. She widens her perpetually crossed eyes. "I'm Emma Blakely," the girl manages through small, sticky fingers. "Welcome to our home." Lucy laughs, both at Emma's odd pretensions, and the confirmation of her own strengthening hunch: this one can only be her father's elder sister, disfigured and disappeared as a young child before he was born, somehow preserved here in the forest. Lucy's heart beats faster with delight, with wonder. What enchantment has she stumbled into?

Red-headed Kathryn cannot stop giggling, a mix of nerves and excitement. (KATHRYN, 1206–1223, her only memorial: "Run!") Kathryn smiles conspiratorially at Lucy, taking and squeezing her hand. "Warmest welcome." She pulls Lucy's arm long as she speaks, examining the lace sleeves of Lucy's nightgown with an undisguised hunger.

Across the clearing, Imogen frowns at them, face solemn. (IMOGEN, 1468–1486, walked into the wood and was not seen again.) "Don't mind her," says Kathryn, grabbing and swinging Lucy's other hand. "She'll only try to set you against us, to make you hate your time here. And there's no use rushing that."

Imogen does not contradict Kathryn. The only mother among them, Imogen carries the weight of her second, unborn child beneath her skirts. Imogen's eyes are filled with unexpected pity. For me? Lucy wonders, and for the first time since encountering these women feels a surge of fear.

The cold intensifies when Alys steps out from between the trees as if from nowhere. (No one left to remember ALYS, 591–605. Alys, the last of her kind.) Alys's teeth are honed to knives. At first glance, Lucy thinks her thirteen, perhaps younger, but her eyes display her true age: round and placid, so dark they almost lack pupils. She says nothing, only watches.

Lucy takes a long breath, banishing her hesitations. She thinks of the book she hid under the floorboard before climbing out her window, the time she has spent praying to unknown old gods, testing her own fantastic assertions, honing ancient desires.

Lucy smiles at these gathered women, straightens like a queen, her head held high. (LUCY MARGARET, 1867–1888, very slim and pale.) She lets Kathryn and Emma regale her with tales of forest animals, long-remembered friends and brothers, while the other four hover nearby, silent. Helen picks butterwort and tries to weave a garland; Mary watches Helen's hands, her own mouth puckering. Alys stands still at the edge of the trees, barely blinking. Imogen wrings out her skirts.

After several hours Lucy pauses Emma mid-description of her favorite dog's best collar. She asks Kathryn what she might do next, where she might go to find shelter. How she can now take action, channel strength from this new wood.

"There is nothing to do," Kathryn tells her with a bitter laugh, brushing her red locks behind one shoulder. "Nowhere to go. Nothing to take from."

"Every so often the wood opens up for travelers," Mary interjects. "You take well enough from them when it does."

"Every so often," repeats Kathryn, sighing. "But it all happens so quickly, and the men who pass through are never quite right. That's why we're so pleased to have you here. Finally someone new. It's been a very long time."

THERE ARE NO seasons in this shadow wood, only the low cradle of midsummer. Mellow, drifting sun. Trees choose their deciduousness, shift as they see fit. Light filters in through bowers, dappling the tangled undergrowth; a stream babbles gently over stones. Compared to where the women have been, it is paradise; still, they miss winter. They remember the dry burn of their cheeks in the cold, plump bursting drops of rain, sharp-scented autumn with its pungent decay. Once inside the wood, these women cannot leave it. Once offered its asylum, they may not again defect. Their years in the forest unwind at both ends, ever-rolling scrolls that conceal both the finish and start. Several weeks, they think, sometimes, several lifetimes.

And what is there to do here, with no fairy feuds to thrill them, no mad kings wandering, no lovers in disguise? The women sit, they weave flower crowns, they dream and remember. They make pets of the immortal squirrels and badgers preserved here beside them, build forts of fallen branches, watch clouds travel the sky. They listen for the outside world, waiting for those rare evenings when men with muddled minds pass briefly by. The women doze in glens and hollows. They sit, unseen, and watch their only entertainment: the evolution of the great house, Urizon. They see its inhabitants come and go. They wonder what it might be like to die.

AFTER THE POWER she's discovered, the promise of her books, Lucy is not content to sit idly by, waiting. Something that had begun to shift within her in those final months at home now undertakes its most permanent migration. Lucy will not be locked away. She will not stoop to pick flowers, chase fauna. Lucy wants to move mountains, raise armies, amass followers, be praised. Above all she wants a daughter to continue her singular evolution.

"Wanting too much will bring you trouble," says Imogen, a hand atop her ever-swollen stomach.

Helen, fingering her raised scar necklace, nods. "Much better not to want at all."

"We live here now," says Mary, chewing a birch twig, her eyes narrow and suspicious. "This is your world." This is their world. So they believe, and so it is, until the day they find the child.

Mrs. Blott had other duties to attend to—cleaning and cooking, helping Peter with his correspondence—and thus we could not visit Mother Farrow as often as I would have liked. I was, of course, forbidden to go see her on my own. Between visits, I would imagine myself part of the tales that she told me, would stand with my eyes squeezed shut at the border between the wood and our garden and whisper a wish for my own witch's familiar, for a friend.

This wish was granted on the morning of my eighth birthday, when I found Marlowe in the wood behind Urizon. He was a puppy then, a fuzzy black cowering little darling, nestled under a downed tree branch, and I heard him before I ever saw him: a high-pitched whimper that I dodged under the foliage at the edge of our backyard to get to, accidentally reviving a rabbit-gnawed shrub. When I finally caught sight of him, soft and downy, his eyes still blue, his coat so crimped he could have been a little lamb, I could not bring myself to leave him. Instead I drew closer. I knew what would happen if I held him. It had happened with Mr. Abbott's lost terrier when it wandered into our yard: the poor stupid little Scottie was terrified, shaking as it flickered between life and death in my arms.

This was on my mind when I saw Marlowe, but as I approached he got excited, wagging his little puppy tail, and it was all that I could do not to trip over myself in the getting to him. I prepared myself to reckon with the guilt I would feel upon reaching him, whether it be shame that I could not provide the warmth his young body desired, or remorse at my lack of restraint. He was so precious, so dear, so clearly starved for a companion—I could not resist kneeling on the undergrowth and offering my hand. I had only just turned eight, after all.

"Hello, pretty puppy," said I, and Marlowe put his soft, wet nose right on me.

I flinched and pulled away, expecting him to stiffen at my touch, but he just reached out his candy-pink tongue and licked my fingers. At this point I let out a whoop of joy and gathered him in my arms, savoring the feel of his beating heart and his warm, breathing body, and raced with him back to the house to show my father.

I remember that first time holding Marlowe as one of the most pleasurable moments of my young life. All humans crave touch, the fundamental feeling that life burns inside another. For me the sustained touch of another living body was like opening a door that had been shut for a very long time, kicking it wide open and letting in the light. It felt like sun against my skin, but better, stronger. If my belief in the old ways and Mother Farrow's stories had been shrouded like her small and slippered feet, discovering Marlowe seemed proof of the hooves' existence. Life was mightier, more beautiful, and kinder than I had ever imagined. I could feel Marlowe's heart pound, the swell of his chest, the shiver of his pleasure as he pressed against my arm. I realized then that the world must be full of things of which I would never conceive unless directly encountered.

Peter was cautious, but could not bring himself to make me cast my new companion out. "Careful now," he said when I held out the puppy, who had fallen asleep in my arms.

"He's unchanged! No need to be careful. Nothing happens when I touch him, absolutely nothing at all!"

Peter's eyes watered behind his glasses. His nose wrinkled and twitched.

"I'll keep him outside," I promised, never intending to do so. "I'll let him live on the back terrace and I'll care for him. You'll never know he's there." I held the puppy up to Peter, in hopes the animal's sweetness might do more to sway him than my own excited face.

Peter sighed, closed his eyes, rubbed their corners. I knew that I had won. We'd keep the dog. We named him Marlowe, and he accompanied me everywhere.

MARLOWE QUICKLY BECAME my dearest confidant and friend. He slept with me at night, sat at my feet while I studied. He would race down the dark hallways at Urizon, chasing after a squirrel or a bird he'd seen through the front window, Mrs. Blott racing after him, scolding him for tracking mud. He came with us to Mother Farrow's, and would sit listening to her stories as if he understood them. He liked to dig in my garden of sand, where sometimes he might bury me a tree branch or a stone.

At age eleven, I was raking in that garden with my fingers when I came across something tender—something soft and squished and feathery. Clearing away the sand, I found interred a common sparrow, clearly meant to be dead, a sizable chunk of its breast torn away by what I guessed were Marlowe's teeth. The bird was shivering and convulsing. It cheeped loudly enough that Marlowe heard it fifty yards away, but its shredded chest did not cleave together. Shocked, I did not think to touch it again, and instead watched it hobble about the yard, finding its bearings, readjusting its idea of itself as alive.

Other than the odd caterpillar or dried snail, I had never before resurrected an obviously dead creature. Foliage, yes, but that was different, more like resuscitation than surgery, simply painting in color to a landscape sadly drained. I had certainly never brought a body back to life and let it linger. Bodies that should not be moving—desiccated bodies, broken bodies—piqued my interest, but frightened me. I would never have intentionally revived one.

The sparrow hopped off the stone barricade at the lowest tier of garden, and headed for the front line of the trees. I reasoned it was best to go after it, and turn the bird back. But despite reason I sat still in the sandbox, listening to its strangled cheeps, staring at the trail of blood it left behind. I knew that I was breaking Peter's third rule—*If a living or a dead thing is touched, you will immediately return it to its natural state*—yet I did nothing. How did the sparrow breathe, I wondered, with its chest so fully open? Could it eat? How long would it survive?

"Poor thing," I said to Marlowe, who had come to sit beside me, showing no apparent guilt at having orchestrated the lurid event. "Perhaps a fox will find it. Or a wolf."

Both aroused and repulsed by my own fascination, I resolved not to tell Peter of my actions. My intentions had been innocent—all I had done was take a handful of sand—but I was nonetheless complicit, my responsibility heightened by the curiosity that had prevented me from reversing course. Flustered, I told Marlowe very firmly that he mustn't play a trick like this again.

Once I could no longer hear the resurrected sparrow, I stood and rolled my shirtsleeves, preparing to go back inside. Mrs. Blott did not like me to track sand through the house, so I sat at the edge of the terrace to brush myself off before I entered. It was there that she found me, shaking grains from my shoes.

She carried a bucket of water and a pole with a rag tied to the top, and I assumed that she had planned to wash the windows. Rather than starting the work, she came and sat down next to me.

"Maisie, girl, we've had some news," Mrs. Blott said. Her eyes were swollen into slits. I was suddenly afraid.

"What?" I asked, thinking of the bird. Had someone found it so quickly in the wood? Did they suspect me? Would I be punished?

"Mother Farrow, as you know," began Mrs. Blott, and I released a ragged breath, "has been ill for a very long time. She's lived a fine life, a long one. We've just had a call from the village telling us that she's passed on."

"Passed on to where?" I said, confused.

"To the next life," said Mrs. Blott.

"Do you mean," I asked slowly, "that Mother Farrow is dead?"

Mrs. Blott nodded, let out a sigh. Had I been a different child, she might have reached out for my hand. Instead, she laced her own fingers together and regarded me with a tender expression.

"I'm very sorry" was all I could say in response. My heart was beating quickly, my cheeks flushed. I bit down on my lip, hoping physical pain would delay my mounting emotional distress. "I really didn't mean to hurt her."

"Why, child, you didn't hurt her. She was sick and very old. It was her time."

I kicked Mrs. Blott's washing bucket, splashing myself with a wave of soapy water, then sat back down and grabbed one of my shoes, smacking it hard against the stone terrace until the final grains of sand flew loose. Though empty, I whacked the shoe again, again, again, then in a fit of frustration hurled it down into the garden.

"Maisie!" said Mrs. Blott, surprised. "You know a lady does not throw shoes." Her words were a reprimand, but her tone was soft. She came closer, put a careful hand on my clothed back.

It was midday, and I could hear the insects buzzing, watched a fat, hairy bumblebee meander toward a single red daylily. The sun was high and bright, but I felt chilled.

"We all pass on, in the end," said Mrs. Blott. "After a long, full life, we all want peace."

I WAS NOT consoled by Mrs. Blott's words. Mother Farrow's death had been an omen, I was certain. Whatever force was watching me was telling me, *Take care.* I knew my guilt, I wore it as my skin. For weeks I could not close my eyes without seeing that sparrow, its guts protruding, its feathers matted with blood. While waiting for sleep I'd be accosted by an image of a horse's legs nailed to a woman's body, Mother Farrow's gruesome feet. I did not think I'd replaced her life with the sparrow's. I knew that the rules were not so simple, the logic not so clean. But I had interfered with something. The bird's new life timed so exactly to the news of Mother Farrow's death was no accident. It could not be. Of this I was certain.

"What you do," Peter had told me, "who you are, goes against nature. You must be vigilant. Be cautious. Take care."

Chastened, I took care for five years straight.

My Shadowed Double

At the start of the first new millennium for all except Alys—although how could they know it? Why would they care?—Lucy spots a sparrow tripping through the forest. The bird's chest is mangled, exposing a sagging crop heavy with predigested food, a tattered purple liver, a pulsating heart. Its gruesomeness fascinates her.

Lucy follows as the sparrow hops a bloody trail; she tracks it over hills, through undergrowth, past groves and under roots, until it leads her to the base of an old oak tree, where a single slender finger rises like a sapling from the dirt, pointing toward the trees above, the sky. Lucy stoops and grasps, expecting some ingredient for enchantment, a dried-up digit, the severed finger of a birth-strangled babe. She is surprised to realize that her discovery has roots. Digging, Lucy finds that it attaches to a hand, the hand to an arm, the arm to a young girl, approximately eleven, pale but miraculously breathing.

"Emma," pants Lucy, "come and help me."

Her young cohort, eternally age five, has followed both Lucy and bird, then tried to hide behind an oak tree. Emma steps cautiously out to where Lucy is kneeling, raking her hands through the soil.

"It's dirty," Emma says through the thumb stuck in her mouth, positioned so that her closed fist nearly covers her large birthmark. Her other hand twists the tarnished locket that she wears around her neck. "Mother said not to get dirty."

Lucy looks Emma over, taking in the ripped tiers of her skirt, her mud-caked hemline, her twig-ravaged sleeves. She resists an exasperated sigh. "Go fetch the others, then," she orders. "Quickly!"

Alone with the buried child—the sparrow having achieved its goal and fallen into a sleep suspiciously like death, Emma off to seek assistance—Lucy looks on her discovery. The girl, as yet, is just a dirty face, a bit of bare chest, an arm and elbow, but Lucy has every reason to believe that the rest of her is there under the clod, equally pale, equally motionless. Lucy is already staking her claim to the girl—to her mind, discovery is tantamount to birthing. But this girl has spent years waiting. She has grown here in the forest's rich earth. Lucy reaches a long-nailed finger toward a cheek, removing an unhappy earthworm, the traces of fungus. The girl's skin is quite cold, but electric.

IS THIS WOODLAND girl alive? The women hear her breathing as they carefully unearth her, the same slow and steady rhythms of the breathing of the trees. A heart is beating. But the eyes remain closed; the body does not twitch.

"Careful not to let her neck drop," instructs Lucy, having stepped back to direct her companions. Kathryn rolls her eyes at Helen, who shrugs and positions her hand at the base of the girl's skull, as if she were a newborn. Alys takes one arm, massaging the small fingers, and Imogen carefully takes the other. Emma wrinkles her nose as she brushes clumps of dirt off the girl's icy body. Mary struggles to lift her unshod feet.

The women set their newfound treasure on a makeshift wooden dais in the center of a glen, position her hands atop her chest, comb out her dark hair. The frozen girl's nose is narrow, her veined eyelids large and far apart, so that once opened they will overcome the rest of her small face, those permanently pursed lips, her high, pronounced cheekbones.

"She looks like my sister Marian," mumbles Emma.

"She looks like an evil spirit." Imogen crosses herself quickly.

"She looks like the girl at Urizon," says Helen. "The girl with the powers. The one that they hide."

4

Mrs. Blott died on a Sunday evening. I was sixteen. She was eighty years of age. Because she never came to us on Mondays (those were her days, and hers alone), it wasn't until Tuesday at approximately ten in the morning that I knocked on the door of Peter's study. He was seated at his massive fir desk, his back curved downward at an uncomfortable angle so that he could examine whatever was laid out before him, a magnifying apparatus strapped over his glasses and extended such that its rotating lenses practically touched the yellowed paper. He was muttering something to himself about inaccurate translations and pigheaded students.

He hadn't heard me. I cleared my throat. When he looked up, the magnifier covering his eyes spun and retracted.

"Maisie," said Peter, "have you come with my tea?"

It was obvious that I was not holding anything remotely tea-like, so I ignored his question and walked a few feet into the room, dodging piles of books and a sad, sticky plate with the remainder of last night's dinner.

"Mrs. Blott hasn't been by yet," I said. "It's three hours after her usual time." I think he blinked at me, but it was difficult to tell behind the goggles.

"Well, then"—Peter stifled a yawn—"might you start the kettle?"

"Yes," I said, "I will. But the point is that I'm worried about her."

"I'm sure you've no cause to be worried," said my father, who rarely was, "but if it makes you feel better, you could pop round. After the tea."

Peter had recently extended me the privilege of walking to Mrs. Blott's house, so long as I took the main road, called ahead to tell her I was coming, avoided conversation if I came across a traveler, and brought Marlowe. It was a gesture of his faith in me. He and Mrs. Blott had taken me on occasional chaperoned outings, to her house, to Mother Farrow's, once a picnic by the sea, but only lately could I set out on my own.

I was not yet a woman, in the scientific sense, and several months prior I had brought this to Peter's attention, having realized that my own biological progression was delayed after finishing a remarkably dry essay on anatomy. Did this mean that I would never be grown, was condemned to always be my father's child? Flustered at first, Peter had rerouted my questioning to a more general discussion of adulthood, and together we'd determined my new boundaries. His was a sort of illusionist's trick, loosening my lead so that I might not notice the bit in my mouth. And it worked; I was elated. I forgot the subtle swelling of my breasts, stopped searching for the blood that would mark me as grown. I ignored the dreams, those scarce remembered snatches, in which my body became liquid with desire.

I brought Peter his tea and bundled into my raincoat and wellies, for it was raining that day, a persistent sort of drool. I called Mrs. Blott's house, and when she did not answer I left a quick message: I was concerned. I'd be there soon. I walked for twenty minutes on the road and rang her buzzer when I got there, my fingers stiff and purplish from the cold. I shook droplets of water off my boots and the hood of my jacket. After a minute, when Mrs. Blott still hadn't come, I rang again.

By this time the foreboding indigestion in my chest had sunk into my stomach. It wasn't like Mrs. Blott to sleep this late into the morning. It wasn't like her to be tardy. I fished in my pocket for her key, a little silver thing that she had given Peter years ago in case of emergency, and that we'd never had cause to use before. It felt strange to be letting myself in. I felt dizzy and intrusive as I twisted the key in the lock and the door opened inward with a pleasant creak.

The house was dark. It was a cottage, really, two levels with five small rooms and uneven flooring. She'd decorated in pastel florals, each room curtained and cushioned in a different muted bloom. It had been sixteen years since her husband passed, but Mrs. Blott had not replaced him, her only companion a mottled brown-and-orange tabby cat named Abingdon, who mewed when I entered and sauntered up to greet me. The entrance was dark. I stepped back.

"Hello?" I whispered. Abingdon hissed at Marlowe, who followed me through the kitchen and up the stairs to Mrs. Blott's bedroom door. "Hello?" It was slightly cracked, and so I pushed it open.

There was Mrs. Blott, slumped in her rocker. Her face had swollen into something alien and doughy. A blanket lay draped across one side of her body, covering one of her legs, but had slipped down to expose her flannel nightgown, her pasty ankle, a bouquet of plump veins curdling up under her skin. Her eyes were still open.

My instinct was to touch her: just the pad of a finger, a gentle stroke upon the cheek. My hand drifted toward her, and I let it linger until the knock of a tree branch against the upstairs window startled me back to my senses. Peter would not like it if I touched her, not without his permission. I'd disobeyed him in the past, but never so directly, never to such momentous effect. I lowered my arm.

Abingdon mewed again, and I jumped to avoid his slinking across me. I realized that his food and water bowls must be empty. I closed Mrs. Blott's door and in the drizzly morning light proceeded down the stairs to feed him. Once Abingdon was gleefully crunching away, I went to the telephone by the window and called my father.

Peter didn't use a mobile phone, having neglected to ever recharge the old model he'd gotten when I was a child, which meant he had to tear himself from his desk and make the walk into the hallway to answer. Not until my third time dialing did he pick up, and then he sounded confused, as if he couldn't fathom why on earth someone should be trying to reach him through such a ridiculous contraption.

"It's me," I said, and his nerves seemed to settle. "I think that Mrs. Blott is dead."

It will seem strange, I'm sure, that I, at sixteen, should speak so nonchalantly. Mrs. Blott was the closest thing I'd had to a mother; her loss would bring repercussions I could not foresee. But I'd grown in death. We were bedfellows, friends. Though I'd not yet called in for collection, I was certain that we owed each other favors.

Surely, I thought, I would revive Mrs. Blott, once Peter came and gave permission. And he would give permission—in that first hour of shock and denial, I could not imagine otherwise. Peter's rules explicitly forbid me from touching a dead *thing*, not a dead *person*. Not someone with a name we knew, a purpose. I had touched her before, as a baby and at seven when I reached to get a toy and brushed her ankle. It did not seem to me that this particular circumstance was any different, that my life would change at all, save the excitements of the day. For all of my informal education, I had lived in an experimental bubble where cause and effect were entirely reversible. Mrs. Blott had always been there, so to me it seemed she always would be.

I HUNG UP the phone to discover Marlowe and Abingdon the cat circling each other warily, sizing each other up. Marlowe was attempting to nuzzle poor Abingdon, who wanted none of it and bared both teeth and claws. I watched them with amused detachment as I waited for Peter, who'd said he would come promptly. I knew that even if he took the car or his bicycle it would still be some time before he'd gathered himself and made it out the door.

My eyes fell on Mrs. Blott's bookshelf. At age twelve I had discovered that by placing a pile of heavy textbooks atop an ottoman in Urizon's library, I could see the books that Peter had deliberately shelved out of my reach, a rather comical selection, including recent children's literature and school stories that might give me too great an understanding of a more conventional childhood. Most were books I had outgrown by the time that I found them, but the right angle and a careful stretch might bring one down, upon which the contraband nature of its content would excite me far more than a tale of young Bill's boarding school days should. Some of them were marked with initials, and I imagined they'd been paged through by my mother. I pictured her as a child, devouring these stories, setting aside her favorites in the hope she'd someday share them with her daughter. I pretended she was reading them aloud to me. But I had never heard her voice, and could not settle on its tone: sometimes I heard her sweet and lilting, sometimes throaty and mysterious. This became yet another reminder of my loss.

I had not inspected Mrs. Blott's library on previous visits, and now that I did I saw that it had little in common with ours. I sidestepped Marlowe and Abingdon to scan it: mostly novels with lovers gazing lustily across their tattered covers, many of which I recognized, having taken them from Mrs. Blott's handbag to read by flashlight under my covers and then guiltily returned, eager to research the difference between viscount and duke, the finer points of male circumcision. Among these familiar titles I now noticed that the lowest shelf held new ones, the novels double-shelved to make room for experimental manifestos, books of mathematical proofs, a massive tome titled *Principles of Genetics*. I looked at these with curiosity. Something was afoot.

Abingdon's purrs revved like an engine, and he padded closer toward the kitchen door, where a key turned in the lock.

Peter, I knew, did not have a key, as our copy sat snug on the key ring in my pocket. I froze, my left hand reaching toward *Principles of Genetics*. I listened as the door squealed open and some heavy bags were dropped. A throat cleared.

"Why hello," a voice said.

I turned around. The voice belonged to a young man, a boy, really, barely older or taller than me. It was a surprisingly deep voice for such a body. It did not match the curling, unkempt hair, the anorak dripping on the carpet, certainly not the puzzled expression wrinkling the ruddy, blond-browed face.

"Hello," I said in turn. "And who are you?"

It happened he was Mrs. Blott's great-nephew.

"Mrs. Blott doesn't have a great-nephew," I told him.

"I regret to inform you, she does, as evidenced by my standing here."

"I regret to inform *you* that even if you are who you claim to be, she doesn't anymore," I said. "Mrs. Blott is dead."

At this the nephew's jaw fell open, so that I could see into the abyss that was his moist and pinkish mouth. His face contorted, first falling slack, then wrinkling and contracting, finally settling on a perplexed, pursed sort of frown. His chin was trembling. Would he cry, I wondered? As a result of what I'd told him? I regretted my rash choice of words, and I decided that I'd better make amends.

"She's upstairs, if you'd like to see her."

My thinking was that I could guide this great-nephew to Mrs. Blott's bedroom. Once there I would casually reach out and touch her hand, to find, in fact, that she was not dead after all, but simply sleeping. What a stupid, scared little girl I had been. I was sorry for the trouble.

I thought myself quite clever.

I said, "I can take you, if you'd like."

"You can take me," the nephew repeated, still stunned. "You can take me up the stairs. Have you called the police?"

"I've spoken with my father."

"And he's called them then, has he?"

"Well, I don't know."

He moved toward the telephone in the kitchen, in his dazed state almost tripping on a hand-woven rug.

"Stop!" I shouted, rather louder than intended. From upstairs, Marlowe heard me and came tapping down to join us, growling at the stranger. He was sluicing something in his mouth, and I was aware that he smelled very much like wet animal. I rooted my fingers in his coat. "Stop," I said again, this time more restrained. "We don't need to call the police. My father is on his way."

"Your father is on his way," the nephew repeated.

"You don't have to keep mimicking me," I said. "In fact, I'd rather that you didn't."

"Would you?" His brows raised. "And who are you?"

"Who am *I*?" The question offended me. "I'm . . ." I paused, suddenly aware that there was no easy way to explain who I was, my relationship to Mrs. Blott, what I was doing in her cottage in the dark on this very wet Tuesday, and why it was vital to not phone the police. I settled on my name. "I'm Maisie Cothay."

"Ah." The nephew nodded. He shrugged off his coat and draped it on a kitchen chair, coming closer to where I was standing. The immediate shock of his great-aunt's death had begun to dissipate, leaving him still solemn, but now competent.

"You know me?"

"From the family she works for. She's mentioned you."

"She doesn't *work* for us," I scoffed. "And she never mentioned you."

Speaking warily, his words seemingly rote, he told me that his mother was the daughter of Mrs. Blott's estranged sister. He had visited her in Coeurs Crossing once when he was small, and then again for a longer stretch of time when he was older. Upon deciding to enroll at the university nearby, it had seemed prudent to avoid the cost of housing on its campus and move in with Mrs. Blott for his first term. He had now been living with her for several happy months and was just returning from a weekend-long trip to the city.

"Matthew Hareven," he said, and he held out his hand. I shied away.

His forthrightness made me uncomfortable. He was the first person near my own age I had ever encountered, and I found it odd that Mrs. Blott had never brought him up. Surely it wouldn't have been difficult for her to slip him into casual conversation, to let me know she had a nephew, to let me know that he was here. And why did he want to stay here with her anyway, so far from his fellow students? I was suspicious. I looked around for Marlowe, to find he'd disappeared back up the stairs.

"So," said Matthew, "Maisie Cothay. What do you intend to do next?" He was looking at me drily. I sensed that he might be having me on, and said as much. "Not in the least," said Matthew, face still drained of color, seeming infinitely more tired than he had in that first moment that we'd met. "If we aren't going to call the police, I'm simply curious as to what you suggest we do next."

I wondered if this was how all young men dealt with death. My instinct told me they did not, that he was different, or that perhaps he'd been prepared. He seemed on the verge of either tears or laughter. That pallor to his face, which I'd assumed was grief, could very well be malice. How would he react to find that Mrs. Blott was not dead, after all?

"We'll go upstairs to see her," I said, my plan of resurrection intact, "but first you will take off those wet shoes. We'll not track mud through her house."

Matthew slipped out of his squelchy brown boots and followed me up the stairs, which creaked under his weight.

When we arrived, the door to Mrs. Blott's bedroom had been pushed fully open. Marlowe sat there at her feet, half covered in her blanket. He was making a sound with his mouth, a wet, sucking sound.

"Marlowe!" I said, and he lifted his head.

Matthew and I looked at him for what felt a long while. Finally Matthew took a slow, unsteady breath, and spoke.

"Your dog is chewing on my aunt."

And he was. Her frail, blue-veined ankle was resting in Marlowe's jaw. He had been sucking, nibbling, gnawing persistently the way he was wont to with a bone. There were tooth marks in her thin, old skin, and in some spots little smears of red. Her calf had turned the angry purple of clotted blood caught in raw meat.

"You bad boy! Get out of here this instant!" I shooed Marlowe away from the rocker and out of the room. He obeyed at once, barely whimpering as he abandoned what had been, to him, a spectacular treat.

It was clear now that I would be unable to attribute Mrs. Blott's unresponsiveness to an unusually heavy sleep. People did not slumber soundly while canines feasted on their ankles. Ankles did not flop down at such inclines once dropped from canines' jaws. Nor did living bodies smell quite so . . . sour.

My head felt light. I grasped for the bedpost to steady myself.

Matthew moved to comfort me, reaching out to rest a hand against my shoulder. I recoiled.

"Don't!"

His eyes narrowed.

"I'm sorry," I cut in before he could speak. "I didn't mean to startle you. I just . . . I just prefer not to be touched."

"Right then," said Matthew, rubbing his eyes as if only just awakened.

At that moment, the doorbell, our savior, sounded noisily. It was Peter. I could see him through the window, standing at the kitchen door, not at all dressed for the weather in his good black shoes and a pair of khaki pants, clinging to his umbrella, which the rising wind swung wildly about.

I took a towel from the closet and went down to let Peter in. Abingdon the cat had gone to cower in a corner, and, not seeing Marlowe, I assumed that he had gone to do the same.

"As you should," I said aloud. "Shame on you."

When I opened the kitchen door, Peter frowned and took the towel from me, wiped the lenses of his glasses, and lifted his head to the ceiling, where the floorboards complained as Matthew headed toward the stairs.

"So, you've got her up again, have you?" Peter said. He wasn't angry with me, merely disappointed. He looked at me as if this was inevitable: that I would rouse her, that I would disregard his explicit instructions—which, in fact, I might have had it not been for the dog. Still I generally listened to my father, and I wanted the credit that such frustrating obedience deserved.

"It's her nephew, actually," I said, pouting.

Peter nodded. "Ah, yes."

"You mean she told you? You mean you knew that he was here?"

"Of course. Why did you think I had you call her before setting out?"

I shot out my breath in a huff. I was flummoxed and unsure of what to say.

Then two things happened in rapid succession.

The first was that Abingdon, sensing my distress, had come to comfort me. Without my noticing he had climbed the kitchen counter, pushing off his back legs to catapult toward me, his front paws brushing against the strip of bare skin above my collar. Even as it happened I berated myself for not being more careful. Abingdon's hair shocked out as though he had been electrified. He stiffened and fell to the floor with a thud.

The second vital thing was that Matthew had made it down the stairs in time to see the whole affair. He looked from Peter to me to the now-still Abingdon, then back at each of us in turn. The lines of his forehead crinkled in concentrated thought.

He turned to me. "Did you just kill that cat?"

"I did not," I said, pursing my mouth into a frown. "He simply fell."

"It certainly looked as if—" While Matthew spoke I crouched down next to Abingdon, causing Peter to cut in and interrupt.

"Maisie, please do not touch that animal."

"I hadn't planned on it!" I snapped, although I did not know if this was true. All I knew was that I had now lost two friends in the course of a few short hours, thus lowering my count by exactly half.

"Cats are meant to land on their feet, though," Matthew continued, standing on the lowest step and speaking toward the ceiling. "A bad jump shouldn't kill a cat."

"Let's leave off the cat for the moment," said Peter, taking off his suit coat and wringing it out with his hands. "How is our good friend Mrs. Blott?" He was leaving a large puddle. I hoped no one would slip.

"Well," I said, sniffing, still squatted down by Abingdon, "Mrs. Blott seems to be deceased."

"Surprising," said Peter, "because she'd seemed in perfect health—"

"There's a reason that it's the cat who is said to have nine lives—"

"—just last Friday when we saw her. I would have guessed that she'd—"

"It is the cat, isn't it, who is said to have—"

"—another several years at least."

Despite the noise, my mind was racing. I'd been lied to—or at least misled—about Matthew. My dog had developed a disposition for the dead. Mrs. Blott and Abingdon had each crossed to a less preferable plane of existence, and I was feeling sick over all of it. I reached down to Abingdon and stroked him deliberately with a finger. He shuddered back to life, yawning and stretching.

"There," I said, "now we've dealt with the cat."

Matthew's voice faded. He swayed a bit, but caught himself on the wooden banister and lowered himself slowly into a seated position on the stairs. He stared at me.

"Maisie," said Peter. "We've discussed this."

"I'm sorry, but things were getting rather overwhelming. It was necessary that someone take control." *Control* was not a word I used with Peter. It felt dangerous and delicious to do so now. I turned to Matthew. "Wouldn't you say?"

Matthew blinked. His mouth moved without emitting sound. He kept jerking his head as if his memory was a magnetic drawing board that given a good shake would be swept clean. He tugged a lock of hair. "If you're asking me," he said finally, slowly, "I don't know that I . . . I wonder . . . Could you show me that again?"

There was a new sort of reverence to him, and I liked it. With the tip of my finger I touched Abingdon's tail. The cat froze, and keeled over.

"Marvelous!" said Matthew.

"Maisie!" said Peter, stepping between me and the now-inert tabby. "You know better. That's enough."

"But you must let me bring him back now," I said. "One last time."

"I am under no such obligation. I think the animal has already been through quite enough." Peter positioned his body to hide the cat from my view. He knelt and placed a firm yet gentle hand on my shirt. "I know it's difficult, darling. But we'll let things rest as nature intended. We are not supreme beings. We mustn't allow ourselves the hubris to think we can bend nature without consequence. We will bury the cat with Mrs. Blott."

Upstairs, Marlowe was whimpering. I felt that I, who rarely cried, might do the same. "You can't bury both of them," I blubbered. "Nature did not intend for us to be so completely *alone*." I saw Peter lift his thumb as if to mitigate my sniffling, then carefully pull back. He dug into his pocket for a handkerchief.

"Darling," he said, holding it out to me.

I bit down on my lip, taking his offering and blowing my nose loudly. I was embarrassed to have made such a display in front of Matthew. I thought that he would see me as a child. But I turned to him to find his eyes sparkling.

"You know," he said, mostly to Peter, who had straightened, "she's right. This trick of hers . . . if this is something she can do, then it can't be unnatural. It necessarily must be as . . . nature intended. At least as much as nature intends anything."

I was crouched, looking at the clean and tiled floor. Matthew and Peter both stood over me, one on either side, each his own colossus of experience and thought. Peter gave me a tender look; Matthew's eyes were sharp.

I felt then that I had two distinct choices. I could lower myself further, let my weight down off my ankles, sit on Mrs. Blott's recently mopped tiles, and let Peter try to comfort me. Or I could rise, push up on the balls of my feet until I'd straightened, lay my hand in blessing over Abingdon, climb up the stairs to revive Mrs. Blott, then step into my wellies and out of the door. I took a deep and careful breath.

As I exhaled, Marlowe came prancing through the kitchen with Mrs. Blott's shinbone in his mouth. His jaws were clamped around her ankle and the rest of it, up where it had once joined to make her knee, was being dragged across the floor, straws that I assumed must be her tendons leaving a slimy red wake to show his path. He made for the kitchen door, the inner part of which Peter had absentmindedly left cracked. Marlowe prodded with his nose, and it swung open.

"How the devil did he detach it from the rest of her?" said Peter.

I watched my dog, tail wagging, disappear into the mist. The trail he left behind him was softened by the rain, but still visible.

I stood, my body burning with a new, frightening decision.

I took my coat from its hanger and slipped my feet into their boots. I looked at Peter, who looked back at me, slightly shocked, and at Matthew, expression inscrutable. I belted my raincoat around me and stepped out the door.

Part

II

The Dark to Logic's Light

In the wood, the years pass like hours, the hours like centuries. Rabbit kits born at the start of long-lost springs maintain their downy ears, pinched noses. Young deer wobble for decades on matchstick legs, baby hedgehogs who have shed first sets of quills do not, for all their effort, grow into the next set. But the frozen girl ages: her breasts bloom, dark hair lengthens, cheekbones sharpen.

What is this girl? All of the Blakely women wonder. Is she a demon, biding her time? Some sort of savior? The dark twin of the girl at Urizon? One of their own, unborn, daughters made flesh? The girl was born within the wood, not taken later, like the rest of them. There is nothing of the outside world upon her. Nothing broken. No scarred flesh.

Helen pays homage to the creature in the clearing, watching as the girl's limbs lengthen, her hair begins to curl, and remembers her own brief pubescence. Helen pines not for her mortal life but for her childhood, lost to her long before she woke in this new wood. Even before the frozen girl's resurrection, Helen was drawn to her double: that child wrapped in coats and layered stockings, locked away at Helen's former home. The living girl, always so dutiful, always tightening the laces at her wrists, adjusting the brim of her hat. Helen has long wanted to run to her and shake her, tell her to cast off her clothing, tell her that once she is a woman all her freedom will be gone.

When the child first removed her gloves, turning green seedlings brown, reviving dead grass with her palms, Helen had stood with the other Blakelys and watched with jealous eyes. "Yes," she whispered, though aware the girl heard nothing. "Take your pleasure while you can." Helen felt compelled to reach out, and tried to take a few steps past the forest, ready to climb the wooden fence and slip into the yard. But even as she did, she was halted by a painful inner wrenching, as if she'd tried and failed to broach the boundaries of her body, as if she'd peeled off her skin. The trees rustled their disapproval. Like all living things, these are protective of their children; like all children, Helen feels the need to stretch her own branches, to grow.

"I heard her speaking with that boy," reported Emma, once Helen's wits had returned, "and now she's stopped wearing the hat. Why did she ever wear it? She has nothing ugly to hide."

Immune to Emma's questioning, Helen did not try to answer. Familiar with Helen's silences, Emma did not force her to respond. Instead, Emma turned to Mary, who has also kept vigil, watching the home that had once been her own.

"Why does she hide there, all covered up, with just that dog for company?" asked Emma.

Mary sucked her teeth, smiled sharply. "They think she's something special," she said, her face tight with disapproval. "But that's a girl like any other. Locked up. Afraid. It's the one in the hollow who will save us, when she wakes. It's the one in the hollow you should praise."

Mary observes both girls, the cursed one and her double in the clearing, as they grow leaner, grow longer. While the Cothay girl throws balls for the strange woodland creature she calls dog to run after, the other lies cold and still, but breathing. When the Cothay girl fiddles with her sandbox and leaves sandwich crusts for squirrels, the other rests, heartbeat steady and slow. The sleeping girl is biding her time. She is waiting. Mary understands waiting. Mary has always found herself waiting, both in past life and in present. The girl is waiting for something, but what, Mary cannot be sure.

* * *

THE FROZEN GIRL'S cheekbones grow hollow, her nipples peak and swell.

Lucy and Kathryn stand by her side, watching. "This girl," Lucy tells Kathryn, "is the height of evolution."

"Of what?" Kathryn giggles at the unfamiliar word.

"She's the fulfillment of a promise, a centuries-old spell of protection. I read of her, of a daughter, a child within a tree. Spirals to death and back again. She is the key."

Early on, back at Urizon, when the doctors saw that her menses did not come, Lucy had been told that a child of her own was impossible, that in her frail condition she could never nourish life. Now she feels the old book has answered her need. That the wood has been a surrogate, absorbing her desires, building from them, crafting her this gift. Lucy is sure the girl will wake soon, and be pliable, an extension of Lucy herself. A daughter: a way out of the forest, a connection to the future, a way back into the world.

"The wood doesn't just give you what you want," warns Kathryn, frowning, twirling a lock of her red hair, eyeing the frozen girl's darkening pubis. "It's not a wood that grants you wishes. If it did, I'd have so many more young men . . . the pretty blond one Helen worshipped, Imogen's husband, that blue-eyed boy with black hair we've seen sneaking around the house . . ." Kathryn sighs, shuddering in her chemise, twisting a stiff nipple with her forefinger and thumb. Kathryn has never wanted children. From a young girl, she has known to tell her partner to withdraw, to keep her body free of seed. She's laughed as she rinsed men's stymied futures from her thighs and her breasts in the stream. She sees the fluids of young men's pleasure as accessories to her own unquenched appetite.

"The wood doesn't care what we want. It doesn't know what it is to be human," says Kathryn, who for years has known gnawing libido, fulfilled only biannually at the high seasons when the forest lets down its guard, lowering its veil to let strangers wander through. Pretty Kathryn, seventeen for over seven hundred years. Kathryn dines on these unwary visitors, teasing them, taking them, leaving them empty, sending them stumbling back to mothers and wives. "The wood has its own plans, its own ideas," says Kathryn. "I hope it uses her as bait to lure in some excitement."

LUCY IGNORES KATHRYN'S warning. She watches the girl's double at Urizon and belittles Peter Cothay's shoddy parenting while praising herself for her own: she uses her skirts to wipe her frozen daughter's brow, detangles the girl's hair with her fingers, sings her lullabies. She asks an offering from each of her sisters, to adorn the child in laudatory jewels. The others are eager to share their remaining worldly treasures, despite differing in their ideas of how such tribute will resolve. All but Imogen.

Imogen, the woodcutter's wife, her stomach still swollen with the child who has been gestating for centuries. Imogen, who will not speak of the loss that she wears as an albatross, that stagnation inside her, the plight of these seven frozen women in physical form, a future with no future at all.

"Do you ever feel it kicking?" Lucy asks her.

Imogen does not respond. Imogen, so pious, still praying to a God the rest have long since abandoned. It takes all of Lucy's cunning, all her coddling and convincing, to get Imogen to part with the wedding ring she'd brought into the wood.

"If the girl is your savior reborn, you would not want her to forget you," Lucy reasons. "You would not want to be the only one left here, while the rest of us ascend to her heaven. You would not want to be alone here, once the rest of us are gone."

Lucy finds her logic sound, and when Imogen concedes, she praises herself. She is too single-minded to realize that Imogen has only given in to stop her prattling, to end an argument that might go on for years if Lucy is not appeased.

No savior of Imogen's would ever need material gifts of splendor.

Imogen believes the frozen girl to be a dark spirit, her captor. The women's faults bound to the forest, the culmination of their long-tainted bloodline, a reminder of their guilt. She could be the original evil incarnate: that first taste of forbidden knowledge, the disobedience that cast her whole kind from the bosom of Eden. Or the girl could be the final punishment, once she has awakened. *You abandoned your purpose as wife and as mother,* Imogen imagines her saying; *with your longing, you have done this to yourself.*

5

It was a thirty-minute walk from Mrs. Blott's house to Urizon, but only half that distance through the wood. That morning I'd thought about shortening my journey by cutting through, and elected against it out of practicality: Peter would be livid, I would certainly be lost. The trees here were tricky, shifting things.

Yet after all that had transpired that afternoon, I no longer cared. I left Mrs. Blott, Matthew, and my father behind and marched into the forest with Marlowe as my guide. He showed no remorse as he trotted along with his usual happy posture, tail upright and swinging. He dodged fallen branches and bulldozed mushroom spores, all the while dragging the shinbone, muddying the tissue at its knee. On occasion, he encountered a stubborn rock or root pile and had to turn back and nudge at the leg with his nose, or prod at it with one of his front paws to help it overcome the obstacle.

I followed a safe distance behind, squeamish at the sight of the limb. I tried to disassociate the object in front of me from the woman who had raised me from an infant, tried to lock up thoughts of her passing in the same way we'd store canned foods in the cellar, or chopped wood in the shed. With every step I tried to crush my grief, my anger. I envisioned the emotions writhing deep within me as a living being half buried, gasping for air as I pressed the heel of my boot to its throat, pushing it deeper.

Thump went the shinbone, over sharp, angled rock face. It should bleed, I thought; why did it not bleed? Upon returning to Urizon I would ask Mrs. Blott about her previous experience with corpses, her hypertension, blood in female bodies. But I could not ask Mrs. Blott. I was dizzy, I was so very tired.

Why could I not ask her? Because Mrs. Blott was old, because she, herself, was tired. Oh, but why hadn't she called me when she felt the end was coming, before she sat down in that rocker, if she'd been so tired, if she'd known? What good was I to her if she chose not to use my only talent? Was she so ready to be rid of me? Was she so frightened, so angry with her lot in later life, that she, like Mother Farrow, like my own mother before her, would rather "pass on"? I was angry with her, suddenly. This old woman who'd pretended to care for me, secretly counting down the days until one of us was gone. She had not told me about her nephew, Matthew. She was the closest thing I would know to a mother, yet it seemed that she had not thought me her family at all.

At first, frustration fueling me, I barreled through the forest. But as the rain softened, so did my resolve, and after some time walking I was calm enough to finally take stock of my surroundings. I was deep inside the forest; I could not see the cottage, Urizon, the road. Here, the birds were mostly quiet, the animals waiting out the weather. The longer and farther we'd traveled, the taller and the thicker the trunks of the trees, the hungrier the moss at their roots. I saw myself quite small amid the vastness.

Marlowe paused to relieve himself, laying the shinbone at my feet. I looked up to try to find the sky through thickly clustered branches, and saw only brief patches of storm-foreboding gray. I could not tell what time it was or how long we'd been walking, and my stomach kept reminding me it needed to be fed.

"I want to go home," I said to Marlowe, who had crept over to nuzzle my knee. "I'm tired. Take me home." In answer, he licked my proffered hand with a sloppy tongue, collected his new toy, and continued, pausing to be sure I was still following behind. I wiped my hand on my skirt.

I felt that Peter must be worried. It would have taken him a moment to recover after I'd left, from my outburst and from Marlowe's odd behavior, but when he realized I had meant it, that I actually had gone, he would be frantic. Peter was frightened of the forest as I'd never known him frightened of anything; he'd spent many years instructing me to be afraid as well. I was trying to distract myself from mounting panic when I tripped over something on the ground—the shinbone.

Marlowe had dropped the limb at the base of an old oak tree, and was digging furiously in the soil at its roots. It was a massive tree, the trunk easily fifty times the circumference of my body, the bark wizened and textured, bulbous with knots. Branches spread above us, wandering so far from their base that were it not for the sturdy junction of append-age to trunk, I might have worried they would tumble down and crush us. I whistled to Marlowe, which normally would have been enough for him to drop what he was doing and heed me, but he paid no mind.

"Marlowe," I said, giving him another whistle and then patting at my knee. Nothing. I could have tried to wrestle the leg from him, but even as I stepped forward, I realized that I didn't have the stomach for it. Marlowe panted through his work, and I suddenly felt I could not take another step, that I could hardly remain standing. I smoothed out my jacket and collapsed next to the oak tree, so tired that I almost touched it in the process.

As Marlowe dragged the shinbone to his newly burrowed hole, I closed my eyes and slept.

MY STOMACH WAS still grumbling, and in a sort of haze I saw myself surrounded by the foodstuffs of the forest, at the head of some glorious table that had sprung from the ground fully formed. In my vision I was feasting on venison by the fistful, eating it raw between handfuls of bright berries while a shy young roe deer looked on. I was at once, in the way that such dreams can happen, both within my body and be-yond it. I could taste the gamy flesh and the tartness of the berries, and simultaneously see myself as if from far away: my eyes shut in ecstasy, the mix of blood and juices a deep red as they roiled past my chin. My hair was darker than I knew it to be, loose and waving, and on my head I wore a crown made of what looked like polished bone. The greens and browns and gray mists of the forest, the starkness of the red on my pale skin, the sense that I was caught in something merciless and wild, sent a chill through me. The other self lowered her hands. She turned to me. Her palms and her face were dirtied with blood; her eyes were closed, her eyelids veined and thin, almost translucent. She opened those eyes with their dark thick lashes, and instead of my own green ones they were deep and endless black, no whites at all, just darkness.

I RECOILED FROM my dream into waking and found myself sprawled on the tree root, my neck and chest sticky with sweat. I wiped crust from the corners of my eyes and spittle from the sides of my mouth. Turning, I found Marlowe covering his prize with soil.

"Are you finished, then?" I asked him, forcing off the unsettling vision. "Let's go back." I vaguely remembered having come through two large spruce trees, and looked around to try to find them.

I blinked. Was I still dreaming? Not only did I not see the spruces, I was clearly not in the same wood in which I had fallen asleep. The trees just in front of me seemed to have doubled in size, and had somehow arranged themselves along a new path. The light had changed from gray to lavender. It was very disconcerting. I looked for the black-eyed girl I'd seen in my dream, thinking perhaps she might be real after all, but she was nowhere to be found.

My hands clenched, reaching for Marlowe: I knew my dog's stance when he was frightened, and was comforted to realize that his breathing was calm. In fact, he seemed almost excited. His tail shot upward and it beat against my knee.

Unlike the muddy mess I'd slogged through earlier, our new route was carpeted in fresh green grass. I crouched down to examine it, and caught a whiff of lushness I associated with the very height of summer—once the plants and trees are fully grown, before the sun has bleached them. One particular blade was so bright a green, so delicate and sweet, I could not help but reach out to it. My fingers hovered so close I thought I felt the pulse of its life, a quick humming vibration animating the air between us. My father's words from hours before returned to me: "We must not have the hubris to think we can bend nature without consequence."

But why should nature constantly bend me? I sucked in a sudden breath, and before I could reason myself out of it, reached down to grab a thick handful of grass.

It remained green.

I gasped, then frowned, disbelieving, and released the clump to twirl a single blade between my fingers. I held it so close that I could feel my own breath warm against my hand. The grass was rubbery, young, not yet hardened into the papery blade it would become. I knew that if I pressed it in my palm it would release its verdant juices and would smear into a fragrant, grassy pulp. It was softer than expected, as smooth as the untraveled skin between my breasts, and I felt the same thrill of connection that I might were a hand to reach out and caress me. My breath grew soft and shallow, my lower pelvis tight. I shuddered, and felt myself opening to experiences I had not yet imagined.

Ahead of me, Marlowe barked, beckoning. Heart full and fearful, I stood up to follow him, sliding the bit of grass into my pocket.

The nascent path wound in a mazelike spiral that seemed to take me deeper toward the heart of the wood. Instead of gnarled branches, the trees here had smooth and stately trunks. I reached out to stroke one, and was pleased to find that my touch had no effect.

After years of tripping over things and taking special care to watch my footfalls, of plastic tarps and varnishes and waves of shame each time I looked down at my body, I had stumbled into a world in which I was welcome. Here it was easy to push past my thoughts of Mrs. Blott, her nephew, my frustrated father and his rules. I touched as many tree trunks as I could, stroking their bark, kissing them. They grew so tall that their leaves hung far above my reach, or else I surely would have touched those too. At one point, overcome, I lay facedown in the grass, inhaling its sweet scent, removing my jacket and spreading my arms, moving them up and down by my sides like a child making an angel in the snow. The blades tickled my bare arms and neck. The

world that I had watched from my window, separated from me by protective glass, became real in those moments; the difference between
reading a story and embarking on adventure, between dreaming a kiss
and receiving one.

Eventually, urged on by Marlowe's whimpering, I stood to follow
him farther. Faint birdsong reached us through the branches. I noticed
a spotted chipmunk dash across my path, a plump pink earthworm
slink over my shoes. Luscious moss blanketed stones, ferns growing
intricately patterned in soft, paler greens beside them. Unlike in the
forest by Urizon, no dead leaves crowded the ground. The air was clear
and sweet and dry; the sun was tender.

Not twenty minutes after we had started down this trail, Marlowe
barked with glee and turned a corner, disappearing from view. I raced
to join him, and to my surprise saw Urizon just ahead of us, marvelous
against the evening sky.

Shifting Galaxies

It has been so long. It has been such a long time. Alys can stand, still and silent, for years, watching the trees sway in the breeze. She can practice the movements—a flick of a wrist, a glyph drawn in the dirt—that bring her closer to her clansmen. Ask the oaks to stop and listen, call the poplars from their clearings, murmur old words that tell even older stories. The twitch of a finger reroutes a vine that has trapped a little wood mouse. A whisper calls forth a limb that holds a nest of owlets: their mouths stretched wide, forever waiting for their mother to return. Alys struggles to remember a life before this forest, cannot remember why she conjured this eternity. She is ready for the life that comes after.

The girl in the bower, the girl with red lips, creamy skin, smooth black curls—the girl who does not shiver in her nakedness, but wears it calmly, proudly. If Alys leans in very close, she can watch the girl's heartbeat flutter behind the supple breast, the dark pink nipple, the row of ribs climbing from waist to sternum. If Alys leans in very close, she can hear the purr of the girl breathing, in and out, out and in. If she holds her hand up to the lips, she can feel the bursts of breath, vital and warm.

The breath stops. The girl coughs.

Alys steps back. Something is coming.

THE OTHER BLAKELY women sense the change—the networks of roots and fungus that keep trees in communion sending messengers: vines tugging their shirtsleeves, paths rerouting at their feet. *Come at once*, the wood says, *something is different*. Eager, the Blakelys arrive.

From close by—could it be coming from within?—a distant, inconsistent shuffling, strewn with labored breathing and occasional canine

grunts, sounds from the foot of the girl's pallet. In front of the women
the dirt swirls without impetus, collapsing in on itself like a home with
a rotting foundation. The child Emma gasps. Imogen reaches for her
hand.

It is a sinkhole, thinks Imogen, an undertow of darkness that has finally come to eat us. She gives Emma's stubby fingers an instinctual pat.

"Where is it all going?" Kathryn asks of the twigs, the unmoored
seedlings, the scurrying wood lice that struggle to escape the deep-
ening hole. Mary kicks Kathryn's ankle with the heel of her boot.
"Ouch!"

"Hush."

An object is appearing, a shape molting out of darkness, shedding
soil. At first Imogen thinks it a leg of mutton, a rotting piece of someone's half-eaten supper. But as it emerges, this odd flower, from the
ground, Imogen sees it is the knee joint of a human: a wrinkled calf,
an engorged ankle, five plump toes. Imogen shudders. Her eyes dart
around the circle to gauge how her companions will respond. Though
they've spent centuries together, they have long behaved as bears, sol-
itary creatures mostly content to roam separate domains. Imogen does
not know their histories, though she assumes all have known some
sort of darkness. Who comes from carnage? Not Kathryn, who hides
her eyes under her palms. Not Mary, who swallows heavily, nor Lucy,
whose pale face tinges green. Not Emma, who cries out again, but this
time finds no comfort. Perhaps Helen, unblinking. Or Alys, who stares
at the shinbone, eternal serenity unwavering.

Swift as it appeared, the shinbone once again is gone, buried under
the dirt that rises fine as sand into their eyes.

"Look," says Emma, moving forward. She takes a step to break the
circle but is brushed aside by Lucy, sweeping ahead, hovering over the
black-eyed girl, whose lids, for the first time, twitch faintly of their own
accord.

The girl's eyes open. They are an inky pitch, an endless dark.

Leaning down toward the black-eyed girl, Lucy tells her, "Do not
be afraid."

6

Moving forward, I frowned at Urizon's silhouette, so abrupt, interrupting the tree line. I looked back to view the path I'd traveled, trying to determine how I'd suddenly found my way home. But though I'd only gone a foot or so since turning that last corner, behind me, the route had quite fully disappeared. My spiral path was gone; the wood was the same unruly wilderness it always had been. When I turned again to observe it from the lawn, it looked as it had looked for all sixteen years of my life.

I squeezed my eyes shut, let them open, but the trick had no effect. There was the knot in the old oak tree where robins made their nests. There was the rotted, peeling fence post, cocked at its odd angle. Everything was as it should be, as it had been when I left.

Was the other wood a dream, I wondered, a delusion? Chilly and damp, I put on my coat and peered through the tangle of trees. Nothing seemed especially unusual. I reached into my pocket for the blade of fresh grass I had hoarded upon its discovery, and understood the extent of my desire only once it emerged, still green, unaltered by my hand.

My forest was real—a shadow forest that existed alongside my everyday wood, intangible and shifting, but always beside me. It had not exiled me entirely. I wanted to return at once, but I supposed that its caution was fitting: I was a foreign body, to be excised until the wood knew more precisely what I was. It had spat me out and then contracted its long tongue, but was not closed to me forever. The blade of grass was proof.

My stomach gave a violent growl. Soon, I promised myself, I would return to decipher the wood's meaning, but for now I was hungry, back at home, shivering. Dry clothes and dinner were my most pressing concerns.

I stepped over the fence onto the Blakely property and climbed the steps to the back terrace, suddenly worried over what I would tell Peter about the day's events. He would be angry, of course, that I'd so obviously disobeyed him, but I hoped that the distraction of my new discovery would save me from a lecture. A lamp was on in his study, and I expected to find him there frowning, muttering, absorbed in the papers he'd been staring at that morning when I'd left. He'd be mourning Mrs. Blott as much as I was, though he likely wouldn't show it. Perhaps I could be of some comfort.

I hung my jacket on a hook in a back closet, where it dripped comfortably onto Peter's boots, and made my way down the dark hallway, rehearsing an explanation of the afternoon inside my head:

I got lost chasing Marlowe.

I must have acted out of shock.

I had a bizarre vision of a girl who looked just like me, picnicking with terrible manners.

The last I spoke aloud as I reached the study door and pushed it open with my shoulder: "I'm very, very sorry, and prepared for any punishment you've . . ."

My eyes took in the window, cracked open, a bit of breeze rustling the pages of a manuscript. The dirty dinner plate, its contents now congealing. The tea gone cold. Peter's binocular contraption zipped into its canvas case, abandoned in his armchair. Peter, himself, nowhere to be found.

"Hello?" I raised my voice so that it echoed through the hallway, into the dark kitchen, the library. I moved through the house, flipping switches to fill sitting rooms with light, one after another. All were empty.

The car was gone from the driveway, and I realized he must still be at Mrs. Blott's house, handling whatever it was that one handled after natural death had occurred. Perhaps he was needed for paperwork, had decided to sit with the body, might have been asked by the nephew to stay. My breath caught a bit at the thought of the two of them together, tending to the joint that had once held the limb now buried by the oak tree. Did they cover Mrs. Blott in her favorite quilt, the blue one with the little white knit flowers? I hoped that they had. Maybe even now Matthew and Peter were digging as Marlowe had dug, forcing their full weight behind their shovels, flicking raindrops from their cheeks, preparing a new home in the ground for what remained of Mrs. Blott. I knew that when I reached the cottage the true loss of her would hit me; the fist of my sore heart would unfurl and stretch its fingers into the empty spaces her passing had left.

I went to our telephone and picked up the receiver, but could not bring myself to dial the number for the cottage. Mrs. Blott could not answer, Peter would surely be confused, and I had no desire to make awkward conversation with Matthew. Still, how could I not be there? I called for Marlowe, retrieved my jacket and a flashlight, grabbed a pastry from the kitchen, and set out.

WE TOOK THE main road, which was well paved and lit sparingly by flickering streetlamps. Through the murmur of a softened rain, I listened for the rumble of a car, a bicycle's sputter, some fellow traveler on the road. Nothing passed us.

The only other life I sensed on our half-hour walk was the forest, dark and whispering beside me. It had always been there beckoning, a regular temptation, but where before the wonder had been one of possibilities—shimmering futures like fish to be caught—the sport had changed so that I was the one being baited. The memory of the shadow self I'd seen was a hook in my heart, the lure lax but set to tighten any moment. The thought that I might suddenly be reeled in without notice frightened me. Even more difficult to parse was the notion that I wanted, even needed, this bond with the forest. I had left some vital part of myself, barely discovered, in the touch of the shadow wood's tree bark, in the depths of my shadow self's eyes. I worried that my feet would redirect me, my subconscious would send me back into the wild before I'd had the chance to talk things through with Peter, or say goodbye to Mrs. Blott. I was relieved to finally reach her cottage, bright and cozy, smoke puffing from its stone-piled chimney with every appearance of normalcy, even if I knew she did not wait for me inside.

I'd left my key when I set out that afternoon, and was thus reduced to knocking like a stranger, covering my fist with my jacket so as not to disturb the wooden door. I scolded myself for forgetting my gloves, which could have allowed me a more meaningful farewell, a stroke of Mrs. Blott's cheek, a clasp of her hand. Perhaps I could find a pair inside.

The wind picked up, pushing off my hood. What could Matthew and Peter be doing? Cold and wet, suddenly quite tired, I pounded again.

"Coming!" came Matthew's muffled voice, along with a squeak I imagined to be a chair across the floor. He opened the door and squinted. "Maisie?" he said.

Matthew's hair was mussed. One cheek was pink, engraved with the pattern of whatever had been pressed against it. He smelled like plain soap and rosemary. He blinked.

"What's the matter?" he asked me, stifling a yawn.

"Have you been sleeping?" I noted the disdain in my voice, but did not try to check it. How could he go to bed a few short hours after finding his aunt lifeless, leave my bumbling father on his own to settle her affairs?

"Stand back and let me in," I said, "it's cold out here, and I need to see Peter at once."

"What?" Matthew cracked his neck, stretching, still sloughing off sleep. I stepped past him into the kitchen. The table held a cup of tea, a ragged notepad, an open textbook with the pages he'd used as a pillow bent down at their corners.

"He's upstairs, yes? With the body? Or have you sent him off into the village?"

"What?" Matthew frowned at me, his nose wrinkled, his hair almost golden in the light of the dying kitchen fire.

"My father. The body," I said slowly. "Mrs. Blott? Your great-aunt? Her leg is gone, but you still have the rest of her. Or did you clean her up, and bury her, and find time for a nap in these three hours I've been gone?"

"What?"

"Oh, don't be useless." I started up the stairs, calling out, "Peter?"

"Maisie," said Matthew.

I paused. The second floor was quiet and dark. When I looked back, I saw that Matthew's face had resolved into a serious expression. I felt a chill incongruous with the toasty cottage, Marlowe sprawled comfortably by the door, the familiar hydrangea pattern of the quilted cotton curtains.

"Maisie," said Matthew, his voice low, "it hasn't been three hours since you left—it's been three days."

The Silver Necklace

Emma, 1817

When Emma Blakely was born, the first thing her mother noticed was the birthmark: a palm-sized patch on the baby's cheek, the angry pink of a fading burn. The accoucheur assured her it was common in infants, though likely a sign that the girl would be wild. Cecilia Blakely was most displeased. Cecilia liked smooth-skinned, quiet children who kept, most days, to the nursery, children who could be paraded in front of her guests and made to perform the songs the governess had taught them in sweet, reedy sopranos; children to be applauded and praised. Children like Emma's older sisters. She did not want a child who would embarrass her through poor performance, poor behavior, or poor looks.

Because the mark was not a danger to the child, the doctors Cecilia consulted all advised she leave it be; any attempt to surgically correct it would result in a scar cruder than the original marking. They said it was merely a sign Cecilia had eaten too many strawberries during pregnancy. The girl would never be a beauty, but she still might have a fine life, develop other skills deemed admirable by a husband.

EMMA LEARNED OF her own ugliness at an early age. Her favorite doll had smooth ivory skin, the rouge marks round on the apple of each cheek.

"Like me," Emma said proudly to her eldest sister, holding up the little figure with its helmet of curls and soft cloth body. She pressed the doll's cool china cheek to her own.

"Not like you," the sister scoffed. "More like Grandmother, or Mother. Your mark is too large, and much too bright. You're ugly."

Emma dropped the doll to the floor, letting it land facedown on the thin nursery carpet.

"Besides," continued that same sister, primly, "yours is only on the one cheek, and it doesn't wipe off. Everyone knows that beautiful women look the same from one side to the other." The sister knelt to retrieve the doll, straightening its petticoats, brushing a bit of dust from its forehead. Emma hoped that its nose might have chipped in the fall; that the rouge of one cheek might sport a fracture. When her sister sat the doll down on a rocking chair, hands crossed demurely over its skirts, Emma saw that its downward plunge had done nothing. The face was still vacant, serene, symmetrical.

Emma was left at the house when her sisters went into the city. She was warned not to stray to the edge of the yard, where passersby might see her. Eventually she was no longer invited to perform for the guests with her sisters, and would sit up in the nursery with the governess when company came, listening to the clinking of silverware, the parade of voices laughing down below.

CECILIA BLAKELY FELT sorry for her youngest daughter. Loved her, in her way. Emma's sister was right: everyone did know that beauty was symmetrical, that symmetry and balance, not just in appearance but in management of household, in marriage, in bearing, was the secret to the gentry's success. Cecilia's youngest had burst from the womb at extreme disadvantage, consequently putting her nearest relations at extreme disadvantage. No one of any worth would want Emma as such, and with so many other daughters to consider, the Blakelys could scarce afford the sort of dowry that might influence a husband. The only solution to Emma was to slice the mark off, but no doctor would attempt it. Lye soap did nothing. Lavender and liniments and laudanum all failed. Cecilia had nightmares of her child grown old, confined to an attic, sold off to the circus. She shuddered when she saw Emma's face in the light.

And so she decided that despite her reservations, despite a firm faith in the ordinary and a lifetime of belittling the silliness of villagers and their myths, she'd venture down from the great house, disguised in her serving maid's shawl, and beg for aid from the wisewoman who lived by the river. It was September, the year 1817.

"Ask the wood," advised the woman. "Draw a circle in the dirt and tell the trees what you desire. Leave the girl there overnight, and they will grant you what you wish."

And so as a last, desperate resort, Cecilia took her little daughter to the forest. She dressed the child in a hooded fur cloak that would cover the birthmark and, said the wisewoman, scare away the wolves. Emma rubbed its plushness against her unmarred cheek. She was used to luxury, having spent her short life at Urizon, but had never felt something quite so sensual, lined in such a lovely, lusty hue.

"Where are we going?" Emma asked her mother, who had paused at the lowest tier of the back garden. Cecilia said nothing. Her mouth had turned lipless. She sniffed.

After a brief journey on an unmarked path, angling around prickly branches and ducking to avoid low-flying birds, Cecilia stopped near a patch of purple hyssop. As instructed, she drew a series of spirals in the dirt, then spread a checkered blanket at their center.

"Sit," she said to Emma, who had never seen her mother even crouch to pluck a flower. Emma was hesitant. "Sit," said Cecilia again. Emma sat.

"You must stay here tonight." Cecilia's voice already sounded far away, though she'd moved only a few feet from her daughter. "I've packed you a basket with supper and snacks. Don't eat too much at once. And don't get dirty."

"What will you eat?" asked Emma. "Won't you stay with me?"

Cecilia ran her tongue over her top set of teeth. "No," she said. "No, you'll be here alone. But this will fix you. When I come for you tomorrow, you'll be beautiful."

Emma nodded. It was early autumn, and her new cloak was warm. The basket was filled with breads and cakes, and Emma nibbled at the edge of a scone while she watched her mother leave. It would be worth a night in the wood, she thought, to be beautiful. To protect herself and her family from the feeling that clotted in her throat when people pointed or laughed. She lifted two fingers to her cheek, feeling for the mark, but without view of her reflection she could not distinguish fair skin from foul.

Emma sang to herself. She ate several biscuits. She watched the sun-cast shadows of leaves stretch their borders and expand with the twilight, until the wood was entirely in shade.

Emma thought it to be long past her bedtime—the air had grown chilly, the sounds of the forest were sharp. Emma shivered. Every crack of a twig, every rustle of leaves, could be a creature about to attack her. The darkness made the stretch of wood seem endless. Emma tried to keep up with her singing, but found her voice thinning and quavering, until her courage failed her and her song fully died out.

"Mother?" Emma whispered. From the edge of her circle came two glowing sets of eyes, four yellow orbs, each with its own black, pin-pricked pupil.

Emma burrowed deeper into her cape, pulled its hood over her head until her face was covered by sanguine silk lining. The newspaper had reported the slaughter of the last wolf in the region just several months prior to her outing. Her father had read the account of its death aloud to the family, applauding the industrious hunters, savoring the gory details. Emma had wondered how they knew that single wolf had been the last one.

The wolves came cautiously closer in slow, languid lopes. Emma could feel the air crackle as they sniffed, could hear the heavy panting of their breath. She hoped the scent of the beast that had first worn the skin now resting on her shoulders remained, deterring them from whatever nastiness awaited little girls in the night wood. That was what Cecilia had promised when presenting Emma with the cape. She said the wisewoman had blessed it. It would keep Emma from harm.

But the wolves were so close that Emma felt the musky heat of them. A tear escaped each of her eyes, wetting the cloak's lining. When she shook the hood away, she saw a black snout stretch across Cecilia's circle of protection.

The wolf licked Emma's cheek with a long, wet tongue, like a cat grooming its young. Emma was frozen, her heart pelting her ribs. Instinctively, she held out a hand, as she would to her own dear pets. The wolf opened its mouth. Spittle hung from sharp teeth. Strong jaws snapped shut.

They closed around the place where Emma's hand had been mere seconds before. The animal took a step forward, onto the blanket where Emma had been seated. The girl was gone. The wolves gathered.

THROUGH THE VEIL of the forest Emma heard them, their howls echoing from far away. She shrugged off her fur-lined cloak, much too warm for the new midsummer climate. She covered her eyes against the sudden burst of light.

I sat at Mrs. Blott's kitchen table, drumming my fingers on a plastic place mat set out to protect me from its wood, while Matthew relayed the events that had transpired, to his knowledge, three days prior.

At first, as I'd predicted, he and Peter had stood dumbstruck as they watched me follow Marlowe into the rain. I imagined Peter watching me go, my green rain jacket receding, hood pulled tight atop my head. I'd been so proud of my defiance. I'd stomped through Mrs. Blott's garden, fraught with the knowledge she'd no longer see it bloom.

"That was the last I saw your father. He said he hoped you had gone home," Matthew told me, "but he seemed pretty nervous. His mouth was sort of . . ." He contorted his own into a perfect mimicry of Peter under pressure, the jaw stretched in an uncomfortable way so that when closed, all of the teeth sat misaligned.

"He kept on saying you'd be at Urizon," Matthew went on. "I told him if you weren't there, to call and let me know."

Peter had nodded again, put on his coat, and set off with an unusual air of dreaminess about him (or so Matthew described it. I told him that Peter often had that air when he had found some pressing problem, as if his mind were miles away from us, his thoughts slow-drifting clouds).

Left alone to deal with Mrs. Blott's body, Matthew had ventured up the stairs to examine the postmortem injury. The amputation, he told me, had been messy, its aftereffects foul.

"When I phoned the police, I pleaded ignorance. Said I thought it was an animal attack, that I'd found the front door open. They came . . . ," he said, and here his voice finally cracked. Again he rubbed at his right eyebrow. "The undertaker came for the body soon after. She was cremated the next day. I buried her cat in the yard."

"And Peter?" I asked.

"I never heard. I assumed you two were safely back at home."

"And we'd made no effort to contact you? We just left Mrs. Blott to . . ." I was unsure of how to finish.

Matthew shrugged, though not unkindly. "Can I get you a drink?" he asked. "Something to eat?"

Any disturbance he felt at my current situation, my father's disappearance, the malleability of time, Matthew hid under that expression of competent concern, much as he had when first confronted with my power. He filled a kettle, fought thrice to light the stove, and opened his aunt's pantry to a wide array of treasures. Realization did not dawn until he'd spread four types of biscuits on a plate, at which point I was pleased to see his steady eyes reveal a hint of panic.

"Can you have . . . ," he started. "Does . . . *all that* . . . happen when you eat? How do you . . ."

My diet was the same as any other, though I used my back molars more consistently than Peter or Mrs. Blott. Peter had always stressed the need for silverware, the import of small bites so that I could avoid my lips. I was adept at wriggling a variety of foods through straws, hinging my jaw to fit full cabbage leaves, and, of course, finding excuses when the meals that I was served weren't to my taste. Mrs. Blott had always managed our cooking. We had more of these same biscuits in the freezer at Urizon. Each bite of her baked goods, I knew, would bring me further from her, as if once I'd eaten the last of her stores she would be gone from me completely. I tried not to dwell on the image of an empty pantry, echoing her empty cottage.

I'd been hungry on arrival, but found my appetite gone.

"If Peter isn't here," I said, ignoring Matthew's half question, "then he must be out looking for me. Unless he's already back home." I stood. "He must be worried. I should go."

"Why don't we call your house?" said Matthew. "See if your father answers?"

I let the phone ring twenty times. We'd disconnected our machine. I remembered the message that I'd left for Mrs. Blott that very morning, so it seemed, letting her know that I'd be by. "I have to go," I said.

"Let me drive you. Just give me five minutes to get ready."

MATTHEW INSISTED ON accompanying me inside Urizon proper. He'd put on a sweatshirt adorned with his college's mascot, a bear, and I followed its scowl through the house as we searched it for Peter. I found myself glad to have him with me to push open wooden doors, remove dust sheets from sculptures, crack dry jokes at portraits; I was amazed by Matthew's ease with the unknown. I would not, until much later, understand the calculation of the comfort he provided, the care with which he examined each possible choice before he acted, the tone of each word before he spoke.

He could tell I was afraid, although I tried hard not to show it. Voice loud, hair curling down onto his collar, the Matthew I met that night was jovial, even funny, doing what he could to abate my fears. Our quest for my father proved more futile with each empty room's alibi, the enormity of my isolation growing larger as the house around me tripled in size.

"You know," Matthew said, an hour in, lifting the key lid of a dust-covered piano to pluck several sour notes, "I once visited the village, as a child. My aunt told me this whole estate was empty. It's weird to be inside after imagining what it would be like for so many years."

We'd unveiled the old music room: a plump, retired cello, a stringless harp, shelves stuffed with pencil-marked sheet music. I lingered in the doorway, watching him sound out the melody of an old children's song.

"You didn't know that we lived here? That Mrs. Blott helped us with the house?"

Matthew shook his head. "Not when I was younger. There were

rumors, of course, but she always denied them. Said I was imagining things when I thought I'd seen a kid here. Back then she said that she cleaned houses around town."

"And now?"

"When I came a few months ago, she admitted she was working for the Cothays. Painted your father as . . . unfriendly. Never even mentioned you."

"Because of my curse."

Matthew played three crashing, tuneless chords, then slammed the cover. His eyes met mine. "I don't believe in curses."

If I'd been too distracted by my father's disappearance, my time in the wood, to reflect on the fact of being alone in my house with a boy, the bluntness of this comment and the directness of his gaze brought me immediately to my senses. The tops of my ears burned. I could not think of a response.

My embarrassment was heightened when Matthew opened the door to my bedroom, moving quickly ahead of me before I could inform him that we'd find nothing of value in my unmade bed, the clothes strewn on the carpet. He realized at once the room was mine, and stepped awkwardly to the side, his back hitting the picture frame that held Peter's rules for me, sending it crashing to the dresser.

"I'm sorry." Matthew winced. I shrugged, and tried to direct him away, but he lifted the frame by its edges and turned it over to investigate the damage.

"You don't have to . . . ," I started, then gave up when I saw that he had read the text immediately, his lips pursed in thought.

"They're only guidelines," I mumbled.

"So you aren't allowed to touch anything."

"It's from when I was little."

"You've lived your while life without holding hands, or hugging. Without picking flowers or pulling leaves off trees. Without petting a dog or—"

"I have a dog," I interrupted. "I have Marlowe. I can pet him."

"Still," said Matthew. "I can't even imagine what that must be like. To never be held. To always have to worry. You've got remarkable restraint. Mind-blowing control. It's truly impressive." He looked at me, but though his words expressed awe, his eyes held pity.

"Can we just leave it? We need to stay focused on Peter." I knew that I'd been rude, but was not sure how to correct it. I swallowed. "Let's just go back into the study. Maybe there's something else there. He likely wouldn't leave a note, but we might find some clue as to his whereabouts." I sighed. "Or he could very well just pop up in the morning. He's not the type to think of . . . details. Or of how I might worry. Not to say that I am." The last I blustered through, aware that the force of my teeth had started my lip bleeding, that the fierce red taste of it likely now colored my gums.

"Hmm," said Matthew. He yawned. It was very late, and I remembered that I'd woken him. I knew I should relieve him, thank him for his help, suggest he best be on his way back to the cottage, but could not bring myself to do so. Avoiding his gaze, I chewed a thumbnail, keratin clicking against my lower teeth.

"I could stay here for the night," Matthew said carefully, not entirely successful in masking the white lie that followed: "It would be easier than having to drive all the way back. It's very late. And we can do a better search of your father's office in the morning, when we're fresh. I can sleep in that purple bedroom upstairs."

"It's violet," I corrected automatically, then closed my eyes and nodded, afraid to display the depth of my gratitude.

"The violet bedroom, then." Matthew moved toward the door. "You should try to get some sleep. We'll find a way to reach your father in the morning."

My stomach dropped as I watched him go, the shuffle of his feet, the cowlick at the back of his blond head. I didn't think to guide him to the bathroom, find him clean towels, perform any of the tasks I knew from reading books of etiquette a good hostess should. I was pleased to have Matthew stay with me, unsure of what I would have done without his kindness. Still, I was anxious. His questions were reasonable, hardly disrespectful, yet there had been something about them that unhinged me. Of all that had occurred the past few days, all of the strangeness I'd encountered since Mrs. Blott's death, Matthew was clearly the least of my troubles. And yet my body found him most unsettling.

The Dirtied Family Crest

Mary, 1708

As a young girl, Mary Blakely was quiet. Shy not in the alluring way of the prudish, those women whose reticence men sense and prod like a dog tracking fear, but rather gauche in her detachment. Chewing her fingernails and mumbling. Staring too intensely at those parts of her companions they would rather go unnoticed: a rector's bursting pimple, a country gentleman's long nose. What suitors her father found were not lured by her dowry, not even when increased by half.

Mary despised her own awkwardness, the sharpness of her elbows, the bulge of her gut. She watched her younger sisters married off and sent away. She watched her younger brother Frederick take a wife.

THE YEAR WAS 1707. Jane Mulhollan, now Jane Blakely, had been at Urizon six months but did not yet know how noises carried, the echoes allowed by the curvature of stairwells, the hollow panels that cradled small sounds, ferrying her words from where she sat in the library with Frederick to the place where Mary stood listening at the top of the front stairs.

"So you must find a way," said Jane, a plump, dimpled thing in a blue sack-back gown, already secure in her role as head of household. Twenty years Mary's junior, and given to ejecting sympathetic little sighs each time she settled in a chair or a divan. "We haven't the money to keep her. And it is foolishness to think that at her age . . ."

A murmur as her husband, Frederick, spoke in an undertone. Then her reply:

"You've had years to look. She has had years to become ready. All women know the time will come when they must either—" A thump as the library door closed.

That night, Mary combed her hair one hundred strokes with the silver-backed hairbrush that had once been her mother's, but belonged now to Jane. The furniture was Jane's now, the table settings, the fire-wood, the old Blakely heirlooms. The flower beds in the garden. The chambermaid. The cook.

Soon, the house itself would be taken from Mary, given to Jane. All its thick walls, its firm foundations. The nursery, where she'd played with her young sisters. The kitchen garden she'd planted with such care. The turret, where she'd sat gazing out at the road, daydreaming of the prince who would see past her sallow face, her thinning hair, the wrinkles that framed her small eyes. All given to Jane.

That haughty girl of seventeen, waving a hand like a queen, as if she were the lady of some far finer house. Mary wished Jane a pain-ful end, such suffering as she herself had suffered when watching Jane stand in the door of the church, listening to wedding bells knell, seeing Frederick touch Jane's shoulder, hearing the moans they made at night. Mary could no longer breathe for the air that Jane sucked from Urizon. She sat daily with her needlework, waiting for Jane's dress to tighten and Jane's skin to flush, for the day Jane would announce that she was carrying Frederick's child.

Jane dismissed the valet who had been with the Blakelys since be-fore Mary's birth. "He's much too old," the girl tutted. "Imagine him encountering our guests! He'd surely scare them."

Jane cleared all the tallow candles out from the cellar. "That smell!" She giggled, unable to consider a future in which the family might need them for light.

Jane rearranged the front sitting room, removing the tasteful drap-eries Mary's mother had chosen, installing gaudy replacements. She sent the settee out to become firewood, bringing in a hideous new piece painted to look as if it were made all of gold.

Mary watched the changes unfold—fists clenched, fingernails scarring her palms—unable to prevent them.

Without a husband, Mary's choices were few. She might be a nursemaid to her brother's children, live in a cold room at the back of the house, wear plain dresses and hide from the guests. She might go to the church and spend her days cloistered, praying to a God she did not trust. Perhaps one of her sisters would take her.

In the mirror, Mary's face was so white with powder as to appear ghostly. The black with which she'd tried to paint her eyebrows in the fashion of the day, as Jane did hers, had smeared onto the bridge of her sharp nose. Lines creased her forehead, sliced the sides of her mouth. *Old maid. Unwanted.*

I should eat the child's heart when Jane births it, thought Mary. I should seek out the waters of youth and drink my fill. Spin the years backward. Unfair, to have just one attempt at ripeness, a few brief years of possibility before sweetness turns to rot.

FREDERICK AND JANE did have a child, a little girl, golden and plump. Mary held her at the christening, and though Jane's own sister was named godmother, it was Mary who knew instinctively to bounce the baby, whisper her to sleep, support her soft skull with a bent elbow. If dropped, that tiny skull would crack, its small brain spilling out onto the floor. Mary felt such power standing over the cradle, the ornate wood carved like a coffin, the infant swaddled so intensely she appeared to be embalmed.

Jane's mother and sister came to live at Urizon, claiming that Jane needed help with mothering, though all of the unpalatable aspects of her role had been assumed by a girl from the village soon after the child's birth. The Mulhollan family filled the estate with activity, and filled Jane with a greater sense of her own importance.

Frederick shared his sister's lack of initiative, and had thus far avoided the unpleasant task of casting Mary out. Yet it was coming. Drawing her new motherhood as weapon, with the support of her nearest relations, Jane pressed Frederick to act.

Again, Mary stood at the top of the stairs, and heard the group of them gathered in the library.

". . . enough of this silliness . . ."

". . . propriety to think of . . ."

"It must happen at once, without delay."

The trilling of one voice replaced by another, each new instrument taking up the tune so its fellow could rest. Mary heard Frederick yield, heard them formulate a plan.

She went to the wood.

SINCE JANE'S FAMILY had arrived at Urizon, making far more of a hassle than two medium-sized women had the right, Mary had taken to long walks out in the forest. That evening she kept to the edge of the tree line, nervous of losing her way in the dark. She debated her dwindling options. She did not speak out loud, but the wood heard.

8

The next was to be a day of disappointment—in myself, as I could not access Peter's computer, and in Matthew, who, incurious the night prior, now struggled to focus on the task at hand. He appeared full of questions, but midway through would bite his lip and swallow each one down, casting me sidelong glances and a furrowed brow instead of further conversation.

"When you get sick, do you— Never mind." He ducked his head, diving into a file cabinet.

"If you eat meat, does it— Sorry." He scratched his neck.

"Has it been since birth—" Matthew stopped himself, punctuating the abrupt silence with the click of a pen cap.

"Just ask me," I said.

"No, it's okay. I'll stop. I'm sorry." He blushed, busying himself with Peter's computer for a moment before jerking up again. "It's just—I've been around babies. I can't even imagine how you could have been an infant, and then raised with this . . . condition. Let alone how your mother could have carried out the pregnancy."

"She didn't."

"Didn't what?"

"She didn't carry out the pregnancy. She died." I scrubbed my voice of all inflection, but felt a surge of frustration toward Matthew for having been the first to make me say the words aloud. I'd always known that my gestation killed my mother, but speaking it gave the fact a new, tangible weight.

Matthew blinked at me. "I'm sorry," he said. "That must still be very hard for you."

I shrugged. He watched me, waiting for me to say more. When I was silent, he busied himself at Peter's desk, trying to hack my father's files.

"Could the passcode be a birth date?" he asked, face lit by the computer monitor's unnatural glow. I remained in the doorway of the study, my hands folded under my armpits, embarrassed and afraid. Each false start of Matthew's had made me feel more like an artifact, alone in a forgotten museum, abandoned by my caretakers. Each stifled question made it clear that I was nothing like the other girls that Matthew had encountered. I'd known that I was different, but with his curiosity thus piqued, I fully felt it.

My father had rarely followed through, but I'd lived always under threat of his punishment. Who would tell me, without Mrs. Blott or Peter, when to brush my hair, to tidy, how to behave around others? Who would comfort me when I awoke, sheets sweated through from nightmares? Who would fend off nosy Mr. Pepper, bring our mail in from the village, start the fire in the library in the evenings, quiz me on my reading, tell me not to play with Marlowe in the hall? Equally important, who would make sure that Peter had eaten enough dinner, remembered to bathe, to take some time away from books? Who would make him laugh when he was mad at a rude colleague or upset he'd been passed over for a departmental award?

Who else out there would love him? Who here would love me?

If my world had been a painting hung flat across a wall, its frame had fallen and its canvas now curled inward, rolling and distorting the image I had known.

"When was your father born?" Matthew asked.

I shrugged, pressing myself into a corner, where the edge of my ear struck a bookshelf. The wood shivered. I felt sick. The trouble with bookshelves, with assembled wood in general, was the paneling—if two unrelated pieces had been grafted together postmortem, once revived they would express immense dislike. Peter had once described such craftsmanship as comparable to a postcolonial nation, borders drawn without regard to indigenous rule. This particular shelf wrenched itself from its wooden backing, sending stacks of books and papers to the ground. I touched it again, and turned to find Matthew looking from the files spilled across the carpet to the lowermost shelf, to the upmost, to the hand I had used to correct my mistake. He seemed thoughtful.

"Are you afraid of me?" I asked him.

He smiled and shook his head, pushing back from Peter's desk to kneel beside me as I straightened up the mess. To tidy was a feat of engineering, transfiguring my skirt into a mitten, shimmying to straighten the stacks.

"What, then?" I kept my eyes down on a set of plans, drawn to scale, of a medieval jailhouse, feigning interest in Peter's handwritten aside about the improbability of its size.

"I know my questions are the last thing you need right now. I'm sorry for prying. It's just that from a biological perspective, you're phenomenal," he told me. I felt my chest expand, though I could not tell if I could claim the compliment, or if he'd meant it toward some higher, unknown force. "I'd love to study you." He stared at me intently, then flushed. The color suited him, warming the few freckles on his cheeks. "I mean the things you can do," he corrected. "From a scientific perspective, of course."

It was his turn, now, to fuss with Peter's papers. He flipped through a dog-eared pamphlet, a schedule for an academic conference, a few pages that were dated like a diary, a handwritten recipe. I struggled to make sense of the ache in my chest.

"Wait," Matthew said. "What's this?"

He had come across a map, creased and fat from having been folded incorrectly, and pushed aside a file cart to spread it across the carpet, unveiling a full, miniaturized depiction of our region. A mug stain made a waxing crescent moon over a row of squares that stood for Coeurs Crossing. To the west was labeled Matthew's university, to the south the city, surrounded by suburbs, fading out into moorland and small farms. Peter had drawn a star to represent Urizon, his wide hand designating it and the surrounding forest as home.

Peter's handwriting was everywhere—crammed into corners,

covering geographic landmarks, crawling all around the compass rose. It was largely indecipherable, but I could make out a few mathematical formulas, a proper noun or two. A select list of Blakely women's names with birth and death dates scribbled next to them had been erased and rewritten so often that the paper had ripped and been patched at the back with clean scraps and tape. I didn't recognize them all, though Lucy, born in 1867, had to be that great-grandaunt whose picture hung in our hallway, Helen, born in 1650, the pale subject of the painting nearby. The final name and birth date was my own. This last was written in the rich blue ballpoint pen Peter had received as a gift from a colleague just a week before, and the writing made him seem both far away and still close by. The diffusion of him frightened me.

Still, what gave me greatest pause were the three spiraling circles that my father had drawn across the full length of the map, all connected by a single, careful pen stroke. Three twisting snail shells. Six snakes, each pair entwined, converging in the center of the wood beside Urizon. Looking at them made me dizzy, like those hypnotic mazes that would hide inside my eyes if I stared too long at their patterns without blinking, imposing their ghosts onto the next plain space I'd see.

Matthew ran a finger along the uppermost circle, whose middle curled to a peak south and west of Urizon and then spun out to encompass Mr. Abbott's land, along the west edge of the wood. There were, I realized, two ways of looking at each spiral, impossible to catch concurrently except for at their centers, where, if I squinted, the curls looked like small clasped hands. Another optical illusion, the lumpy vase that hid between the lovers, forcing distinction between shadow and light. One path in toward the center, Matthew's index finger turning, and the opposite path out.

"Two ways of moving about your death," I whispered to myself, quoting a poet whose name, just then, escaped me.

The second spiral lay across the unlabeled moors to the south and the east of Urizon—Peter had jotted some coordinates in red pen over a smear of poorly erased pencil. The third spiral was drawn directly south, over the city.

The spirals were so like the path I'd walked in the strange forest—Peter must have known it waited for me. He must think me still wandering in the wood. Of course he would have gone off to find me.

"This is it," I announced, excitement mounting. "We've found him! I'll just follow all these lines, and there he'll be."

Matthew opened his mouth as if to say something, but before any sound escaped, he frowned instead, twirling his hair.

"What is it?" I said. "What were you about to say?"

He waited, debating with himself, then finally answered. "No offense, but that's ridiculous . . . You aren't a kid spy in some novel. This isn't some treasure hunt. And if your father left the map, that means he didn't bring it with him, so he can't be following it."

"It's our best and only clue," I said.

"Exactly."

I thought this twist of my words a dirty trick.

"And even if it really were a map of where he's gone," Matthew continued, "all you've got is his vicinity, some stops he maybe plans to make. Tell me, where's the destination? It's not like you can just set out and find him." My impending protest must have been obvious, because before I could respond Matthew changed tactics. "Okay," he said, swallowing his condescension in an attempt that might have worked had I been ten years old and blind to the clear effort that he took. "Let's say you're right, this is a map of your father's journey to . . . whatever. None of these places are far enough away that he'd be gone for very long. Your house is even on the route. The best bet you've got is to just wait it out." He paused. "My school term ends this week, but if you'd like I can wait with you."

"No."

"I only meant," said Matthew, reddening, "that I'd understand if you didn't want to be all alone in the house. After Aunt Abby's death, your . . . recent experience. But if you think you're well enough to handle things, I can obviously—"

"I didn't mean that *you* shouldn't stay," I said flatly. "Only that *I* won't. By which I mean, I'm going to go."

"Go?"

"To find my father. My name is on this list. The spirals all connect in the wood where he last saw me. He must be looking for me."

Matthew pressed his knuckles to his nose. "Oh, come on. You don't know that. You don't know anything about his timing. You've nothing to go on. And besides . . ." He stopped, considering his phrasing, "I'd been under the impression you preferred to be alone."

At once, I saw my path to victory. I knew precisely what Matthew meant, and the tact that it had taken to arrive there, but I blinked like a fool and asked him, "Why?" When he frowned, I continued, "I don't follow your logic. Did you not just suggest I might need company?"

This was a strategy I'd employed throughout my childhood, most commonly on Mrs. Blott when she assigned me a task I found distasteful. I had learned the game from Peter, who was expert at exploiting fallacies, and whose explanations of such appeared far less manipulative than my own. I generally tried to hide behind a mask of naïveté, to imply that I had no ulterior motive, yet even at my most successful I could never disguise my glee at setting up a verbal trap and catching my partner in a snare of their own making.

Matthew did not take my bait. "What will you do if you go after him?" he said.

I thought for a moment. "I'll learn about the things he's studying. These circles and numbers. My involvement, why he's written down my name." However successful my improvised plan proved to be was secondary; anything seemed a choice alternative to sitting locked up at Urizon and unfolding my inadequacies, taking in the loss of Peter, Mrs. Blott. Better prepare for a new journey than contemplate the meaning of the one I had just taken, better sort through the tangible mystery of the map than parse the strangeness of my time spent in the wood and the pull that I now felt to return.

"How will you get there? Wherever there is."

I squinted. "I suppose I'll have to walk. Or I can bicycle. Neither seems especially difficult."

"You can't be serious."

"I am." And to prove it I reached for the map, let my bare hands spin the paper so the spirals seemed to twirl, the shaded forest shimmering, before I pulled away. I was daring Matthew, testing his generosity, stretching the bond that death and mystery had lately formed between us. *Will you really*, I was silently asking, *let me take this journey on my own? Is it true that you're enamored of my body? Do you think you're being practical? Or are you afraid?*

Had Matthew not risen to my unspoken challenge, I cannot say that I'd actually have left Urizon. I'd been made bold by recent trauma, and mine was the sort of courage that would dissipate once enough time had passed. Matthew was right, there was the outline of a trip but no real substance, and it would not have taken long for me to realize the flaws in my plan.

But out of curiosity, compassion, or perhaps because he'd nothing more pressing to do, Matthew decided that his role in my story was not finished. His fascination intrigued me. His earlier insistence that he paid no mind to curses made me question my conception of my body. Was it possible to be both simultaneously frightened and awed? Already, though at the time I did not know it, my life and Matthew's were entwined on both sides of the moment that he cocked his head, and frowned at me, and told me that in four days, once his last exam was over, he would help me to explore the nearest spiral if my father had not yet returned.

The Promise Ring

Helen, 1666

The daughter of a wealthy engineer, Helen was one of the first generation of Blakelys to live at Urizon just after the great house was built in the spring of 1653. Her father William had left the village of Coeurs Crossing as a young man, setting out to make his fortune by championing new methods of waterpower and hydraulic development. Helen was three years old when William returned, successful, to raze the old family property, erasing any sign of what the Blakelys had once been. The frame of the little house Helen was born in had been easily demolished, but when the workmen went to pry up the tiles in the cellar, they were seized by superstition, claiming to feel strange chills each time they bent down with the shovel. Pushing through, they found a dirt-laden manuscript buried beneath the floor, nestled next to an odd wooden carving. The man who took both discoveries to the woodpile found himself sobbing unexplainably once he set them down there, his partner struck with the same melancholy until the objects were removed and returned to the site of the house.

They did not ask the owner's permission. William Blakely did not know of the carving until it was embedded in the woodwork of the servants' stairs, at which point it was too late to remove it. He never knew of the manuscript, slipped onto a shelf at the back of the library.

Aside from these small remnants of the old world, William and his wife made their home a paragon of new money propriety. Urizon was lavishly decorated in the finest trappings of the age, impeccably staffed. The children were provided the best governesses, tutelage in music and painting, instruction in etiquette. William was determined to surpass his feudal roots, to establish the family as significant not only in Coeurs Crossing but the county, the commonwealth, even the unexplored reaches of the world. Such a task would be difficult, but not fully impossible. With money, William thought he might do it. With money, and with marriage. Which is, perhaps, why Helen's actions struck him such a blow.

The Blakelys' cook had a young son named Simon, a rosy-cheeked child who grew into an earnest young man. At six, he had been Helen's playmate. By sixteen, the two were very much in love. Helen heard her father grumble that the boy had no ambition, content to live a quiet life in the village, having declined William's offer to serve as head coachman or groom. But Helen found such quiet comforting, and noble. She admired Simon's love of the land, the common people. She admired his ability to be happy. Helen had only vague memories of her earliest childhood, that time before her family was moneyed, but in them she remembered her mother as kinder, her own life more free. With Simon, she felt seen. She felt valued for more than her mastery of manners. Every chance she found, she slipped away with him, at first exploring the forest and village, and then spending hours simply talking, until words turned to touches, and the two shared stolen moments in the wood.

The youngest of the Blakely daughters, Helen was the last to be given her dowry, but the day did finally come when a man with means and title required a wife, petitioned her father, and was promised her. The transaction was presented to Helen as a joyous one, her mother clucking and kissing her, her father beaming with pride. Helen—who until that very moment had lived in blissful denial of her role as William's pawn, who'd seen her mother and the governesses' instructions as the enemy, her father as ally, who knew of William's ambition, but had always believed his love for her to eclipse any love of fame and title—felt her heart tighten with panic. William had always praised his daughter's needlework, her poetry, the striking figure she cut in her favorite dress. He had laughed off her mother's concerns that Helen spent too much time out of doors, claiming that as long as her complexion didn't suffer, he saw no harm in a child of his enjoying the gardens, the sky. Surely, thought Helen, his love meant that her needs would be considered, her unease about the match would be addressed.

But as preparations for the nuptials continued, Helen found that her concerns went unheeded.

"He's so old," Helen said of her unwanted paramour, "past fifty."

"Nonsense," said her father. "He can handle a healthy young girl."

"I haven't even met him," whispered Helen. "I don't know him."

"He was here at the house several months ago, attending your mother's birthday celebration. The gentleman in red. You remember."

"I don't," said Helen, close to tears. "I don't remember. I can't marry him. I certainly don't love him."

"Love"—her father chuckled—"has not a thing to do with marriage." He folded the letter he'd been writing, the heated wax dripping like thick burgundy blood. As he stamped the Blakely seal, he spoke more firmly than he had before, settling his daughter's fate: "And you'll do as I say."

"I won't," said Helen. She froze, afraid of her own brashness. Stone-faced, William slowly rose, menacing as he came around the desk. He stood still for a moment in front of his daughter, and then slapped her.

Helen recoiled, her empty hand flying to her cheek, which had never before felt her father's wrath. William grabbed her other wrist and twisted.

"You will," he said coldly before leaving Helen there in his study. "Your new husband will be here tomorrow."

Helen's cheek stung from the blow. Her wrist was raw. She was too stunned to cry, and instead felt an utter blankness. This could not be her life; she could not stand it. Helen imagined the emptiness she'd feel as she climbed into this older man's carriage, as she looked back for a last time at the lengthening drive. She imagined suffering through his dinners and balls, his age-spotted hands upon her body, being smothered by his sweaty, hirsute chest. Helen shuddered. If only I could stay a child, she thought. If only we were simpler, hadn't come into such money.

The thing to do, of course, was to escape to Simon. Run immediately to his house in the village, despite the distance, the rocks tearing her slippers, the midsummer heat, and collapse into his thick, hardworking arms. She pounded her fists against his front door, inhaled the comfortable, acrid smell of him when the door opened.

"What's the matter?" Simon asked, but Helen could not answer through the sudden gush of tears. He led her into the house, rubbing her back, pushing the hair from her eyes—touches more tender for the novelty of happening not out in shaded forest but the candlelight of his home. When Helen had recovered herself, she squeezed Simon's hand so tightly that he thought she would draw blood.

"We have to leave." Helen's voice was hoarse from crying. "We have to leave now."

"Hush," Simon said into her forehead. "You're safe here with me. We can work it all out in the morning."

"There isn't time. We must go now."

"It's all right," whispered Simon, "we're together. It's late. Try to calm yourself. Try to sleep."

She stayed that night, for the first time, on Simon's straw mattress, traced her finger across the curled hair on his arms. She welcomed him inside her, the pressure painful at first, but then comforting, making her whole.

Helen was content to cut all ties to the Blakelys, stay forever wrapped in Simon, live off hard, honest work, and raise his child. Her renunciation complete, she fell asleep against the slow swell of his chest.

She awoke some hours later to the sound of angry voices, the heavy wheeze of horses, the wails of Simon's mother.

"They are coming," said Simon.

"Who?" Helen grasped his hand, squeezing it white.

"Your father. Your brother. Men from the house."

Helen dressed herself as quickly as possible. The men burst through just as she slipped a final sleeve onto her shoulder, but before she could work out the intricacies of her heavily boned bodice, which she'd only ever laced with housemaids' help. She let it drop to the floor with a clatter, her underdress displaying the pert fullness of her breasts.

AT WILLIAM'S INSTRUCTION, Simon was dragged to a tree at the edge of the forest. Helen's mother made her daughter watch as they tied Simon's wrists to level branches, tore his shirt from his back, exposed the flesh and muscle, rippling and brown. The titled man who had won Helen's hand sat atop his horse some distance away, watching, a bland expression on his face.

"You mustn't make a sound," said Helen's mother. "Act either pleased with his capture, or as if you are too startled to care." She pinched Helen's arm.

Helen's throat was thick with tears, her body motionless.

William's valet hit Simon with a knotted, nine-tailed whip. At first Simon was silent, bit through his lip to bury the pain, but as the lashing continued, he could not help but shout.

Once Simon had been reduced to a whimpering mass of blood and pus, once his back was a long rug of woven welt marks, the man with the whip stepped back. He turned to William.

"Will that do?" he asked gruffly.

William was silent and still. He looked at the diminished Simon for a cold, endless minute before asking his daughter's betrothed.

"Is it punishment enough?" William's voice showed no emotion, did not betray his own sense of whether justice was fulfilled.

Helen clasped her mother's hand. The horseman, her fiancé, cast a long last look at Simon. He took a military pistol from his coat.

HELEN WAS GIVEN a month to prepare her trousseau while the fiancé awaited her back at his estate, a six-day journey south of Urizon. She did not cry. She did not beg her parents' lenience, or forgiveness. Instead, she moved about the house in a permanent haze, stuck in the lost place between sleep and wakefulness. Salt in her tea, slippers on backward. One morning she took one of the hunting dogs out past the yard, brought him on a tether down into the forest. Climbed a tree and made herself a noose.

At first, when she opened her eyes, Helen thought herself caught, stuck somehow between her life and what came after it, a bit of bread lodged in the back of a throat.

"Simon?" she whispered.

She heard only the trees rustling around her, moving to hide the great house from her view.

9

Four days passed quickly with no sign of Peter, although every night I dreamed him in the forest. I dreamed his face in the gnarly bark of trees, his body bolstered by tangling vines. I dreamed a sapling oak tree had come thrusting from his breastbone, its trunk his heart, its roots his arteries and veins. In the dream I knelt beside him and I grasped his trembling hand, and it was my touch that set free the sapling, sent it towering, erupting, far past where my eyes could see. I would awake and reassure myself a dream recurred did not mean a reality. Still, I couldn't shake the feeling that a seed had sprouted through me since I'd entered that strange shadow forest, that its trees were now entangling my mind, becoming an obsession. I couldn't shake the feeling that my father was in danger, and that I somehow was its cause.

In the mornings, despite fog or cold weather, Matthew would leave before the sun had risen fully to go jogging. Cup of tea in hand, I watched him through the window, his hair held with a sweatband, leaning down to stretch his calves on the veranda. He'd then plod grunting and huffing off down the main road, to return an hour later, wet and flushed.

"Where do you go?" I asked him.

"No place in particular."

"Then why bother going?"

"It clears my head."

Shaking mine, I did not press the question. Activity, to me, was endeavored for effect. I participated in experiments so Peter could be paid after publishing his studies. I read books so I could have some understanding of the world outside my door, so that I might, upon reshelving

them, gaze proudly at the empire I'd conquered. Even the myths that
I delighted in hearing served a practical purpose, teaching me how
to behave, while at the same time showing me a sordid history that
helped me take comfort in the relative stability of my present. I did not
yet understand ritual for its own sake, as a way of making meaning.

While Matthew was gone, I searched our bookshelves, poring through
fairy tales and histories of our village, none of which led me any closer
to the purpose of the spirals and the map. I hoped to find some record
of the Blakelys, my mother's family, whose names Peter had written
next to mine. He'd always been reluctant to discuss them, claiming
that we had no information, with my mother gone there was no way to
answer my questions. I'd long suspected this was deflection, and now
I knew for sure he had been hiding his own knowledge of my heritage.

From the library I could watch for Matthew's return. I was growing
to appreciate his presence at Urizon. He was useful around the house:
quick to start the fire, good with Marlowe, exceptionally tidy. As my
first contemporary, I found him infinitely interesting to watch. He had
a habit of tugging at his hair when he was thinking, of chewing on his
pencil while studying, of crinkling his eyes when he laughed, which
he did easily and often. Matthew was a better cook than me, and in the
evenings I would sit at the kitchen table while he conjured dinner out
of what we had left in the pantry.

"How do you know how to do that?" I gestured toward the large
pot that bubbled on the stove.

"What? Make pasta?" Matthew smiled. "The directions are right
there on the box."

"All of it. The setting up and cleaning up and planning. All the
things that Mrs. Blott would do for Peter and me. Did she teach you?"

"Well, when you're one of seven kids, you get used to taking care of
the others." He rummaged in the cupboard for a potholder.

"Seven!"

"I know," said Matthew with a smile. "I say that to my mother all
the time."

"Seven brothers and sisters." I couldn't imagine having even one.

"Well, six. I'm number seven. Or I guess I'm number two—there's my older brother, me, then all the others." Matthew took the pot of pasta from the stove and a rush of steam obscured him as he drained it.

"They must miss you, now that you're away at school."

Matthew shrugged. "Maybe a little."

I found myself missing him when he was gone during the day. I told myself it wasn't him precisely, but human company—an ear other than Marlowe's to discuss the day's events and plan tomorrow. Still, each time I heard a noise from the front yard I looked up from my research, hoping that Matthew had returned. Often, the sound was just a car barreling by on its way into town, though twice I spotted a man on a motorbike, parked outside our front gate, staring up at Urizon. At first sighting, I ignored him, assuming him enamored with the beauty of our large estate, the structure of the house. When he appeared again the next day, this time turning off the engine, climbing down off his bike, I thought he must need some assistance. I bookmarked my page and left the library, stepping out our side door, ready to offer what guidance I could. By the time I reached the front lawn, my thin blanket shielding me from the breeze, my slippers wet with dew, the man was gone. The only sign he hadn't been imagined was the faint whiff of exhaust that lingered at the edge of the drive. Prior to Peter's disappearance and my journey through the wood, this stranger might have consumed me. I might have spent hours dissecting his intentions, imagining he'd come to kidnap or to rescue me, to steal Urizon's meager treasures. Now that I was mired in an actual mystery, I barely paid him mind, dismissing him as a curious tourist—it was not uncommon for a few a year to make their way to our estate, much to Peter's chagrin and my excitement—while focusing my attention on the more pressing questions at hand.

Had my father actually gone to find me? If so, did he believe this map held some vital clue? After all, it was focused on the forest where he had last seen me, and he'd written my name across the bottom. But then why wouldn't he have taken it with him? And in the back of my mind the niggling question: Had he left me here on purpose? Now that

Mrs. Blott was gone, was Peter afraid to be alone with me, tired of caring for me, ready to resume the life he'd led before I was born? This last thought crept up on me regularly. Each time I brushed it away, trying to convince myself that it was ridiculous while fearing it to be true.

On the day of our departure, Matthew skipped his morning exercise to sit for an exam, reciting absurd combinations of letters and numbers as he packed up his study sheets and laced his boots. I was to have myself ready upon his return, an instruction repeated the night prior, and again as he was walking out the door. He need not have worried—I was eager to begin our search. When he pulled into the drive some hours later, I was quickly out the back door and clambering over textbooks, clearing room for myself in the front seat of his car, and for Marlowe in the back seat just behind me.

"Are you sure you should be so close to the . . ." Matthew gestured toward his leather valise, twisting almost fully around to move it over. "Oh," he said, "I think the seats are leather, too."

"They aren't," I said snippily, "they're just an imitation. But even if they were I would be fine."

I knew I should not take offense at questions asked in my best interest, and it was only this past year that I'd discovered it was safe to touch a hide, so long as it was tanned. Under controlled conditions I had stroked a strip of leather, and upon its failure to react, became rather too ambitious. The Blakelys had amassed a great deal of taxidermy, which I next suggested that we try, not realizing that some amateur artisan had done a shoddy job with the animals' preservation, and quickly learning that a hollowed, chemicalized beast was no more domesticated than its organ-endowed brother, breaking a Blakely family heirloom, and begging the question, said Peter, of what made up a soul. None of this seemed fit to share with Matthew in the moment.

We drove past the turnoff to Mrs. Blott's cottage, Mr. Abbott's bungalow, the post office. We rounded the curve that would take us through the village.

* * *

WHILE SEARCHING PETER'S office I had come across a letter written by William Blakely, founder of Urizon, to a noble he was courting for his daughter, claiming that the village of Coeurs Crossing hadn't come to prominence until Urizon itself was erected. William's assertion was subject to debate, as no one else would ever call the village prominent, and it had in fact existed long before his estate as home to farmers and foresters, families who could trace their roots back thousands of years. In the latter half of the last century, as Urizon fell from favor and fame, the village had fared only slightly better. Its population fell within the low thousands. Coeurs Crossing lacked the charm of some of the quainter locales of similar size, and thus the wealthy had bypassed it when choosing where to build their country homes, leaving us little in the way of municipal resources. The nearest hospital was an hour's drive away. The university and its surrounding town absorbed most would-be tourists. Back when the modern trade roads were built—the highways that would carry timber and coal and other northern resources to the thriving cities of the south—the villagers of Coeurs Crossing had protested the felling of a certain grove of trees, claiming their spiritual significance more meaningful than the money that would come from steady travel. Thus the grove near Coeurs Crossing was spared, the highways diverted elsewhere, leaving the village in relative obscurity.

This grove, a part of the same wood that bordered my home, lent our region a frightening aura that even the sunniest days could not entirely overcome. Refusing its removal tied the village to the sorts of superstitions Peter studied, reinforced the rumors of a woodland power, the tales of a Blakely family curse. In my mind, the Coeurs Crossing that sat beside the wood was dark and dusty, eerie and empty as Urizon's shuttered rooms, filled with grim faces and ominous birds circling low skies. The few glimpses I'd been given of the village during my childhood had all reinforced this notion. Before my birth, Peter's studies had been largely anthropological—he had a keen interest in folklore, in the ceremonies that began as sacred ritual long before the dawn of what we called civilization and had continued in truncated forms ever since. When we were not experimenting, he'd return to these former occupations. Sometimes, if I'd been good, he'd let me join him.

"The early savage," Peter once told me, biting into a cherry turnover with relish, "believed in sympathetic magic. He did his work on imitations of the object that he wanted to affect. A poppet, for example, or a ripened fruit to represent the sun. In this regard, his ritual had all the trappings of modern scientific theories of cause and effect."

We were seated at the top of Urthon Hill, the highest point on the Blakely property, which looked out over the dirt road to the village. Mrs. Blott had prepared us a picnic, and I sat on a frayed blanket, nibbling at a biscuit and drinking lemonade. I was ten, and unimpressed.

"Their philosophical model," continued Peter, "was quite advanced compared to the religious frenzies that followed. To practice our Western religion is to ascribe the cause of everything to the will of some great power, a mercurial creature whose favor we might court. Quite the opposite of scientific methodology. The savage never pandered. He saw himself as catalyst to action, responsible for nature, for the summer, for the rains."

Below us, villagers were gathering, their outfits brightly colored, their faces masked, knocking each other about like sea-swirled marbles. One man (the Wild Man, said Peter), was dressed all in brown, adorned in leaves and white-budded branches that made him seem born of the hawthorn, wide as its blossoming expanse. He sat atop a stocky piebald horse and waited for the others to ready themselves. From our perch high above them we could not hear his words, just the twittering of voices, his playful growl, bursts of joyous laughter, the cymbalcrash of girls' delighted screams. Had they thought to look up, they might have seen us: two small figures looking down from our high tower, observing.

"The Wild Man will ride three times around the center of the village," said my father, "and when he's finished he'll decapitate a frog. In the past the people thought that they were having some impact on the season, that they'd chosen this evening and through ritual were asking their gods to make it the longest of the year. As if they were the true cause of midsummer, midwinter. As if they controlled the passage of the time. Today, we've abandoned such pretense. Now we simply repeat what has always been practiced, too superstitious, too silly, to question things."

"Might we join them?" I asked.

We might not.

"So it always is," said Peter, by way of explanation, "that the layman partakes in his ritual, blind to the true powers that be."

"Might I don a mask and watch from down below?"

I might not.

"Too dangerous," I remembered Peter saying, jotting something in his notebook, "far too wild."

I'd imagined my own wildness was transmuted through these rituals in the village, was the consequence of some mistreated toad or misheard prayer. I'd assumed every villager as chary as Tom Pepper, the solicitor, whose small eyes scanned our sitting room twice over before he would sit down to take his tea. Who knew what spirits could be watching, what ancient impulse lay in wait? Now, in Matthew's car, counting streetlamps and stop signs, I realized the debauchery I'd witnessed was uncommon, as repressed beneath these carefully paved streets as my own impulse under Peter's regulations.

The sun was out in full force as Matthew drove past the lower school, the grocer's, the whitewashed fences and wooden swing sets and neatly parked cars. Coeurs Crossing was pedestrian, comfortable and quiet, with no sign of the savagery that Peter had insisted waited just outside our door. It was all painted picket fences, cozy pubs, well-labeled road signs. Cobbled streets and schools, neatly parked cars. A young boy rode a bicycle. A man in coveralls pruned a flowering bush at the side of a church. I leaned my forehead on the car window, paralyzed by awe.

How was this here, so near Urizon? How had I not known, when I looked down from our hilltop, what it was that I saw? I felt a sudden stab of loss at my discovery—the tangible existence of a modern village that, for me, had shared a space with far-off planets, fairy castles—the

existence of a village with playgrounds and blue plastic bins for its re-
cycling, with signs posted on streetlamps advertising a found kitten,
with flagpoles and tulips and a stray football rolling down a hill. We
drove past the firehouse, the tailor, a little shop called Holzmeier's proclaiming that it sold "metaphysical souvenirs," which Matthew and I
tried to make a guess at.

"Ale glasses." I giggled, drunk on novelty.

"Local witches' littlest fingers."

"Holy breast milk."

"Quilts made by somebody's grandmother."

Mrs. Blott's face flashed through my mind, followed by Peter's. This
was not the time for laughter, for indulgence. This was not the time to
push my boundaries outward, expand the borders of my own sorry self.

"I think," I said, all humor gone, "it would be best if we go in and
find out for ourselves."

"What, inside the building?" Matthew shook his head, inhaling
sharply as he braked for a young child chasing a ball into the street.
He rolled his shoulders, regaining composure. "I've been in that shop
before. It's very small—too many things we might knock into."

"We?"

"Besides, it's all your usual mumbo-jumbo. Piles of fancy books in
front, cult meetings in the back, trying to profit off all sorts of superstitions."

"That sounds useful," I said. "That is exactly what we need."
Though its facade was modest, the same discolored brick and brown-
trussed plaster as the shops that surrounded it, I felt that were a bogey-
man watching me, sharpening his claws, this shop would be his prime
location. If there was a darkness comparable to my own that remained
in Coeurs Crossing, this was surely where it hid.

"Some quack selling us evil eyes and cow's blood?" Matthew
frowned.

"Piles of books. Superstitions. Experts who might know about the
map and the spirals."

"I wouldn't call the folks who work there experts," said Matthew.

"More expert than we are."

"Maisie, I'm telling you, it's useless. And too crowded to comfortably have you poke around asking questions. What if you accidentally brushed against a walking stick, or some old freeze-dried rat?"

"I'd think the superstitious sorts would love that," I said. Matthew grimaced. "But really, you're making it sound even more enticing. Just the sort of place that Peter might have made acquaintances, the sort of people who might know about his work. What if I wait for you here, and you just bring the map and ask them? Find out what they know. There's no harm can come from asking."

This last must have been an expression I'd read somewhere, as it was certainly not one that my father or Mrs. Blott had ever used with me. As a child, my harm had all begun with asking: What would happen if I touched this; how could that possibly hurt? Better, I'd been taught, to firmly corral curiosity. I would find out when I was older, they said, and should save the sorts of questions whose answers spawned action for Peter's experiments and labs.

But Peter was gone. Until he had come home again, all experiments would have to be my own.

Matthew sighed. "All right," he said, "if you promise to stay in the car with the dog, I'll go in and see about the spirals. You should keep the map here. Just in case."

He parked the car a short walk from the shop's entrance, behind a large, unlabeled van, its back hatch propped with cardboard boxes, apparently in the midst of being unloaded.

"Stay here," he instructed. I could not tell if this direction was intended for myself or for my dog. I scowled. As Matthew exited the car, three chatting mothers passed along the sidewalk with their baby carriages, and I sank lower in my seat, cowering from their gossip, as if just by looking at me they might learn of my curse. I remembered the one trip to the ocean I'd taken with Peter, the anonymity of the endless pebbled beaches and rising tides. My father had never explained his logic, why I was welcome to journey (under strict supervision) to a place so far from home, and yet forbidden to visit the village. I'd understood instinctively: Coeurs Crossing was too near us, too incestuous, too small. It would be too difficult to contain gossip if the village discovered my dangers.

Once Matthew had gone I pressed the locks down on the car doors, but then promptly pulled them up again, ashamed of my anxiety. Still slumped, half hidden by the dashboard, I stared directly ahead, watching as two men returned to the white van in front of me. They wore matching jackets, embroidered at the chest with red lettering I was too far away to read, although I could tell that the boxes they transferred from the souvenir shop were heavy, requiring both men to grip each one. Sacred rocks, I imagined, or statues.

Marlowe squeezed in beside me, brushing up against the glove box. Suddenly aware that this could be my only chance to investigate Matthew's car without him in it, I pulled myself up and pushed Marlowe away to examine its contents: a broken pencil, his car insurance, an empty bag of chocolate candy, a single little girl's pink glove. Why just the one? Was a little girl waiting somewhere with its partner? Was it stolen? Did Matthew's outer kindness hide some dark depravity, an anger that would compel him to come across a child and snatch away her—

Of course not: the surname Hareven was written next to a phone number in blocky letters on the glove's inner tag. A daughter? He was much too young. He'd mentioned younger siblings. A sister, then. It was easy to imagine Matthew holding a tiny, ungloved hand. It suddenly occurred to me that Matthew'd had a full life before he had met me. How naive I'd been to imagine myself his only company, simply because he was mine. A torso hid under his T-shirt; in his head, thoughts all his own. When he went jogging, closed the violet bedroom door, he did not disappear into some void, Paleocene and stagnant, waiting for my consciousness to summon him. I shuddered and reached back for Marlowe.

The couriers in front of me returned from their second trip, slamming the van doors. Before they could climb into the front seat, they were stopped by a new man, much younger, dark-haired and tall with a striped scarf and chiseled jaw. The three spoke for a while, the larger of the workmen gesticulating grandly, broad shoulders heaving as he seemed to either chuckle or to cry. Eventually the two workers climbed into their van and pulled away, leaving the younger man behind. There was something familiar about him, although I could not place it. He adjusted his scarf, looked straight at the car without appearing to see me, and ducked into the shop.

The street was quiet. I twisted the pink glove in my hands, staring at the phone number as though it might give me a glimpse into Matthew's other life. I gained no insight, though the handwriting was soon branded onto my mind. I thrust it back into the glove box. The car's digital clock had turned off with its engine, so I did not know how long I had been waiting. I felt it had been too long; maybe something had gone wrong. Just as I steeled myself to open the car door and step outside, prepared to blame Marlowe if questioned, Matthew emerged, carrying a handful of pamphlets and some sort of dangling charm. I yanked my hand from the door handle and tried to look innocent.

"Well?" I asked as he clicked in his seat belt. "Did they have good advice? What did you find? Come on, now take me step by step. What happened?"

Matthew turned to face me. "I went inside, they asked what they could help with—"

"They?"

"An elderly couple. A woman and a man."

"They were the only ones there?"

"Those two and a customer. And someone in the back, unloading boxes."

"And the elderly couple told you what, exactly?"

"Calm down, you'll disappoint yourself. It's not at all exciting. They know your father, though not well. He came in years ago before your mother died, but has barely been seen in the village since. They suggested I speak with my aunt . . ." He bit his lip. "They hadn't realized . . . For such a small place it's amazing how slowly word gets around here."

"The maps?"

"I didn't ask about the maps. Only the spirals, which, I was told, mean either the holy trinity or phases of the moon. Or the movement of the stars. Or life, death, and resurrection. Or a triple goddess. Or the interconnection of everything. Or mind, body, and spirit. Or a mother and her child. Or a whole host of other options, spelled out in these booklets, which I think they must have printed off some website that we could have found ourselves."

"So much to work with!"

"No," said Matthew, starting the engine, "not so much to work with. We have nothing. If the spirals mean everything, they basically mean nothing. We'd do better to forget it all and stick to what we know. We'd do better, in fact, to head back to your house and wait for Peter."

"Just because something can be interpreted in different ways doesn't make its meaning useless," I said. "You must see some value in having gone into the shop."

"Yes," said Matthew. "The single useful thing they mentioned is the cemetery just outside Coeurs Crossing. Apparently it's got your spiral symbol carved into some of the gravestones. If you still insist on spending the afternoon searching, it seems like the place to start."

The Wedding Band

Imogen, 1486

Miles and Imogen married for love, neither family rich enough in property or title to object to the union, and for a few halcyon months following their wedding in the spring of the year 1484, the two were happy. Miles had steady work chopping and delivering wood to the neighboring village, and spoke of taking an apprentice. Imogen was busy with her duties as wife, excited by the novelty of keeping her own house. She had been taught by her mother to find joy in life's daily patterns—sweeping the floors, treating the stains on Miles's shirts, churning the butter. She sensed herself building a life out of these patterns, and took comfort in the fact that through them she could glimpse her future just as well as any oracle or seer. She would bear Miles's children, wash their clothes and cook their meals, she would go to church on saint's days and Sabbaths. As the children grew, they'd learn to do the same, and one day Miles and Imogen would have grandchildren to coddle.

A proper wife, Imogen worshipped her husband second only to her God. She tended to the livestock: their two plump pigs, the bony cow her father had given as her dowry. She tried to have a proper supper ready for Miles when he came back from the forest, conjuring hearty meals from nothing even when meat was scarce. She went to his bed happily, holding her tongue when he twisted her body too roughly or his beard scratched her cheek. She prayed for him daily.

And Miles would come home to his wife with wildflowers in hand, with tales of wolf kits he had spotted in shaded glens, bright cloth he had bought in the village. His smile would widen upon seeing Imogen there in the doorway of their cottage, and together they would thank God for granting them such happiness.

When Imogen told Miles that she was with child, he kissed a trail across her stomach, and with tender, calloused hands he cupped her breasts. He marveled at the elasticity of his wife's skin, the pop of her navel. He wanted her more once she was no longer simply herself, once he had claimed her so completely. Their lovemaking, for Miles, became a sort of onanism. When he thrust he'd imagine himself and not his wife as the recipient, himself in small, pure form, slowly devouring her. He could not explain the sudden onset of such solipsistic desire, nor did he understand the void left in its wake once the baby was born. He was no longer content with just Imogen, once he had known her as an embodiment of himself.

The day of his son's birth, Miles paced the trees outside their cottage. His own mother had died several hours after bearing his brother, and Imogen assumed this initial anxiety stemmed from the fear of a similar loss. Yet even after both the child and Imogen were declared healthy, Miles remained anxious. Imogen watched him for signs of the sweating sickness that had swept a nearby town, but his apprehension was not trailed by shivering or fever. Was he worried that the child was not his? He had no reason to suspect her of unfaithfulness: the boy had his gray eyes, his father's auburn hair. Still, Miles would not hold his baby. He would not look at his wife. He took to frequenting the far side of the village, returning late, smelling of ale and other women's bodies. Imogen prayed for him, but no saints seemed to hear her.

In the night, when the child cried and Imogen rose from the bed she shared with Miles to feed him, she might catch her husband watching her nurse. Lit by the dying fire, he looked gaunt and old and jealous. Jealous of what? Imogen wondered. If anyone had cause to be jealous, it was Imogen herself, raising Miles's child while he found comfort with others. And yet she did not feel jealousy, rather sadness at Miles's new affliction, at her own inability to please him. She felt she must not have tried hard enough, that it was not Miles to blame but her own failure to excite him. Imogen saw no other way to reconcile her husband's behavior with his previous elation, could not otherwise understand such disdain from a man she thought she knew, her own simple woodcutter, who'd wooed her with sweet words and gentle smiles.

As time passed and Miles grew more distant, Imogen felt she had to act. She attempted to seduce him, but their lovemaking was wooden, passion drained. She tasted other women on his breath. She was afraid to tell Miles of the second child, whispered the news late at night, hoping he might be asleep. But Miles was not, and to his wife's surprise, he was thrilled at her announcement. He leaped up and kissed her, smiling his old smile for the first time in months. He swore to be faithful. He cried in Imogen's arms, and she promised to forgive him.

THEIR LAST WINTER together was a harsh one, early snows destroying crops, blocking passages for trade. Firewood was in demand and Miles delivered, but many of his usual customers were unable to pay. Their small family kept warm, but went hungry.

Imogen heard no more rumors about Miles. She was pleased with his renewed attentions, to herself and to their son. Still, the dark season seemed endless, and Miles was often gone. In the house, one son crying at her feet, another sucking life inside her, Imogen grew restless. She imagined Miles kissing the neck of another, imagined him dry in the whorehouse while his own roof leaked.

One night it grew increasingly late; it grew unbearable. *Be patient*, she instructed herself. *Have faith in him, faith in the Lord*. The hours passed. Miles did not return. The drip of melting snow through the crack in the roof grew ever louder. Her son's whimpering increased. The child within her womb twisted and writhed. Imogen could no longer be patient. She bundled herself and her child into their warmest clothing and set out to hunt for Miles.

ALL IT TOOK was a single moment: Imogen's feet cold in the snow, her son pulling her skirt, her husband off with another village whore.

They were hungry, there'd soon be another mouth to feed. The child tugging. Her husband gone. *Who does he think he is now, getting his fill of that woman*— The cupboard at home, bare. Wind blasting, ice in Imogen's bones. Her child whimpering. *If only*—

Imogen squeezed her eyes shut, shook her head, tried to banish sinful thoughts. She reached back for her son, who she'd brushed off her skirts in uncharacteristic frustration. There was no one behind her. The wind had softened; the snow had disappeared.

"I didn't mean it," Imogen said aloud, sinking to her knees. "I didn't mean any of it."

But the only response was the low whisper of trees.

10

Regarding the disposal of bodies, I knew more of ancient practice than modern. A picture I remembered from one of Peter's books displayed a burial mound, a small hill like a tumor squatted green upon a meadow, marked by rings of upright stones. These mounds were man-made, though I could not imagine how a man might mold the earth in such a way. I could not imagine how a king, upon his death, might ask his retinue to follow, to crawl into his cave, close their eyes, and take their own last breaths. Voicing my disbelief to Peter, he'd explained that mine was a concern that stemmed entirely from the culture I'd been raised in. There were still, today, societies, he told me, where a wife might end her life with loss of husband, strap herself onto his funeral pyre and embrace his flames.

"But not a husband's loss of wife?"

"Besides," said my father, ignoring the question, "your conception of a life is fully Western, fully modern. We've lost that innate sense of service, no longer need to see our kings as gods. What need was there, back then, to live on without your maker, your captain, your light?"

Burial in itself was a difficult concept to me, though I supposed dark ground was preferable to being wild beasts' vittles. In the grave-yards, I knew, the buried waited for salvation, revelation, words that meant their lives would become more. What if, I once said, giggling, I was to dig them up and fulfill this desire? Would the dead wander, brittle-boned and fleshless, through the village? Would they take to their shrunken patellas and pray? Peter had not laughed, and told me not to belittle what others believed, which seemed contrary to other things he'd said to me. I could only assume that he was thinking of

my mother, her own grave site, the life he had lived in her wake. I had
asked him where she was buried, if we could make a visit to her grave.
His only response was to shake his head and sigh. He seemed so lost, so
dejected, so unlike the Peter I knew, that I did not press him further.

COEURS CROSSING'S GRAVEYARD was a jumbled collection of
stones, a menagerie of styles and faded colors. A marble angel stood
watch at the gated entrance, arms spread wide, her eyes closed, moldy
wings whitewashed with bird droppings. The hill beside her had once
been a sacred landmark, ravaged by raiders some centuries back, and
among the neatly ordered graves the stubby foundations of a ruined
church burst from the grass like old, worn teeth, its only lasting wall
covered in moss, a reminder that the whole place was a palimpsest,
dead buried upon other dead, the past never erased.

Matthew explored a small chapel at the cemetery's center while I
walked the rows of tombstones, looking for the spiral pattern, squinting to read names of the deceased. My mother's grave I found in the
far corner, surrounded by her fellow dead Blakelys—MARIAN JEAN,
1810–1852; JANE PATIENCE MULHOLLAN, 1690–1772; EMMA CORDELIA,
1812–1817. This last was just a child, and I pictured her miniature
toes, her tiny fingers, her compacted skull decomposing under my ten-
nis shoes. Below her name, carved in her stone, was a crude rendering
of Peter's triple spirals. *Life, death, and resurrection. The interconnection
of everything. A mother and her child.*

And then I saw it, LAURA ANN, engraved in curling letters, a hairline
fracture splitting the top of her stone. No spiral for my mother, no angel, no rose. No words of comfort, written mainly for the living, which
might grant her guidance from her first life to the next. Marlowe settled by her side, curling himself into a fluffy ball, and I noticed that his
coat was precisely the shade of the soil on which he lay.

"Mother," I whispered, testing the word, bending to touch the rough
granite.

What need was there to live without your maker?

At ten years old, in my princess-print pajamas and an old pair of rain boots, I had snuck out of the house a good four hours after my bedtime and used my touch to bypass the padlock on the door of our wooden garden shed. Peter found me rifling through broken flowerpots and tangled hoses.

"What is this, Maisie? It's past midnight."

I was looking for a shovel.

"And why do you need a shovel?"

"I need to dig up a grave."

Peter, in his bathrobe and slippers, sank down next to me onto the floor of the shed. He sighed and adjusted his glasses.

"You need to dig up a grave," he repeated.

Of course I did not dig up a grave, not that or any other evening. Peter patiently explained that it would take more than a child with a shovel to unearth my mother's coffin and lift it from the ground. Even with the right equipment, if it were opened, I would not look on my mother, just a dry tangle of bones.

"How do we find her, then?" I asked him.

Peter tapped the side of his head with a finger. "In our memories," he told me. He tapped the left side of his chest. "In our hearts."

In the years following, I'd tried not to think much about my mother. In part, this was because it seemed she did not think of me—not now, where she lay buried under layers of soil in the Blakely plot, nor years ago at my conception. Had she felt me, there inside her? In those first few weeks of life, as I'd curdled to creation, had she sensed the small sprout of me suckling? A secret, Peter called me, a grand surprise she had been waiting to unveil. But he could not know that. We could not know she'd been aware of my existence at all.

Your mother waits for you. Ever since I'd first heard Mother Farrow's tale of the mother whose love rescued her child, I had dreamed of our reunion. I'd imagined, despite myself, that one day I would wake to find my mother leaning over me, stroking my forehead, whispering her forgiveness, assuring me of her love. This fantasy required a sort of mental balancing act, a recognized delusion that sat opposite the scale

from practicality. I had to cast aside all logic to even entertain the possibility, yet I knowingly found myself wondering: Was the murmur of
the trees beside Urizon proof of Mother Farrow's story, or merely the
swagger of the wind trying to make itself known? In the indifferent
light of day I knew my mother was not waiting for me, watching me.
She'd never once come to offer me rescue from the prison of my body,
nor the stifling confinement of the house. Hoping for her was foolish; it
would only lead to heartache. And still, late at night, I would wake in
my room in the darkness, and wish, despite myself, its walls might be
her womb.

UPON ENTERING THE graveyard, Matthew and I had been alone,
but now I saw that we'd acquired company. Several yards to my left,
Matthew was making conversation with a stocky woman carrying an
elaborate, ribboned wreath. To my right a figure crouched beside a
headstone, uncomfortably close, having slipped in beside me and Marlowe without catching our attention. As he stood I could see that he
was a young man, tall and handsome, with dark hair and a strong, dimpled chin. He had thin lips, a straight nose, thick, shapely eyebrows.
The same man I'd seen speaking with the workers by the van, who had
gone into the souvenir shop after Matthew. Up close he was undeni-
ably handsome, reminding me of the figures on the covers of some of
Mrs. Blott's more torrid romance novels.

Marlowe followed my gaze and scrambled up, displacing dirt, cata-
pulting two muddy front paws onto the young man's chest and nearly
knocking him over.

"Marlowe!" I said. "Naughty!" In such a place I should have had
my dog on a leash, and now I silently blamed Matthew for not making the suggestion. To this new young man: "I'm sorry, he's generally
calmer. I hope he hasn't disturbed your . . ." Was mourning the appropriate word to use? The stranger was far more self-possessed than the
blubbering woman still speaking with Matthew, calmer than I was as I

appraised my mother's headstone, but why else would he have come to a graveyard if not to pay respects to the deceased?

"Not at all," the young man said, stooping down to ruffle Marlowe's ears. "You're a pretty boy now, aren't you?" He straightened and held out a hand for me to shake. "I'm Rafe."

Flustered, I bent into a semblance of a curtsy, almost tripping on a partially concealed grave and grabbing a statue to steady myself. A bit of moss brightened. I took a step closer to Rafe, trying to hide its transformation.

"A fascinating family, the Blakelys," Rafe said, gesturing toward the stone that had stopped me. "A sordid, tragic history, theirs. There's a woman in the village that keeps up their old estate, though I've never heard of anyone visiting. Some remarkable rumors surrounding the family, as recent as that gravestone there, for Laura."

"What rumors?" The question fell out of my mouth at mention of my mother's name, but Rafe just smiled at me, offering no answer. He pulled a notebook from his jacket pocket and uncapped a ballpoint pen. I hoped I hadn't somehow offended him. My pulse quickened, my whole body buzzing with curiosity. I felt as if my mother, long imprisoned, was now crying to be freed. I bit my lip. "Are you a historian?"

"You could call me that. Certainly a student of a history as interesting as this." Rafe grinned again, apparently unfazed by my awkwardness. He cleared some dirt off the headstone beside him, jotted something in the notebook, then looked up at me. His eyes were very blue, a shade I'd only ever read about in books.

"You're here for research, then?" I said, heartened. "Here to learn more about . . . the family?"

"I am."

"Maisie!" called Matthew, having escaped the grieving woman and suddenly aware of my new interaction. "Are you ready to go?" His casual tone almost hid the note of urgency beneath it.

"Just a minute!" I called back.

"Maisie," said Rafe with a bow. "A lovely name. It's good to meet you. Who's your friend?"

"Matthew," I said as he came closer to us, frowning and tugging at a stray lock of hair. "His name is Matthew. He's . . . his great-aunt was Mrs. Blott," I said, desperate to hear more. When Rafe looked at me quizzically, I foolishly continued, "Mrs. Blott, the one who keeps—kept—house at Urizon."

"Ah!" said Rafe with confident enthusiasm. "Well." He tapped his fingers in a quick pattern against the edge of the grave, and twice clicked his teeth. Matthew was just a few headstones away, and widening his eyes in an exaggerated gesture that seemed an attempt at a warning. "I wouldn't normally do this, but I simply can't help myself," Rafe said. "Would you come join me for a coffee? I have about a million questions regarding Urizon, and it seems that you two have an inside scoop." Rafe's teeth were very white. They glistened when he smiled. "In return, if you've an interest in the Blakelys, I've got several juicy stories I can share."

The Bit of Braided Wire

Kathryn, 1223

Kathryn was born, in the year 1206 of her Lord, with an insatiable hunger.

For food, at first. She was a chubby child, worrying her mother with the rate at which she'd finish her pottage, the cause of countless conversations between parents about how they would keep Kathryn and four elder brothers fed. But by thirteen, Kathryn's appetites had shifted. She shed her baby fat and blossomed, a new need unfolding, a different desire.

Kathryn's mother came across her on the shore of a stream where she'd been sent to do the washing. Dirtied clothing sat in small piles around the girl, including her own underthings. Her auburn hair gleamed in the light, falling over her bare shoulders, bright against her breasts. Her head was tucked, fingers exploring, mouth caught in a delicate *Oh*.

The mother ran to the rock on which her daughter sat and took her by the hair, yanked her up, and slapped her. Beat her with the washing bat, three smacks against pert backside, three throbbing red welts. This behavior was improper. It was sinful. It would lead her to her end.

Perhaps, as Kathryn's father claimed, such punishment did not make an impression. A harsher beating was warranted, a stronger assault. Or perhaps there is no way to punish appetite, which only grows with abstinence, consuming both desirer and desired.

AT FIFTEEN, SIXTEEN, seventeen, Kathryn still wanted. She'd steal off to the wood with the cousin of a neighbor, to the barn with the miller, to the river with a groom. Her family knew, the hamlet knew, but none who might act on the knowledge could ever catch her at it. Her mother pleaded with her to be modest, cried and begged. Her father beat her. When Kathryn carried pails of water up the hill to her home, when she worked in the garden, women would pull their daughters closer, whisper harsh words, throw stones, spit. It did not bother Kathryn. She cared nothing for gossip. She was adept at dodging curses. She was never afraid.

Her brothers disapproved of their sister's reputation. Kathryn laughed at their mumbling, the burn of their cheeks. She only truly cared for one of them: handsome Owen, three years Kathryn's elder and her double in complexion. As a small child Kathryn would cling to him, ignoring the others when they tried to entertain her, preferring him over either parent. Owen would bounce his sister on his knee, tend to her bruises. Then came a day on which his sister on his lap set his groin stirring and he pushed Kathryn off, ashamed and stuttering.

Thereafter Owen could not ignore the urges that he felt toward Kathryn. He would watch her bathing, trace his fingers across his own hip bone, thinking of hers. He would dream of the white dip of her neck.

He told no one of his feelings, and would never act upon them; Owen was an honorable man. As they grew older, he was wed to the daughter of an influential socman, a clever young girl who he loved dearly. Still, Owen blushed each time he passed his sister.

Kathryn, for her part, did all that she could to tease him. Would walk behind him and breathe soft against his neck, loosen the top of her dress, bend so he could see her freckled bosom. She would lick her lips and smile.

WITH THE COMING of each spring, the people of their hamlet gathered for a festival. They welcomed warmth with rituals—the drowning of an effigy, a Wild Man dressed in roughage—and concluded with a bonfire and a large amount of ale. So much ale that Owen, aglow with the drink, eventually succumbed to his beautiful sister. They coupled in a barn at the edge of the wood, faces flushed, two pairs of sea-green eyes in mirrored reflection. She nibbled his ear, he sucked on her breasts. He entered her, both gasping. Her nails left red roots on his back.

Owen's wife found them asleep, their limbs tangled together. No question of identity, their matching red-brown hair and small, peaked noses, each sleeping with bent arm above a head. In shock, Owen's wife screamed for her mother, for her father, for someone, quick, to come.

Sacrilege, they said, for a brother to lie with his sister. Action must be taken. Something must be done.

THEY TOOK OWEN first. Brought him, clothed, to the stockade. His wife, once her head had cleared, was sobbing, begging her father to spare him. He had done wrong, yes, but he still had her love. A whipping, perhaps, some sort of fine, and his lesson would be learned. It was not Owen, but Kathryn, who needed punishment.

Owen's father-in-law agreed to spare his life, but only under two conditions. The first: Owen would be banished, could never set foot in the hamlet again. The second: they'd instead take the head from his whore sister's neck.

Kathryn's parents pleaded, but Owen's father-in-law, churchmen behind him, would not be deterred. Owen was given a rucksack with few supplies and sent out of the village, went stumbling, shamefaced, off into the unknown. Kathryn was locked in an underground room of the parish church. She'd have three days to reflect on her behavior, then would be burned ceremoniously. A warning. An example.

Kathryn's mother sat stone-faced on the hard-packed dirt outside her daughter's prison, cursing her own failure, silent for the first two days of the girl's condemnation. On the morning of the third day,

Owen's wife appeared. Kathryn could hear the two women whispering, but could not make out what they said. The door swung open.

Kathryn's sister-in-law stood at the entrance to the cell, her eyes decades older than they'd been the week before, swollen and red like two battered fists.

"My father will be back soon," she said. "Run."

11

It took some haggling to convince Matthew to accept Rafe's invitation, but when he saw I would not be swayed he finally conceded. The roadside café he selected as safe house for our gathering was remarkable only in its bareness—wobbling tables, harsh overhead lighting, a haggard woman wiping down a counter, her hair tied with a rag. There were few customers. We sat at a booth in the back, sipping weak but steaming coffee, picking at a plate of chips, positioned so I could see Marlowe, chafing at his bonds where Matthew had insisted we tie him up outside.

"You're suspicious, I see, and so I'd like to start with all my cards out clearly on the table," Rafe said to Matthew, opening his palms. He turned to me. "You've told me you're connected to Urizon. Now, correct me if I'm wrong, but you look very much like my friend Peter Cothay. You were at his wife's grave. . . . Am I right to assume a relation?"

I nodded. Matthew, sitting next to me, coughed into his drink.

"I knew it!" said Rafe, his expression taking on a look of wild glee before he caught himself and calmed it. "I knew you'd have the . . ." He shook his head, took a sip of water, and began anew. "Peter Cothay is a colleague of mine," he said. "We've been working together for the past year on a theory I've developed. Or that he developed, really, but that I've been very eager to adopt."

"Bullshit," said Matthew. "Prove it." I kicked him for his rudeness, but Rafe appeared unfazed. From his coat pocket he produced a stack of letters, all in my father's hand, dated from the past fifteen months. Matthew flipped through them while I read over his shoulder.

*. . . if we assume the wood itself was larger, we can widen our scope
and begin to look . . .*

. . . from the south, in approx the yr 600 (AD?) . . .

*. . . can be translated to mean "lifeblood" or family, so there'd be no
need for . . .*

. . . once you prove the physics of it, they'll be hard-pressed . . .

Matthew skimmed faster than me, put the letters down before I had
finished. "All right. So he's a colleague," he said, pushing the pile toward Rafe. "But why does it matter? What can we do for you?"

"You're going to have to bear with me," Rafe said. He had, for the
past while, been leaning toward us, his elbows set upon the table, voice
deliberately low. Now he leaned back in assessment, as if trying to de-
cide if we were worthy of the coming information. "Keep open minds.
Most social anthropologists, archaeologists, even, are more concerned
with history than practical application. I admit, to the skeptic, the idea
I'm about to pose could seem a joke."

Matthew sat very still, watching Rafe with eyebrows raised, his
mouth already skewed skeptical. I thought that any minute he'd declare it time to leave, that we were done with this diversion.

"We promise to believe you," I said, stressing the collective.

"All right"—Rafe took in a large breath—"here it is: I've found
proof of the existence of a very special passage in the wood beside Urizon. But it needs . . . a lot of help with its unlocking. That's what I was
after in the graveyard. That's why I'm curious to hear about your ties to
the house. I understand that others call it pseudoscience—most of my
peers think that I'm mad—but there is so much of the world we close
our eyes to. So much of ourselves we, in our modern age, dismiss."

"Unlocking?"

"One of the texts your father studies is concerned with a ritual leading to a woodland prophet. There's a series of processional routes the
ancients would travel to find her—you'll be familiar with cursuses, I'm
sure"—I nodded emphatically, although we were not—"and ley lines,
of course. Certain stops along the way functioned like keys. Travelers

made pilgrimage to certain sacred places, as if unlocking dead bolts before opening a door. It's all written out, the directions are all there if you can make the right translation, and I think that I've done it. I think that we can get inside." Rafe exhaled, smiled, and looked to us for validation.

"I don't understand," said Matthew flatly.

"You mean a tunnel?" I said. "What, under the ground?"

"Not quite." Rafe took another sip of water. "More of a . . . path to a different dimension. Well, no, dimension is the wrong way to phrase it. If you haven't got the background in the history, it can become a bit tricky to explain. Think of a spirit world. A holy place. Not a literal passage, but . . . metaphysical."

I thought that Matthew might start laughing. Near us, someone's mobile device beeped. The woman working the counter argued with a man who didn't have the correct change for his purchase. Outside, Marlowe tugged at his bonds.

I felt that I had begun a large jigsaw puzzle on a surface half its size—my mind was not wide enough to lay out all the pieces, but I could carefully examine little pockets and, by squinting, visualize how they'd combine. Rafe's explanation took so much of the experience I'd struggled with and wrapped it up so very neatly. I had gone missing and found myself in some other dimension; Peter's research held the clues. The visions and the forest that I'd had no way to parse—here was my guide. Peter wanted to open the strange, shadow forest, to enter Rafe's metaphysical world; he thought that I was there and had gone off to find me. Likely, he was waiting for me now.

"Could this be useful?" Using my sweater as a grip, I took Peter's map from my pocket, pushing it across the table toward Rafe, ignoring Matthew's quick intake of breath as I laid bare our only evidence. I watched as Rafe unfolded it, his eyes round with his luck. He traced the spirals, whispered the women's names.

"Where did you find this?"

"Am I right? Is it directions to your passage?"

"Cothay wrote to me about this. We'd been planning an expedition, speaking regularly, and then we got into a slight . . . disagreement. Words were said, the fault was mostly mine. For a few weeks' time we stopped all correspondence. Then I wrote him an apology, but I've heard nothing back. He's not the type to hold a grudge. I'd thought he'd, well, I didn't know what happened, but I'd hoped . . . and now it seems he's gone ahead and done the work without me. You've given me exactly what I need to get through."

"Through?"

"To the holy place. The other world. The undiscovered country."

"You think that's where Peter has gone?" I asked. Matthew kicked me again. "I mean, where he would have gone if for some reason he so happened to be missing?"

"I'm certain that it would be. And if you're all right with my copying these coordinates, very soon that's where I'll be, too." Rafe's hands were shaking, his eyes glistened bright. His desperation was palpable, and compared to Matthew's stoicism seemed a hand extended.

"This is absurd," said Matthew.

"It isn't," I said, turning to Rafe, "and I will let you use our map."

"Really?" Rafe's hopeful smile extended into a wide grin, revealing rows of porcelain-white teeth, a set of dimples.

"If," I said, "and only if, you'll let me through the passage with you."

A car sounded a long, low honk from the highway. The woman at the counter stifled a burp. Matthew suddenly seemed very tired.

"That isn't happening." He turned to me. "You're going to forget this whole debacle. We'll go back to your house and we'll wait there."

"Your house?" Rafe said. "To wait there?"

I glared at Matthew. "You see," I said, "Peter Cothay is my father." I saw no reason not to tell Rafe everything, believing, as I did, that he'd laid bare his plans to me. "Peter is gone, and we've been out looking for him. I intend to keep looking, regardless of what Matthew, here, thinks."

"This is a joke," said Matthew.

"It isn't!"

"Would you," Matthew asked Rafe, jaw tight, his milky coffee sloshing on the table, "mind giving us a moment alone?"

"Not at all."

Abuzz with discovery, Rafe moved to the other end of the café, took his notebook from his pocket, and started scribbling. Matthew sat with his arms crossed, watching me watch our new companion.

"What?" I said, bristling.

Still no words, only that condescending focus.

"You've made your point," I said, although much of it I had yet to decipher. "Will you please speak?"

"Do you really think it's a good idea to go off with a boy you barely know on some fool's errand?"

"I didn't know *you* when I first met you," I replied, aware of the silliness of the sentence and the petulance in my tone. "And I can take care of myself."

"In my experience," said Matthew through his teeth, as if I had not said a thing, "it is not a good idea for a young girl to run off with a strange man."

I bristled at whatever he appeared to be implying, determined not to let him humiliate me. "I thought you'd said he was a boy."

"What?"

"Man or boy, which is he?"

"Does it matter? Regardless, you shouldn't go with him. This whole thing is highly suspicious. Sure, he has letters from Peter, but he just told us they'd had a falling-out. Something feels wrong here. I'd say that if you thought it over, you'd agree."

I opened my mouth, but was not sure how to respond. To me, very little ever felt right—I'd built a life around denying gut reactions, curbing my instincts. How was the nagging feeling that I had regarding Rafe any different from the urges I had always been told to suppress?

"Be smart," Matthew continued. "A wild-goose chase across the country? Unlocking ancient invisible doors? Come on, Maisie. I know you've spent years locked away, but you're in the real world now. Be reasonable."

"I am being reasonable—"

"*Use* your head."

"It's a giant lead. Our only lead. You don't know Peter—this is just like him. And he would want me to come—"

"Really? You really think that's what he'd want? After holing up for years, keeping you quiet, he'd want you to run off on this ridiculous quest? I've been lenient, so far we've followed all your whims, but as your current guardian I—"

"You are *not* my guardian."

"Well, if I were in any official capacity, you can be sure that I'd—"

"Even if you were, it wouldn't matter. I'd go then, and I'm going now. I don't care what you say."

There was a long pause while we looked at each other. Finally, Matthew sighed.

"So you're set on this?"

IN HINDSIGHT, RAFE'S involvement in my tale is all too simple, too serendipitous. How could he so easily tell I was related to the Blakelys? Why was he so quick to share the theory of the wood? And of course he had just told us that a multitude of scholars had made criticisms of the very theory I was eager to believe.

What I did not know then was the history of the ley line: a collection of purportedly meaningful points—burial mounds, churches, mountain peaks, lakes—that when charted on a map can be connected with a single stroke of the pen. The amateur archaeologist who'd coined the term was thrilled at his discovery. Surely when the old antiquarian looked up to see a chain of fairy lights, monuments, and megaliths in geometric pattern, he'd uncovered ancient wisdom, found some key. Surely these patterns meant something! But give each individual monument and megalith its own symbol, mark them on the map, and count their abundance: his atlas becomes the night sky, a dense collection of such wonders. His ley line becomes a constellation, a pattern imposed to make sense of the world. Not the word passed from the prophetess on high, but a tale he, himself, has written.

Still, I was looking for a prophesy—I saw my curse as proof that there was more to Peter's maps than met the eye. I had been flailing about, seeking a guide, afraid to be the sole check on my body and its powers, afraid of my new feelings toward the forest. Afraid that some terrible harm had befallen my father, that he was gone forever, that I'd always be alone. Rafe's theory suited my own desperation, and as so many do, I found it easier to believe, to cling to its inherently flawed structure, than to admit I was adrift in an indifferent world, alone.

"I don't see why I shouldn't be set on it," I said. "What else am I to do? Sit home and wait?"

Matthew gave me another long look. I was about to leave, go and get Rafe to begin planning, when he finally spoke.

"You're being swayed because he's handsome." His voice was very matter-of-fact. "And because you're angry with me. I wish you'd reconsider."

In this moment there was nothing patronizing about Matthew, just a sort of weariness. He closed his eyes and lifted his face to the ceiling, then opened them and looked at me again.

"All right." He sighed. "I'm coming with you."

"Ha," I said. "I don't need you to come with me."

"I know you don't. But humor me."

"No thanks, I'd rather not."

"I don't care what you'd rather," said Matthew. "I'm coming."

"Fine," I said.

"Fine." Matthew used the heels of his palms to push the hair from his face. "Just promise me this: that you'll be careful. That you'll try hard not to give yourself away."

"I don't see why it's me you're frightened for," I said. "I've got an excellent defense."

The Brooch of Hammered Iron

Alys, 605

Alys was nine when she first saw the soldiers. The year was 600 AD. She'd followed her little cousin Madenn to the stream, ostensibly racing, but letting the younger girl gain ground. Spring had fully displaced winter, which meant the ice that crusted the water had finally melted, the rains restored their favorite swimming spot, which in the weak afternoon light would be frigid, but flowing. Madenn's flaxen hair streamed loose behind her, a beacon leading Alys through the trees. Every so often Madenn looked back and laughed, the sound waxing and waning with the turn of her head.

Alys fell farther behind Madenn, but she knew what lay ahead: Madenn would untie her belt and slip out of her smock while still running, would leave the garments on the ground and make her way into the water, singing, splashing, spitting fountains through her teeth. Celebration done, Madenn would lie on her back, yellow hair spread like sea reeds, dancing while the rest of her was still, and wait for Alys's approach, hoping to frighten her. As it had been the year before, as it would be the year after, and on and on until the time came to be wed.

But rather than immersed and naked, Alys found her cousin clothed, and pressed against the wide trunk of an oak tree. Madenn held a finger to her mouth, and cocked her chin to signal to Alys what had stopped her.

Two creatures knelt before the water, armored like locusts, protected by hard metal shells that they peeled slowly from their bodies, the pieces clanging together, the creatures voicing sounds that Alys did not understand. Once stripped, they revealed themselves to be men, broad-shouldered and bulging, with hair cropped close across their foreheads, pronouncing their ears. They entered the stream, yelping when struck by the cold, sitting to cover themselves fully.

Two metal shields the size of Madenn sat abandoned on the rocky plane beside them, as did a longsword, a thick dagger, and a spear.

Alys crouched down, retrieved a dart from her boot. As she did, Madenn placed a small hand over her cousin's and shook her head. "Fire," Madenn whispered, seeing, as her own mother could, beyond the present to a future that had, in the brief measure of a moment, shifted into something dangerous and uncharted. "Bloody death." Alys laced her fingers through Madenn's and squeezed. The two slipped quietly away, back to their home, to warn the others.

IT WOULD BE three years before those soldiers returned, three years of Madenn campaigning for a rally, whispering warnings, insisting they must strike first or be struck. She had seen fire, she pressed those of her clan, had seen destruction.

Madenn's brother Fionn echoed her concerns. He'd followed the rumors of southern invaders more closely than Madenn or Alys, greeting those who'd seen the conquerors with questions, voicing his own thoughts on strategy to anyone who'd listen, itching for the glory of war. He offered himself as envoy, asked his father to petition neighboring clans to join together, but each peaceful day that passed convinced the rest that the cousins were wrong. The empire's hand had already exceeded its grasp; there was talk of revolt among its armies. There was no need—in truth no way—for them to act. Where would the clan even stage an attack, if threat was imminent? The seat of the alien empire, a several months' journey away? The men tousled Fionn's hair and called him child. The women told Madenn and Alys not to be frightened.

Then, at the height of the summer when Alys was twelve, the cousins saw crushed meadows that proved enemy movement. By autumn, most of those who'd laughed at their warnings were dead. Together, the survivors retreated to the forest, using their knowledge of the wood to taunt the soldiers who now camped atop the place that had once been their home. The insurgents ruined food stores, rerouted rivers, captured boys meant to relay news from one foreign camp to the next.

"We will rout you," the conquerors hissed in a mangled version of Alys's tongue, "we will civilize you. You will be ours." They burned whatever land they could, hoping to smoke out the natives. They uprooted the old burial mounds, laughed at the old gods.

"The people practice savage rituals," read one letter that Fionn intercepted, the translation forced out of the errand boy before his early death. "Their women run wild, their men are unclean. They are lucky to have come under our influence."

HIDDEN IN THEIR sacred groves, shielded in the deepest tract of wood, the cousins plotted. While Fionn and Alys, fierce in firelight, mapped strategy, Madenn dove deep as she could into their history, her visions mining the remains of the old ways, building quiet communion with the trees. "Here before us," Madenn swore, "and here long after." Alys watched as her cousin mixed berries and blood, scratching pictures onto dry hide, disregarding her mother, who claimed that to capture a word was to empty it of power, to tame what should be wild.

Fionn refused to hide forever in the forest, despite his sister's faith that the trees would protect them. His father gone, Fionn knew that he must take revenge, must stand against invaders to uphold the family name. Madenn eventually agreed. There would be a final barrage, led by the hundred of their kind still remaining, however unlikely its success: if they failed, they must fail gloriously, martyred to freedom, avenging their dead. And if they failed, Madenn promised, she'd preserve them. They would be remembered not in the eyes of the conquerors, savage and stubborn, but forever in the sheets of hide she'd bound into a book.

In swirling symbols drawn with blood and berries, Madenn wrote the story of the world that she wanted, the wisdom she'd learned from her mother, the promise of rebirth and a return to what was true. She drew a tree scarred with a spiral, a small human figure half hidden in its heart. A crested bird at the edge of a vast forest. An open palm held to a knife's blade. It was a prayer, Madenn said, for the forest, for the meadows that burned, the crushed stems of the lilies, the uprooted trees. To tell the story, Madenn reasoned, was to harness its power. A prophetess, Fionn called his sister, handing her a sharpened spear.

MADENN DIED IN the first rush, a longsword to her throat. Alys stabbed the soldier that defiled her cousin's body. In her shock, she had no time to invoke the land's power, forgot to make the symbols Madenn thought might bring them aid. She knelt next to her cousin and stared into those vacant eyes, pressing a dirty finger to the wound. It was too much, in the crux of the combat, on the fields that stank of sweat and blood and piss, to remember the world as it had been, the quiet of a meadow, the babble of a stream. Those fireside tales of trees that defended men, tales told in whispers, a last leaf of hope as the clan was cut down, proved themselves only stories. Amid the corpses of their comrades, Alys and Fionn were taken alive, symbols of their crushed rebellion.

AT THE EDGE of the wood, in a cage recently vacated by some larger animal, the gristle of its meal mixed with its still fragrant waste, Alys saw Madenn's blood crumbling quick under her fingernails, the remains of Madenn's promise drying black upon her hands. She felt a trickle of wet between her legs. Alys took the angry red from where, inside and out, she had been broken, made an ink of her own blood and her cousin's, reaching through her prison bars and smearing Madenn's symbols—the spiral, the hand clutching a knife, the crested bird—

onto a splintered piece of wood. Alys whispered a word to her family, the forest. She pressed her forehead to the iron bars of her prison, and felt them dissolve.

ONCE FREED, ALYS cursed the thieves, the lives and land they'd taken. She called on the forest, itself under ambush, for aid. She'd doubted Madenn's claims that the forest would listen, wondered why the trees would help if there was nothing that they wanted she could give. But now her clan's sacrifice was scattered all around her, bone and blood blossoming from the ground. Alys felt herself clutching at the forest in desperation. *Preserve us*, she prayed.

The trees shivered, listening, afraid of the changes that had come upon them suddenly: these men with steel and fire, the destruction of their ancestors a day's journey away. The trees foresaw charred, chalky stumps, molten skeletons, fleeing woodland creatures spitted and skinned. There would be fields where once was forest, steel structures where once their kin rose tall. *Preserve us all.*

Alys's eyes were shut, her flooded heart heavy. The trees knelt down to her, acknowledging her pain. She was so young. She was afraid. She did not bargain with the fact that preservation has its own meaning to trees, whose lives span centuries, whose reach is slow, who experience years as humans do moments. Eternity, for Alys, would last longer. Preservation meant stasis, not fulfillment. Preservation was more sister to suppression than release. This she would learn once it was already too late.

Sore from the soldiers who'd used her, the shackles they had locked around her wrists, Alys hid her heart inside an old oak tree. She took Madenn's book from where it was concealed in the undergrowth and buried it deeper. She took the blood she'd used to paint her way to freedom to call to the forest, scarring the wood deep with Madenn's symbols. Alys placed a splintered branch at the edge of the trees in memorial, a challenge and a curse.

She stood alone that evening at the top of Urthon Hill, wind gusting, slapping her dark hair against her cheek. Far below her, men sang bawdy songs of conquest, sparks hissed and popped in campfires, horses snorted nervous whinnies. The sky reeled with shifting galaxies of stars.

Alys shut her eyes and disappeared into the wood.

Part

III

12

We returned to Urizon that evening, our plan to collect Rafe
from his rented room in Coeurs Crossing the next day. Matthew was to drive us, as Rafe did not have any vehicle but his motorbike, the existence of which was, to Matthew, another blot on Rafe's
general character. My first view of that bike standing sleek against the
graveyard fence explained the feeling of familiarity I'd had outside
Holzmeier's—it had been Rafe parked by Urizon on those first days
after Peter's disappearance. When I asked why he'd left so quickly, Rafe
explained he hadn't wanted to intrude. Matthew rolled his eyes, and
on our return home stomped up the stairs muttering something about
the idiocy of those who forgo helmets. I could hear him still pacing the
length of the hallway while Marlowe and I prepared for bed.

That night I dreamed of Rafe. I imagined he was with me on Urizon's lawn, watching me. Together we rose out of our bodies, ghostly
figures floating out over the yew trees, drifting far out past the house,
past alders and hazels, hawthorns and pines, past the road, past the
barley, into the heart of the old forest, where Rafe undressed me, tenderly unfastening each button of my blouse. He pressed his mouth to
my neck and I ached for him, held him, my fingers tearing through
his shirt and grasping his shoulders, twisting at his skin. His mouth
was soft and warm against mine, his torso pressed so close I thought
us caught up in some ritual, some ancient exchange: he'd entered me
so fully that parts of him flowed through my veins, now he was me,
now the me and he and we were interchangeable, were one. I awoke
gasping, my fingers sticky with a transparent sap, stiff from exploring
my body.

*   *   *

AFTER A QUICK, early breakfast, I bustled through the house, check-
ing to see nothing was forgotten, peering into Peter's study, tearing
through the kitchen, digging through my dresser drawers a sixth, then
seventh time.

"That's the last of it?" Matthew asked when I'd finished my search,
nodding toward the carpetbag I'd stuffed with any book that seemed
relevant and now struggled to carry down two sets of stairs. I nodded
and he took the heavy bag without acknowledging its weight, hefting
it easily over a shoulder. "Make sure you have the key to lock the house
behind you."

I blinked at him, confused.

"Maisie?"

"It's just we never lock it. I don't know who you think will come by."

Matthew gave me a strange look.

"I'm sure I have a key somewhere," I said, "but it does seem rather
silly if we haven't ever—"

"Fine," said Matthew, "don't lock the door."

"Besides," I continued, starting with him to the car, "Marlowe will
see no one disturbs things."

"What, you aren't going to bring him?" Matthew stopped suddenly,
turning himself to face me. I could not tell if his expression was one of
condescension or concern.

"Of course not," I scoffed. "He'll be much happier here. Clearly I'd
like to have him with me, but we all know that wouldn't be practical."

I had not yet put words to the emotions that I felt regarding Marlowe, but I knew as soon as I'd spoken them this plan was for the best. I
was leaving, and Marlowe must stay at Urizon. I could not picture him
without Urizon's garden to reign over, could not imagine him confined
for hours to the back of a car, tied up as he'd been outside the café. He
belonged here, and to take him from his home would be not only cruel
but impossible. Marlowe *was* the grounds, the forest. My decision was
simple as that.

Matthew squeezed his eyes shut, wincing, crinkling his nose. "Not practical," he repeated. "Well, if we're gone awhile, then who is going to feed him? Who'll make sure he gets outside?"

It was my turn to look quizzically at Matthew. "Marlowe's not a cat," I said.

"Not a cat." He was falling into that tic of repeating me, the one I so despised. After a moment, he shrugged and walked toward the car.

I crouched and called to Marlowe, who came over at once, his tail wagging, his claws clipping the drive.

"You're a good boy," I told him. "And I'll come back to you soon."

Marlowe nuzzled me and I felt my throat tighten. I buried my face in his neck and inhaled his familiar scent, pressing close as if to fuse us, trying to hold on to the feeling of life against my skin.

"Stay," I said, though he seemed not to need instruction. He watched me as I moved toward the waiting car, which chugged comfortably, billowing gray smoke. I took my place in the back seat, squished against suitcases, leaving the front free for Rafe.

I kept my head turned and my eyes on Marlowe as the car pulled away. I watched him sitting there, growing ever smaller, watched the house and the gardens grow smaller, until we were out onto the main road and I was, at last, leaving home.

RAFE WAS WAITING for us at his bed-and-breakfast, his own luggage compact, shirt freshly ironed. He took the map and unfolded it wide across the front seats once he'd settled next to Matthew.

"We aren't far from that one," I said, pointing, stretching the limits of my seat belt to lean forward, very careful not to brush against Rafe's neck. The mark I referenced was the nearest to Urizon, at the farthest edge of Mr. Abbott's extensive property.

"Excellent!" said Rafe. "I'd say that's a wonderful start. We'll head there directly."

Matthew rolled his eyes. "So you show up at each of these spots and do what exactly? Some chanting? Dance around? Is that how this game's played?"

"We simply have to be there," Rafe said pleasantly. "It's like running an engine to get the heat going. Or raising one leg of a bridge. Do you see?"

I did not see, though I'd be damned if I'd admit it. Matthew's expression informed us that not only did he not see but he doubted the legitimacy of anything Rafe said. I kicked the back of his seat, hoping he'd understand my warning and stop voicing his doubts, but he didn't turn around. Rafe ignored both of us.

"We'll travel here," he said, brushing a mote of dust from the map, "and then this river, and then on to our final destination in the city, after which we just need to apply the right force . . . then we're through."

"Okay," said Matthew, his voice rather louder than necessary, "and how exactly do you intend to meet up with Maisie's father? We'll just happen upon him in one of these spots?"

"Why, yes," Rafe answered. "If we're lucky. Otherwise, once we've ensured the door is open, we can follow him right through."

"Of course," Matthew muttered, "through the magic door. Makes perfect sense."

THOUGH IN NO rush to endear himself to Matthew, Rafe did expend much energy on me. He was enamored of my father, turning around to pepper me with all sorts of questions about Peter's upbringing and schooling, very few of which I was able to answer.

"So once he'd finished his graduate studies, he came straight to Coeurs Crossing?"

I bit my lip, my jaw skewed, wondering.

"Surely you help him, though? With all the research? You seem like the type who wouldn't mind spending days in the stacks." Rafe turned back to me, nodding in admiration. I had no idea what he meant by stacks, but I would take any compliment he offered. The experiences he projected upon me—time spent in libraries establishing theories, attending parties where I charmed prominent scholars—seemed like those I could have had, with opportunity. I wanted to be the girl he thought I was; I liked myself more through his eyes.

As we drove on, Rafe spoke of Peter's studies. He was well versed in the legends of the forest, and the catalogue of missing Blakely women. He even thought he knew where they had gone.

"Imagine a holding place," he said. "A slice of time outside of time, where all those women who should be dead are still living."

"Like a memory."

"What do you mean?"

"The way a memory is real, but also not real." I spoke quickly, with bravado. "If time is one long line and we're all moving across it, there has to be a place we're headed, and a place that we've just left. Obviously, the memory is the place that we left." Rafe seemed impressed.

"That works if you believe in the concept of progress," said Matthew, chiming in for the first time in half an hour of conversation. "If you think progress is a fallacy, then there's no destination. We're just barreling forward blindly."

"I didn't say a *destination*, I said a *place*. And just because we aren't in the place we've come from, doesn't mean we haven't left it."

"So what you're saying is the opposite of Schrödinger's cat." Matthew smiled.

"What?"

"The cat in the box," said Rafe. "Does the cat actually exist in the closed box if you can't see it? A famous philosophical quandary."

"I don't care about philosophy," I said, frowning. "I'm talking about physics."

"So was he," Rafe smiled, approvingly. "Physics and philosophy, science and stories, are more intertwined then *some*"—he looked at Matthew—"might make it seem. Those fables about your family aren't nothing. They're clues. They're a way to move through time, both figuratively and literally."

"So instead of moving in the straight line, you want to start doubling back," I said, nodding. "To start moving in spirals."

"Exactly! For decades scholars have thought it was words that held the secret to entry," said Rafe. "But it seems clear to me it's movement. It's *presence* that's needed. *Physicality*. Skin"—he winked—"on skin. Wouldn't you say?"

"Yes," I said. "Physicality. Of course."

"I knew you'd understand."

I wondered how much Rafe actually knew about me. He showed no sign of having been aware of my existence before our first encounter in the graveyard. I was certain that Peter had taken great pains to hide any connection between the research he published as the Toymaker and the anthropological work that he did under his own name. Rafe's language was likely haphazard, his discussion of the physical meant not to frighten me but rather to provoke the response he must be used to from girls softened by his smile. Still, I felt anxious. I tried to appear normal. I kept my fingers hidden in the sleeves of my jacket. I shifted in my seat so that Rafe would not accidentally touch me while gesticulating. He did seem quite clever. I hoped he hadn't guessed.

"Here," he had said, outside that café at the edge of the highway, leaning down to pet a dog tied next to Marlowe. "Let him sniff your fingers, Maisie, he's a sweet one. Come give him a pat."

"Here," in Matthew's car, passing back a paper bag, "it's just dried fruit and nuts, if you're hungry."

"Look! Go pick that flower. The color would be gorgeous in your hair."

He doesn't know, I told myself. How could he?

The Undiscovered Country

Deep in the wood, Imogen stalks a roaming roebuck, its tufty bottom a white shock against tangles of green. Her feet are blistered, her gut aches, yet she follows, for she feels she must do something, find some semblance of release for the pressure that has tightened her spine since the black-eyed girl awoke.

This wood makes all the women hunters. They know the animals within can never die, but cannot help but make chase. There is no better show of human power than to be proud purveyor of death, to attempt slaughter. To kill for sport, for indulgence, speaks to the infinite depths of human desire, an innate need to demonstrate the irreversible, to have lasting effect. Here, where time flows like honey, where their own deaths have died, the women need and they need, and it frightens them. During the hunt, that need abates.

The buck crashes into the black-eyed girl's grove, paying the frozen child no mind, crossing a short distance and then pausing, looking back in hopes that stillness will lull his pursuer to submission. A yellow butterfly dances about his black nostrils, forcing him to sneeze in a sharp burst of breath.

Although Imogen does stop short when she breaks into the clearing, it is not because of the buck. Her impediment is the black-eyed girl herself, still lying motionless and silent on her pallet. Imogen sees the girl and stumbles, hands clutching her large, laden stomach. The color drains from her face. She crosses herself, whispering a prayer of protection.

Once Imogen has withdrawn her attention, the roebuck decides the chase has passed. Several hundred feet away, he nibbles at a bush, grunting as he digests, while Imogen stands staring at the black-eyed girl. Her anger shifts to something less tangible, water to mist.

Suddenly, the buck coughs and emits a distressed bleat, full-throated and low. He collapses, foam erupting from his mouth. Imogen watches. Nothing sickens in this shadow wood. In her centuries in residence, she has seen nothing die. She goes to the roebuck, strokes his neck and coos to him. She notices a cluster of bright berries tucked under the leaves where he had stopped to eat.

The animal twitches, his back leg manic, splayed at an improper angle, hummingbird quick. And then the convulsions slow until they cease altogether, the last notes of the roebuck's life played out. His glassy eyes remain open.

Imogen runs a finger along the short fringe of his lashes, the knobbled stubs of his velvety antlers, the jaunty tips of his shapely ears. She goes to the roughage and plucks a stem of three ovular berries, their red almost translucent in the light. She rubs the branch between two fingers, spinning it, making the berries dance. She carries them to the black-eyed girl.

Solemnly, fully aware of the sin she is committing, Imogen holds the fruit to the black-eyed girl's mouth. The black-eyed girl cannot turn her head or curse her. She cannot spit the sweet back in Imogen's face, which is stoic as she exits the clearing.

The black-eyed girl blinks. She swallows the berries, relishing their juices. What might kill a roebuck will not harm her, not here in this wood. A different hunger gently prods her, a patient reminder, polite. *Soon*, she tells it, *soon*.

She wiggles her largest left toe.

13

Rafe was emphatic that without traveling each stop along the path, we'd be accomplishing nothing, which meant first one long twisting trek through muddy fields and sparse groves, and then another as we made our way back along the outer rings, walking in the opposite direction. Only then, said Rafe, could we fully explore the spiral's center. Matthew said the whole affair reminded him of groups that went in search of missing bodies. Rafe whistled as we walked, his spirits high.

"Ever since I can remember, I've been set on doing things correctly," he said, grinning. "Whether showing all my work at complex math problems when I was a kid, or slaving over ancient runes' translations during my graduate studies. Better to do it slowly and correctly the first time than have to start all over, am I right? It's always bothered the bejeezus out of my mother, who'd ask why I needed so long to tie a shoelace, or why I was ignoring my little sister's scraped knee. I'd tell her I wasn't ignoring anything, just focused. I'd say to get what you want out of life, it's important to have singular focus, wouldn't you?"

I was behind him, so he didn't see me nod.

Matthew, who'd gone on ahead of us, unconcerned with proper foot placement, was not yet so far that he could not hear Rafe's speech. He didn't make a sound, but in response strayed deliberately from the path, so that rather than tracing a spiral he was walking toward our ultimate location in a diagonal line.

It was dark by the time Rafe and I joined him back at the outer edge of that first spiral, where we had left the car.

"We're going to call it a night," Matthew said. "It's too dark to do anything else."

"Too dark to look for Peter? But he might be in trouble. We should keep on through the night, just in case."

Matthew shook his head. "We've waited this long already. And we'll be more effective at . . . whatever this is . . . with a few hours of sleep."

"Why don't you rest here, and Maisie and I will head back into—" Rafe started.

"No," said Matthew. "We'll stick together, and we'll wait until it's light."

Rafe shrugged, then winked at me. "Whatever you say, Captain. Don't worry, Maisie." He put a hand on my sleeve, and I tried not to startle at the contact, to wait the appropriate amount of time before pulling away. "A few hours won't make much difference. I've got a quick call to make. Be back soon."

I watched him walk off with his mobile phone, tracking his movements by its unnatural light, and tried to parse the meaning of that wink while Matthew prepared a place for us to sleep. If Rafe said a few hours wouldn't matter, then they wouldn't. He knew more about my father's journey than I did. And along with his interest in Peter and the forest, Rafe was apparently now interested in me. Unlike Matthew's interest—cold and cautious, scientific—I felt a heat from Rafe's attentions. I felt a strength in the curves of my hips and the heft of my breasts, a power budding every time Rafe looked at me.

When he returned, we spent the night as we would for most of our journey: myself sprawled across the back seat, Matthew and Rafe out on blankets in the grass, flanking each side of the car. It was like camping trips he'd taken as a kid, Matthew insisted. Rafe told me that he liked to see the stars.

WE RETURNED TO the center of the spiral the next morning to discover an abandoned, three-walled structure that had been hidden by the mist the night before. We were, I realized, at the westernmost edge of the forest that bordered Urizon, though it seemed hardly the same being, its trees slimmer and spread much farther apart, its floor level, the grass lush. Mother Farrow had told me that at one point this whole continent was forest, webs of wood from coast to coast. Like an emperor expanding his holdings, one original tree must have seeded and spread, until a migratory bird might look down to see green in all directions.

"I thought there was a lock we had to fasten. Or unfasten," said Matthew, leaning against the far side of the building, watching us walk around the structure with his arms crossed over his chest.

"Not a literal one," said Rafe. Again he put a hand on my sleeve, giving my clothed shoulder a squeeze of recognition, as if to suggest that I understood what Matthew did not. This time, I did not startle at his touch.

We could see the sky through the rifts in the roof. A gray morning light made a brief halo over Matthew's hair, then was gone as wispy clouds sailed past to block it. A thin stream of sweat had gathered between my breasts, another at my temple.

On the side opposite from which Matthew had parked, we found what seemed to be a cellar—a dug-in pit, lined at the bottom with stone. A fossilized ladder led from the side of the barn down into the hole.

"Looks like an old jail cell," said Matthew, behind me. "See the remains of the chains?"

THE NEXT LEG of our drive was spent debating the significance of the jail cell, and discussing the meaning of the spirals and their role in Rafe's research. Matthew took the stance that we were wasting time, our efforts clearly amounting to nothing.

"What, you were expecting some rift in the sky? Some blaze of light? That isn't how it works. Unrealistic." Rafe shook his head, half smiling.

"Something, at least," said Matthew, pulling onto the main highway.

"There is something," Rafe countered. "A sort of electricity. You can feel it, Maisie, can't you?"

I nodded, though the charge surging through my body seemed to have more to do with Rafe himself than our recent accomplishment. I noticed every time he shifted weight in front of me, aware of his slightest adjustment. Was he equally attuned to my movements? At times I thought I caught him looking at me, his expression one of thoughtful satisfaction. I wanted to unsettle him. When I leaned down to retie my shoelace, I deliberately repositioned my shirt so that the tops of my breasts were just visible, pressed together.

Once we had exhausted the topics of rituals and deities and doors, I found myself dallying with flirtatious repartee, at which I was not adept, but was aided by the loud bursts of sound that periodically exploded from the engine of the car and distracted from my worst faux pas.

"So you've never seen the city? You are in for quite a treat," Rafe said.

"I know I am, especially seeing it with you. I'm sure there's more that we can see . . . together."

I caught the reflection of Matthew's rolling eyes in the rearview mirror.

WE STOPPED AT a roadside oasis for something to eat after I'd spent twenty minutes remarking to no one in particular that we hadn't done much the night before regarding dinner. Matthew went in to order us some sandwiches and coffee, leaving me alone, for the moment, with Rafe. We got out of the car to stretch our legs, the small dirt parking lot empty around us, despite Matthew's worry that there'd be a crowd inside.

"Your hair looks pretty like that," said Rafe. "Did you have it that way before?"

My body tingled with the compliment, urging me toward him. I wasn't sure how to respond, but before I could embarrass myself I started coughing, my throat suddenly blocked.

"Maisie?"

My face was hot, my head felt buoyant. Rafe gave me a large thump on the back, which only increased my discomfort. "Are you choking?" he asked, and I shook my head, although I thought perhaps I was, and the panic that accompanied this thought made me gag harder.

Rafe wrung his hands, then pressed them against his own abdomen, as if practicing for how he might assist me. Luckily, we had no need for his experimentation. After a moment, the guilty parties showed themselves: three perfectly round red berries came up in a swirl of bile and landed on the grass. I cleared my throat, embarrassed and confused. I'd had a scone for breakfast, and a cheese sandwich the night before. There had been no berries. I had not eaten any berries.

"I'll grab some water for you," Rafe said, dashing over to the car.

"I must not have chewed them properly," I mumbled. "Silly of me." Had I imagined it? But, no, Rafe had seen them too. Were they some sort of warning? A reminder of the dangers that awaited if I listened to the urges I had recently discovered, if I gave myself to Rafe? A punishment for wanting.

I shook off the thought, "I'm fine." A viscous wetness like an amniotic sac held the berries, clustered in the grass. "I'm fine," I repeated. But I could not rid myself of the bitter taste the berries had left upon my tongue.

A Few Brief Years of Possibility

The black-eyed girl lies on her bier and blinks up at the silhouettes of branches, wisps of cloud. A bold bird hovers close above her, while others warble his praise from their perch on the outstretched finger of a nearby poplar. These wrens have teased the black-eyed girl for weeks, now. They've grown reckless, diving and cheeping, showing off for their brothers. Beautiful, dull targets, putting themselves within reach.

Look!

Closer comes this spotted wren, closer, closer. *Here*, he thinks, *what fun*. He has learned from the others, watched them experiment, rejoiced each time they returned to the tree branch, boasting of success.

The foolish wren emits a mating call, darts back, giving a sly, beady look to his intended paramour. He whistles. Down he comes. A wing brushes the black-eyed girl's cheek.

Her hand shoots up, reflexes newly tight, a spring come suddenly uncoiled. The black-eyed girl grabs the wren. She feels his oily skin against her own, the straw blades of his feathers.

She squeezes.

ACROSS THE CLEARING, Mary watches the bird, hears the gush of his insides collapsing. Afraid, but too curious to run, she hides behind a large tree. Cheek pressed to bark, she peers carefully around until her own eyes meet those black ones, upon which Mary twitches and then disappears from the black-eyed girl's view. Mary takes several slow breaths, bracing herself against the tree trunk, observed by a rabbit that has halted his consumption of a sprig of purple flowers. She hisses at the animal, hoping to frighten him away, but the rabbit merely frowns at Mary and continues his meal.

Mary's mythology is limited. Despite all Lucy has told her of toppling empires, breaking ground, Mary can think of only one use for a child of the forest. Mary wants the black-eyed girl to grant her wishes. Ideally there will be three, a proper number, but Mary is not so proud that she'd falter at just one. And if the girl has only one wish to bestow upon the women of the forest, Mary is determined to make that wish her own.

After all, Mary has the most to wish for. The others in the forest are preserved in youthful beauty, their skin forever smooth and tight, their hair never to gray. Mary remains middle-aged, fleshy and afraid, reminded of mortality even while she knows she'll live forever. She'd sacrifice the centuries to come for one more year at two and twenty, for invisible pores, for knees that do not creak. She stands frozen between fear and longing, hoping to summon a courage that has failed her before.

Ask, Mary commands herself, *go ask it*.

It, the wish, or it, the wish-giver? Much easier to crush sympathy with words stripped of their meaning, to be forceful with a creature known as *it*, rather than *she*. To use language to devalue a body.

Mary steps out from her shelter, inches toward the girl. She sniffs, and wipes her nose against a sleeve.

One black eye winks.

Mary flees the clearing as quickly as her clumsy feet allow.

14

When we stopped the car at early evening to relieve our bladders by some blossoming elders, Matthew took advantage of my sudden separation from Rafe. Twilight had risen and the sky was now a fading purple-blue, spread wider above us than I had ever seen it, prickled with emergent bursts of stars. The rising land swelled like a mother with child.

"Stop mooning over him," Matthew said quietly to me once Rafe was out of hearing. "Nothing good will come of it."

"What do you mean?" I knew exactly what he meant.

"This thing with Rafe. Just end it now."

"I cannot imagine of what you might be speaking," I said, thrilled to confirm that our flirtation had been more than just my fancy.

"He can't touch you. You can't touch him. What kind of love affair does that make? And besides, he's so much older. If you have any sense, you'll stop this before you expose yourself."

I made a face at Matthew. I did not need his warning to know it was a dangerous game I played with Rafe. I could not hide the desire that emanated off my skin. I wondered how close I could get, how close I could bring him, how much I could make him want my body before pulling it away. Did I want him to reach for me, to press my flesh to his? My body seemed to want it, but my body could never be trusted. My body was a wild thing I had tamed into submission, and yet part of me knew at any second it might lash out, it might fight me. I knew that Matthew was right, and I hated him for it.

And what if the intimacy Rafe wanted was more than the physical? Perhaps, as Matthew claimed, his motivations were not as transparent as they seemed. Perhaps he'd want to know me underneath the skin, the secret of my feelings toward my body, rather than the flesh itself. This thought was even more intimate, even more frightening, than imagining him tangled up inside me. I was caught up in these thoughts as the boys shuffled back into the car, as Matthew tried to turn the engine, as it gave an awful squeak.

"Dammit," he said softly, one of the few times I had ever heard him swear, "the ignition won't catch."

"Let me have at it." Rafe hopped back out the side and bent down to examine the front of the car, which even in the growing darkness released a visible hiss of steam. Matthew moved to join him, lifted its hood. I scrambled out so as not to be excluded, for the moment setting aside my questions about Rafe.

The various gears and wires that comprised the car's engine looked to me like a monster, one who'd come out at the wrong end of a fight, with small steel grommets freckling its complexion, hair like oily gray noodles, big black bulging eyes. I reached out to touch it.

"Careful," said Rafe, his arm stopping mine. He'd only touched my shirtsleeve, but the pressure of his palm made me shiver.

"I see the problem, I think," Matthew said, brushing his hair back from his brow, leaving a small streak of grease across his forehead. He frowned and bent over the engine, his torso disappearing into the monster's maw.

"We should call for a mechanic," said Rafe, "get it towed."

"We've been out of range of mobile service for the past hour." Matthew's voice echoed from the inside of the car. He resurfaced to cough loudly, then dove back into the wreckage.

"I'll walk back to the turnoff for the town we passed," said Rafe. "If they don't have someone there who can help us, I can at the very least ask to use a phone." He turned to look at me. "Maisie, why don't you come with me?"

At this Matthew sprang so quickly from under the hood that he slammed his head against it.

"No," he said, "Maisie stays here. You can move faster on your own."

"I'm actually—"

"No." It was the tone Peter used when he would not be persuaded, the vowel extended, punctuated with a strong purse of the lips. Matthew was not my father, had no legal power over me, but the similar force of his denial made me see myself a child. Tired and decidedly uninterested in the prospect of another long walk, I decided that I wouldn't press the issue. I shrugged.

"I guess that's settled, then." Rafe met my eyes. "But I'll be back soon. Don't worry, Maisie, this will all be fine. Probably best not to mess with things until we get word from the experts."

Matthew emerged once more to scowl. Rafe grinned, patted the pockets of his jacket, and set off down the road, walking quickly. When he was out of sight, Matthew returned to the engine.

"Rafe just said not to—" I started, but was silenced by the steely expression on Matthew's face when he looked up at me.

So I sat on the side of the road and watched him fiddle about, unsure of how he could see clearly in the fast-dying twilight. What if another car needed to pass us, I wondered, with Matthew elbow-deep in gears and wires? What if Rafe did not return before true darkness? I chewed my fingernails as Matthew traveled from driver's seat to hood, testing his handiwork, finding it lacking. Again and again, attempt and fail, another tweak, the pitiful sputter of whatever would not catch.

Eventually I curled into myself, hugging my knees, drowsy.

I WAS WRENCHED from my nap by the hack of Matthew's cough, the crash of his body against metal, the slither of his jacket as he slid from the car's hood to the road. I jumped up, hobbling toward him on stiff legs.

The night had settled into variegated darkness, a full moon and clear sky casting thin shafts of light. Matthew's body was crumpled on the ground in front of the car. A steady hiss came from below the car's hood, and as I rushed over I caught the whiff of a sour heady smell, burning and rotten. Had Matthew inhaled some sort of gas that made him dizzy? Instinctively, I grabbed Matthew by his uninjured arm, using my sleeve to shield him from my touch, and dragged him off the road. I knelt to examine him further and found a raw red burn at his elbow and a blossoming blister, the size and color of a plum, upon his palm. I pushed with knees and elbows, trying to turn his body over, and saw his eyes were open, pupils huge. He started convulsing, his head slapping irregularly, hard against the ground.

I took my jacket and rested it atop him to keep warm, but Matthew continued to toss about as if lost in some nightmare, his gray eyes open and glazed, their veins red and spindly. I tried to hold him still, but it was useless. His neck whipped one way, then the next, in rapid succession.

Sitting cross-legged next to him, I spread my skirt over my knees. I slid the fabric under Matthew's head, taking care not to touch him, and eventually shimmied it up into my lap.

"There," I whispered, my lips so close that had he been in his right mind I'm sure he would have felt my breath. "That's more comfortable, isn't it?"

Confined by my folded legs, the head thrashing slowed, then ceased altogether. Some hair had jostled out over Matthew's forehead, prickling up against his eye, and I regretted not having had the presence of mind to grab gloves from my bag before going to him.

"Rafe?" I let out a hoarse whisper, the loudest I could manage without using my full voice. Unsure of how long I had slept, I didn't know how long we'd been out here, how long Rafe had been gone. I heard no response. I called again, and louder. Still nothing.

Matthew's breath was slowing, the moaning stopped.

"We told you to let the mechanic take care of it," I whispered. That wayward lock of hair was sopping, more brown than it was gold.

Dread settled as a weight in my chest, making my limbs heavy, pulling me down. I felt that we were sinking, that the sky was widening and growing ever farther away.

"Rafe!" I called out, almost screaming. "Rafe!"

Then Matthew was no longer breathing at all. A reddish liquid dribbled from the corner of his mouth. His eyes rolled back, showing just their moony whites. His forehead shone with sweat. His jaw was clenched, his shoulders shuddering, each seizure striking my body as I tried to hold him still.

And so I did the only thing I could. Steeling myself, feeling an aching in my chest, I swept my fingertips across Matthew's forehead, combing the hair back from his face. At my touch I felt his body cool, grow stiff. I took a breath.

There had been very few times in my life that I had touched another person. In recent memory, there was nothing: Matthew was the first since I'd been made to understand my father's rules. I waited several long seconds before reaching back down, savoring the sweet anticipation, knowing I might never touch bare skin again. Finally I pressed two of my fingers to a lymph node in his neck, holding them there until I felt his pulse.

Matthew's eyes fluttered closed. His chest rose with breath.

My body was numb; I felt as if the blood had all drained out of me. "Thank goodness," I whispered. I tucked the jacket around Matthew, whose color had softened, who mumbled in his sleep. Strange, I thought, that I could see him so clearly. Had a cloud unleashed the moon?

It had not. I turned and found myself in the beam of a truck's headlights, saw Rafe climbing down from the passenger's-side door. A woman sat in the driver's seat, her face in shadow.

"Maisie!" Rafe ran to me. "What happened? When we pulled up, I could have sworn Matthew had . . . it looked like he was . . ."

I could have kissed him, and squeezed my fingers to fists to keep from reaching for his hand.

"The engine sparked," I said slowly. "There was a small electrocution. It was frightening, but I think he'll be all right."

The woman came to join us, surveying Matthew and his car.

"Not much to do out here, tonight," she said. "In the morning we can call and get you towed, find out what we'll have to do to fix you. I can bring you three back with me, give you a place to pass the night, but if you need a hospital, that's different. Have to push on toward the city, several hours."

"We don't," Matthew croaked, sitting up blearily.

I considered protesting, insisting we get Matthew to a doctor, but I knew that I had cured him, and to press the issue further would raise questions that I did not want unearthed. Unless he already suspected, there was no way for Rafe to know what he had seen, to understand what had happened with Matthew. Still, I felt suddenly exposed.

Matthew was stretching, yawning, circling his right wrist. I caught a flash of his confusion, saw the moment that he brushed it away. When he stood, he lacked balance, and Rafe offered his arm. I stayed put.

"Can we keep the car here, overnight?" Matthew asked, accepting Rafe's arm without acknowledging its source. "No harm will come to it?"

"Not with the hood still smoking. Not if you lock it up tight."

Matthew nodded. His eyes shot again to his wrist as he flexed it, then to the woman.

"I'll have an estimate tomorrow," she said. "Find out how much repairs will cost you, how long repairs will be."

The Ceremonials

This is what we'll do," says Lucy. The other women gather around her, looking every so often in the direction of the black-eyed girl's clearing, some hundred yards away. Equally nervous and excited. "There is a ritual," says Lucy. "A drowning. I learned of it in a sacred book—an old tradition from the east, a way to end the winter, welcome summer and spring. Perhaps a way to let the wood know that we're ready to end our long season here. A way to strengthen our daughter."

Mary, focused, nodding. Emma curious. Imogen frightened. Kathryn sucking on an index finger. Helen, perpetually dazed.

"The drowning of death," says Alys. All turn to her, surprised to hear her speak. Lucy's eyes widen. She cannot know her sacred book was authored by Alys's cousin Madenn, that the ritual she speaks of was carried thousands of miles across mountains and sea by great-grandmothers, brought south with settlers, north with Alys's mother's marriage.

"The drowning of death," Lucy repeats. "We make an effigy, immerse it, and in doing so we bid farewell to old seasons, we welcome in the new."

"A poppet?" asks Imogen, shuddering at the word, the mere mention of which, in her former life, led women to the pyre. "Of the girl?"

"A poppet of death." Lucy frowns at her. "Not of the child."

But Imogen knows that death and the black-eyed girl are one and the same.

"What about the other girl?" asks Kathryn. "The living one. Will we be drowning her too?"

"We aren't drowning anyone," says Lucy. "It's symbolic."

"Well, if it's just symbolic, then what will it do?" Helen asks.

Helen is the last of the women from whom Lucy expects argument.
She squeezes her eyes shut, exasperated, and speaks very slowly, as if
addressing a child.

"It's a sign, like a prayer, to the gods or to nature. We banish death,
we banish winter, we banish whatever force has kept our woodland
daughter silent and still for so long."

"But just the other day Mary saw her take that——" Emma begins.

"Enough," says Lucy. "Will you join me?"

Helen looks to Alys, who is silent. Mary will, of course; the steady
spaniel always loyal to her mistress. Kathryn loves change, any excitement. Emma likes the idea of crafting a doll. Imogen likes the idea of
destroying a doll, the possibility that this could be the black-eyed
girl's destruction. Helen waits to see what Alys will say before deciding.

It stirs a strange melancholy for Alys to hear her family's rituals
distilled thus by Lucy. The spring before the soldiers took the river—
that spring which, centuries ago, preceded this eternal summer—Alys
and the women of her clan had brought their own effigy to the water,
welcoming the changing season, celebrating the turn from death to
rebirth. What that ritual actually did now seems irrelevant—whether
it was Alys impacting the river and the season, or the season indeli-
bly marking Alys, does not matter. That she took action, that she
noticed and honored each differing sensation, that she loved the land,
her body—that was the resurrection. That was what the land desired,
what it deserved.

Alys nods. She'll follow Lucy. She'll make communion with her
family one last time.

15

I must have drifted off in the back of the mechanic's truck, for I had no recollection of arriving at any destination, nor of being carried into the foreign room in which I found myself the next morning. Venturing down a flight of narrow stairs, I discovered my companions gathered at the center of an open garage, and right away I understood why the mechanic, Ginny Ranke, had gone to such trouble to solicit our business. The place was outfitted for at least ten other cars, but Matthew's sat alone in a back corner. The other ready spaces showed no sign of recent use. In a far corner, a generator buzzed with monotonous static. A mountain of tires emitted a chemical smell.

"At least four hours to fix the engine," said Ginny, "and another few days or so to get in all the parts." The shelves lining the garage were filled with car parts, so I did not understand why we couldn't be en route by evening. "Not much around nearby," Ginny told us, "but for extra cost I'll take care of your meals."

WE PASSED SEVERAL days with no deliveries in sight, though we did have a roof to sleep under, and a freezer's worth of sustenance to heat at our leisure, which Matthew claimed put us in a much better spot than we might otherwise have found ourselves. Ginny told us to be patient, that she'd put in all the orders, that deliveries weren't as prompt out here on the moors as we were used to in the cities. I was not used to any deliveries, prompt or no, and was surprised to learn that people made careers of couriering, were paid to transport packages, left always to wonder what might be inside.

"What if they're bringing something dangerous?" I asked, "or something uniquely wonderful? Don't they want to open up the boxes and find out what they're carrying?"

"They're used to not knowing," said Matthew. "And it's illegal to tamper with other people's mail."

"Maybe they did tamper, this time," said Rafe. "Maybe some delivery-man needed a new battery. Maybe that's why our order is taking so long."

Rafe was restless—he spent almost an hour outside, pacing while talking on his mobile, and when he returned to the garage he seemed unsettled. I understood his anxiety. We both knew that each delayed day meant we fell farther behind Peter, who must be long ahead of us, perhaps even already in the wood. Matthew studied his anatomy textbooks while Rafe and I twiddled our thumbs waiting, every so often offering a quick glance up to let me know he was not totally engaged in his studies and at least halfway listening to the stories that Rafe told me to pass time.

Rafe claimed that these were tales he'd come across during his work, and that each was of vital importance to the legend of the enchanted wood that we hoped to enter. In one, a father killed his child in an attempt to seek out magic. In another, a young doctor gave up his fiancée in exchange for secret words. In a third, a man's body was bled slowly, until he appeared to be a ghost.

"Impossible," Matthew broke in at the close of that one. "A person can't survive without blood. Slicing an artery would mean the man died instantly. If the witch was going to take that much blood it would have to be done slowly, letting the body replenish before she took more."

"It's just a story," I said.

"A story of a sacrifice," Rafe added, looking at me hungrily. "And a brave one, at that."

Matthew sighed and closed his book, swinging a leg over the bench that he was seated on to face us. He seemed about to speak, but then he shook his head slowly, as if he felt sorry for us, as if he had already attained the wisdom we were trying so desperately to reach and found it wanting. As if Rafe's stories, which I saw as clues to help me find my father, told us nothing. He rolled his shoulders, and walked out of the room.

AT THE END of the third day of waiting, I decided that enough was enough.

"We aren't so far from the second spiral that we can't wake up early and walk there. It would take, what, two hours, to get us to the start?"

"That's a lot of extra walking," said Matthew, "and then more walking once you got there. And then the walk back."

"I'm game for it," said Rafe. "Why don't we go, just the two of us, Maisie?"

Matthew scoffed. I turned to him, smirking. "Aren't you the one who told me I should move for moving's sake? I would think you'd like the exercise."

Matthew shrugged, his mouth a lipless line, and busied himself packing up his knapsack.

BEFORE THE SUN rose the next morning, we set out in the direction of the river, which appeared to intersect the second spiral on our map. There was a town just past the water, said Ginny, where we could stop and have lunch before heading back her way. She was fairly certain that by then she'd have the parts to fix the car.

We followed the spiral path as closely as was possible, yet found no sign of the river.

"You must have gotten the coordinates wrong," said Matthew as we finished the final curve of the outer loop, the sun more than midway through its trip across the sky. "Or made a wrong turn. We should break off or go back."

"This is it," said Rafe, tone clipped. "I measured it precisely. If we take a true path to the center, we should find the river soon."

"That logic makes absolutely no sense," said Matthew, pushing damp hair off his neck and cracking his shoulders. "We've just spent hours walking in circles, with no river in sight. At this rate, we might as well just walk until we've reached the city."

"If we ignore the map," Rafe countered, "we're likely to get lost. Better to keep a sharp eye out and hope we find the river."

"Ridiculous."

"No, likely."

This seemed to me more a battle of wills than a pragmatic assessment of our problem. Matthew's theory seemed more sensible, but I hated to choose one side over the other. I let myself fall behind, contemplating the scenery.

The stretches of wood that had marked the first leg of our travels had grown smaller and farther between, usurped by long laps of moorland, purpled with heather and spackled with rock. It was a landscape more lonesome and majestic than any I had known. If the forest filled me with awe at the earth, the strength of the life that burst through it, this country was the saga of the sky: its infinity, the way the clouds hung low like honey as it settled into tea. Even the walking could have been heavenly, were it not for thirst and hunger, and the boys' continued bickering about whether or not we were lost.

Matthew was walking slowly, having decided to seek out a side road despite Rafe's concerns. Both had resorted to mumbling their grievances under their breaths. I lapsed farther behind, now deliberately avoiding them, and so I was the one to spot the first signs of the others on our route.

First came shadows on the crags, undulating, growing, and then I heard the sound of chanting to my left. Voices blended with the rush of the wind, which seemed stronger than it had been, and bittersweet, ruffling the heather in hefty swells. I cracked my knuckles.

"Maisie!" Rafe called. "What are you—"

I put a finger to my lips in an exaggerated gesture that I hoped he and Matthew would recognize, and turned to point beside me.

A group of seven women, all dressed in rags, came in a slow procession across the road, dividing me from my companions. They wore flowers in their hair and tied as necklaces, braided into bracelets, around their heads as wreaths. Their ages ranged from around five years to mid-thirties, their shapes and colors varied, but each with equally clear eyes and determined, pursed mouths. In the bleak, cloud-filtered sunlight, they might have been specters, or ghosts. They crossed in front of me, not heeding.

I tried to hail them, but they gave me no acknowledgment, simply continued with their singing, which I realized was in a tongue I did not understand. It sounded slippery, susurrant, from some other unknown world.

They moved like a gaggle of geese, their dresses rustling, their song not quite in tune. The tallest two women were gathered at the center of the group, carrying between them a small box shaped like a coffin. I positioned myself to better see it: an open casket, lined in leaves. Resting inside was the branch of what I thought to be a beech tree, with an ill-fitting green apple tied carefully with twigs onto one end.

At the back of the procession was the smallest of the gathering, a little girl who skipped along, struggling to match pace. A large port-wine stain marred her cheek, and her eyes were thin and narrow. As she reached the far side of the road, she, alone, looked back.

After a moment to process my surprise I hurried after the women, paying no mind to Rafe and Matthew calling after me, then hustling to follow behind. I caught up with the youngest of the mourners just as the group was slowing to a stop beside a half-hidden stream. It was small but not stagnant, shimmering deliciously, nestled between two walls of tall grass the way a bonnet's ribbon might hide in the folds of a fat woman's chin.

The women seemed reverent of the water. None of them were touching it, their chanting continuing and rippling across it like skipped stones. Though tranquil when they reached it, the wind, their words, the ceremonials, were stirring, somehow stretching the stream, helping it awaken. Like a wound renting, small and pinkish at first and then pooling with blood, it seemed to widen. The tall grasses around it seemed to wane.

Matthew appeared next to me, clutching my sleeve.

The pallbearers lowered their child-sized coffin, and the other women moved to make way. One, tall and narrow, with a long solemn face that seemed to have paused mid-melting—the hollows under her eyes sinking low past her cheekbones, her skin inordinately pale and veined, her lips a shade of blue—knelt next to the box as if in prayer. The other six bowed their heads beside her. Their chanting stopped.

The pale woman lifted the branch from the box and took it slowly to the water, where she plunged it, apple downward, into the stream as a sword might plunge into flesh. The moor was silent as I watched her, the wind suddenly calm. She held her effigy submerged with such force one might have thought it was a man that she was drowning. The other women gave a cheer and resumed chanting, this time louder, almost raucous. The pale one hurled the stick into the stream, which had continued to stretch and expand. Its water moved faster now, its width five times the size it had been, its movement forming rapids that frothed and spat white foam. And then there came several incomprehensible moments that even now I'd claim to be the most intriguing of my life.

I could not say where I was or what was happening around me. I felt but could not quite perceive a strange green sky and rumbling thunder, snow and rain and sunshine all at once, bells playing distant music, bone-deep vigor, cool crisp air. I could hear, but not feel, myself laughing. And then all at once it seemed that I'd forgotten how to breathe, that my lungs had paused mid-motion, were being squeezed by some great fist. I found myself coughing, unable to reject the sudden liquid that was pooling in my chest, creeping up behind my nose, pouring out of me as though I was a conduit, a fountain. I retched, and felt a strong hand slap my back. My body was burning, my skin prickling for lack of air.

The violent retching ceased. Matthew thumped me on the back, and I came to myself. I blinked to see the women, and found they'd transformed with the water: they were girls now. Simple girls wearing swimming costumes, playing in the river, splashing one another and giggling. I saw no sign of the child with her port-wine stain, the woman with the sickly blue lips. Rafe was kneeling at the bank of the newly formed river, cupping his hands to take a drink. I stood back with Matthew.

"What do you make of it?" I asked him, struggling to catch my breath.

"Of this?" His voice was low. "We can assume the water's safe, if they're here swimming, though I'd recommend against jumping in to join them. It's amazing that you heard them from the road. We would have gone right past the river if you hadn't followed their noise."

"No." I shook my head. "I mean the . . . changing . . . the colors . . . the way the water . . . When those women . . ." I stopped. He was looking at me curiously.

"Your fit of coughing just now?"

"Yes. No. I don't . . ." The front of my shirt, my shoes, were all dry, as was the grass before me. There was no visible sign of my struggle, no way to explain my experience without heightening the differences between me and these girls by the river, no way to describe my body without showing him how little I truly understood it. I shook my head and moved to join Rafe at the water.

Your Mother, Waiting

L ucy returns to the clearing to find the black-eyed girl upright, seated with her legs hanging over her stone bed frame. All the feathers have been plucked from the crushed wren—*It loves me, loves me not*—and lie around her, scattered in a downy fairy ring. The bird's scabby carcass has been thrown to lie beside the dead roebuck, which has already melted fully into undergrowth, the only signs of its history its yellowing ribs, its still symmetrical antlers.

Lucy brushes away a clump of feathers and kneels before the black-eyed girl, reaching up for her hands: "For everything, I thank you."

The black-eyed girl is stronger, but not yet strong enough to laugh at Lucy, the pomposity of her rituals, the solemnity with which she speaks. She presses her jagged fingernails, too short to cause pain, into Lucy's palm, and hears a quick intake of breath. She cocks her head and smiles.

Lucy straightens her shoulders. Points to herself and says slowly, loudly, "Lucy."

Tedious. The black-eyed girl clears her throat and tries to speak, but is capable only of the sort of animal grunting that confirms Lucy's surmise.

"So much to teach you"—Lucy's eyes gleam—"so much that we two can create."

16

To no surprise of mine, Rafe made quick work of gathering information from the girls. He befriended the littlest one, eight years old at most, who wore a neon-pink two-piece bathing suit and an elaborate braid in her hair.

"Colette says that the water's rarely warm enough to swim in. That's why all these ladies are out in full force today. Colette says it's only this one spot, really, the exact center of our second spiral, that has some sort of current that keeps it from being too cold." Rafe flicked a finger at me, sending several water droplets in a mist across my cheek. It felt wonderful, and I gave only a brief thought to the countless invisible organisms I'd no doubt disrupted.

"Does she now?" said Matthew, coming toward us and stooping to fill a canteen. He produced a previously unseen canister of orange liquid, and squeezed in two large drops before handing it to me. "Wait sixty seconds before you take a drink."

Once I'd sated myself, I examined the girls who'd so mysteriously shifted shape. So much bare skin—some brown, some milky white, some sunburned red and peeling. One floated on her back, her stomach spilling from her soaking string bikini, her hair spread like seaweed behind her. Another spit water through her teeth. Several older ones, particularly pretty, flocked to young Colette when she splashed back into the river, fluttering their lashes and twirling their hair, making bovine eyes in our direction.

"For you, I'm sure," I said, frowning, pointing them out to Rafe. He shrugged and smiled, more pleased with himself than apologetic.

"We should look for a topographical map when we get back to the garage," he said. "I'm curious to see if this river connects in some way to the one near Coeurs Crossing. My guess is they share the same source, that water's bound up in the ritual. I'd bet the last spiral turns out to be right by the major river—"

Rafe stopped himself, acknowledging little Colette as she skipped forward, twirling the wet end of her braid, her suit dripping onto his shoes.

"My sisters and cousins wonder if you might come back to join us for a meal," she said. "My mother made a large dinner, and it is only fitting that you might . . ." Here she looked over her shoulder at the aforementioned sisters and cousins now emerging from the water, their heads making insistent nods as they wrapped themselves in towels. "That you might join us."

Before Rafe could answer, both Matthew and I responded at once.

"Of course!" Despite the strong sense that I'd developed legitimate competition for my paramour's affections, I was thrilled. My hunger trumped any brewing jealousy. Most exciting was the thought that I would finally participate in the sort of friendly gathering I'd only ever accessed from afar. Our quest had given me courage, and I saw myself a far cry from the frightened girl who'd hidden from the baby carriages in Matthew's car back in Coeurs Crossing.

But with just as much vigor, Matthew declined the invitation. "Really, thank you kindly, but we must be on our way." He widened his eyes at me, the gesture I'd begun to see as his attempt to keep me in line.

"Don't be an idiot," I told him. To Colette: "We'd love to join you. In fact, Rafe here is a scholar interested in the area. He studies under my father, a renowned anthropologist. Perhaps you've heard of him?" I commandeered our guide and started toward the crowd of her cousins and sisters. "In any case, I'm sure that Rafe is eager to interview you for their research. And, as it turns out, we have been looking for a place to stop for food."

"Wonderful," said Colette, her voice loud enough that the rest of the girls could hear and dissolve into simpering fools, clutching each other and giggling. The most composed of the group took a steadying breath, smiled, and offered me her hand in introduction. In the instant that I hesitated, Matthew intervened.

"Please excuse my own poor sister"—he placed himself in front of me and took the offered palm in both of his—"but she is unwell. Unfortunately"—and here he lowered his voice to a whisper, as if in my imagined affliction I had suddenly gone deaf—"the disease that has hold of her organs has progressed into her brain, so she often forgets her sad state of health. You can imagine the shock that it has given our poor mother." Matthew had taken the girl's goose-pimpled arm and was steering her away from me, over to Rafe, who looked on, amused. "If it's not too much to ask of you, perhaps we could send Rafe to bring a small selection back. I'd hate to fully decline your invitation. At the moment we're en route to find a doctor who might cure my poor sister, but to bring her to your family now would likely be unwise. We would not want to thank you for your kindness by infecting you with her . . . germs."

Colette, looking alarmed, increased the distance between us, shielding herself with a large yellow towel. I was lost for words.

"I assure you that Rafe, here, is fully vaccinated." Matthew offered him the girl on his arm. "And truly a most charming visitor. He'll go with you, won't you, Rafe?"

And thus, ever so simply, I'd been strong-armed by Matthew, who returned to my side, feigning concern for my health as Rafe was ushered off by the swarm of scantily clad girls.

"Now don't you worry," Rafe whispered as he passed me. "They're none of them as interesting as you." He winked before disappearing into his flock of admirers.

When they were gone, I pulled myself away from Matthew.

"Your sister?" I hissed at him. "Your poor, sick sister, of questionable mental skill?"

"I had to think quickly. I really think we managed pretty well, given the circumstances."

"*We?* I'm hungry *now*. And I am perfectly capable of managing myself. Is this another attempt to keep me hidden? Keep me from causing *harm?*"

"You're not the only one who can cause harm," Matthew reasoned with frustrating composure, as always making me feel silly for my own impassioned response.

"But you apparently don't trust me not to hurt them. You think I can't control myself. You made that very clear from the beginning, but I'd think you could admit that I might do things on my own. I don't need you here to help me. I don't want you here. I'm not a child. I'm not your toy."

"Maisie, I—"

"And," I continued, voice rising, both in anger and in an attempt to rid myself of the memory of my recent fits of coughing and delusion, the fear that his words might be true, "to tell that girl that *I'm* the sick one? When just the other night you were frothing at the mouth? Of course you haven't thanked me, of course it isn't possible that *I* might have helped *you*. Because *I'm* just a—"

"Maisie." Matthew took both of my shirtsleeves in his hands, holding me still amid my ranting. I tried to pull away, but he was stronger than expected. He looked directly into my eyes, his expression serious, perhaps even sad. It was sobering.

I could hear the water rushing with intensity beside us, like a river of children running barefoot. The wind had picked up, ruffling Matthew's hair, pressing my own against my cheek. I smelled clover, and salt, and subtle hints of him, of rosemary.

Matthew's face was very close to mine, his breath a breeze against me, his lips pillowed and pursed.

I did not know what to do. I hit him.

My elbow, encased in my shirtsleeve, jutted back and then jerked upward, making contact squarely with his jaw. His hands flew up to check the damage. His eyes grew wide with shock. I turned away from him, tripping over myself as I ran back toward the main road, and when I reached it, I kept running, back, I thought, to before our confrontation, before my vision, back to the garage, where I hoped Rafe would soon return.

I was afraid. And I was angry. Who was Matthew to belittle my feelings? To sweep me up in some attempt at (was it?) romance in his symptomatic need to have his way? I stopped finally, panting, at the edge of the moor, a stitch in my side, limbs jittery from exercise and hunger. The world stretched silently around me. For a moment I thought that I had gone the wrong direction, I would sicken, I would starve.

And then I spotted Matthew walking leisurely behind me, a speck on the horizon, his yellow hair distinct.

I let him join me, though I did not have the energy to continue our discussion. We walked the main road without speaking, and kept several feet between us. By the time we were in view of the garage, I could almost convince myself it all had been imagined, were it not for the dull pain in my elbow, the redness visible under Matthew's chin. We met eyes before walking the final few feet, and I felt that we were tacitly agreeing to ignore what had happened.

WHEN WE RETURNED to the garage, the parts needed for Matthew's car had, by some providence, arrived. Ginny was hidden under the carriage, and did not emerge to ask us about the success of our trip. I sat in one corner of the garage waiting area, thumbing through a magazine, picking at the blisters on my heels, while Matthew flopped down in another, staring at a wall. At one point he got up to microwave a frozen pizza, and silently offered me a slice. I let it sit on the coffee table, crust hardening, too stubborn to sate my growing hunger.

Rafe did not return until late in the evening. He rushed through the swinging doors with a paper bag of goodies in hand, leaping across the waiting room to reach me.

"Those girls saw Cothay just a week ago, passing through their town for research," he said breathlessly. "We're on the right track. They said he was headed to the city. Even left word where he'd be staying—the address of a hotel. Said he'd be there for two weeks at the least."

"Did he?" Matthew frowned. "Why would he tell them that?"

"In case they thought of more to tell him. The spirals, anthropology, you know."

I nodded, heart racing, though I did not know.

"Not very specific . . . ," muttered Matthew. "And I thought you'd said earlier he'd gone through to a different world, the door . . ."

"Oh, give it up," I told him, pushing the paper plate he'd set down earlier, now flimsy with grease, in his direction. I turned to Rafe. "I hope you wrote down this address."

The Cycling of the Seasons

Lucy helps the black-eyed girl stand, walks with her around the clearing, brushes her hair from her eyes. The woodland birds have abandoned the glade, and, songs conspicuously absent, their two footfalls are the only nearby sounds: Lucy's firm and patient, the black-eyed girl's coltish and weak. They are on their seventh lap when the black-eyed girl falls forward. Her chest tightens. Again she feels as though she's gone deep underwater. The blue seeps out of the sky, replaced by a glowing, celestial green. A burst of lightning. The distant sound of city traffic: car horns honking, sirens' screams. The black-eyed girl laughs, and her own voice is of a higher pitch than she would have imagined. She lifts her chin to see a full, starlit sky.

Then the scene recedes, and the black-eyed girl is back in the clearing, aware of her breasts, a sparkling below her stomach. A new sort of wanting, urgent and deep. A hunger that starts in her groin and rises upward: a commandment to take all that she desires. To lap blood from her fingers and suck marrow from bone. To nibble earlobes, guzzle sweat from skin. To feast.

Lucy, frozen where she stands, is unable to hide her anxiety.

"Hello," says the black-eyed girl, licking her wet lips.

17

Imagine all your life the world is green and brown and quiet. Your days pass slowly. You celebrate the sun. All magic is of trees and dappled shadows, all mountains peaked eruptions from an old ancestral earth, a ground so sacred there has been no cause to name it. The old story, told to me by Mother Farrow in the months before her death, is that in ancient times when a passerby peeled a ring of bark from a tree, his punishment was to be nailed to the stripped spot by his navel, walked around and around until his organs all uncoiled and wrapped about the trunk as its new skin.

The closer we got to the city, the stronger the signs of those ancient times' decay. Trees had been cleared to make way for identical square houses, long paved highways, domed monstrosities that Rafe explained were factories and labs. At the first glimpse of these outskirts, it felt silly to think of my own village's rites for early spring. Here were confident assertions of progress in action. Here steel was king, and science, and the sense that modern man might conquer all with his behest.

The road curved around to reveal the city before us—hulking, unreal, gray with smoke. I clenched the sticky edges of my seat. The land itself seemed at once barren and productive, spiked with towering buildings the likes of which I'd never seen before. Silver smokestacks coughed brown clouds into the sky. Cable-wired bridges crossed rainbow-oiled water. Pedicabs transported streams of people to and fro. I could not help but gawk. The air smelled like tar and burned biscuits.

Rafe turned back to grin at me. "The city," he said proudly, holding out his open palms.

I supposed I saw its beauty, although it was a different sort than I had ever known. My fascination lay in all the elements behind it—the markets and machinery, the grinding gears, the cranes—more than the brick or steel or stonework of the buildings' stern facades. I wondered what was hidden inside all those outer casings. What soft center was so precious that a steel structure was needed to protect it from the earth and air and sky? At home, I felt you saw the heart of something simply by looking; here, mystery prevailed. Like Matthew's stoic face, the city's harsh exterior hid its true intentions.

People were everywhere, caught up in eddies of their own collective making, carrying one another in waves across the pavement. They seemed a collection of various species: one genus of neckties and umbrellas and suits; another of sneakers and visors, sporting fold-out maps and mobile phones, weaving in and out of the more assured crowd.

We moved from the shiny, slick center of the city to an area filled with warehouses and vans making deliveries, through a neighborhood of shops and pubs and churches, to another lined with single-family homes. I was overwhelmed with the sheer amount of city there was to discover: the slivers of public parks and railways we could just see from the road, the number of stores that we drove past, mere blocks from their identical brothers, covered in neon advertisements. Eventually Rafe told Matthew to park in a crowded public lot in an older area, less glossy than those earlier streets and skyscrapers, but equally bustling. I got out of the car as if setting foot on land after a long journey at sea, my body tentative and shaking.

It did not take us long to find the last spiral's location. We slipped through side streets and alleys, at one point even passing through the lobby of a building that Rafe told me was a bank—a cold, high-ceilinged space that smelled of grubby boots and iron—and dodged cars with angry drivers when our coordinates coincided with traffic-filled streets. I drew into myself, wrapping my arms across my chest, at times closing my eyes when the crowds around us were too dense, as if I could make myself invisible and thus escape the overwhelming press of bodies. Matthew noticed and shielded me as best he could, his eyes constantly alert to incoming throngs of people, his elbows wide to give us space. At one point his hand guided the small of my back through my jacket. I was grateful, but once we were through the worst of the crowds I shook him off. I had not forgotten our encounter by the river; the awkwardness still palpable between us.

The center of the final spiral proved to be another river, as Rafe had suspected. The last point of the triangle, south and east from the first. We stood under a bridge, toxic water lapping at our toes, and at Rafe's explicit direction I plunged a stick into the silt, mimicking the actions of the ritual I'd recently envisioned on the moors. It sizzled, as if frying in oil, and dissolved almost instantly.

Matthew's skepticism, never quite masked, had reached its peak, and he sighed all the way through Rafe's recitations, which neither of us understood, but which I at least tried to honor with reverent attention.

I felt uneasy, but could not say why. Was it a result of our performance, the change in aura that Rafe claimed we had ignited? Or was it merely my continued discomfort with Matthew, the intensity of being in the city? Again, we saw no sign of my father.

"He must be at his hotel," said Rafe once we'd returned to the car, tapping a hand against the dashboard, jiggling his leg as we stalled in the slowly oozing traffic. He repeated the address he had been given, the location where the girls by the river had promised we'd find Peter.

THE HOTEL WAS a small and unassuming building, a wedge of plain gray stone the same as others all around it, with a row of shaded windows and a weather-worn sign freshly painted to spell out the word LODGING. It didn't seem the sort of place Peter would choose on his own—too nondescript, lacking history or character. Matthew pulled the car into a neighboring alley.

"Peter must be inside," said Rafe, spilling out the side door and coming around to help me carry my belongings. He did not look any worse for his past hours traipsing the city, barely rumpled, certainly not irritable or dirty, as Matthew and I did.

"I'll go in with you." Matthew said from the front seat.

"Don't be silly." I stretched my legs. "You should go home to see your parents. Don't they live nearby?"

Matthew ignored me and turned off the engine. I shot Rafe an exasperated look. I did not have time for Matthew and his changing moods, nor the murkiness of my own feelings about what had transpired between us. Was he jealous of Rafe? Had that been the source of his advances? More likely he'd been trying to manipulate me, the gesture by the river meant to placate my frustration, to control me. I shook my head in an effort to forcibly remove all thought that those warnings about Rafe might be founded. Luckily, I would not have to deal with them much longer. Now that we'd reached Peter, Matthew and I would part. This could well be, I thought suddenly, the last time I would see him. The thought made me unexpectedly sad, and I brushed it away.

The air outside was pleasant, but immediately upon entering the hotel we were met with an oppressive warmth. We walked into a cramped entryway, wires crawling through a patch of unfinished ceiling, the stale smell of industrially washed curtains not quite overpowering a lingering odor of cat. A sloping desk sat unattended beside a row of keys dangling unevenly from hooks in the wall. They reminded me of specimens, each key a neatly labeled bit or bob: *Room 7* a fox paw, *Room 12* a pinned moth, *Room 20* a tagged flower.

"It doesn't look as if anyone has stayed here in some time," muttered Matthew. As if in response, a large cat loped out of the shadows, looked at him disdainfully, and yawned. "Here's hoping no guests are allergic."

I scowled. Matthew had on his expression of derisive incredulity. It was clear he did not trust the path that led us here, which meant that he did not trust Peter. He obviously did not trust me. I widened my eyes to demonstrate my annoyance, and Matthew simply cocked an eyebrow, widening his eyes back at me.

Rafe leaned over the desk to find a small silver bell, and tapped at it impatiently until we heard a rustling behind a nearby door, from which emerged a heavyset man, bleary-eyed, unshaven, wearing an unbuttoned shirt with an embroidered red logo, like an external heart across his chest. He had a single dead tooth just to the right of his two front ones, bluish black in color. I tried not to stare.

"What do you want?" the man asked before he'd even looked at us.

"Poor customer service," Matthew said under his breath.

"We are looking for Peter Cothay," said Rafe slowly, louder, I thought, than was necessary in the small space. "We were told he's staying here. Do you know which room he's in?"

The man scratched the back of his neck. He smiled, rotted tooth on full display.

"Yes," he said, "Mr. . . . Yes. Um . . . room sixteen. But he's gone out. Yes, he's gone out for the day."

"He'll be back soon?" I asked.

The man shot Rafe a look—was my question inappropriate?—then turned back to me and shrugged. "How should I know?"

"Why don't we get a room as well?" suggested Rafe. "Clean up and have something to eat while we wait. I'm sure he won't be too long. We've found him at last, Maisie!" He could barely contain his excitement.

"A good idea." I turned to Matthew. "You can leave now. We'll be fine."

"I'll wait, too, until you see him." Matthew crossed his arms over his chest, planting himself in the fusty carpet beside me. I sighed. My back to Rafe and the hotel man, I spoke softly, close to his ear.

"*Stop* trying to protect me," I said through my teeth. "It's humiliating." I could feel the heat of the others' eyes on us. My insides simmered with exasperation. "Rafe will wait with me. Peter will be back soon. As I've told you, I can take care of myself. Please leave already. Just go."

"You don't think anything about this is shifty? You don't have *any* feeling that maybe something isn't right?" Matthew took no care to lower his voice.

"Stop it," I hissed. "You're embarrassing me!"

"You're embarrassing yourself," he said. "Come on, Maisie." Matthew steered me by the shoulder, one hand carefully set atop my jacket, turning me toward the door. "We're going now." After two steps I jerked away, the force of my elbow throwing him off balance. He gave me a look of surprise, tinged with hurt. I moved back toward Rafe and pressed myself against the welcome desk.

"Please stop," I said, tears swelling in my throat. "If you want to go so much, then just get going. I don't want you here with me. I never did."

Matthew opened his mouth to respond, but again I said, "Please."

He looked at me for a long time. I felt a strange ache in my chest. Finally, he nodded.

"All right," said Matthew. "All right, then." He turned away from me, and toward the door. I could see where the bruise I'd made on his chin the day before had begun to yellow. My fingers twitched at my side, wanting, of their own accord, to touch it. I had prevailed; Matthew was leaving. So why did I still think I might cry?

I assumed that he would turn himself around to say goodbye. He didn't. I watched him leave, heard the door slam behind him, and felt that tightness in my chest reach an intensity I thought must be its peak. I turned to Rafe.

"About that room."

A Bedeviled Family Line

The black-eyed girl stretches, twisting her body one way, then the next. She rolls her neck.

"What can we bring you?" asks Lucy, worrying her fingers, taking a step forward and then falling back as it becomes clear that the black-eyed girl won't answer. "What comes next? What do we have to do in order to escape?"

The black-eyed girl raises an eyebrow.

"You can speak," Lucy says. "Can't you?"

But the black-eyed girl chooses not to speak to Lucy. Instead she cocks an ear, listening to the world outside the forest. She brings a finger to her lips and sucks, lubricating the knuckle, using her teeth to remove the dirty emerald ring long pressed upon it, which she spits to the ground.

Lucy falls to her knees to retrieve the ring, then scrambles to gather the rest of the jewelry—the iron brooch, the plain gold band, the promise ring—that trails the black-eyed girl as she walks slowly from the clearing. The silver chain torn from the neck. The wire bracelet unwoven. The fallen Blakely crest, pressed facedown in dirt.

18

The hotel room was much like the entryway: stuffy and drab. It had two twin beds with copper frames, made up with stiff, flowered bedspreads. These looked even less comfortable than the carpeted floor, which boasted scars from recent vacuuming, uneven stripes like poorly harvested crops across its length. A gray plastic desk held a stack of brochures with suggestions for what to do while visiting the city. Atop the bureau sat a television, the first I'd seen in person, which displayed only a static snow once turned on.

At any other time, I would have been excited to explore these new surroundings, bland as they were, but my enthusiasm was tempered by the sour taste left by Matthew's parting. I felt the anxiety of our lack of resolution, compounded by mounting anticipation of reunion with my father. Had I been unduly short with Matthew? Would Peter be angry with me for pushing him away, for failing to heed his directives of caution?

I thought of Mrs. Blott, Matthew's blood relation, and had a sinking premonition that he would suffer a similar fate. Whatever fever I'd abated might return. His exhaustion might lead him to an accident. I wanted to race after him, bolt through the building to apologize, beg him to explain his motives in that moment by the water. I restrained myself.

"Why don't you start off in the bathroom?" Rafe offered, opening a door I had not realized led to an attached bath, with a cramped shower stall, a plain white toilet, a streaky mirror in which I could fully examine the toll travel had taken on my face. I thanked him and closed myself in, remembering suddenly that I was in a hotel room, with

Rafe. The battle I'd avoided for these past few days had now been thrust upon me.

There was work to be done if I were to make myself appealing, beginning with the basics of hygiene I'd neglected these past several days. Fortunately, everything in the bathroom was safe for me to touch, and not just after having been refined by human working; these basins were porcelain, faucet heads metal. Nothing here lived, which meant, consequently, that nothing here died. The whole room, and city, too, I realized, was artificial, which I thought even more remarkable than if it had been dead. Dead things became living, by time's inevitable passing if not by my expediting touch, their decay and dissolution eventually becoming food for their successors, nourishing new life. But these things were the whole extent of what they'd be forever. They had reached the pinnacle of their existence, and I was sad for them.

I imagined Rafe with me as I showered, the water running down his shoulders, my mouth on his neck, my tongue against his teeth. I wondered if he was imagining the same. When I stepped back into the room, he was seated on one of the beds, flipping through a notebook. The television hummed, its wavering fuzz dissolving every minute or so into blurred, discolored faces, as if the people trapped inside its wires were struggling, not quite failing, to break through. Help them, I thought, though I knew that they had no true need. A covered tray sat on the desk, atop the tourism brochures.

"You must be starving," Rafe said. "Would you believe this place does room service?"

My mouth twisted, confused.

"Room service," repeated Rafe, "a meal delivered to our room from the hotel kitchen. Here—" He stood and offered me his arm, ready to escort me to the desk. Because we both wore long sleeves, I took it, and let my hand linger.

Rafe offered me the plastic desk chair and I sat down, excited for my dinner, although I was growing restless, unnerved by the pressure of our intimacy, how he licked sauce from his lips, the way his head cocked toward the incoherent drone of the TV. The tension between where Rafe sat on the bed and my place at the desk grew increasingly hard to ignore.

"Any word from Peter yet?" I asked, both eager to see my father and afraid of what might happen were no one to intervene.

Rafe shook his head. "I asked the man up front to let us know. He'll send him up when he arrives. Just enjoy yourself! Your first hotel! I'm sure he'll be here soon."

I smiled and tried to comply, but could not make myself at ease.

"You mustn't worry." Rafe grinned, and jumped suddenly up from his seat. He collected our used dishes and piled them on the tray, then reached for a gleaming silver pitcher. "Have some tea," he instructed, already pouring. I nodded my consent, and lifted the cup once he'd placed it in front of me. The drink was the perfect temperature, having cooled a bit during our meal, and it tasted of licorice with some under-lying, sweeter sort of herb. Certainly not my preferred flavor, but I did not wish to be rude. I drank.

"Tell me more about what to expect with Peter. What we'll do once he arrives," I said, in an attempt at innocuous conversation.

Rafe shrugged. "My part isn't all that interesting. I'll just do what needs to be done." As when clouds clear quickly from an otherwise blue sky, his eyes took on a sudden intensity. They looked directly into mine, and made me shudder. "It's important to remember, Maisie," he said, "that we all do what needs to be done, when it comes down to it."

I did not understand, but before I could ask him to explain himself, a crashing sound came from below our room's window. The backfiring of a van, the screech of tires. I lifted my eyes toward the noise and felt my stomach churning, my head begin to spin. My body tilted off my chair. I felt Rafe's large hands catch me, squeeze my sleeved arms, turn me around.

"Remember," he said, his eyes pinpricks, his voice rough.

And then I was falling and all was dark.

Part

IV

Inaccurate Translations

When Peter Cothay pulled into Urizon's drive, the great house stood strict and imposing, and quite obviously empty. All that greeted Peter was the dog—if you could call the creature such, which Maisie did—its canine form restless and panting, whining like it knew something vital.

"What?" he asked as he entered through the kitchen, walked the hallway to his study, Marlowe nipping at his heels. "What have I missed?"

Within hours of Mrs. Blott's passing, Peter had realized that Maisie must be trapped inside the forest. Abandoning precautions, he had traveled the spiral path to rescue her, spending weeks paying homage to the history, whispering the old prayers. He knew precisely where she'd gone, and how to find her. He knew he must complete the final step. And still a part of him imagined that his daughter would greet him upon his return to the estate. A part of him hoped that the late nights, the travel, the research—his whole life's work—would in the end amount to nothing.

PETER GREW OUT of short pants at finishing school, where upon hearing his first fairy story he developed an interest in the exotic—ancient practice, modern myth—that bordered on obsession. He did not stumble blindly to Urizon. Curiosity piqued, Peter sought out

Laura Blakely and married her, knowing full well her family's past. Captivated by the whispers, the old tales of the wood, he believed himself capable of solving the riddle that had eluded other scholars of his kind for centuries. He was sure that he could find an explanation for the strangeness of the forest that bordered the estate, for the villagers who emerged from the tree line at the solstices with accounts of woodland spirits and wandering oaks, their minds unhinged, eyes wild, the erratic disappearances of years of Blakely women. Seeking out answers might take time, but Peter Cothay was nothing if not patient. He envisioned a comfortable future, a career at the nearby university, a book or two published, a few months of each year spent exploring while Laura kept house.

He did not expect to lose his wife so quickly. He did not expect to raise a little girl all on his own. He'd stood in the icy night air outside the hospital the night of his daughter's birth and smoked his first cigarette in years. Pounded his chest to clear the coughing. Cleaned his glasses with a shirtsleeve. Decided he'd give it a go.

How difficult could it be, Peter had asked himself, to act as lone parent? With a large property, some money, a new friend willing to assist—how much would his life, already drifting off its axis, truly change once the girl was brought home? If anything, a little Blakely girl could help him where her mother had failed. He'd expected to find Laura Blakely strange, tainted by the stories of her family. Instead, she had been sweet, attentive, a bit absentminded—overall profoundly normal. She did not sleepwalk or mumble spells or wake screaming from arcane nightmares. Yet Peter was surprised at the ease with which she fit into his life; how much he cared for her. It was fitting that some small bit of Laura would continue in the form of her daughter. A memorial to the mother; a continuation of the family line.

For years he saw his child as an experiment. Maisie did not make much noise, or take up much space in the house. She was excellent research. The case study Peter published was met with wide acclaim, touted as the first of its kind in its amalgam of folklore and science, if occasionally scorned by certain colleagues who thought it an unserious pursuit. But Peter was quite serious. He took note of the little girl's development, tested her limits. He watched the wood, waiting for a sign that the child was an extension of its power, might hold the answers to the Blakely family curse. Some days he would forget to feed her, to dispose of soiled diapers. He would find himself chastised by Mrs. Blott, scolded for thoughtlessness, even called cruel.

But time bred love. His regard for his daughter had grown. He wanted, now, to be a set of armor, to replace her heart with his. He might have been a better father, might have dandled her or whatnot on his knee, but there was this: if he could, Peter Cothay would stretch himself around his only child like a membrane, so that the dark parts of the world would never find her, so that she would always be the full golden yolk of a hen's egg before it breaks.

HE WAS SURPRISED to find his study in a state of disarray. Not that Peter saw himself a paragon of organization, but the sloppy way the papers had been piled, the displacement of the dust on the desk— someone had been there. His suspicion was confirmed when he opened the file drawer and saw only a dusting of mouse droppings where should have been his working copy of his map.

Peter knew at once who'd taken it. Rafe's letter of apology, read and reread, still sat crumpled in the pocket of his jacket.

Rafe, who had written him years ago asking for patronage, needing a mentor. Rafe, who believed Peter's theories when others had laughed. Rafe, who'd seen only hand-drawn copies of the symbols in the book Peter had found under the floorboards after Laura's death, before Maisie burst from within her. Rafe, who said he'd come up with the proper translations.

"Blood," Rafe had insisted, blue eyes eager, seated across from

Peter in that roadside café. "There's absolutely no question. The symbol means blood."

"It could mean lifeblood." Peter shook his head, turning the paper so that he could see it more clearly. "It could mean roots, or family."

"No." Rafe had pounded his fist on the Formica table, attracting the attention of the tired-looking woman at the counter. Peter gave him a stern look, and Rafe continued with his voice considerably lower. "It's clearly blood—a sacrifice of blood."

"But how can it be actual blood? A body of blood that keeps living? That's impossible. My boy, the runes mean family. A sacrifice of family. A family that continues even after the wood has been opened, the sacrifice made."

"No, it has to be blood," Rafe pressed. "Look at this symbol of a body here, these lines leading into the forest. The knife slitting the palms, the two palms pressed together. It's the only explanation. Blood explains why it's so difficult, why it takes so long. You have to calculate the time it takes for the blood to replenish in the body—use iron supplements, folic acid—it may have been impossible hundreds of years ago, but not with all the medical advances we have now."

Peter had listened for another few minutes, then come up with some nonsense about a class to teach, a paper to grade. He'd hurried home to Maisie, unperturbed by Rafe's adamancy until the next day, when Mrs. Blott had brought the mail in from town.

Peter remembered Rafe's words, scrawled onto a sheet of notebook paper, stuffed hastily into the envelope:

Cothay, I'm right about the blood, where it should come from. I know you are the Toymaker. You know that to open that forest we will need blood from the Child.

Peter had thrown the scrap of paper in the fire, watched its edges blacken, the flames lick the words away. After that, he could have sworn some of his old notebooks were missing, the ones with the notes he'd eventually turn to published studies, the ones that tied his daughter to the subject of his work. Was that how Rafe knew? Because he'd stolen the evidence, somehow snuck into the house?

Peter put the work first, always. Pursuit of knowledge was the goal, at the cost of all else. He'd respected Rafe because Rafe was the same: could spend hours bent over a manuscript, neglecting meals, mothers' birthdays, pretty girls. Peter had seen himself in Rafe, and thus he knew the boy was capable of going to the furthest ends, would justify each action, no matter who it hurt, as a sacrifice to knowledge. It was only now he realized that fatherhood had changed him. He'd found a limit to who he was willing to hurt, to what he was willing to give. Somehow, without warning, a love had crept up on Peter Cothay, a love he had never imagined.

ON HIS WAY into the wood, walking down the last terrace, Peter paused at the plot that had been turnips back when Laura was alive to tend the gardens, the plot that he'd transformed for his daughter, digging out years of rocks and old roots, their spindly anchors stretching deeper than he ever knew they could. Yanking them free, he'd remembered the rubbery blue cord that connected the last vestige of his wife to his new daughter. The odd curving scissors, their blades like the beak of a bird, gleaming in the fluorescence of the delivery room. Laura on the operating table, her upper body covered by a thin paper sheet. The nurses could not close her eyes, so they had kept the body covered by a series of paper sheets that wilted in the warm damp of the hospital room, its climate curated and stifling. Peter could not resist raising the sheet once when he was alone with Laura and her strange, swelling stomach. His wife had not withered—her skin was cold but bright. Fingernails the same length, freshly manicured. That splotch of pink polish on her left index finger still boasting the whorl of his thumbprint—*Careful*, she'd said, laughing, *they haven't dried yet. Now I'll have to do it over.*

A physician's assistant found him there, staring. She ushered Peter out. He had not looked again.

PETER KNELT BY the sandbox, a recent rain making his digging difficult and slow. Despite his dirtied shirt cuffs, the scrape of wet sand on his hands, he did not stop until he'd found the soggy edge of a plastic bag, explored its borders to feel for the flimsy cover of a book.

It was still there, where he had hidden it, weeks earlier. The book that had saved him after Laura's death, when he'd thought himself lost, peeking out from a floorboard in what would become Maisie's nursery. The book with its promises, its cryptic instructions, its symbols and ambiguous translations. Rafe had not stolen it, which meant he must have been stymied. Without the book's instructions, Rafe could not have gone further in his quest to harvest blood. He could not know how or where or when—he must have given up. Peter reburied the manuscript quickly, relieved.

There'd been a day, a winter morning, on which Maisie—maybe six years old—had rushed up to the nursery, abandoning an intricate performance with her dolls to do his work. She'd looked up at him, so trusting, chatting while he readied a scalpel, a swab of antiseptic, a vial with which to collect her blood. The instruments gleamed in the pale light that reflected off the snow outside, and in his gloved hands they'd felt so cold. A sacrifice of blood, he'd thought, picturing the runes in the book—a knife held to a palm, a prostrate body—while watching his daughter's small, heart-shaped mouth, the freckles scattered across her cheeks, the bit of sleep still scabbing the corner of an eye.

"Go back and play, dear," he'd told her.

Her face fell. "I thought that we were going to play together."

"We will, darling. Soon. But the plans that I had for today . . . We'll reschedule."

They had not rescheduled this particular experiment, the harvest of her blood. Blood, a word with so many meanings, so many uses, so many goals. As Peter's love for Maisie deepened, his understanding deepened with it, and he saw that blood meant more than the mere fluids of the body. Peter was his daughter's blood, just as surely as the cruor that ran though her. Now that he knew love's dual brand of pain and satisfaction, Peter knew that the sacrifice the book asked for could not be simple bloodshed, the slicing of a palm, no matter how Rafe made the case.

Peter would have to bring himself, a sacrifice of family, to the forest to complete the ancient ritual. He'd go inside, he'd find his girl. He'd save her.

The Shimmering Thing

The black-eyed girl waits for Peter. She hears him fumbling at the edge of the forest, watches him step tentatively past the trees. She cracks her knuckles, relishing each pop of cartilage. She whispers, and her voice echoes through the wood, a low hum that finds all the Blakely women: "Come to me." They do.

19

I dreamed myself as a very small child, playing in the wood beside Urizon. I was running, and Marlowe was with me. We were chasing something slippery as it twisted between oaks and rocks and poplars, always far ahead of us, always out of sight. I could not make out what it was, but I felt it was a part of me, or, more precisely, that I was a part of it, one of its belongings, a piece it had let go and was now luring home. It whispered to me: *Come.*

The running was marvelous, air exploding through me in long, lovely bursts, sweet-smelling trees spilling past me. I laughed, and Marlowe barked, and as our shimmering enchantress danced across the trees ahead, I felt myself to be eternal.

And then I tripped upon a thick tree root, a giant's finger extended in punishment. The clear sky clouded over. I lurched forward and caught myself with the palms of my hands, feeling the forest floor scrape mean across my wrists. I was bleeding. When I looked up, there was Rafe, silent and watching me. With him were Matthew, Ginny from the auto repair shop, Mrs. Blott. Mother Farrow was there, and the solicitor, and the man from the hotel, and little Colette and her sisters. Almost every living person I had ever encountered had planted him or herself in a line like garden flowers and was staring at me, brows bent, disapproving.

And my blood mixed with the earth's blood, the soil, and that dust-dry soil turned fertile.

I lay there on the forest floor, the heels of my hands, my wrists, speckled with burgundy. I looked at them, held them proffered out together as if waiting to be bound, and the blood crawled slowly down my palms out to my fingers, in teardrops to the ground.

Then, finally, Peter, his hair mussed, his glasses askew. He knelt with me, his back to the watchers, my judges, the crowd. He wrapped my wrists in a cold, clean bandage. Up high, above the trees, from the slight corner of an eye, I saw the shimmering thing glint over branches, turn and take flight across the sky.

I AWOKE IN a small, damp room to the slicing blades of a gray plastic fan, face creaking one way then the other, watching me like a passing driver taking in the thrill of an accident. In one corner sat a simple metal cot. In another an old toilet bowl, missing its cover. My body ached. I was alone. My wrists were bound with cold metal.

As fear increased my heart rate I could feel myself weaken, and I tried to take slow, calming breaths.

"Rafe?" I called. "Peter?"

Nothing.

"Well, then," I said, trying to hold my voice steady.

I stretched out to examine my body. My stockings were gone. I felt exhausted and sore, angry and throbbing both inside and out. My arms and legs were swirled with various bruises, yellow-green and purple, no longer fresh. At the joint of my right arm was a thick wad of cotton, held to my skin with strips of tape. It smarted when I flexed, and with trepidation I wriggled off the wrap to find the cause: a swollen pink mark upon the vein.

Before I could explore myself further, I heard a noise just outside. I did not have time to try to replace the bandage, but curled back into my corner and resumed my previous position, closing my eyes halfway so I might seem to be asleep but still observe my situation. I'd read novels in which prisoners conned their captors in just such a way, and I racked my thoughts for lessons to remember. All the while I struggled to breathe slowly, to breathe deep.

The sounds that I had heard came from two figures who entered the room dressed toe to finger in white uniforms, wearing goggles and masks that hid all but their foreheads.

"Look, she's lost her bandage," said the first. "We'll have to tie it tighter after this." How did I know that voice, a drawl both foreign and familiar?

"She's looking peaky," said the second. "You think we've taken too much blood?"

"She's breathing, isn't she? We're doing fine."

My stomach dropped. With half-closed eyes, I looked again around the room and found two small windows, recently cleaned, framed very high on one wall. Pink puffs of insulation were tucked into the unfinished ceiling.

One of the men came over, lifting my hand, which, with the cuffs, brought the other up with it.

"A shame." He sighed. I could feel the bumpy texture of his gloves against my skin.

Suddenly a sharp pain pierced my sore arm, and my eyes flew open. The man had inserted a large needle into the pink juncture at my joint, a needle that led to a long tube, through which my blood was now spiraling, collecting in a glass jar the size of one of Mrs. Blott's canned blueberry jellies. My heart rate rose, pumping the blood faster, filling the first inch of the jar.

The man with the needle was looking at me through his plastic goggles. His blue eyes met mine. I could not help myself. I screamed.

He was startled, and his confusion gave me time to act. I yanked my arm away, leaving in the needle and its cylinder but detaching the coiled tube.

"Coulton, do something!" He ducked around to catch my flailing arms, squeezing until a fount of blood exploded from the truncated needle. "Hurry!"

"I'm doing it," said the other man, presumably Coulton, his back to me so that it was impossible to see exactly what it was that he was doing. I flailed and kicked and yelled, doing everything in my power to escape the first man's grasp.

"Matthew!" I cried. "Peter!"

The man held my arms with viselike hands, twisting at my skin, pressing with cruel fingers. It became harder to fight him; my body, with the blood I'd lost, grew tired.

"Hurry up, would you?" he hissed.

Coulton chuckled, lifted his mask, and I saw he was the man from the hotel. How had I not realized? He was grinning, his dead tooth gleaming, his stubbled cheeks glowing with success, hands planted on his hips as he surveyed his small kingdom, and I suddenly hated myself for my obliviousness. I'd seen this man, not long ago, outside the Holzmeiers' shop in Coeurs Crossing, finishing a delivery, shaking hands with Rafe. That red logo on his chest, the one I'd overlooked in passing, announced affiliation proudly: BEAUFORT LOGISTICS, in curled red script. That glimpsed handshake . . .

I swallowed hard. It couldn't be, it couldn't.

As Coulton readied a syringe filled with clear liquid, to my shame lifting my dress to find my thigh, I gave one last wrench of my body, called out for help one last time.

"Peter!" My throat burned. "Rafe!"

Then the liquid went through me and I felt myself soften, felt sleep fall like a blanket across my mind. I turned my head to shoot a final glare at my audience, and saw the first man remove his mask as well.

He balled his fists into his pockets, his face harsh, his mouth a line. His eyes would not meet mine. He was nodding at Coulton, reconnecting my tube. On his gloves were red starbursts of my blood.

As unconsciousness took me, as my body felt remote and old and nothing, I whispered his name again: "Rafe."

My Father's Hand

The black-eyed girl stands at the edge of the forest, watching for Peter's approach. He has not seen her. He navigates, he thinks, by the angle of the light, though in truth he is wandering blindly, the black-eyed girl guiding him to where the women wait for him, the black-eyed girl preparing to open the wood.

"I told you he would come," hisses Mary, standing back in the group of seven women who flank their new leader. "A fool, like all the rest of them, deserving of his lot."

"Don't say such things," says Imogen.

The black-eyed girl ignores them; she'll be finished with them soon. She hums a low note, and raises one arm. Peter's gaze follows, neck stretching back. He sees the swirl of sky, amassing clouds that smell of rain. He rubs two fingers under his glasses. He sees the women. Sees the black-eyed girl. He stills himself, breathes deep.

"I've done it," Peter whispers, filled more with awe than fear. "I was right! I knew . . . I knew it! Maisie, my darling! How long have you been in here? More importantly, do you know where *here* is? What you're caught in . . ." He pauses, sensing that something is different. These are not his child's eyes. "My daughter . . . Could you . . . Could you be?"

"The girl you've raised to be so docile?" The black-eyed girl's tone has no inflection; her voice is low and harsh. "The girl you've gelded? The child whose purpose you've concealed?"

"You're not . . ." Peter's voice quavers. He coughs. He is not prepared for animosity. He expected to be lauded as rescuer, the lost women to bow or praise him, to cry ghostly tears of joy. He expected his child to blink up at him, her green eyes his own, whispering *Father, you have saved me, I forgive you all your faults.* "I will not let you harm my daughter."

"No. It's too late for that," says the black-eyed girl. "You've done the harm yourself."

"She is a child," Peter says. "Give her back to me at once. I don't know what you are, what you've become here in this forest, but its remedy is surely not the conquest of my daughter, her corruption, the betrayal of her free will. All those things that will——" He pauses, because the black-eyed girl has stepped forward. She has inhaled the stink of the Blakely women and exhaled a low, guttural note. It stops Peter cold. He should feel excited, having completed the ritual, yet he only feels unease.

"You are too late," the black-eyed girl tells him. "I have you."

"Well, I think that's quite a stretch to say that you——" Peter cannot resist the belaboring of semantics. Finally, something familiar. He has not been *had*, this plan has been his all along: to trace the spirals, find the passage, help his daughter to escape. He did not think to find her kidnapped, transformed so fully, surrounded by such foul-smelling women in such fascinating attire. If they simply set the child free, he will help them. Peter will do all in his power to join their cause. The girl will be left out of it, and all will soon be well. His rhetorical powers, his evidence . . .

"You see here, *I* found you. I completed the rites, followed the ley lines. I opened the wood."

He is interrupted by the black-eyed girl's humorless laugh. "*You?* You've done nothing. And there is nothing you can do."

Peter frowns. "Well, if there's nothing to be done, I don't see why we should keep arguing." He means this as belittling, but it comes across as sullen. The women sense him teetering, peering over the edge at the distance he might fall.

Alys steps forward. The others try to mask their surprise.

"The child's power is growing," says Alys, looking only at Peter, ignoring the tittering behind her, the black-eyed girl's stare. "The door will be unlocked."

"I've already unlocked the door," Peter says, frowning.

"No." Alys is stone-faced. "You have not."

Peter, lost in thought: The door, he thinks, the borders. Rules made to be followed, lines drawn not to be crossed. He must remind the child, the real child, once he has found her. He must reiterate the lessons he's conveyed throughout the years. Must reinforce the boundaries. Much to be done. He turns to take his child and go, certain that once free from this wood she'll return to her previous form.

But the black-eyed girl is not obedient. She is not Peter's daughter. She knows nothing of human morality, nothing of empathy or ethics, nothing of borders. The black-eyed girl knows only the unflinching path of nature, the electricity of hunger. She cocks her head, she licks her lips, she takes a slow step forward.

But before she can act, Alys raises a dirt-blackened hand. A vine spirals up from the ground and arrests Peter mid-step, curling around his ankle, yanking, so that he plunges forward to the ground. His top teeth hit the lower with a satisfying crack. The vine lengthens, continues to coil, snaking across Peter's torso and noosing his wrists. It rolls him onto his back, so that his head hangs crooked. Wide leaves grow up around him like a cloak.

The black-eyed girl nods at Alys, saying nothing. The others hold their breath until the girl has fully left the clearing, until all sound and all scent of her is gone. Relieved, they erupt into a boil of nervous laughter, and disperse without talk of when they all will meet again.

Their world is changing, and they cannot yet predict it. The wood shifts shape before their eyes. The tree that now holds Peter will grow tall.

20

At first I refused to admit the reality of my situation. I was not, I assured myself, trapped here. I could at any time call out for Rafe and he would come to me, explain that this had all been some fantastic misunderstanding. Peter would arrive at any moment and we'd laugh about how frightened I had been, how I had imagined myself a prisoner. In preparation for that moment, entirely overwhelmed, I tried to force a laugh, a chuckle, any familiar sound to make light of what had happened, to show anyone watching I was in on the game. Instead, I vomited my lunch into a corner and then cried myself to sleep.

WHEN NEXT I awoke, I was determined to be more resilient. Certain I could save myself, I concentrated all my energy on unleashing the shackles at my wrists. I shimmied until my skin was raw, hoping to find some angle that would let me slip out of them, at which point I imagined I might do the same with the door. When that plan failed, I chipped a tooth trying to break the hinges, and the rawness left behind by the missing enamel shocked me into recognition: I was stuck here. I was entirely vulnerable. My skin prickled, and I began to sweat despite the chill of concrete floors and bare walls, the whoosh of the indifferent fan clicking in the corner. After a moment, whatever warmth my rage instilled in me abated, and I curled onto the lumpy cot, shivering.

I wished myself curled under a quilt at Urizon, Marlowe nestled beside me, listening to the familiar patter of rain on the roof. I wished myself holding a blade of green grass in the forest, the ground soft and buoyant beneath me, the trees guiding me home. I wished myself sitting in Mrs. Blott's kitchen while she boiled water for tea, could almost see the strain of the apron stretched around her waist, the bob of her gray bun as she assured me she could cure whatever ailed me.

Of course she couldn't help me now. Mrs. Blott, my mother— neither hid in the high ledges of the narrow windows, ready to spring forth and grant my wishes. Marlowe did not, as I prayed he might, come snarling and scratching outside my prison door. Matthew and Peter did not pound down the cellar stairs, demanding retribution. The forest did not stretch itself to claim me. There was nothing organic on which I could use my body: the room was cleared of every trace of dirt or germs, let alone any wooden joists or cabinetry. The only life here was my own.

My own, and then Coulton's when he appeared to make his harvest, coming up suddenly behind me while I slept, wrenching my bruised arms to gather blood. His breath was sour, and his mass increased the temperature of the normally cool room. He had a greedy energy that sucked in those around him, a current of charisma that was difficult to fight. The first time he came I was too shocked to speak, too hazy from the drugs and the blood loss to process what he was doing. I thought I must have been imagining things. Why would he want my blood? He'd taken too much to merely be testing it. But the second time he came, I saw I had not been mistaken.

"Why are you doing this?" I asked outright, trying to sound reasonable, as if I were just a casual acquaintance asking about the weather or what we were having for dinner. "If you tell me, maybe I can help you."

"What, now you're cooperating? You don't fool me, you little savage." Coulton smacked the cuff of a rubber glove against his wrist and stuck his needle in me with no other warning. I gasped. "That's what you get."

"Please, you don't have to do this," I whispered. "Whatever you want to know, I'll tell you."

"*Have* to?" Coulton leaned toward me, stroking my cheek with a gloved finger. When that finger reached my lips, he pressed down, hard. "Have to," he said to himself, smiling.

AT HIS NEXT appearance I spat at him, hoping he'd be frightened by me. I had no clearer idea of what he was doing, but from the precautions he took when he approached me I assumed that the dangers of my body were clear. When he chuckled in response, I tried to trip him as he moved toward me with his needle, tried to yank my arm away when he relaxed his grip. Failing that, I turned away from him, scowling.

"Where's Rafe?" I said, staring at the wall, my voice weaker than I wanted it to be. "I need to talk to him."

"Oh, you *need* to, do you?" Coulton grinned, yanking me up from the cot. He walked me several feet, uncomfortably shackled. "Well, in that case, Your Highness, we'll just summon him." He twisted the top onto the jar of blood he'd collected and pulled the needle from my arm at an angle, so that it stretched my already sore skin. I opened my mouth to protest, but was silenced by a quick smack to my backside, a spanking somewhere between what Coulton might provide a lover, or a child. My lip quivered, but I was determined not to let him see me cry.

He left for a moment and then reemerged with a chipped blue plate holding a bit of bread, a small paper cup with several medium-sized pills, and a cup of cloudy water.

"Take the vitamins before you eat," he said before slamming and relocking the door. "The food will help them stay down."

I sniffed at the bread and pushed it aside. I dumped the pills in the broken toilet in the corner of my cell. The water my body would not let me refuse, so I drank it, despising every swallow.

TIME PASSED. AS I faded in and out of sleep, I noted the traveling shadows cast through my two windows, the revolving trays of pills I would not take and food I would not eat: at first a cold bowl of soup, then a limp salad, then some sort of soggy noodle.

They did not trust me with a fork, and seemed to know that I could not use my fingers, leaving me a small plastic spoon with which to avoid letting the food touch my lips. Its sides were sharp enough to slice the noodles into smaller bites, but not enough to use as a weapon.

Coulton came at various intervals to take my blood and scold me for my lethargy. At some point I realized he was drugging me. It was a struggle to keep myself alert. My next full conscious recollection was of his large bulk leaning over me, insisting that I eat.

"Rafe was right about you, wasn't he?" Coulton's face was covered, all but his eyes, which seemed to relish my confusion. "A feisty thing at first, but not to worry, we'll soon break you."

I snarled at him, refusing the hot broth he offered, refusing the small part of myself that was grateful for his company after all the hours alone.

"Up to you. Just remember that force-feeding is a nasty business. Better to take your lunch in through your mouth than a tube down your throat."

I looked down at my arms, pocked with pinpricks and bruises, and imagined the rest of my body subjected to similar force. I'd read my histories, and I knew about the suffragettes who'd suffered in the city prisons, their hunger strikes stymied, their mouths clamped with steel, the phallic rubber wrangled down their throats to send the gush of liquid they'd resisted roiling down into their bellies. I shuddered.

Hating myself for my cowardice, I took the mug and drank the briny soup.

"There's a girl," said Coulton. He knelt and proceeded to prick me in the crook of my arm. One smooth strip of forehead shone between his goggles and the cap covering his hair—my one chance at escape, I thought, if only I could touch it. He whistled, ugly and off-key, and I imagined the squeal he would make when he discovered I'd outwitted him, would kill him. It would happen, I insisted to myself, it had to.

The soup was too rich for my empty stomach, and I'd downed it too quickly. I coughed, and it returned in an oil-sheened, salty bile, diluting the glass jar of my blood. Coulton raised his eyebrows, saying nothing. He poured his ruined harvest into the toilet, where it splashed up on the seat.

"We'll try again in an hour," he said before he left.

I STARED AT that toilet for hours, waiting for the moans that meant the moving of its pipes. I watched the crack under the door for shadows that could give me some clue to the space just beyond. I counted the same stains on the wall, praying that each effort would yield different results, that something about the room would somehow, magically, be different. It never was.

Each time I heard a body on the stairs I braced myself for Rafe's appearance, but if he came it was only ever while I slept. The thought enraged me—Rafe standing over my prone body, Rafe's gloved hands prodding me, exploring without permission. Rafe laughing at his fortune, my stupidity. Rafe's shadow looming, sharp and twisted against the gray basement wall.

I thought relentlessly about the events that had led to my capture: what Rafe must have known, must have been thinking. I could not revisit our journey together without burning with shame. To think I'd imagined that Rafe cared for me romantically. To think I'd followed him. To think I'd abandoned my father to whatever unknown fate. For I was certain, with each day that passed, our quest had all been artifice—there was no ancient ritual, no task to heal the land. Rafe had baited that idiot story, knowing I'd not question it, knowing I'd bite, knowing eventually he'd have me on my own.

I imagined him at a local bar, laughing with Coulton, bragging about how easy it would be to seduce me. *I'll tell her there's a prophecy.* The calls he had made nightly throughout our travels were likely updating Coulton on his progress. There was no worried family to check in on. There were no spirals. He must have overheard Matthew asking about the map at the Holzmeiers' store, and known precisely how to fool us.

Were the letters from Peter even real? *I told her I was also trying to find her father, and she bought the whole thing. What a simpleton. How easy.* I replayed the scene in my head, looping over and over: Rafe guffawing, the foam of his drink frothing as they toasted my naïveté, the rest of the pub's patrons judging me, vastly entertained. Rafe had been mocking me from the moment that we'd met, once he had realized I was care-less. And I, silly girl, conceited as I was, thought he had wanted me. That, maybe, he could love me.

But all Rafe wanted was my blood, though I could not guess what he did with it. Clearly from their precautions, Rafe and Coulton were aware of my curse. "How?" I yelled at the shut door. "How did you know? What are you doing?" I kicked at the toilet in the corner until my toes bruised green and purple. I overturned my mattress, wailing until my throat was raw. Nobody came; no one was listening.

I CLOSED MY eyes and envisioned that strange day in the forest, how the tree bark had felt against my fingers, how the birdsong had been beckoning me, how afterward I'd dreamed of the wood calling me home. Frightened, I had thought those dreams the danger. How I wished now I was trapped there, amid soil and buds, tangled in thorn-bushes, my wrists cuffed by vines instead of metal. A bitter part of me whispered that I could have been exploring that wood freely, had I not let the impossible desire for Rafe overcome all my good sense.

The thought that pained me most as I stared at the bare ceiling or picked at the meager stuffing of my cot, the truth that was worse than any stab of Coulton's needle, was the flagrance of my own culpabil-ity. Rafe had no doubt played his part, but I'd embraced mine with-out question, eagerly casting myself as the gullible fool. As I'd proven since my dangerous gestation, from the moment that my mother's heart stopped beating I was capable of only destruction. I'd been careless, out of control, I had followed my desires too blithely. My father had been right to hide me away for so long. Despite a lifetime of warning, I had placed my trust where I clearly should not have, and, as Peter had predicted, was undone.

Mrs. Blott's romance novels had taught as gospel that some men would break girls' hearts. I had always thought them simple, the ingénues blinded by their handsome, ill-intentioned suitors, those who gave the men their whole lives and got heartache in return. Yet here I'd done precisely this, let long-lashed eyes and a chiseled jaw lead me far from the path of Peter's instruction.

And where was Peter? What had happened to my father? I knew even less of his whereabouts than I had before leaving Urizon. Had he taken sick somewhere? Was he waiting for me to come to him, to nurse him? Had he died? Had he willfully abandoned me to live a life unburdened by my care, by my questions, my curse? Could he have any inkling I was stuck here in this airless room, no way to seek him out? That not even my body was my own? My stupid body, whose lusts and night imaginings had gotten the better of my judgment, despite what I now realized were warnings, despite Matthew's direct doubts.

How it hurt to think of Matthew, who'd tried so hard to protect me. My only ally, who I'd ordered out the door when his advice ran counter to my desires. Matthew, who had left without a farewell, on such poor terms that he would not turn to face me, would not watch me stumble into what he knew to be a trap.

An Ink of Her Own Blood

In the outside world it is the height of summer—the evening when darkness appears almost fully banished, when children are tucked into bed in awe of a sun that has conquered the sky. Here in the forest, it is eternally the same slow summer evening as the Blakely women go about their business—Emma trying to catch a wood mouse, Mary picking her teeth with a twig—not realizing that it is one of only two nights a year the veil will lower without a sacrifice from those who would enter, one of two nights when villagers will stumble in, the trees claiming their bodies, altering their minds.

The black-eyed girl blinks at the women—Imogen kneeling in prayer, Kathryn attempting to pleasure herself upon a tree stump—fascinated by all that they do not see, despite the many years they've had to hone their vision. These trapped Blakely women are no different from the villagers outside the wood, performing their antiquated rituals. Thinking the earth moves as a result of their actions, rather than prompting them. Thinking that walking in a spiral has significance, that tales are told more for their listeners than their tellers.

The black-eyed girl watches Lucy attempting a potion of berries and bark, Helen braiding a noose out of vines. She returns to her clearing, sits cross-legged on her pallet, where she digs her fingernails into the wood, scraping perfectly curled shavings of the sort Lucy is unable to summon. She smiles when the splinters pierce her palms, holding her hands to the light. She does not try to remove the shards of wood.

When the men come, only two this season—one pimply and hairless, the other so tall that he struggles to navigate the trees—the black-eyed girl closes her eyes and tilts her head to listen. She hears Kathryn's delight, her heavy breathing as she tells the younger, *Come*. She hears the other become tangled in a spiderweb, a thousand-year-old net of sticky fibers that sweeps from ancient tree to tree. His breath is also quick and heavy, his moan of fear not so different from his neighbor's moan of pleasure. But when the evening ends, this man will not go free.

ALYS STANDS IN the black-eyed girl's clearing, her mouth tight with memory. The way the black-eyed girl is seated with her legs tucked in, head cocked so that her hair falls just so. Her eyes fully closed, but faintly fluttering. Alys pictures her young cousin Madenn in communion with the wood, buried deep in a vision. The glow of the firelight, the gold of her hair. The wonder in her eyes once they opened.

The black-eyed girl does not need grandmothers and mothers to teach her the ways of the forest. She does not need books to tell her how to commune with the trees. The black-eyed girl is a part of the forest that made her; she is the shift, the difference, the element of randomness requisite for any evolution. Even now she can open the wood at her will, as she did for Peter Cothay. Soon, once she knows her womanhood, the wood will open for all the Blakely women. The season will finally change.

When she is ready, the black-eyed girl opens her dark eyes. She greets Alys with a slow and knowing nod.

21

In the days that followed, hours of anger interspersed with monot-
ony: the dullness of the colorless room, the endless boredom. The
weightlessness of my drugged body. The sound of my blood drip-
dripping down into Coulton's jars. A song stuck in my head, an old
lullaby that Mrs. Blott once sang me, the same two lines of melody
repeated. The thrum of the plastic-bladed fan. I paced the room,
crouched in its corners, searching for some means of escape. I waited
for Rafe.

One morning a mouse scampered out from a crack in a wall. I
pounced, freezing the creature at my touch. Coulton kicked it out the
open door before I could revive it. But the mouse had to have come
from somewhere, and, excited, I spent the next few hours trying to
peel back the plaster and paint in search of its nest. I used my elbow
to make the hole larger, and after what felt like decades of work had
made a small opening the size of my fist. I pushed my cot to the side, trying to hide my plan from Coulton when he returned the next morning.

Upon opening the door, Coulton looked from my torn fingernails
to the rearranged cot, to the dusty motes of plaster I'd been unable to
sweep into the toilet. With his boot, he kicked the cot aside, revealing
my means of escape. I thought that he might punish me. Instead he just
laughed.

"It's several feet of concrete past the drywall. Good luck clawing
your way through that. You're more likely to squeeze yourself through
the pipes or find a way up to the window."

I followed his gaze. The windows were at least ten feet above us and
not even large enough to fit my emaciated arms. I could not hide my

disappointment, my exhaustion. I gave an elbow to the effort, punching the plaster in an attempt at defiance, but as I watched my blood pour into Coulton's cup, I felt my spirit spill out with it.

TOO AFRAID TO contemplate my future, I tried to maintain hope by retelling the stories of my childhood. I could track each stage of my life by the stories I'd been told. Stories were blueprints for selfhood, ways to mold myself and my surroundings into what I needed them to be. Stories had taught me what to want, and how to want it. Maybe now they'd help to set me free.

I told myself the tale of the woodcutter's wife, lost in the forest. Fantasies of fairy princesses fooling their captors. Sudden storms that swept evil tyrants from their reigns. I rehearsed Mother Farrow's old yarn about a village mother rescuing her daughter with a foolish and fervent insistence, as if it would save me. As if my mother, even now, would save me. But for every story of a mother's love, there was a tale of blood-drained bodies, of a dumbfounded prince. A story of a disobedient child.

One of our village rumors, a tale no one could place but all insisted must be true, I had heard first from our solicitor, Tom Pepper, during one of his annual trips to Urizon to discuss the Blakely estate. Mr. Pepper, I knew, hoped to frighten me into politeness with his telling, scare away what misbehaviors I had planned. I was never disobedient, always treated his visits with the respect that I felt they—the only regular outside contact I received at the house other than Mrs. Blott and Peter—deserved. Still, he told me this:

There once was a mischievous little girl who was too curious by half, picking the locks of cupboards, eavesdropping, muddying her dresses, throwing massive tantrums that could be heard far from her home. She belched loudly in company. She uprooted garden flowers. She'd run, in the nude, down the main street of the village, her mother chasing after, trying to put her in the bath. This was a common sight to see, said Mr. Pepper, and the village butcher soon learned to time his closing shop with the slap of the girl's footfalls, the moaning of her poor, flustered mother, bath towel flapping in the breeze.

What to do about the child? How to teach her to obey? The slap of a birch switch could not calm her, nor a stern telling-off from her father, not even a prayer of expulsion to release whatever demon had her heart. All advice was empty, the child could not be tamed. The parents, especially the mother, were at their wits' end.

There was, at the time, an old wisewoman living by the river, and to her the distressed mother finally crawled.

"What to do about my child?" the mother cawed, once she'd arrived. (Cawed, I imagined, because the voice Mr. Pepper put on for her was high-pitched and crackly, not convincing in the slightest, but distinctive enough to stick in the craw of my memory.)

"Hmm," said the old wisewoman (in a breathy falsetto, punctuated every so often by manly Pepper throat-clearings and coughs). "A child who will not heed her elders. That is bad news, indeed."

"But what is to be done?" the mother asked. "I have tried everything."

The wisewoman gave her a beady-eyed smile. "Take the girl out to the forest," she said. "Give her a blanket to rest on, and a knife."

The wisewoman gave the mother a charm to call the wolves close enough to scare the girl, but not so close to hurt her. "Wait at the edge of the clearing," she instructed, "and when you hear the child scream you must not go to her. Wait, wait, until you hear nothing. You will find her asleep. You can carry her home, and she will never trouble you again."

The mother found this a strange tactic, but she had exhausted all other options. She took the girl to the wood, gave her a blanket and a penknife, then retreated some distance away, where she would wait. She followed the wisewoman's instructions, muttered the wolf spell, and listened to the child's screams until they ceased. Then back she went, to collect her sleeping daughter.

But the girl was not sleeping. The girl was angry, waiting, ready to pounce. She ran full force at her mother, penknife in hand, sounding an otherworldly yawp. She slashed her mother's right cheek, then the left. With another long cry, she leaped a log and disappeared into the trees.

The mother returned to the village, blood coating her face. In time, the wounds healed into perfectly symmetrical scars, constant reminders of her guilt and of her failure, of her wild little girl lost to the wood. The villagers assured her there was nothing else she might have done, nothing else one could do with such a disobedient daughter, though when she was out of earshot they blamed her for having birthed the demon child in the first place. At times, woodsmen or hunters would remark upon a fearsome forest sight: a small child jumping out from bushes before scurrying away. An angry, feral sprite.

THE MORE TIME passed, the more my rotten core seemed obvious, my complicity clear. My captors knew that I was guilty. "If it hurts, you have only yourself to blame," Coulton would tell me if I yanked my arm away because my veins were too swollen for his needle. "Almost as if you're asking for it," he remarked when he saw I had yet again tried to peel the plaster from the wall. My punishment for this was a quick slap to the cheek; his gloved hands scorched my skin. When he returned to find me itching, my nails drawing blood, he clucked his tongue as Mrs. Blott had when I came in late for dinner. "You're a menace to yourself, my girl. Can't imagine what harm you'd do to other folks around you. Lucky you're here with us, where we can help you. Good thing you had Rafe looking out for you." Coulton's words struck me harder than the burn of his gloved palm.

I thought, for the millionth time, on the events that had preceded my capture, but this time I replayed them with a crucial narrative difference. Matthew had been scared to let me go with the girls by the river. For all his talk of camping, I knew we'd spent nights in his car because he worried what would happen if he let me in a house. Peter had held me at Urizon, forbidding me the simplest sorts of travel. It was clear I needed guidance, that everyone I knew and loved had constantly been trying to keep me in line. Rafe's efforts now were unconventional, were painful. And yet what if his intentions were another thing that I had gotten wrong?

I hadn't seen Rafe since my arrival, but that didn't mean he wasn't thinking of me, watching me. Perhaps, I thought suddenly, the only way to free myself was to prove myself docile. Perhaps I had been set on a path to perdition that Rafe was now trying to counter. Perhaps, in my imprisonment, I really had been saved.

I had spent hours with Rafe, falling asleep beside him, sharing stories. I knew Rafe, and Rafe was no monster. Could all this be for my own good? This bloodletting a cousin to the remedy used for centuries when a patient displayed misaligned humors? Was Rafe using my blood in a way Peter had never imagined, to understand my failings, to cure me? Rafe had told me to trust him, that he knew what he was doing. Was there any way this work was for the best? It fit as well as, if not better than, every other explanation I had previously arrived at to explain my current condition and Rafe's role in it.

I knew my power to be dangerous, my existence to be a source of shame. I'd killed my mother, driven my father, now Rafe, to what appeared obsessive madness. The trouble, I began to see, was never Rafe, was never Coulton. The trouble was that in the hour that I needed them most I had bristled at the rules Peter imposed, thinking my defiance brave, my disobedience something special. I'd been selfish and stupid. I despised myself.

I deserved this treatment. Maybe it would wash me clean.

I STOPPED STRUGGLING, I stopped sneering. I sat meekly when Coulton came to me.

"She's a changed woman," said Coulton, crouching to come level with my seat on the floor, straightening a straw so I could drink the cloudy water he'd provided. "Seems we've tamed the beast, eh?"

Tamed. A word for a wild girl made obedient. A word for a hawk with clipped wings, a declawed tiger. A word that made me safe.

One evening a violent storm sent rain leaking in through the windows, and I used a bowl left over from my breakfast to catch the drops. I watched the beads of water as they raced down the wall, chasing

each other at first, and then combining as they reached their destination.

"Resourceful. Your boy Rafe would be proud," Coulton told me
when he saw my jerry-rigging. He nodded and brought me a larger
bucket and a mop with which to clean up the rest.

I shuffled awkwardly in my chains, but sopped up most of the water.
I tidied the mess I had made of the plaster, brushing the chips of paint
into a pile. I washed myself, wiping my armpits, rinsing the sweat between my thighs. I ate my bitter soups, swallowed my crackers, forced
down boiled potatoes and cold gruel and stale breads. I held my arm
out when Coulton reached for me, unflinching at the prick of the needle, steady when he gave my head a pat before he left.

Each time I heard the locks click into place, I thought that surely
Rafe would be next to unbolt them. Each time I looked up to see Coulton, I felt my hope shrink. I became the pit of the fruit that had once
been me, my meat eaten slowly, bite by fleshy bite.

RAFE DID NOT come.

He was not coming.

Perhaps he had decided I could not be cured. Perhaps he'd sold me.
Perhaps my life would end here in this basement room, with Coulton.
Perhaps I was to be the body drained of blood.

Please just kill me, I prayed silently, as I did now every time Coulton
came to check my temperature, stick me with his needles. *Kill me now
and make it quick. If you aren't going to set me free, just kill me.* For wasn't
this already a sort of living death? Nothing to look at, nothing to listen
to, nothing to touch. The sunlight that crept in through the basement
windows was weakened by the frosted glass, and though I could move
myself into its clouded beams I could not feel its power.

AS A CHILD, I'd asked my father, "What is death?"

Heaving earthward on a far point of our property, a large tree was threatening the byway. Mr. Abbott had told Peter to cut it down, claiming that it could, at any time, flatten his Trixie, the little terrier soon to suffer a less common fate at my hands. Supported by a last leg of trunk not yet splintered by the force of its leaning, the tree arched long over the spackled path that split our land from Abbott's, a seldom-weeded trail that made a line—I had been told by Mother Farrow—from Urizon to a burial mound at the northernmost tip of the wood. Peter caught me by the tail of my oversized jacket as I tried to pass under the tree arch, my weight at age four no match for the grip of his fist.

"Why does the tree bend," I said, "if it's not making an entrance?"

"Because it's dead," said my father.

So I asked Peter the question that all parents must one day prepare to answer, the question that all children will eventually ask: "What is death?"

Peter released his hold on my jacket. He crouched down on the gravel and gestured for me to mimic his action. He lost his balance slightly while wiping the lenses of his glasses, preparing to speak.

"See these thick roots here, all stretching? See how they reach past the road, past the base of this tree? They fought with the roots of another species, and that lucky tree came out the winner."

With this verbal sleight of hand, Peter had answered the much easier question: *why. Why* is this tree dead? A different wonder altogether, fascinating in the concrete traceability of its answer, opposing the unknowable *what*, the impossible *where* of the question I'd asked. What was death? My father, still living, could not tell me.

What really happened when I fingered a ladybug, fell to my knees upon the grass, or patted poor Trixie? Where was my mother? Where would I go now if I yanked off the bandages plastered to my arms, squeezed the skin at the inside of my elbow, heightening the blood flow?

Was death, as I had long suspected, darkness? I imagined a fathomless, floating nothing. No needles or pills or sweaty men with foul breath leaning over me. Just peace.

A Body Drained of Blood

Kathryn no longer knows what to make of the black-eyed girl risen from her bier, now that she is a sentient, blinking being, rather than a fresh-kept corpse. She is unsettled by the appetite with which the black-eyed girl watches the women, her undisguised hunger. Kathryn has spied the girl kneeling before the old corpse of a roebuck, her fingers tearing into its stiff body, raising the rotted flesh to her lips. The first death in the forest in centuries. Now Kathryn finds herself jumping at the crackle of a pine cone, the echo of a wood thrush, the scrape of a penknife against twigs. Will it be now? Has the black-eyed girl come for her? The wait is torturous.

She tries to focus her attention instead on those traveling the forest, the other breed of unlike body to consider, within and yet still so far from her reach. It feels to Kathryn like centuries since midsummer, although Lucy tells her it was just the other day that the wood opened, that Kathryn had her dalliance with that young man from the town. Kathryn had hoped that the awakening of the girl would mean a difference, that the wood would let her lovers stay longer, enter more often. Kathryn has been disappointed with the black-eyed girl's slow stalking of the forest creatures, her apparent disdain for Kathryn's needs. If she can open the wood on a whim, why not use it to all of their advantages?

This is not to say that Kathryn does not respect the black-eyed girl. She does. Hers is a boundless respect born of fear. She tries to work up her courage to ask the girl for favors, to start a simple conversation, but the uncanny darkness of those eyes, the languid movements . . . Each time Kathryn gathers her courage, she imagines the girl hissing at her. She imagines her own body torn open, the black-eyed girl fingering her unbound muscles, tasting her blood.

*   *   *

SHE GOES WITH Lucy to gather a bouquet of bluebell and honey-suckle to lay at the black-eyed girl's altar. As she stoops to pluck a flower, Kathryn feels someone moving in the *other* wood beside them, kneeling where she kneels. Mumbling. Praying. A man.

"I can see him," Kathryn says. Though still shut, the veil has been thinner since its recent midsummer opening, in a way it never has been before. Kathryn hears movement, smells cologne, catches sight of shadowy profiles. "I can feel him."

"Don't be ridiculous," says Lucy.

"Perhaps if you were to ask the girl to bring him inside . . ."

"Contain yourself," says Lucy. "He's clearly trying to come in. As if he thinks he's owed entrance. I know of men like that. He isn't worth the risk."

"But she let the other's father—"

"That was different."

A rush of air sputters through Kathryn's lips. "Imagine," she says, "the wind screaming. Imagine the scrape of his boots. I wonder if it has snowed. I wonder if the snow has melted."

"Silliness," says Lucy. "Besides, it is summer, remember?"

Kathryn sighs again, brimming with desire. She turns and leaves Lucy. She thinks of the dark-haired boy with blue eyes, lithe and mus-cular. The boy she's seen before, a shadow slipping through Urizon. He'd peered in through a back window, sweating through his white collared shirt, and Kathryn could see the ripple of his biceps, could easily imagine the rest of his lean body underneath.

She pictures him now, and tries to reach for him with her mind, fol-lowing his scent. When she inhales, an overwhelming new odor arrests her. Bullfrogs sing mating songs, trees shiver in the breeze. Kathryn inhales again and stops, looking down at her clogs, which are grimy with age, but still boast small patches of their original color. They are sinking into new-formed mud, a rich red stew of sticky earth. Kathryn kneels, sinking her hands into foreign soil. When she lifts them, her fingers are stained red with blood.

22

Days piled up like playing cards, with only occasional distinctions to separate one from the next: an unusually hot bowl of gruel, a new regimen of vitamins, a rainstorm against the windows, a heavy, dreamless sleep. I had given up my fantasies of Rafe trying to cure me. Surely by now those intentions would be clear. I had become the model captive, and it had not been enough. I had fooled myself again, working so hard to be what I thought Rafe wanted. I was finished with that now. I had done more than enough pandering. I had only enough energy to blink my eyes, to sigh a bit, submit to Coulton's bloodletting. But just as I was losing myself, becoming the four walls of my prison, my warden's tactics took a turn. Coulton came to me one day without needles, without food. He stood by the door, his eyes appraising.

"How much," I asked him finally, voice hoarse from lack of use, "have you been making off each vial of my blood?" The most rational motivation I had landed on was money.

Coulton chuckled and removed his goggles. I thought of my father, removing his own. *Maisie, have you come in with my tea?*

"Not nearly enough, my dear accountant," said Coulton. "If there's coin to be had, I've been kept out of it, though I'm pleased to see you're interested in profit." His one dead tooth was shinier than the others, a magnet for saliva, fascinating in its rot. I wondered if my touch might stain it white.

"Serves you right," I said.

Coulton laughed. He beckoned me closer, as if ready to confide. When I did not succumb, he sighed, and leaned back in the folding chair he'd brought to the room with him. It was blue plastic. It creaked under his weight.

"It's been a strange few weeks," Coulton said, straightening his shoulders, "for both of us, I reckon. Not a pleasant task, draining a living body, collecting the amount of blood your boy claims he needs. Not work I'd be a part of if it weren't for his knowledge of some unsavory activities of my own."

"Rafe is blackmailing you."

"And so you likely wonder why it is I'm smiling." Coulton had not been, but grinned widely now, displaying that awful front tooth. "I'm smiling because our friend here has gone off on some adventure. Left you all alone with Coulton, and we're going to have some fun. Just like you, I'm interested in profit. I'm interested in what we two, together, can do to make a profit. Do you follow?"

I did not.

"You see, the other day I came across a mouse you killed some weeks ago. I'd meant to throw it out, but, well, you know how things go. Kicked it into the hallway, forgot it. Anyway, imagine my delight to find the thing had never rotted. No smell. A little stiff, icy corpse, just the same as I'd last seen it." He waited for me to respond, but I held my face firm. "Now imagine: squirrels and foxes, kittens and dogs, lining the shelves at a place like your Holzmeier's. Showing none of the signs of decay you'd expect—simply frozen. Like taxidermy without all the mess. No need to pay for someone to skin the beasts, to stuff them. Cut out the middleman, as they say." Coulton crossed his arms and leaned back in his chair, pleased. I hoped he would tip over.

"You mean you want to sell dead animals?"

"Frozen witch's familiars," he corrected, "for twice the usual price." His dead tooth, I noticed suddenly, had a spot of remaining white at its corner, the white paw of an otherwise black cat.

"Let me see Rafe again," I said. "Let me talk to him."

Coulton laughed outright. "You think that would make a difference? Besides, as I told you, he's long gone."

"It isn't good if I touch animals. You have to understand. It hurts people more than it helps them, will hurt you . . ." I realized that I was pleading with him, my voice rising, making me seem younger, as desperate as I felt. Coulton cackled. Changing tactics, aware that our time to talk was limited, that soon he would be gone and I'd be sitting here alone, I steadied my voice and continued: "Nobody thinks it's real. The souvenirs you sell to Holzmeier's. A joke, it's all just silly."

"Oh, no, little one, they're set in their beliefs. The people know what they want. Who are we to deny them? A special thing, it is, is witchcraft."

"I'm not a witch," I said.

"So say they all."

PERHAPS THIS WAS how I would die: mauled by some wild animal, or starved to death as I barricaded myself behind my cot. I swore that I would not play Coulton's game, that I would hide from any beast that he brought me, no matter how vicious, no matter how sweet, no matter how much I craved touch after weeks without Marlowe.

Coulton brought his sacrifices into my underground chamber, and from the look of things (his red-rimmed eyes, his claw-scratched hands), the task of collecting them had not been pleasant. The animals cried, scrabbling in their boxes, and Coulton grimaced when he dumped them in with me, seeming almost sorry as he double-locked the door behind him.

My first was an angry dog, a stray, from the look of it, roughly the size of Marlowe. Snarling, maybe rabid, it bared sharp yellow teeth. Saliva gleamed like spiderwebs, slid slowly from its jowls.

"I won't hurt you," I whispered, aware as the words left my lips how unlikely they were. I held out my hands, palms open in surrender.

Unfortunately, the animal saw this as a sign of aggression. The dog lunged toward me. For a moment I debated holding to my word, simply sitting and submitting to its bite, but an image of what Coulton might do with my injured body flashed through my mind. I was gripped by a rage as intense as if the damage had already been done.

Our collision was a frenzied burst of action, a firecracker popping and then hissing, sizzling still. I left the encounter with a tooth mark at my shoulder, scratches across my chest, a purplish-yellow bruise budding just beneath the skin. The dog left as a corpse.

I stared at the dead animal. The dog seemed smaller, once stilled, less enemy than comrade, afraid and abused, not so different from myself. Perhaps all it needed was a thorough grooming, some affection, and it would have become a companion comparable to Marlowe. Or perhaps this dog had been content to roam the moorland, to be citizen of crags and grass and sky. Who could know, now, what its life might have held, had it not intertwined with mine?

I forced myself to sit with these thoughts. I had killed, with aim to kill and kill completely. For the first time, I had tried to end a life, and with success. I'd have imagined shame and guilt, a sense of failure, but as I looked on the stilled animal I felt only a full-body numbness. I felt tired, and centuries old.

I THOUGHT OF another story, one every child of Coeurs Crossing knew by heart. I'd heard it first from Mother Farrow, and after had perused our library at Urizon, looking for some mention in a history of our region that might further flesh it out. I'd found several references that could make the tale true, though Peter cautioned me that it was legend, and as such embellished and altered over the years, like an old car whose parts have been slowly replaced until little remains of its initial model.

Once there was a great empire to the south that wanted our country in its fold. (*Country* being, here, a very loose term for the land and the spattering of native tribes that nursed it. This was centuries ago; before the rise of modern cities, before men sailed across the sea.) As one of the northernmost settlements, the land that would, in time, become our village was spared the greedy empire's initial rapes and pillages. Those who lived there were left mostly to themselves. Of course, this could not last. Eventually the empire sent its troops to take the land

and civilize its people. Some fought, many surrendered, even more were killed.

At this point in the story, the history books revered the brave soldiers who crushed one final pocket of resistance. Led, it is said, by a brother and a sister, one of the stronger forest cults would not submit. They used guerrilla tactics and crude weaponry in an attempt to hold back their would-be oppressors. They caused enough of a to-do to be remembered in their conquerors' books, but could not halt the tide of what those books called progress.

The southern troops were stronger, in number and in weaponry and skill, and they thoroughly routed the rebels. The siblings were captured and taken to their enemy's camp, rumored to have rested on the spot where Urizon would be built centuries later. The sister was tortured, kept prisoner, used most foully, until she escaped one spring morning right from under the empire's eyes. The brother was sent south and made to fight. This was a common enough punishment in those times. These were the days when crowds would gather at arenas to watch gladiatorial combat, cheering as men battled to the death. Mother Farrow claimed the brother became a champion fighter, the most ferocious, the most cunning, of thousands. She told me this with pride, smacking her tongue against toothless old gums.

Looking down at the dog, contemplating my own situation, I reasoned myself a sort of gladiator: imprisoned, ripped from my home to be thrown into a slapdash arena with no choice but to fight to the death. There was no reason to feel guilty about what I had done. Did the gladiator wonder what became of the subjects of his triumph? He did not. That brother, I was sure, had killed countless wild animals. He'd killed men. His only thought his own survival, the brief burst of his victory, no matter its price.

MY SPOILS INCREASED. There passed a stream of weeks of orchestrated killings. Days of dodging bites and blows that brought me to exhaustion, a repetition that stripped me of any lingering sympathy toward the animals I killed. And with each death, these beasts renewed me: I absorbed their will to live, their instinct to fight. They reminded me an outside world existed, a world to which I was determined to return.

In my readings as a child, I'd been enamored by the Greco-Roman god Charon, the ferryman who ushered souls across the river that divided the land of the living from that of the dead. I'd seen him as an ancient compatriot, the god in whose image I'd been made. To pay Charon for passage from one harbor to the next, coins were placed upon the eyes of corpses, hidden under their tongues. I saw each animal I met as my own payment to old Charon, who would surely love a life force more than coin, and might ferry me from this living death to the realm of life outside. It was, I knew, when I let myself think back to who I'd been before my capture, a weak justification for my actions. But in my collusion with death I'd had my first true taste of agency, of power. I'd discovered that I liked it.

There was a moment before the final moment—as each animal looked at me, aware that it was breathing its last breath—that felt like being known for who I truly was. A me that I had always been, but hidden. A fire that I had refused to acknowledge was slowly being stoked, a hunger that I'd long tried to ignore could not be sated.

Toymaker and Child

In his new home, this soaring elder, Peter has much time to reflect. He can sense the tree's disdain for its visitor: unlike its roots' fungi, whose fibers suck nutrients but offer protection in return, Peter's presence offers no advantage. *Out*, the tree whispers in a tongue not known to man, though Peter feels its fibers fighting against him. A new verse to add to the song of its desire: *More light. Taller. Wider. Out.* The elder feels each tear in the fabric of its trunk and tries to heal the fissures, pressing Peter tighter, forcing him to contort his body, knocking his glasses, which Helen had rescued from the forest floor, out of his reach.

In a way, Peter thinks, this penitentiary is an honor. He remembers the great wizard Merlin trapped in his own ancient oak tree, and for a moment feels his chest swell with pride. What would his colleagues say, those venerated academics that had doubted the fusion of folklore and science, if they saw him here now? He'd always believed he was destined for greatness, for discovery. Peter had dreamed—

His shoulders sag, unable to continue the pretense. He cannot lie to himself any longer. This is penance.

Above him, around him, the elder dreams of soil. Dreams of glassy, glinting snow. Dreams of its own greatness—*taller, wider, more light*. It knows nothing of self-sabotage, regret, or restitution.

Peter knows that his behaviors warrant this punishment. Stuck here alone, Peter has no escape from the accusations flung at him by the stranger his daughter has become. Her words reverberate, sticking to the walls of his mind, rankling. What more suitable fate for a man who has tried to own a body—for now Peter acknowledges the tests, the rules he imposed on his daughter, as such—than the confinement of his own? This is the natural conclusion of his studies, a clever response from the forest and the women that it breeds, the women who have taken his daughter. He wonders what they have done to her.

He has a sudden vision of Maisie as a young girl—how she'd tug at his hand, those gardening gloves floppy around her tiny wrists, and lead him to an object of her childhood fascination: a tree with a twisted trunk, a squirrel without a tail, an old arrowhead. She'd looked up at him with such innocence, such trust. She'd been so helpless, unaware of her burgeoning power. She had needed him. And what had he seen when he looked at her? What had Peter needed? A testing site? A key?

If she ever returns to the clearing, what Maisie has become will look at him with her strange, altered eyes; her girlhood gone, and with it all small wonders. Whatever Maisie had been, what she might have been, Peter believes he has ruined. He presses his forehead against the wall of wood and cries for all that they have lost.

23

I made my offerings—a whining chipmunk, a house cat with a large, puffed tail, a little lamb. I ate all that Coulton offered me to regain my strength. I paced my small room, planning, preparing for whatever might come next, hoping for some chance at escape.

I guessed it had been three weeks since my encounter with the first beast, and I'd just finished battling a monstrous red fox. The thing was evil, vicious as a bull shark, its skinny body scurrying and scratching until I finally touched the white tip of its tail. Coulton had shuffled into my compartment to remove the body. Once he'd bagged the fox, he nodded his usual, silent goodbye, and I thought myself alone for the evening.

But on this particular night, the door opened shortly after Coulton had left. I sat straight up from my cot, body tense, to see Rafe in the doorframe. I'd given up on him weeks ago, yet there he was in front of me, dressed in his white jumpsuit, fully covered but for his face, which grinned rakishly, charming as ever. His audacity infuriated me.

"May I?" Rafe asked me, hand extended toward my blankets. Like an animal I recoiled from him instinctively. "Maisie," Rafe said.

At first I thought to freeze him out, refuse to look his way, ignore what explanation he provided. But my current situation was unchanging. Perhaps I could use this encounter to my advantage. I turned around.

"What do you want?" I said softly.

A smile played carefully across his lips. "I know that you're angry with me."

I blinked at him.

"I know that this is not what you'd imagined when we set out on our quest."

I said nothing. He stood, looking down at me, hands hidden in his pockets. His mouth twisted. He sighed. "I could have gone about it differently, I suppose. But Maisie, all that has happened—I hope you recognize it's necessary, all of it. We'd undone the locks, we needed the last sacrifice. It was so clear you'd been conditioned, your father taught you not to touch anything, not to talk about what you can do. You would never have believed, wouldn't have let me take the blood—I couldn't risk it."

"Oh, come off it," I said. "Like there was ever any reason to run me all around to special *places*, to pretend you cared about my father or his work. Who are you selling my blood to? What are they paying you?"

"Maisie," Rafe said, "I do care. Trust me—"

"Tell me you're joking."

Rafe pulled his hands slowly from his pockets. I couldn't help but flinch.

"We have the same purpose," he said slowly. "To know the forest, to enter it and understand the wood. My whole life, well, since I began this line of research, I've been waiting for you. At first I didn't know it was you, precisely, but when I realized that your father was not *only* Peter Cothay, when I realized that he had you . . . I'm sure you understand the stakes, why I had no other options. I couldn't risk your disagreeing, couldn't risk your saying no. Your blood is the only way in. I'm sure of it." He paused, as if waiting for me to absolve him. I wondered what he'd say if he learned I had already entered that wood without shedding a single drop of blood.

"Why are you here?" I asked, scowling. "Have you come back to see your handiwork? To gloat?"

Rafe seemed surprised. "Maisie, the plan didn't work," he said. "I thought you'd already know. The door hasn't opened. I sat by that forest for weeks waiting, and I know we had the right amount of blood—we had more than enough, more than a body's worth—so I can only imagine that you have to be there with me. That there's something about you, about your presence. That there's something else we've missed."

"My presence?" I laughed harshly.

"I figured you'd have had a sense . . . a vision . . . ," Rafe continued. "Don't you have any intuition? Anything at all?" He stepped closer, so that I could smell his cologne. Again, he smiled.

I turned away from him to stare at the burrow I'd made in the wall, my eyes trained on the flaking plaster. "You must think I'm even stupider than I seem."

"I understand," Rafe said to my back. "You're still angry. But Maisie, you're a miracle of science. You shouldn't be ashamed, you should be proud. When your father talked about the forest, about its history, was there ever any—"

"You're wasting your breath."

"Because you don't know, or because you won't tell me?"

I said nothing.

Rafe sighed. "Eventually I'm going to figure out what it is that went wrong. I'll be back in a day or so. While I'm gone, I hope you'll think about all you could gain if you help me. Think about all I can give you." He set a gloved hand on my shoulder. I jerked away. "By the time I get back," said Rafe slowly, "I'm sure that you'll have reconsidered your involvement." He left the room, bolting the door behind him.

I sat very still, processing Rafe's sudden arrival, his equally sudden departure.

When my captivity had begun, I'd taken comfort in the thought that I knew Rafe, that I could not have sat so close for hours in the car and not seen some glimmer of truth. I had replayed our conversations, reading layers of meaning where there likely were none, turning phrases like rocks to search the soil underneath them. And I'd realized this exercise was futile. My analysis of Rafe's character could be built only on our most recent encounters, any previous behavior necessarily regarded as a part of his well-embodied act. I hadn't known his motives then, but now I saw them clearly: he cared only for his work, and he was willing to excuse whatever torture, whatever cruelty, to achieve its completion. Those stories he'd told me about entering the forest, of sacrifice . . . did he truly believe them? Did he truly believe what he had said to me? That he meant well? That his choices were moral?

It didn't matter. None of it mattered. Well-meaning or not, Rafe had sentenced me to prison; he had been my judge and my jury and my crime. I would not succumb to his body, or his stories. I would not let him take more blood. I'd remain cold and watchful, and I'd kill him if he came again, would lunge toward that unprotected face, that warm, bare skin.

THE NEXT DAY I left the basement for the first time since my capture. Coulton ushered me up some stairs into a different, darker room, windowless and bleak, and placed me in a chair that leaned forward and back. He strapped me in with metal ties that scraped against my skin, then left me to wait, the anticipation its own torture.

I tried to predict what was coming. I thought it sure to be some sort of forced revival, that he'd bring me something dead and have me stroke it back to life. Might he film me? Bring an audience? Or was this what Rafe had meant when he'd insisted that I'd soon reconsider his offer?

Finally, Coulton reentered. He stood before me, eyes gleaming.

"Don't worry"—he smiled—"this will only hurt a moment. We have to keep you fit, don't we? Our dear little sister. Our unending chest of gold."

As he spoke, he prepared his instruments: large, shiny hooks, an oversized magnifying glass, a straight razor that gleamed with brackish light. He slid his hands into a pair of form-fitting rubber gloves, smacking their cuffs against his wrists, and loaded the barrel of a needle with a plum-colored fluid. Involuntarily, I shuddered.

"This will only hurt a moment," he said again. I clenched my teeth against my lip. Coulton tied a band around my poor, abused right arm and plunged the purple liquid into my vein.

Slowly, the plunger's contents took effect. My ankle, which had developed a constant twinge since an encounter two days prior with a feral-looking ferret, no longer pained me. The thumbnail I had bitten to the quick before he'd tied me to the chair stopped the brutal, rhythmic throbbing that kept time to Coulton's words. My body felt light and effervescent, a shell I had found temporary solace in, rather than fully part of me.

With detachment I observed as Coulton took his lancet and carved an inch-long gash into my left forearm. The movement tickled, but didn't hurt. Funny, I thought then, just how delicate my body. How utterly, embarrassingly human.

Look how the blood trickles and pools as Coulton peels away the skin. Look at the swollen pinkness underneath it. How clean it is. How strong.

Once he'd lifted up a sizable square of the skin at the top of my forearm, Coulton used a pair of scissors to cut the peeled part free. He placed his relic on a silver tray beside him, then carried it carefully out.

My arm, bleeding freely, was now twitching. It felt very far away. And then a fire lit my body in a sudden, painful burst. Its onslaught sent me jerking forward, so that the metal ties constraining me cut into my chest. I screamed. As consciousness faded, I noticed that the blood had stained my dress, forming teardrops of red against the dirty white.

24

I dreamed myself back in the clearing where Marlowe had buried the shinbone, walking with great purpose yet unable to name my destination. Although I was sleeping, I felt awake in a way that I had not been before, aware of the world and its wideness. The scene was strange, but did not feel strange. Of course my movements should be guided by some distant, shimmering magnet, a reeling that I felt within my heart, pulling me closer toward . . . I paused, the intensity frightening as I considered my burgeoning bloodlust.

I'd never worried about evil. I'd read tales of horror and found them too elaborate and glamorous, strewn with apparitions, doomed lovers, mysterious curses. Such scintillations were a joke. There was no silver-blooded sexuality about death; there was only the fact of it—the way that it went with the earth. The power I had felt as I'd confronted each new animal was no demon possession—it was me. Each desire that compelled me was mine. If this was true, where was I going? What would I find?

Some questions are birthed, rather than asked, and having been born they will cry until tended. I knew the story of Pandora's box. I knew the cost of Eve tasting the apple. I didn't care. I was led by my desire.

"Maisie." I jumped to hear my father.

"Peter?" I stood in the forest, looking at him as if I'd just peeked in his office door.

"Maisie, my girl," said Peter. He was not standing before me, and yet I could see him, the way he'd turn back from the desk in his office, that circle of glass at his eyes, an eyebrow raised above it. *Have you come with the tea?*

"Maisie?"

I kept walking.

"Maisie!"

ONE MIGHT THINK that with my powers of resurgence I'd be quick
to recover from physical harm, but to my constant frustration, that had
never been the case. My scraped knees required the same time as anyone else's to regenerate skin. When I broke my arm at seven (a silly
story involving a desperate attempt to hush an inconsolable wren by
offering a bit of bread out of a window, all the while trying to keep my
arm off the tree), I had to wait the full six weeks for it to heal.

I was suffering from a square inch of excoriated skin, a gruesome
patch on the inside of my arm below my elbow. Any sudden movement
seemed sure to disturb the clotting process. I winced at my makeshift
bandage, grimacing at the grimy floors of the basement I knew all too
well, the rusted, dirty chains that reappeared around my ankle, the
steady dripping of old water from the ceiling. A headache was ham-
mering through the edges of my skull.

I felt a spasm crawling up my chest, summoned my strength, and sat
up, releasing all the contents of my stomach. My sick splashed across
my blanket, my cot. It stained my paper gown and seeped onto my
bandage. The pain in my arm was an inevitable constant, and I felt a
throbbing tightness in my stomach, as if my bowels were getting ready
to release. Still, the headache and the dizziness seemed to have passed.

A sudden image in my mind: Coulton's hands across my body. My
strip of skin, pink and pulsing. The way he held it to the light as if a
conquest, a lens through which his life would change. My abdomen
curled again. I shuddered, wet dress clinging to my skin. What if Rafe
were to come down here now and see me so pathetic? Surely he'd at
least replace my clothing, rinse my cot. So far he had granted the most
basic human dignities: a bucket of hot water weekly to bathe myself,
food, the lovely drugs that helped me sleep. If he needed my blood, he
needed me alive. He needed to know that, despite my appearance, I

would stay alive. If I died or took sick, his past few months would be for nothing. I thought of Coulton's words: *We have to keep you fit.* If I was seriously ill, what would they do?

It was a gamble, I knew, to even contemplate the question. I poked at my bandage, and the pressure of my fingers sent a darkness to my brain so extreme that I was sure I would be sick again. Would vomit be enough? I didn't think so. They'd give me a shot of something, another sedative. What I needed was to frighten Rafe so much that he'd immediately remove me, not only call for help but carry me off to a hospital. Once I was there, in an emergency room, in some country doctor's office, in his van . . . One thing at a time.

My stomach cramped with my decision, tightening and pulsing. I spit on the fingers of my right hand to clean them, my mouth still sour and dry. Pulling up a corner of my bandage, I gagged at the pus. I had to time this correctly. An artery, once found, would bleed out fast. I couldn't let myself lose consciousness. I sat very still and listened for any sign of movement up above. I had no way to mark the time. How much had passed? Thirty minutes? Three hours?

Then, sound at the top of the stairs. Distant voices.

Bracing myself, my front teeth sharp against my lip, I pressed my fingernail deep into the mess of my injury. The pain was so immense that the room seemed to seesaw. I felt a sticky rush of wetness pooling under me, and was grimly pleased to note that my incontinence would only help my cause. Shifting myself slightly, I prepared to dive again into the abyss of my wound, when I saw the patch of color slowly seeping, turning my gray hospital gown red.

Blood.

Not from my arm, which was producing its own hot seep of infection, but blood from my insides. Deep, thick clots. A flood.

THERE WAS DISGRACE, I had been taught (by books, of course—Peter had never broached the subject, and Mrs. Blott just frowned at me and said I'd learn in time), to monthly bleeding. Menstruation meant uncleanliness. Blood was shameful. It was excess, embarrassing, an obvious sign of sin. And yet I never loved my sinful body more than in that moment, when it delivered me precisely what I needed: both a tangible tool by which to save my own life, and the promise of a future as a woman, a reason to live it.

A quiet current of pride had always run beneath the deep shame of my body: that although I was a monster, I was special. Matthew's attention had strengthened this conviction, as, in a twisted way, had Rafe's. But all at once I saw that pride for what it truly was—a buttress to prevent me from entirely collapsing. I wanted so much to be normal. I wanted to build, rather than conquer, and I'd resigned myself to the fact that I never would.

For the first time in weeks, I felt myself smile.

I WAS READY when Rafe came inside with Coulton. They were mid-conversation, Rafe frustrated and Coulton contrite.

"I didn't know it wouldn't work before I sliced it off, now did I?" he panted, having raced after Rafe, who'd paid no mind to their disparate states of physical fitness. "And if it *had* worked, just imagine—"

"Shut up." Rafe's voice was very quiet. "Maisie?" He took two slow steps toward where I lay splayed on my cot. "*Fuck.*"

My eyes were closed, but with some pride I could imagine the scene that they'd walked into: my naked body curled toward the door, bandaged wrist stretched out to rest precisely on the red stain on my mattress, the bandage itself nearly soaked through. The drying vomit on my lips, the blood like war paint smeared across my right cheekbone, the clumps of my tangly hair. And my pièce de résistance, the slow trickle of the sopping, bloody dress I'd torn and hidden in my left hand, squeezing gently, each drop pooling to the floor.

"*Fuck.* What did you do to her?"

"I told you, just a quick bit off her arm and then—"

"She's going to need a doctor. Where can we take her? Fuck. *Fuck.*"

I heard the rip of cloth, Rafe tearing up the T-shirt that he wore under his jumpsuit, and felt his gloved hands tie a tourniquet above my sopping bandage. It took all I had in me not to scream from the pain.

"Maybe a military doctor. The military hospital . . . we could say that we just found her. We would have to clean this up. For God's sake go get the van. Go get her something to wear."

"Or we could chalk it all up to bad luck. Could be kinder now to let her bleed out. And when her body's still, we——"

"Go!" Rafe roared. He followed Coulton out, the two huffing up the stairs, leaving the basement door open. I opened an eye—was now the time? Not yet, the chain was on my ankle. But soon.

Rafe returned quickly with a new hospital gown and a blanket, which he wrapped around me. Though I was still feigning unconsciousness, he spoke to me as he unbolted my chain, scooped me in his arms, and angled me up the stairs.

"I'm going to take you to a friend of mine. He'll make it all better. You'll be fine. In just no time at all. Like nothing ever happened. It's going to be fine. Maisie, I've got you. You'll see."

In answer, I squeezed my rag harder, my blood dripping down my arm onto Rafe's jacket.

"Go get the cot!" he yelled to Coulton. "We'll strap her to it, strap her in the van." While Coulton did, Rafe carried me outside to where a cargo van, the same one I had seen in Coeurs Crossing, sat waiting. I inhaled my first fresh air in months. The action quickly set me coughing: the van was still running, exhaust fugging from its tail.

"She's moving!" said Rafe. "Thank God."

The inside of the van was clean and quiet. My cot was secured to several ropes against the walls, and I was strapped in with a belt, tightened so that I would not jostle. After conferring, they decided that Rafe would be the one to drive me, while Coulton stayed to clean my mess and any sign of my captivity, on the chance Rafe's doctor friend could not be trusted.

Then we were off. I counted the van's turns, unsure of how far we'd be going, afraid to put my plan in action too soon and have it all come to naught. After we'd been driving smoothly for a bit on what I thought to be a highway, I wiggled my good arm out from its strap, and with all of the strength I could summon, I banged on the side of the van.

"Maisie?" Rafe turned briefly, twice, to see me.

"Rafe," I moaned. "Rafe, the straps are too tight. My hand, Rafe, I think it might . . ."

"Thank God you're up, I'm going to get you to—"

"Please, the straps . . ." I let my voice trail off, needing him to think me even weaker and more tired than I was. "Can we please?"

Rafe pulled over to the side of the road, got out of the van, and came around to the back door. A burst of energy shot through me, nerves and anticipation combatting my pain. I let out a moan of desperation, at first calculated and then all too real as the immensity of what I was about to do finally hit me.

I felt Rafe's weight as he climbed into the van, could smell his aftershave and sweat as he knelt over me. "Let's see here . . ." His breath was hot. "Where does it—" Rafe began, but before he could finish, my hand darted out to brush his neck.

He keeled forward and I tried to squirm away, but there was nowhere to go. His corpse fell over me, his eyes open wide, moving, glassy, toward my own. Fighting a scream, I bit down on my lower lip. Rafe's chin touched my jawline. He twitched, was still, twitched again.

It was as if Rafe knew, in his constant resurrection, what was happening. His hand grasped my throat, choking me, tightening, it seemed, as his life flowed and ebbed. I coughed. I couldn't breathe.

And then, as failure flashed through me, I found one last burst of strength. With a roar, I thrust my bony knee into his groin, then bit down hard on the arm, which had jerked from my neck to my jaw in surprise. I tasted blood through the canvas of his jumpsuit. Taking advantage of the distraction caused by this fresh pain, I pressed my hand to his neck, rolling him off me.

And then Rafe was finished, fully dead, his body slumped across the floor.

I knew I had to move quickly. I undid my straps and relieved Rafe of his jacket, which was thankfully long enough to fall just past my knees. I took the sheet that I'd been lying on, stiff with dried blood, and draped it over Rafe's body. I was about to jump out of the van, onto the gravel of the road that we'd been traveling, but could not resist a last look at my captor. I turned back. One of Rafe's shoes was visible, not quite covered by the sheet, a glob of chewing gum stuck between the treads of the sole. The adrenaline propelling me fell away. I sank to my knees in the back of the van.

As a little girl I'd tripped and fallen in the dirt and a rock had lodged itself in my shin. I was on the back terrace. I stood and went inside, certain I was fine. Perhaps I felt a trickle of wet against my calf, and thought it was water. It was not until Mrs. Blott gasped and told me to move off the carpet that I looked down to see the injury, the black stone under the skin, the rivulets of blood. I screamed, and it was as if my scream unleashed the pain I'd been holding at bay. I still remembered it, the glance, the rock, the onslaught. I stood and took several, shaky steps toward Rafe's body.

I could close my eyes, I knew, succumb to lack of sleep and blood loss, put this moment away as if it had been a dream. Keep walking—as I might have on that carpet, ignoring Mrs. Blott's shock—and laugh and say that what I could not see couldn't hurt me. If I did not dwell on the damage, I could ignore it. Only acknowledgment would break the wall that blockaded my pain. I might feel Rafe just as a twinge in stormy weather, a phantom passing through my thoughts before sleep.

But I had killed him. I had killed him on purpose. It hardly mattered what Rafe had done: he was a man who had been living, and now wasn't. All life, despite the workings of the consciousness it harbored, had its own intrinsic value: Rafe's heart pumped on oblivious to its master's intentions, its beat a force of beauty. Peter had not raised me with religion, but he'd taught me that much. I owed Rafe's life my memory, I owed it my pain. I stretched my bandaged arm back, the gesture futile, as Rafe was too far away for me to touch him, as I knew I could not touch him even if he had been closer. Whatever slight scab had begun to form on my arm ripped free, and two careful drops of blood fell onto the floor. I pulled myself away, tripping out of the van, my arm bleeding freely, and blinked out at the limp countryside, the hazy sheet of summer sky.

SOMEHOW, I FOUND a phone booth. Somehow, I found the proper change in the pocket of Rafe's stolen jacket. Aware of the strange glances I was getting from the few people who passed me, I quickly dialed the first number that came into my mind, catching myself just before I pressed the final digit, saving myself a wasted call. Mrs. Blott would not be home to answer, Abingdon the cat was not home to mew suspiciously at the old-fashioned wall telephone that rang in her kitchen.

There was only one phone number, other than my own, I'd committed to memory. I'd seen it taped to the refrigerator, IN CASE OF EMERGENCY, for four days at Urizon. I'd seen it written in black marker on a little girl's lone glove.

I MADE THE call and then sat on the curb beside the phone booth to wait. I was half naked and shaking, covered in blood, passing in and out of consciousness. A woman knelt next to me, offering help, and I waved her off, my words incomprehensible. Matthew pulled up just as I heard the first murmur of police sirens.

I slumped into the front seat, no mind to the mess I brought with me, the cool plastic a relief against my bare legs.

"Where is he?" Matthew growled.

I shook my head, unable to keep my eyes open.

"Rafe will pay for this, I promise." Matthew slammed the door shut and we sped off, away from the blinking lights, the gathering crowd. "I'll make him pay."

Before I fell asleep, I whispered, "Rafe is gone."

Part

Symmetry and Balance

The black-eyed girl wanders. Birds converse in the canopies above her, out of sight but ruffling the trees as they land and take flight. Small creatures scurry from one patch of undergrowth to another, disappearing into tangled bowers of barberry and thorn. The scent of blood travels on the breeze.

The black-eyed girl stomps through the brushwood and scrub, tracking the odor to a long-abandoned clearing, the apron to a cluster of elders, where a curtain of cobweb hangs stretched between dark-berried trees. Some strands are patchy, barely strung together, others thick and full and white. It is a home built long ago, a place of refuge for the spider at its center, which hangs roughly the size of the black-eyed girl's fist. The creature seems to have a wise face, bright and whiskered, its many eyes as ancient as her own. Its spinnerets shiver. Its web holds one gossamer-clad casualty: a man smothered entirely in silk, with just a small sliver of space through which to breathe.

The black-eyed girl approaches, and deftly stills the spider with a finger. She pulls one of its crisp, freckled legs, stretching until she can hear cracking, see the phlegmy rush of innards as they spill. She lifts the limb to her mouth and slurps its contents. After completing this ritual with all eight of the legs, the black-eyed girl discards the shorn abdomen.

Sensing her, the netted man wriggles in his cobweb, knowing even as he does that he's already met his fate. With a broken branch, the black-eyed girl severs the silk holding him. She takes a fingernail and slices through his packaging, pulling away the webbing until she can see his face, his hooked nose, his eyes wide with terror. Gripping his arm below the shoulder, the black-eyed girl twists until the heavy limb snaps free. She inhales. The meat is bursting and blood-black.

WHEN SHE HAS finished with him, sucking her fingers to lap up the last of the juices, the black-eyed girl turns to find the child, Emma, watching her. One dirty thumb is jammed into the girl's mouth, a gesture that might seem lewd were it not for her size.

"I saw you," says Emma, voice muffled by her hand.

Emma is not a conventionally pleasing child to look at. One brown eye cannot face forward, remains permanently pointed at the bridge of her large nose. That splotchy pink birthmark runs from neck to earlobe, over jaw and left cheek. Her lips form the shape of a small heart. Her slender fingers are flaked with hangnails and crusted with mud.

"Saw what?" the black-eyed girl asks her.

Emma shrugs, sucks her thumb louder and harder, lets escape a pink slip of her tongue. In some ways, Emma is more than a child; in others, as childlike as ever one could be. She spent just five years in the world, and then lost lifetimes in the forest, without mother or father to guide her, without synaptogenesis, or growth. As in the old fable, the grass snake that opens its mouth to let its little ones hide in its gullet, the forest saved Emma from early demise. Unlike the grass snake, it did not let her slither back out of its wide maw once danger had passed.

"You ate the dead man," Emma says, pointing at the remains, the clean bones that litter the clearing.

"I did," the black-eyed girl agrees.

"Did he taste good?" Emma fingers the remnants of the thick cobweb. A cluster of five-pointed elder flowers has been caught, nearly camouflaged in the white of the web, and she picks at the stamens, releasing chalky bursts of pollen. When she wipes her runny nose, she leaves fine yellow streaks across its peak.

"What does good mean?" the black-eyed girl asks her.

"Tasty." Emma shrugs. "Like marzipan. Or veal chops." She smiles. Her eyes widen with the memory of the chops the cook at Urizon made for her fifth birthday, browned in egg and breadcrumbs, dripping with fat, just days before her mother took her out into the forest. A fitting final meal: a calf bred for slaughter, its limbs tied with string so that its muscle could not grow.

"Have you had veal chops?" Emma asks. "I haven't in such a long while."

"I haven't."

"Oh." Emma's hands are knotted in cobweb. "None of the others have ever tried them either. Though Miss Lucy didn't answer when I asked her, so she might have, I suppose." Small fingers weave musty strands. "You aren't like the others."

"No."

"Not like them at all."

The black-eyed girl waits.

"So you can help us."

"Help you, how?" the black-eyed girl asks Emma.

"Help us leave the forest. To escape. I think my mother must be very, very worried," Emma continues. "Wherever she is. Even if she's old and after."

"After?" the black-eyed girl repeats.

"After death," Emma says clearly, removing her thumb, which is red-raw and dimpled from the pressure of her teeth. "I'm very tired of being here," says Emma. "Can you help me?"

The black-eyed girl nods.

She kisses Emma at the center of the strawberry birthmark. The grass snake opens its pink mouth, letting the little girl crawl between the prongs of its forked black tongue. Emma shudders, smiles, is still.

ONCE THE BODY is an empty husk, the black-eyed girl breaks its bones to drink. These bits of Emma make the black-eyed girl grow

strong. The rest will crumble, the immortal little girl a meal for scav-
engers, a heady fertilizer for the trees. Fuel for the forest, now shifting,
its ritual begun.

Branches rustle in new rhythm. The ever-present midday sun loses
its heat. It peaks with seven sharp rays, lustrous and blinding, and begins its long-awaited descent.

A forest hog grunts approval. A nest of red squirrels chatter. Birds
sing louder and faster, excited to share news—

The snake's mouth remains wide. The wood is open.

25

I awoke in a clean room to the sound of someone fiddling with a window frame at the side of my bed. Coulton, I thought at first, my muscles tight. Then I remembered my escape. This must be Matthew, I realized. I fell back into the pillows of the king bed with relief. But when I opened my eyes, I realized it wasn't Matthew—this boy's hair was darker, he was taller, he walked with a cane.

"Don't mind me," he said, "just tightening the frame, here. Draft was coming in, didn't want you getting sicker than you already are."

"Where am I?" I managed. "Who are you?"

"Our house doesn't have a fancy name like yours does." He grinned, and I saw a bit of Matthew in the lines of his smile. "Welcome to Le Chateau Hareven. I'm Charlie." He bowed, and his cane's rubber tip scraped the floor. "I'll go and tell my brother you're awake."

Charlie, I thought to myself, before drifting back to sleep.

MATTHEW HAD TOLD me there were seven Hareven children. Charlie was the eldest, Matthew next, followed by Elizabeth, Ben, the twins Teddy and Avalee, and finally little Tessa. These were far more Harevens than I could have imagined until the bulk of them stood over me, their faces grim, the next time I opened my eyes.

"They've been worried for you."

I lifted my gaze above the children to see their mother, Elodie Hareven herself, framed in the doorway, holding a tray of hot liquids, swirls of steam rising to mask her face. Her voice, like Matthew's, was deeper than I might have expected. Her hair was the same dark gold as Matthew's, her eyes the same ocean-salted gray.

"Clear out, you lot, and give the girl some space."

A general muddle of Harevens tripping over one another, quickly castrated complaints. The gaggle dispersed, and Mrs. Hareven settled the tray of food beside me on the bed. Moving to reach it, I was hindered by my body. My right hand was quite usual, the fingernails bitten, a few knuckles dry with cracked skin, but the left was weighed down by an arm wrapped in bandages to twice its normal size. All other dirt and blood had been rinsed off me. For the first time in ages, my hair was wet and clean.

"Our Matthew," Mrs. Hareven said, "knew what to do with you." The pride in her voice rang out clear and strong. "Fixed you right up, or at least put you on track. Just like him to want to fix things, as always. He said you might feel fuzzy waking, not to worry, it's only the drugs."

"Is he here, then?"

"He will be. Went to close out business. Looking for something, for someone, I think. He wouldn't tell me much. Not that I haven't gotten used to my boys keeping their business from their mother, but in this case, with your sickness and all . . ." She blinked at me, brow creasing, then cast off any visible sign of frustration and molded her face into a vacant and well-practiced smile.

I could not tell if Mrs. Hareven approved of her son's trouble. I wondered what Matthew had told her. I could assume he had at the very least instructed his mother not to touch me. It would have been reckless to leave without such warning; Matthew was anything but reckless. Still, Mrs. Hareven did not seem afraid. Matthew had picked me up, had brought me to his family, to this warm, fluffy bed, to hot broth and bandages. And I knew, despite his caution, that I should not have expected any less.

"I'll leave you to rest," said Mrs. Hareven, shutting the door.

My eyes begged for me to close them, and I wanted nothing more than to sink back into sleep. But there was Peter to find, and several months of misdirection to make up for, and to regain my strength I knew I had to eat. An examination of the bowl Mrs. Hareven had brought found it to be simple broth, still too hot to stomach. A shuffling came from just outside the bedroom, a little girl's giggle, a little boy's cough.

"Is someone there?"

The door cracked open, and two ruddy faces appeared. The twins, Teddy and Avalee, ten-year-old miniature versions of Matthew and their mother. I would learn that there were two strains of Hareven: the stocky blonds who looked like Elodie, and the taller brunettes who took after their father, though when gathered together all were obviously siblings, a certain snub nose repeating across multiple faces, a similar flared nostril when frustrated, a shared shape of the ear. I envied such resemblance, as if it extended past the physical to the bond formed from the time they all had shared. My own childhood seemed even bleaker in comparison.

"Come in," I told the twins, who did so eagerly, Teddy standing by the wardrobe and Avalee climbing up to join me on the bed.

"Be careful not to touch," Teddy admonished. "Mattie says she's very weak."

Avalee looked at me, wide-eyed. "Are you really?"

"I suppose." The conversation was surreal—to be here, wrapped in a cloud, talking with two kind and curious children. I could scarcely believe we existed.

"Can I feed you your soup? I'm good at taking care of sick things. Mattie thinks that I could be a doctor, just like him!" Avalee straightened her shoulders.

"I'm grateful for the offer," I told her, "but I think it might be good for me to spoon it in myself. Stretch the muscles, you know."

Avalee nodded, chattering to me while I ate. She regaled me with tales of her school friends, her family, a horse she had spotted at a stable two towns over that she'd set her sights on buying, once her doctoring money came through. Her brother mostly listened, occasionally piping in to correct some embellished detail. The domesticity, the ease—I

knew I did not deserve these creature comforts, but I was grateful.
As Avalee spoke, my time imprisoned, in the cargo van, Rafe's death,
seemed memories from another world.

I wondered where Peter must be at that very moment, whether he
had someone looking after him, to bring him soup and gossip and to
help him feel at ease. I hoped that he did.

MATTHEW RETURNED WHILE I was napping. When I next opened
my eyes, he was settled into a chair in the corner of my room with a
book and a hot cup of tea. I could hear the younger Harevens chasing
one another around the rooms below us, the dull thumps of their bodies careening into furniture, Mrs. Hareven hushing them. Listening,
I felt safe and serene, a pearl protected by iridescent shell. I watched
Matthew from under half-closed eyes, awash in the midmorning sun.

He had cut his hair quite short during my capture. The severe style
made him look older. He was thinner, quieter, more serious than I remembered him, as if his body had struggled to absorb his recent experience. I wondered how I must look, ragged and gaunt, bled, as I'd
been, like a stuck pig. My bandaged arm throbbed, and I shifted to
relieve some of the pain. Matthew heard me, and looked up.

He was unusually shy with me, pursing his mouth several times before speaking. A flush rose in his cheeks.

"Hello," he said. "How are you feeling?"

"Fine," I said automatically. He raised a brow and I shrugged, irri-
tating my arm even more.

Matthew marked his place in his book with a pen and set it down on
the end table beside him. He stood, stretched, and moved closer.

"May I take a look?" he asked.

I nodded, and he retrieved a pair of latex gloves from his book bag,
snapping them onto his wrists. I flinched unintentionally, a vision of
Coulton doing the same flashing through my mind. I tried to pretend
it away as an itch or a cough, scratching my ear awkwardly while
clearing my throat. Matthew saw my reaction, understood. His eyes

were serious and gentle. "It's all right," he said softly, "you're all right now."

I held out my arm. There was something sensual about the care with which he unwound the white bandage, the tenderness with which he touched my skin despite the barrier of the gloves. The wound was still raw, but the redness had softened, the angry inflammation somewhat calmed.

"You may want to look away," Matthew said. "I mean, you don't have to," he stuttered. "Just . . . might want to." But I was fascinated by the unknown inner parts of myself. I watched the whole way through, as he discarded the used bandage, spread salve across the wound, re-wrapped my arm in soft, fresh gauze. "It's healing well," he told me.

I thanked him, also newly shy. I imagined what might happen were he to remove the gloves, tend to the rest of me with the same intense precision.

"If you want to go back to sleep," he began. "If you want me to go to another . . . move into a different—"

"No." I blushed at my own sureness. "I want you to stay."

IN THE DAYS that followed, I thought myself recovering impressively, although I'd startle at the sound of a car outside the window, a loud crash from the living room below. Matthew assured me all was well, though I did once catch what I thought was a glimpse of anxiety in his eyes as he peered out my open window.

"What is it?" I asked him. "Who's out there?"

Matthew pulled the curtains shut. "It's nothing to worry about. Everything is just fine."

"I wish I could believe that." I forced myself to smile, hoping to show him I was on his side, that for once I appreciated his protectiveness.

"Focus on getting well," Matthew said. "Try to think of happier things."

"Talk to me, then," I said. "Distract me. Tell me about . . . yourself."

And so, over the next few days, he did. I learned about his sister's marriage, of which his mother firmly disapproved, the little niece who was expected several months hence. He told me about university, his lifelong interest in medicine. He told me about his first visit to Urizon.

When Matthew was eight, the Harevens had come to Coeurs Crossing. Gerald, his father, was away on business, a six-month trip that would mean money for the family on the back end, but innumerable headaches for his wife on the front. Charlie, the oldest, was recovering from a terrible accident, a fall that had taken his leg below the knee.

"It was all my fault," Matthew said, squeezing his eyes shut. "I was stupid. I dared him to climb up a tree with heart rot. The whole thing came down on top of him."

The twins had just been born, and her own mother was indisposed, so Elodie Hareven packed up her motley brood of six and moved them temporarily to Aunt Abigail's cottage. It was crowded, and noisy, but Matthew thought it must be a treat for Mrs. Blott, who had been lonely in the years since her husband's passing. She told neither me nor Peter of her guests. In turn, she told her niece nothing of my existence, the nature of Peter's work, the reality of her days at Urizon. The older Hareven children attended the local school, the younger ones played at the cottage.

"I was never alone," Matthew said. "Either busy with schoolwork or helping Mother with the babies, or with Charlie." He chewed on a thumbnail between sentences, uncomfortable, it seemed, with sharing personal details. "I don't remember much of it. I shared a double bed with my brother Ben, and I remember that his feet were always cold. Charlie was past the worst of his injuries, and milking it for all he was worth—he used to call us to his room, then say never mind, he'd forgotten what he wanted, we could leave, then call us back. And so on, you know." I smiled at the thought of young Matthew scuttling to and from his brother's bedside, stiffening his face to hide his mounting frustration.

"He thought it all very funny, though I wasn't entertained. I felt so guilty for my part in the accident, and Charlie clearly knew it. I decided I'd become a doctor someday. Running up and down the stairs, bringing him snacks and books and adjusting his window just so—I tried to see it all as practice. And as penance, I guess."

"And do you still see it as penance?" I asked. Matthew shrugged. "You've been so good to me. So good at taking care of me. You shouldn't feel bad about what you said or did before you knew better, back when you were young."

Matthew smiled. "I'm sure you know that's easier said than done."

Most of that school term was a blur of busywork and simple mathematics, but Matthew did clearly remember one excursion: the Year Threes on a school trip to the forest, led by the new art teacher, who carried a bag of sharpened pencils with which her students would sketch.

"It was my first time in the wood," he said, "though Ben, who was seven, had gone exploring and come back with tales of chattering voices, tree trunks that spanned caverns you could walk across like bridges, mangy wild boars. Mother spanked him and sent him to bed without supper as a warning to the rest of us. She told us that the forest wasn't safe."

"But the art teacher didn't know that?" I asked, anxious. I had a sudden sense that I knew where his story led.

The art teacher had arrived along with the Harevens at the beginning of the school term and was unaware of the wood's dangers. She had the students hold hands as they walked down a back road to a clearing she had come across one weekend and thought perfect for artistic inspiration.

"It went well," Matthew said. "No one was eaten by animals. No one was lost. My sketching, if you don't mind my saying, was quite accurate for age eight, and earned me full marks. I was the last in the line of children walking down the road, returning to the schoolhouse, when our group walked past Urizon."

I bit my lip.

"There was a girl there, in the bushes. A girl in a sun hat and overly large gloves."

I had been six, then. Wrestling with the ivy. I'd come over to watch the children passing.

"I remember," I whispered. "I remember you. You spoke to me."

"I think I said hello, and I let go of the girl's hand that I'd been hold-ing. She went ahead, then called out for me to catch up. We were not, under any circumstances, to let go of our partners."

"You ran after her."

"I did. But that night, after my bath, once I was squeezed in bed with Ben, I asked Mother about you. She passed the question on to Aunt Abigail, who said you were a fantasy, that you must have been imagined. There was a little girl who lived at the house, but she had gone into the city for the season and would not be back for months. There was no way I could have seen her."

Mrs. Blott would not have wanted her nephew exposed to my condi-tion. She would not have wanted me exposed to what I now knew was a harsh, carnivorous world. I could see why she might squelch his curi-osity by saying that the girl Matthew saw was a trick of his mind, that the girl at Urizon was off traveling. I understood, but her words hurt me.

"I wish she'd let you see me," I whispered. "Let me meet you. Your hands . . . you and the others . . . I didn't know that children's hands could touch. I didn't know I was alone until that day, when I first saw you all together."

Matthew looked at me solemnly, giving my confession its due.

Four months after our encounter, he and the rest of the Harevens had returned to the city. Upon leaving, he had asked if they might see me there, invite me for a visit, but Mrs. Blott claimed, by coincidence, that I would be returning to Urizon on the very day they left. The next time that he visited, she promised she would make an introduction. Of course, this was not to be.

Matthew did not return to Mrs. Blott's cottage until he'd turned eigh-teen, and had begun his studies at the university. When pressed, Elodie declared the family too busy for a visit to Aunt Abby, or reasoned that their holidays should be to places they'd not yet explored. But she'd discovered something, thought Matthew, during that six-month stay in Coeurs Crossing, though he never knew just what. Something worri-some. Something that scared her.

"Likely the men who went missing in the wood for several days and lost their minds. I'd imagine your mother wouldn't want that fate for her children."

"Perhaps," Matthew mused.

By now I was two weeks into my recovery. Matthew had spread his story over the hours I was not feverish or sleeping. His armchair was pulled close next to my bed. We could hear the household bustling below, the children stomping through the Hareven home, which, I'd learned that morning on my first trip outside, looked exactly as I had imagined from my bed: comfortable red brick, clean white shutters, flowers adorning every window, a well-manicured lawn. It sat on a cul-de-sac with six other homes, also brick, similar in style but not so close as to be copies. Predictable, suburban. The sight had left me longing for Urizon.

"I knew from the first moment I saw you in the cottage," Matthew said, "that you were the girl that I'd encountered. I never believed I'd imagined you."

"Adults must not think much of children," I said, "to suppose you could deny such a meeting. To call it a dream."

"Adults see a world that suits them. So as long as I didn't bother them about it, both my mother and my aunt decided the matter was closed."

"Well, I will not be denied," I announced, attempting a smile.

Matthew remained solemn. "No, you won't."

I waited for him to continue, but instead he stared at the hands he had clasped in his lap. I wondered what other fantastic parts of childhood had been denied him. I wondered how much of the reality of my own upbringing had been denied me. Were there clues I had missed back at Urizon? I'd always assumed Peter to be truthful, that our work together demanded transparency. How could it be otherwise when so much of its outcome was immediately determined, our experiments' effects established right before my eyes? Peter never coddled me, for as long I remembered had addressed me with the same language he used with his peers. But now he'd disappeared, leaving me no answers to the questions that had crested in his wake.

When, growing up, I had asked about my mother, Peter told me small things: she drank too much coffee, she loved to garden, she had been an only child. They gave me pieces of a life, but not enough to really know her. He'd never talked about himself, his youth, his tastes. I'd never asked, childishly assuming that his life had only truly begun once I was born.

"Do you think," I said slowly, "that perhaps we cannot really know our parents until they have gone?"

Matthew said nothing.

"Do you think we will find Peter in the city?"

"If he's there, he's done a very good job hiding it."

"Do you think he's safe?" I bit down on my lip, "Could he be hurt?"

"I don't know. I looked for him. I was mad at you when I left the hotel—for pushing me away, for ignoring me. But then it seemed so off. Rafe had seemed off the whole time, and you just wouldn't see it. I got halfway home before deciding that I couldn't leave you until I was sure you'd met up with your father, but by then I couldn't remember what route I had taken. I drove around for almost an hour, but I couldn't find the building. Couldn't find any trace of you. I was worried. I asked around the universities for Peter, showed his picture at all the libraries I could think of, even the museums. Right up until you called the other day I was canvassing the places that the two of you might be. No one had any information."

"But I would know if he were in danger, wouldn't I?" I pressed. "I'd sense it somehow . . ." My cheeks reddened as I mumbled, "Just like you knew with me."

Matthew shrugged. "I know it's the last thing you'd want, the last thing either of us do, but still our best bet could be going back for Rafe. He had all of those notes, all Peter's letters . . ."

At this mention of Rafe's name, I froze. There was no way to tell the story of his death without revealing myself as the monster Mrs. Blott had deemed too dangerous to show to her family. Matthew was all I had left; I didn't know where I would be if he abandoned me, too.

"No," I whispered, staring deliberately above Matthew's head.

"If we send someone else, my brother, maybe, to go find him . . . It wouldn't have to be you. I don't think I could even see him without . . ." His mouth puckered, cruel in a way I'd never known him to be. That cruelty was my fault.

"No." The sheer curtains fluttered in the breeze. I heard Matthew take a long, slow breath.

I opened my mouth to say more, but stopped as Matthew's hand reached for mine. He let it rest awkwardly against the comforter atop my knee for just a moment before pulling back and lacing it into his other.

"You don't have to explain," he said. "I saw how you were." He extended his hand again, this time with purpose, squeezing my leg through the bed sheets. I shivered. "We can talk about it later," he said, "when you're ready. For now let's keep our focus on your father."

I nodded, locking my memories away, forcing myself back to the matter at hand. I hadn't thought, in killing Rafe, that I was losing any final trace of Peter. Was Rafe truly our last clue? I thought of the dreams I'd had, Peter as fodder for the forest, his body wrapped in vines, weeds shooting through. I thought of Peter's refusal to cross the line of trees. Matthew's mother frightened of our village. The warnings. The stories. All those women, disappearing. Men forever changed by strange encounters in the wood. The map, the spirals, the quests.

"I think Peter's at home," I said aloud, "or somewhere near it."

Matthew considered this, leaned back in his armchair, reached up as if to tug a lock of hair, clearly forgetting he had cut it. I ached at the emptiness, the awkward dance of his fingers searching for a curl and finding nothing. He scratched at the fuzz above his ear instead.

"School starts again in three days," he said slowly. "I could bring you back with me. But I don't know that our best course of action would be—"

"Yes," I said. "Take me with you. Take me home."

"Are you sure you don't want to make a full recovery here? My mother is happy to have you as long as you—"

"I'm ready to go now." I pushed off my bed sheet to reveal his sister's nightgown and my own spindly shin. "Please."

"We wouldn't leave immediately. First, I'd want to——"

"As soon as we can, then. Please." I had the strong urge to see Marlowe, to fall asleep in my own bed, to give the house a good cleaning. Urizon called to me, needed my care. Now that I realized, I couldn't believe I hadn't felt it before. I could see the house when I closed my eyes, the ivy climbing the trellises, the grass overgrown at the edge of the wood. Every joint and sinew in my body pushed me toward the forest, my stomach twirling as if lengthening with tendrils of its own. To stay at the Harevens' any longer seemed like infidelity, a denial of the Blakely inheritance I'd only just begun to understand. An insult to Peter, who I felt sure was waiting for me at Urizon.

My insistence was enough to persuade Matthew.

"If you think that you're strong enough, we can set out tomorrow morning," he said. "And you do think that you're strong enough?"

I nodded. I wiggled my toes, then slid my legs over the side of the bed, stepping onto soft woven carpet. My head spun a bit when I stood, but cleared quickly. I stretched.

"I'll be fine."

"Then it's settled," said Matthew. "I trust you. I'll go tell my mother the news. Just be careful not to touch the . . ." His voice faded as he caught himself. "Never mind. I know that you will."

A Flood

The forest spools and gathers, holds its breath until evening. In the dark it protracts to take a fuller span of William Blakely's masterpiece, Urizon, Helen's home. Mary's home. Emma's and Lucy's. The ivy moves quickest, sneaking in through the cracks in the stone, under the doors, forcing them wider. The roots of the yard oaks crack like cramped legs and extend themselves, sighing as they stretch against floorboards, popping them loose. Tree branches tap windows. Wild roses, sharp-edged and hideously sweet, thorn through and scent the parlors. The outside comes in. Centuries of stagnation have exploded into action; eternal life, an eternal inertia, releasing all the force it's held at bay.

And in the center of the shadow wood, the black-eyed girl's clearing transfigures, the tide pulling the undergrowth back to make way for her cathedral. The bones of centuries of buried Blakelys past rise from their graves to build a yellow-white palace, displacing the trees and the dirt, forming turrets and battlements, a dark, echoing castle, the black-eyed girl's old bed pallet her throne. To walk here now, you would not know this once was forest, this smooth ground soil, these chandeliers trees.

Lucy, watching, is afraid of her own fear.

"It is well to be afraid," says Mary, patting Lucy's elbow.

"Nonsense," she hisses.

Lucy does not understand the shifting. Fails to grasp the black-eyed girl is now far outside her control, was never hers to begin with. She shakes her head, disbelieving. She thinks to punish the black-eyed girl with a spanking, as she saw the nurses do when her brother misbehaved as a child. To tie the girl up, as she might a naughty dog. This violence, this manifestation of the black-eyed girl's anger—it must be misdirected, intended for the forces that have hurt the women out in the wider world. There must be a way to teach the girl, to help her realize her mistake.

"She is here to protect us," Lucy swears, her voice faltering as she moves with Mary and Imogen around the girl's clearing. The women stand over the jumbled bloodless body that was Emma, contorted and curled, her cracked, empty bones hidden under a thin cobweb shroud.

"We can leave, follow the traveling trees. Hide from the demon at Urizon," Mary says, poking Emma's wrist with a curious finger. She jumps back when the patchy web that covered it reveals splintered bone where the girl's hands should rest. "We must leave," Mary presses. "At once."

Imogen agrees. "Now is our chance, before she finds us. The house's walls will protect us until we can make a better plan."

"I hate the house," says Lucy, still staring. Imogen and Mary call her to follow them, but Lucy does not move. They must tug at her, summon all their strength to remove her from Emma's remains.

"Where are the others?" asks Imogen. "We have to find them, warn them."

"Who knows?" Mary sniffs. "They might be all like this." She gestures toward the little girl, the twisted angle of her pelvis, the drained cheek, once that bright birthmark, now splotchy shades of gray and white. "We have to save ourselves."

Just then they hear a branch breaking, a body approaching, the shrewd movements of a creature on the hunt. Imogen nods at Mary; each take one of Lucy's hands.

"Impossible," says Lucy. "We can't leave now. She'd never hurt us. She's my daughter."

But the forest's door is open, and the others insist. The three of them tumble into autumn, run with the far-grasping wood to Urizon to take refuge in the very place they long ago escaped.

26

Our journey home was somber. We set out before the sun rose—
Matthew's home the only on the block with porch lamps lit,
Mrs. Hareven in the doorway, one arm lifted in farewell, the rest of the
Harevens still sleeping upstairs.

I rode in the front seat of the car, wearing Matthew's sister Elizabeth's blue dress and a pair of her gloves, nervous I might brush Matthew's fingers as they adjusted the temperature or shifted the clutch. I
had never known myself to be so aware of his hands, the small golden
hairs at the tops of his wrists, the notches of his knuckles, the steady
competence of his square fingernails. He'd showered just before we
left, and had a sliver of soap trapped by his right ear, stuck between
his skull and the dip of his cartilage. The error was endearing.

On our trip into the city, the car's speakers had been broken, but in
the interim Matthew had repaired them. He set the radio dial to a crackly
big-band station, and I watched the neighborhood around me shift to
cold, industrial outskirts as a wailing trumpet ushered in the dawn.

Matthew kept glancing at his mirrors, as if afraid we were being
followed. His anxiety was catching, but when I finally twisted around
to view the highway behind us, a wide winding stretch of dirty gray, I
found it empty. Our only fellow traveler was a large truck, just ahead,
carrying livestock.

"Smells like horse dung," I said, as Matthew sped to pass the trailer.
The scent was overwhelming, stronger than the tar that filled the air,
the smoke that coughed out of the factories around us.

"We'll be past this stretch soon," said Matthew, "back into the
country."

I nodded, and chewed my lip. There was so much that I wanted to say to Matthew, about my experience with Coulton, my feelings about Rafe, my immense and impossible gratitude, my poor behavior in the past and how eager I was to make amends, my concerns about my father. So much to say, and yet no way to say it, not with him sitting here, next to me, framed by the sunrise. I could hardly turn to look at him without losing my breath.

A stray thread had escaped from the seam of one of my dress sleeves, and I chose to stare at that instead of Matthew. Three times I brought it to my mouth, trying to catch the string and cut it with my teeth, but was prevented by the movement of the car and my own poor coordination. Giving up, I fiddled with the volume of the radio, making it first very quiet, then quite loud, in the hope that the music might drown out my thoughts. I folded my hands in my lap.

Elizabeth's gloves were faux fleece things with grips across the palms, designed for making snowmen or shoveling out after a storm, far too warm for early autumn. When I looked at them, I felt that these gloved, gray hands were not my own. I wanted to place one atop Matthew's hand, to lace our awkward fingers. Instead, I clutched them in my lap.

HOURS OF URBAN drabness left me longing for the moors, the green vitality of that otherworldly ritual by the river. But when we reached them, all the purple flowers were gone. The grasses had yellowed. The winds were strong and chilly. My teeth chattered.

Eager to be home, we had determined to stop only if absolutely necessary, but after hours in the car, I was uncomfortable, sore from this long period spent sitting and desperate to lie down. Still, I would be damned if I would be the one to suggest a break from driving. Lucky for me, Matthew eventually pulled off onto the shoulder of the road, parking the car before an old wooden outhouse, the weathered sign beside it proclaiming another fifty miles until we reached the next town.

Matthew let me use the outhouse first. Inside I tidied myself the best I could under the circumstances, longing for the hot bath that awaited me at home. I stuffed Elizabeth's gloves into my pocket, flexing my fingers against the chilly outside air, and took in the view while Matthew had his turn.

I guessed we were about two hours from Urizon. Ours was the only vehicle in sight. The outhouse sat on the outskirts of a just-harvested farm, its shorn fields stubbled, the sky so low and damp and gray that though it was midafternoon it felt like evening. A light drizzle had begun, the spitting sort, and I fumbled with the car door, which Matthew had instinctively locked. I gave up after several fruitless seconds.

Hearing a rumble, I at first suspected thunder, then saw large, yellow headlights breaking through the fog, approaching on the main road, soon to pass us. I silently willed Matthew to move quickly, until I realized this was the same livestock transport we'd passed hours ago, its driver a woman of indeterminate age, chewing a toothpick, apparently indifferent to her vehicle's smell. I waved, and she slowed her truck to raise a hand in greeting.

And then I saw another vehicle, an unmarked white van, pull up behind the trailer. The rain began in earnest. The van came closer, catching me in its lights where I stood at the side of the road. As it approached, it slowed to accommodate the dual hazards of the fluctuating weather and Matthew's parked car, and I saw its lone occupant, knew his rheumy eyes, his blotched red skin, his thin-lipped mouth, the gray front tooth that glistened when he smiled. The pleasure on his face made it quite clear that he knew me. It was Coulton.

He rolled down the driver's-side window, ignoring the rain, and called out to me in a voice that was all too familiar. "Looks like my riches have returned to me. Somebody out there's been listening to my prayers!"

He wrenched the wheel of his van in an attempt to turn around, but the ground was slick with recent rain, and the van had not been built for such maneuvers. Instead of turning, Coulton's vehicle sped forward, slamming into the horse transport, which slithered snakelike on the wet road for a moment, before overturning both truck and trailer with a sickening crunch.

My hands stretched in front of me of their own accord, although I knew that I was powerless to prevent the coming carnage. I felt time stop in the second that the horses vaulted through the air. The cab of the truck crackled into flame, the horses screaming, the air filled with blood and dung and gasoline—and I was still unable to react.

"Hurry!" yelled Matthew, already past the shoulder, though I hadn't realized he'd left the outhouse. "We have to get the driver before the whole thing blows."

His words did not move me, but his recklessness did.

"Wait!" I shouted, running after him. Gasoline had pooled at the side of the truck, it would catch soon, we couldn't risk it. Matthew's eyes widened as he realized, and together we crouched behind his car, awaiting the blast.

When it came, the explosion was smaller than expected. I'd thought we would be thrown back, that Matthew's car would shake and shudder, but aside from a bit of horse manure flung onto the windshield, we were largely unaffected. I stood and felt no rush of heat, was struck by no loose bolts. My ears rang, the horses' screams echoing, and it took me a moment to pull my focus from Matthew's lips, the flash of his tongue against teeth, to take in what he was saying.

"The driver!"

Matthew rolled up his shirtsleeves, already soaked, and leaped into the wreckage. It appeared that he had not seen the van. My own instinct was to jump back into his car and abandon the scene, and I felt smaller for it, petty. I forced myself to follow him to the damage. I opened my mouth several times to scream a warning, let him know that Coulton was here, but my voice was overwhelmed by the storm and the brays of the horses.

The rain had already quenched most of the fire, and so we had a clear view of the crushed cab of the truck, the driver slack against the windshield, her neck twisted. That toothpick she'd been chewing had rammed straight through the flesh of her cheek, poking out like an exotic piercing. I gagged.

"Gone," said Matthew, squeezing his eyes shut, trying to regain his composure.

Three of the four horses had flown from the transport and were spread across the road, already dead. The last we could hear screaming in fear within a cage of crushed metal. Matthew and I both tried to lift the trailer to free the animal, but it was quickly apparent that we did not have the strength.

"Its legs are broken," I said, pointing. "It's suffering . . ." I sat on the wet gravel and wiggled my good arm in through a gap. I clucked to the horse, softly. I cooed, hoping to calm it, have it come to my hand, nuzzle me gently, know me as an angel of mercy, a friend. Instead, the poor creature gnashed its teeth and howled, and I had to stretch myself elbow-deep to brush my thumb against the back of its neck. I felt it shudder, stiffen, release a final breath.

The crash site was quiet, the rain softening, the last flames dying out. Matthew sat next to me and closed his eyes. I couldn't tell the origin of the wet across his face. He rubbed his fists against his forehead, scratched his neck. I was frozen in my crouch beside the transport, debating our best option: hide here with the dead horse in the wreckage, or break out into a run and hope that Coulton had been hurt, that his van was too mangled to keep pace with Matthew's car.

"We haven't had service for the past half hour, and I don't know where we'll find a police station, out here, middle of nowhere. We'll have to figure out how to put up some sort of flare to warn other drivers." Matthew got up and walked past the transport, out into the road. "There's a second car!" he exclaimed, turning back to me. "Maisie, why didn't you tell me?"

"Wait," I whispered, pointing. Obscured before by the horse transport, we now could see the van, whose front was bashed in, but had otherwise survived the crash unscathed. Its airbags had deployed, and Coulton sat with his face half buried in a thick ecru balloon, apparently unconscious. Such a sight was more wretched to me than any gore I had just witnessed. Matthew made to move toward the van, but I dug my fingers into his shoulder. "Wait," I said again.

Coulton was stirring. He raised his head, and his eyes opened. He moaned a bit. He rolled his shoulders back, stretching his neck, blinking. Then he turned his head. He noticed us. He smiled.

Matthew froze, then turned toward me, his eyebrows raised in question. Coulton unbuckled his seat belt. Coulton stretched.

Between the van and where I stood in the road next to Matthew lay the ruined bodies of three horses. A brown-and-white beauty, its throat slit by a rogue bit of metal, a clean bone poking from its glossy front leg. A slender roan, bleeding freely from the belly, tail eaten by flames. And the largest, pure black muscle, the sinews of its mouth, its heavy teeth, its eye socket, all visible, flesh and coat almost entirely burned away.

Coulton struggled to open his driver's-side door. I took a breath. I went to the first horse, its white neck matted red, and I kissed the top of its head, watched it struggle to its feet. I went to the second, its entrails unwinding, and stroked its wet ears, saw it sniff at its own innards. I went to the third, its remaining eye open, and ran a finger across the one small still-soft patch of its nose. The eye went wild.

"I'm sorry," I whispered to each of them. The horses stood silent around me. Coulton had exited the van, and was now frozen, staring at the risen beasts in terror. The large black stallion whinnied, the sound all the more fearful from its rippling, skeleton mouth.

"Attack," I told the horses.

They descended on the van.

A Rope Around Her Neck

The black-eyed girl returns to the entrance of the bower where she was once buried, where the poisoned roebuck's antlers wait, crowning the clearing. In any other wood, squirrels would have scavenged them for nutrients, shredding the shaft, teething on the tines. These rest untouched.

Born of the skull, an antler begins with a sweetness: a velutinous, nurturing blanket of fur. Like a child it grows and it hardens; sheds its caul, loses its velvet. When the seasons change, a buck will lose his antlers. New bone will grow in their stead into a crown of resurrection, leaving and returning with each cycle of the earth.

Helen, standing still behind a heather tree, blond curls matted, petticoat torn, watches the black-eyed girl caress the roebuck's antlers. Helen shed her childhood late, but very quickly. She had known, when she let go of that tree limb, waited all the endless drop for the noose to crack her neck, that there would be no ever after. She had hoped, of course, to find Simon, her lover, somewhere, somehow, in the beyond. But Helen sensed that death could very well mean darkness, the same peace that dawned on them equally, and was content to have that be all—the same darkness felt together, as if seeing the same moon from two faraway parts of the earth.

She was surprised, then, by this forest. This perpetual limbo has been a frustrating detour. Helen takes a deep breath and steps forward so the black-eyed girl can see her. Kneeling, she kisses the back of the black-eyed girl's hand.

"Please," says Helen, "take me."

For decades, here in this wood, Helen has tried to end her second life. She slit her own throat with a sharpened rock. She jumped from a thousand-foot maple. *This time*, she'd tell herself, *this time I'll get it right.* But her efforts did not matter. Death was not hers to take.

"Please," she whispers. The black-eyed girl touches the pink neck-lace still scarring Helen's skin. She takes Helen's hand and pulls her to her feet. They are the same height, their eyes level. The black-eyed girl smiles. She lays Helen down on a bed of moss, arranges her golden curls, tidies her dress. She kisses Helen's forehead and closes her eyes with a palm.

27

We took the side road for a while before stopping to clean Matthew's car. The sun appeared suddenly, wrinkling our wet clothes as it dried them, prompting a terrible headache. Matthew made me a new bandage for my arm. We did not look for the police.

"At least now I won't worry he'll come after me," I said.

"I thought I'd seen him parked outside my parents' house," Matthew admitted, jaw clenched tightly. "I should have told you. I should have called in a report."

"You did everything right."

"Maisie . . ."

I shook my head, closed my eyes. We were silent the rest of the drive.

I WANTED A story to calm me, console me, make meaning of the events I had witnessed. I racked my memory, but found nothing. No knight had ever slain a rival with dead horses. No princess had lived happily with a prince who watched her summon beasts from hell. Those naughty little girls of Mr. Pepper's held nothing, now, to me.

WE REACHED COEURS Crossing and made the turn past Mrs. Blott's cottage, shuttered and dark, its eyes squeezed shut, mouth puckered inward. Some primitive corner of my mind asked me why she had turned all the lights off, had let the front garden grow wild. Matthew slowed the car, at first to get an idea of the cottage's upkeep, but then, once we had passed, maintained this pace out of necessity.

The wood, which in memory abided by the main road, waiting to run rampant until out of travelers' sights, had become greedy in my absence. The road between my home and Mrs. Blott's had fully changed. Weeds burst, luscious, from the gravel. Fallen branches made barricades. Twice Matthew stopped, got out to move them, but it was soon apparent that he'd need more than his own strength to clear a straight path for the car.

"I can walk the rest," I told him. "You should go back and park at the cottage."

He looked concerned, made signs of protest, but I swore that I was strong enough. That I needed a moment of solitude, I had to clear my head. As I spoke these words to Matthew, I believed them.

"Are you sure?" he asked me. "Truly?"

I said that I was. I would be fine. Coulton was gone, Rafe was gone, there was no one left to hurt me.

Matthew took a deep breath and scratched at the hair above his ear. He would see to the cottage, he said finally, clean up a bit, then join me. I thanked him, and watched him maneuver the car until it was facing the direction from which we'd come. He gave me a somber, single-fingered salute, and pulled away.

As soon as he was out of sight, I realized I'd made the wrong decision. The quiet of the empty road was an odd sort of quiet, the breeze was the wrong sort of breeze. The forest, I thought suddenly, was watching me, and whispering.

Still, I kept on to Urizon.

I'D ASSUMED MY home would be the same it always had been, the ivy perhaps thicker, the garden overgrown. I'd left in late spring, the drunken landscape thick with fog and dreamlike, as I imagined those moments leading up to one's birth, the misty passages we travel before coming into color, into light. In spring, the gardens smelled mildewed and spongy. Trees offered up yellow buds of leaves.

Then there was Urizon in the summer, when I would sweat through my long sleeves and roll them to my elbows without consequence, spend all day out in my sand plot lazing in the heat while the old stone walls faded and baked. It was summer I'd been gone for, the whole of it, all the long days and blazing suns, the late, rainless thunders with their arduous crackling lights. My first full season not at home.

Now it was autumn, Urizon's lawn bleached, the forest behind it orange-red. Some trees had already shed their leaves, and their bare branches made a latticework for the light to pass through, laying shadows like doilies against the building's facade. An eastern turret pierced the sky, bloodying the late afternoon sun as it descended.

There were more trees than I remembered on the property, encroaching on the house. The ivy was thicker, and the garden appeared eerily overgrown. I could not find the stone bench that had sat beside the pillars marking the estate's entrance. The wood seemed to have eaten it, as it had the front drive. Though spread wide, the house's stance now seemed squat against the exorbitance grown up around it, its closed rooms useless as a paralyzed appendage. It should have been locked up and empty, but lights shone through the ivy covering the windows. The front door hung open. Black smoke rose from a chimney on the west side of the house.

For a moment I was certain this was Peter, home and waiting for me. My body folded into itself with relief, and I smiled. Then I remembered that we did not use the front door, that the foyer had been sheeted and dark for as long as I'd known. The day swirled dizzy.

I heard a rustling in the dry leaves that blanketed the yard and jumped back, fully alert, but it was only my dear Marlowe come to greet me. I laughed at my panic. Marlowe, at least, had not changed in my absence: his coat remained glossy, his body was strong. Joyous, I tripped toward him, my arms spread like wings, and pressed my forehead to his chest, absorbed his heat into my lonely fingers. Marlowe's tail, wagging furiously, got caught up in some brambles, and he gave

me a generous wet kiss once I released him. Then he was off through
the tangled lawn, into the house. I rose to follow.

To enter the house, I had to climb overgrown bushes, finagle through
flower beds, step over upturned benches that vines bolted to the floor.
At one point I lifted my skirt and a twig tore my stocking, leaving
a gash in the fabric and a bare slice of skin that I could not help but
hit against the plants I passed, their patterns inverting, dead leaves
turning green. There were so many that it seemed a pointless task to
go correct them. I struggled to imagine the storm that wreaked such
havoc on the yard, the winds that had cast trees at such odd angles,
the strength of the sun that had encouraged such cancerous growth.

I climbed the three steps that led up to Urizon's front entrance, surprised that after decades of disuse it had been possible for someone
to open the door, that its hinges had not rusted, that weather had not
painted it into another wall. I stepped through and turned to pull it shut
behind me, but found it would not close. A barberry was rooted in the
jamb, growing deep, its trunk firmly planted, branches fanning waxy
fruit. I touched it with a finger, waited and watched as it shriveled and
died. After several firm pushes, the iron door closed over its withered
remains.

"There," I said to myself, pleased to have imposed a bit of order. It
was a small victory, and yet I felt better equipped to deal with whatever
had taken up residence in the rest of the house. I expected a vagrant, a
nest of squirrels, some runaway child from the village. There was no
way to prepare for what lay before me.

Tree roots had burst up through the tiles in the kitchen. Drifts of
dirt covered the appliances, pots had been knocked from their shelves.
Jars of jam were smashed against the table, their glass jeweled in clus-
ters, fruit red as precious gems. The refrigerator sat overturned, its
innards rotting, and I plugged my nose against its smell.

I gazed upon it all with a fascinated detachment, assuming that I
must be sleeping. The changes that had come upon the house would
soon resolve into the home I'd always known, just as the strange

women at the river all those months ago had turned into young girls at play.

"Peter?" I whispered, shutting my eyes when I reached his study door, squeezing my fingernails into my palms in an effort to will myself awake. I took a breath and pushed the door open.

The stump of a hollowed tree, teeming with insects, soft with age, had burst up through his desk. Books were thrown from the shelves by the vines that had replaced them, the closet where he'd kept his robe and slippers was filled with swarms of cicadas. Reeling back, I crushed a spent exoskeleton under my boot, and the crunch it made punctured my panic. The horror of my situation finally filled me. I vomited the lunch I'd shared with Matthew onto the remains of my father's correspondence.

I called for Marlowe, who did not heed me. For the second time that day, recalling the singed horses, I smelled burning. The smoke I'd seen outside Urizon had come from the chimney of the library fireplace. I crept down the hall and pushed open the door, my heart racing.

There they were—the intruders. Three strange women gathered at the far side of the room. One, tall and pale and bony, faced the fire—its paper-fed flames flaring yellower, hotter—one, older and pinch-faced, stood guard at the far door. The last, young and pretty and visibly pregnant, sat on the overstuffed red chaise longue I had so often curled up on, my own favorite spot to sit daydreaming, reading my books, nestling under my blankets with Marlowe. Now my dog was splayed out by the fireplace, belly angled to its warmth, his eyes closed and his breathing slow and steady. He seemed relaxed and vulnerable, as if only his masters moved inside the house. In the past, his comfort would have appeased me. Four months prior I would have immediately let down my guard.

Now, I stood back by the east entrance, the women before me so absorbed in their task that they failed to notice my arrival. As in Peter's office, most of the library books had been pushed to the floor, vines and branches breaking through the wooden backings of the bookshelves to topple them. The tall woman ripped pages out at random, from histories and treatises on science, from my old picture books and glossy tomes of replicated art. A portrait had been pulled from the wall and fully ravaged, the canvas torn so that only the bottommost oil-drawn button of the model's brown morning suit remained, but I thought it the painting of my great-grandfather, John Blakely, that had hung in the hall by the ballroom. On the carpet near Marlowe sat a large pile of laminated papers, unusual symbols, drawings and maps, which I recognized as years of Peter's work.

If ever there would be a time for caution, it was now, myself a stranger in the home that had so altered in my absence. I might have run, telephoned Matthew, might have hid, prepared to fight. I might have done anything other than what I found myself doing next, giving in to my emotion. But I was no longer afraid to exercise my talents; I knew I could protect myself if needed. My father was still missing, and these papers were my only clue to his whereabouts. If I did not act, they, along with centuries of Blakely collections, would be gone.

"What are you doing?" I shouted, rushing forward, reaching down to gather as many manuscripts as I could hold, stumbling on a stump hidden under the carpet.

None of the women turned in my direction. Not even Marlowe acknowledged my outburst. The tall one who'd been supplying the fire with pages continued to do so, not shying from the popping of its blaze or the foul smell of the plastic as it burned.

"Stop it!" I stepped over Marlowe, intending to stop her myself if she would not comply. The woman simply crouched lower, moved closer to the fire, and ripped another page of Peter's notes.

Thinking only of saving my father's small legacy, I grabbed the woman's wrist with the pads of my fingers. I expected her to crumple, drop the papers, and fall forward, into flames. Instead, she clasped my hand in both her own. She turned toward me.

"Maisie," she whispered. Her lips were a peculiar sort of blue.

Her hands were very cold, much colder, I thought, than living hands should be.

"How do you know my name?" I pulled back. Her face was familiar, but I could not quite place it, summoned only a few notes of some forgotten tune.

"I'm your mother," she said. "And I've been waiting for you."

Insatiable Hunger

Kathryn watches Matthew Hareven as he hurries through the forest. She positions herself a little ways behind him, following silently, suppressing a smile. Hundreds of years of education have prepared her for this conquest, this final confession. The veil hiding the forest has lowered. The black-eyed girl stalks her own prey between the trees. Kathryn knows she is nearing her end.

When Matthew stops to get his bearings, Kathryn steps across the boundary of true forest and false. Matthew is startled by her shabby dress, her certainty. The accent of her speech, both foreign and familiar at once.

"Have you lost your way?" Kathryn asks him. Matthew is clever, senses something is not right. But he has lost his way, and he knows that to refuse help at this hour would be unwise. The light, once it begins to fade, goes quickly. Creatures more dangerous than a pretty young woman make their home here in this wood. And on the other side is Maisie—alone, waiting.

"I may be lost," he confesses. "If you could point me toward the Blakely estate, I'd be forever in your debt."

"Oh," says Kathryn, smiling. "I can do much more than that."

He blinks at her, the confusion that descends upon all the men who enter the shadow forest threatening to overtake him. He tries to fight the tide of it, blinking hard to beat back the hazy waves. Then his shoulders loosen, his jaw relaxes. He smiles, and lets Kathryn take his hand.

THE BLACK-EYED GIRL waits until Kathryn has hidden Matthew under a tangle of ivy, nuzzled him, straddled him, coaxed him close to climax, before moving toward the pair. Matthew's eyes are closed, but Kathryn sees her. She pauses to acknowledge the arrival with a nod.

"Mine." The black-eyed girl mouths the word, tasting its shape, listening to the suck of her own saliva as it pools behind her teeth.

Kathryn consents. She presses herself farther, sends Matthew deeper, lifts her small chin up in blessing to the sky.

In the midst of her pleasure, Kathryn summons the thought she has buried, the words she prepared so long ago to declare proudly at the block, before the pyre; the defiance that she swallowed with the creaking of the iron door the morning one fate spared her and another took its place; the thought she hated, and then loved herself for branding into her brain: *I am not sorry. I would do it all again.*

A Sisyphean task, desire's fulfillment: content that will not sour with time and with touch. A spring that will not spoil in summer's heat.

The black-eyed girl cracks Kathryn's neck quickly, suspending her, forever, in her joy.

28

If my mother were alive, had, as foretold by Mother Farrow, been constantly watching me, why had she taken so long to appear? Where
had she been when, as a child, curled fetal on my four-post bed, I pressed
my palms against my neck, my chest, my burgeoning hips, aware that
no one else would? When, months ago, I made eyes at Rafe, lapping up
each drop of his poison? If she truly cared, why had I seen no sign of
her while I was held by Coulton? What use was she if she'd abandoned
me during my hour of greatest need?

And yet—

I had lost so much; I felt it right I should gain something. My time
imprisoned had not fully turned me. Despite all my experience, I was
still disposed to trust. Despite childhood indoctrination, despite betrayal, despite torture—it was the sort of anomaly that made me feel
there was something greater than reason that guided me. Peter would
have said that behaviors are determined by principles, theories. That
the difference between Theory of God and Theory of Not God was
actually quite slim, each a slightly different lens through which to
choose to view the world. One a shade lighter, the other negligibly
darker—what mattered was that both were held up to the eye and used
to filter our experience. It was easier to change the lens than to remove
the vehicle of understanding, easier to adjust my sense of how I fit into
the world than reconceive of the world entirely.

Maybe life was gentler than my previous conceptions had allowed
me to believe. Maybe my mother had spent all these years invisibly
beside me, ready to step in if she was needed, but allowing me to first
learn from my mistakes. Maybe it was she who had inspired my escape,

who could absolve me. Maybe she'd been captured in the forest all this time, could leave its confines only now that some boundary had been broken. This was something to ask her, if I could conquer my sudden shyness. One of so many, many things.

There she was. Sixteen years gone. Come back for me.

"There, there," she said, taking me into her arms, stroking my hair.

A mother who was not only alive, but could hold me. A mother I did not repulse. A mother I had not killed. My chest began to spasm with deep hiccups.

"Coward," hissed one of the remaining two women, who I had quite forgotten in my mother's embrace. I looked past my mother's shoulder to see her. She was beady-eyed, older, with a strong scent of the animal about her. In fact, I realized that my mother was emitting a less-than-choice odor as well, and as I recovered my composure I found myself trying not to gag as she tucked me to her rank, dirt-stained breast. I was no rose myself, still stank of sweat and blood and horses, but this was nothing compared to the aroma of my mother. I was torn between the wonderful new touch of her, and her stench.

I pulled away but kept hold of her hands, marveling at their marble smoothness, their unearthly chill. From this angle I could see her more clearly, and was startled to find that she looked nothing like me. She was porcelain-skinned and veiny, her nose was peaked, her nostrils high and thin. Her lips were the color of crushed blueberries, chapped purple with small white whorls of flesh. Her hair was black and very straight.

I felt I recognized her, and yet she looked nothing like the pictures of my mother I had seen in Peter's albums, a rosy woman, large-breasted and happy.

I fought to create reason around this discrepancy. I supposed this was what death would do.

I was awkward. "Shall I call you . . . Peter, my father, has me call him . . . Peter. Shall I call you Laura?"

The older, hissing woman laughed unkindly. The third, between the other two in age—solemn-faced and sad-eyed, perhaps seven months laden with child—opened her mouth but did not speak.

My mother petted my wrist. "Why, no, my dear." Her fingernails were long and tickled my flesh. "My name is Lucy."

THE ROOM SEEMED to slip one way, then the other, as if the house was balanced on a fulcrum point that had suddenly shifted. I yanked my hands away from the woman and whistled for Marlowe, who awoke to stand beside me, lending me strength.

"Who are you?" I managed, my fingers gripping Marlowe's coat, shivering despite the dry heat of the fire. I glared at the strangers surrounding us. "Why are you burning our library? What are you doing in my house?" Turning to face the blue-lipped, long-nailed woman who had lied to me: "And how dare you pretend to be my mother?"

"Not pretending," she said at once, backing away from me slightly. "A simple misunderstanding. I'll explain."

The oldest woman sucked her teeth and smiled. The third stepped forward and said, "Lucy, that's enough." She positioned herself to block the others from my view, sending the shadow of her swollen stomach across the empty bookshelves. "I'm Imogen," she told me. "These are Lucy and Mary. We've come from the wood because we need your help." She bowed her head as if in supplication, and tendrils of dirty brown hair grazed her cheek. "There is a danger in the forest," she continued, looking up at me, "a creature that will kill us. A creature that means this place harm."

I stared at her, my lower lip fat with incredulity, withholding a laugh. I was finally home after a miserable few months. My father was missing, perhaps dead. My house was destroyed. An impostor had posed as my mother. I felt, in that moment, too tired and spent to fight my own slew of battles, never mind one for these women from the wood. I wanted only to tidy a small space for myself, make a hot cup of tea, and fall asleep.

Still, I was my father's daughter, and I could not stanch his influence rising within me—his need to understand, despite the bitter cost of knowledge, his will to find out facts, with no regard for food or rest.

I knelt to collect Peter's remaining papers, scattered at Imogen's feet, with the thought that I might get a sense of him and what he would advise me to do: a memory of his hand on the pen, a recollected smell. There was nothing.

The fire crackled. I felt the women's eyes on my lowered head, my back. I had to say something. I positioned the last of Peter's papers into an orderly stack. Now that I knew Lucy was not actually my mother, my shyness had abated. I stood and peered around Imogen to find her.

"What do you mean, misunderstanding?" I asked slowly. "The matter of motherhood should be perfectly clear."

Lucy stepped out from where she'd been corralled and reached for my hand. I snapped it back.

"Don't touch me."

"My daughter—"

"I said, *don't*." If she had been a usual life I would have touched her, silenced her, left her there with hardly any guilt and gone to curl under the quilt in my bedroom. "Just tell me what you meant," I said. "Quickly. No more games."

Mary, silent all this while and still maintaining her watch by the west library entrance, smirked at the lot of us. Lucy seemed shocked. I supposed she was not used to being spoken to in this manner. She opened her mouth twice, closed it both times, and crinkled her forehead in thought. Finally, she spoke.

"It was I who found you—the true half of you, in the wood," she said. "I who wanted you. True, I did not birth you, but in this, I am a mother as surely as any who did."

"Found me?" I asked.

"Dug you up from the oak tree." I saw Lucy's long-nailed fingers twitch toward mine.

I guffawed. It was an odd, cryptic answer.

Imogen agreed. "You must tell her the full story," she said, frowning. So they did.

*   *   *

ONCE UPON A time seven women lived hidden in the forest, trapped by rescue, separate from the world. After centuries of sameness these women discovered a child, a small woodland savior buried under an old oak. They tended to her, loved her. When they first entered the wood, the women had all passed through a veil that marked their old lives from the new, a veil that held them in eternal stagnation. This girl was different. She had grown out of the oak in this strange forest— she was of the forest, unlike the others, and continued to grow while the others did not. She looked like me. She grew as I grew. She was also tied to the world outside through me. These women in the wood saw she was different, a break in the pattern of their entrapment. They had come to believe that someday she'd possess the power to set them free.

But although she was a Blakely—the last of their line—this girl was foreign to them. Frightening. The seven women realized they could not tame her. She was ravenous, and fed on the creatures of the wood. She made the wood ravenous, spilling outside its former borders. Some of the women had given themselves to the black-eyed girl willingly. These three in front of me had escaped, but they still felt her hunger. They could not flee far enough; they knew she would come for them. The girl would not heed them, but they thought she might heed me.

"For the longest time," said Lucy, "we thought that she'd not only set us free from the forest but defend us from the evils of this house, from those within it who had harmed us."

"Not all," corrected Imogen. "Not all of us thought she would help us."

Lucy ignored her. "But it's you, my dearest, *you* who have the power. Your fates are intertwined—I don't know how I didn't recognize it sooner. You can break the spell that's bound us all."

IN MOMENTS OF shock one is advised to be seated, to breathe slowly, maintain whatever calm one can. I had always found it odd that this advice made no mention of the calm that asserts itself without maintenance, settles like a frost over the windows of old knowledge, and obfuscates the former view from the new.

I was very calm. I sat on the chaise longue and curled my hands to fists. The stories made sense now—the tales of Blakely's curse, of women missing. Here were my ancestors, in front of me: the women whose portraits I'd studied.

Lucy stood before me, flanked by Mary and Imogen. The fire popped behind them as if nothing had changed, not the house, not my history, when, in fact, we'd all been born anew.

"Are you surprised?" Lucy asked me. "Are you pleased?"

I was neither.

I had always had the sense that I did not belong entirely to myself, that because of my affliction I owed something to the forces that had made me. A year ago, I promptly would have honored any debt. But now, I had grown tired of obligations.

"I don't know why you've dared to call yourself my mother."

"My darling," said Lucy, "I'm the one who found you—"

"You aren't a parent. And you've made no effort to help me find mine."

"What, Peter Cothay? What a mess he's made of all of this, hiding your true purpose, hiding you here. Telling you not to touch things, encouraging your fears, poking his nose where it doesn't belong—"

"Be. Quiet." I had never heard myself so cold, so powerful.

Both Mary and Imogen pulled back from Lucy, trying to dissociate themselves from the source of my anger. I wondered how I must appear to them, to elicit such fear.

Lucy herself produced a burst of nervous laughter. She opened her mouth, forced a smile, then wisely gave up any rebuttal. Her lips trembled. I did not think she was scared of me, unable, as I was, to resort to my usual weapon, armed with her two human associates to my rogue canine one. Lucy was taller than me, stronger, my arm was still bandaged; I'd be no match if we two were to fight. But she needed me, I realized. She could not hurt me. Doing so would gain her nothing, and she had everything to lose.

"Why are you burning our library?"

Lucy nodded, apparently pleased with the question. "There's only one book we need. The rest are useless. They belong to my brother."

"They belong to *me*." I frowned at her. "What is this book you want?"

"An old book, very old—the binding almost fully broken, the paper wrinkly and brown. It has three spirals on the cover, or what passes for the cover. We haven't found it yet. Before I left here I hid it under a floorboard, but somebody has moved it. Your father, no doubt. Do you know where it might be?"

"No." I glared at her, no interest in another old book, another riddle or quest. "And you'll stop burning the rest. You're destroying my home. You're ruining everything."

How badly I wanted to believe this: that Lucy had been impetus for everything, that Lucy was to blame. It was easy to cast her as villain, to say it was she who'd fomented my father's disappearance, my capture, the destruction of the house. That she was responsible for my own defilement, the curse that had kept me confined. I wanted to blame her selfish scheming for the pain I'd caused, the horrors I'd inflicted. I wanted her evil to exonerate my own. I knew that it couldn't, and this recognition strengthened my hatred.

Although unable to destroy Lucy and her companions with my touch, I still might find another tactic. Those bookshelves were quite heavy. The fire was hot. I took a step toward the ancient iron poker.

Unexpectedly, Imogen came toward me, speaking as if she had read my thoughts. "Destroy us if you must," she said, "but know about the wood before you do."

"If I never see the wood again," I said, fully aware that that same wood grew up all around me, thrust its branches through what once had been my home, "I never hear of it again, I never smell it . . ."

"Your young man is there, now. So is your father."

I froze.

"Peter? He *did* go after me! He's been there . . . Why didn't you tell me at once? Why didn't he come with you?"

"He's trapped inside a tree."

"He's—what? And, wait—what did you say, my young man? What, you couldn't mean . . . Matthew?"

Imogen nodded.

"Matthew Hareven? Impossible. I saw him not an hour ago. How could he be . . . How could you even know?"

"Just because we've crossed the old threshold, taken shelter in this house, does not mean that the forest has unleashed us." Imogen looked to the library windows, which had once boasted a wide view of the drive, Urizon's gardens, the lawns, but were now covered over by weeds.

"You can see Matthew?" I asked her. "What's he doing? Is he hurt?"

"He will be," said Imogen, kneeling. She took my hands in her cold ones and looked up at me. She was about to speak, but then her eyes widened with shock. She released a stunted gasp and dropped my hands, pressing her own to the wide mound of her stomach.

"What?" said Lucy, darting forward. "What did you see?"

"I didn't . . ." Imogen's right hand fluttered toward me, her left planted firmly on the lower side of her belly.

"Matthew," I insisted. "Is he in danger?"

"He will be, if you do nothing to stop her," Mary broke in. "He needs you. We all need you."

What did I need, in that moment? To hide under the covers, to pinch myself and hope that I would wake from this worsening nightmare. I needed my mother, or Mrs. Blott or Mother Farrow, someone who loved me not for my peculiar powers, not as a last piece of a centuries-old puzzle, but as myself, in spite of everything. I needed Peter, who had used me, yes, but who, when it most mattered, had gone to find me in the wood. I needed Matthew, who had done the same.

In front of me, Imogen let out a cry. Her eyes were wet, her fingers grasping. I let her clasp my wrist, upon which she released a sudden moan. A gush of liquid flooded from beneath her dress, staining it, darkening the carpet.

"The baby!" Lucy took Imogen's elbow, eyes incredulous. I twisted away from Imogen, her labored breathing, Lucy's hovering, Mary's nose flared with fear and surprise. Imogen howled, and the others tried to lay her on the settee, wiping sweat from her brow. I left them in the library. I went into the wood.

Merciless and Wild

Go on ahead, Matthew had said, *go on, I'll meet you at Urizon.* Matthew, who could balance any chemical equation, did not know how to balance his regard for Maisie Cothay with his fears. He wanted her to know that he trusted her. How many times could he question her choices before she saw him as a captor, as her domineering father, or worse, another Coulton or Rafe? How better to show himself an ally than allowing her to forge her own way?

As soon as he turned around, watched through the rearview mirror as she scrambled over fallen trees, he knew he had been foolish. Better to leave the car and join her, bring her to the cottage with him later, make a plan. Better to risk her wrath than her safety, better to have kept her near.

Was the unease he felt, the danger that he sensed, actual danger, or was it only love acknowledged? The object of his love made tender, appearing softer than she really was, appearing vulnerable in having made him vulnerable. Matthew remembered holding his newborn baby brothers and sisters, watching them take their first steps, their first stumbles, knowing that they must stumble alone. So it was, he thought, with Maisie. Yet he worried for her, missed her. He'd returned the car to his aunt's cottage and turned immediately back toward Urizon. Decided to take the shortcut, through the wood.

WHEN KATHRYN'S SLACK body falls still over Matthew's, her pretty nose fits like a key into the small space above his sternum, locking him, restricting his air. He gags, nudges and tries to wake her. When he cannot, he removes her, and shudders. He fumbles to fasten his trousers, to pull himself from Kathryn's limp arms. His face is ashen.

He notices the black-eyed girl.

"Maisie?" Matthew distances himself from the body, sliding back against the bulge of a tree root and pulling his head into his hands. His shoulders quiver, the edges of his narrow ears flush. He inhales and counts slowly, hold and release, a pattern to make meaning of each breath.

"I didn't . . . ," he says finally. "I thought we said I'd meet you at the house." With each word his chest tightens, with shame, then anger, and finally fear. His fingers twist at his temple, scratch the nape of his neck.

The black-eyed girl says nothing.

"I can only . . . I apologize . . . you finding me in such . . . we haven't said it yet, I mean, not outright, haven't fully, but I thought you'd . . . I'd agreed that if we . . . I don't know what happened. What I was thinking."

Matthew is crying now, the black-eyed girl realizes, a drop of water gathering at the edge of an eye, traveling his cheek. "I want you to know," he pleads fervently, "what happened, there. I wasn't . . . I was not myself."

His tears sit like stars, fat and glistening. The black-eyed girl reaches out to catch one: brushes her hand against his cheekbone, pulls the water to her tongue.

Matthew stiffens.

"Maisie? What—Who are you?" he whispers.

The black-eyed girl strokes his cheek, harvesting a teardrop, pressing her finger to his forehead, gently traveling down the bridge of his nose to reach his lips. She takes Matthew's mind, helps the wood empty his troubles. She welcomes him across the border. Says, "Hush."

29

Forward only, never back. Do not, in your mind, keep a tally of past horrors. Do not question decisions that cannot be unmade, dwell on actions that cannot be undone. The power to equivocate is no power at all, and that you've ever thought it to be is your weakness.

RETURNING TO THE shadow forest proved more complicated than the woodland women led me to believe. I killed several trees, and brought them back when they did not make me an entrance. I knelt in supplication, asked for mercy at the top of my voice. I debated going back to the house and asking Lucy for instructions, looking for the old book she had mentioned, but the thought of Urizon unbridled— overcome by the wilderness I'd found upon my homecoming—was too much to fathom. Eventually I saw nothing else to do but follow Marlowe through the wood until he sat down, expectant, at the foot of a wide-spanning elder.

Marlowe had opened the forest before, after burying Mrs. Blott's shinbone. Perhaps I needed a similar sacrifice, a gift for the wood. Marlowe had brought it a piece of a body. What had I to give? A bit of fingernail? An offering of blood?

I was prepared to unwrap my bandage and reopen my wound when a thought struck me, and I rifled through the pocket of my jacket. There, as I had suddenly been certain it would be, nestled up against the stitching, was the blade of grass I'd plucked my first time through the shadow forest. Even after all these months, it was still green.

I knelt and dug a shallow hole in the dirt at the base of the elder, careful not to brush against its roots. I kissed my blade of grass, set it on the ground, covered it with a layer of displaced soil. I closed my eyes, reached out to Marlowe, and took a deep breath. I opened them to find that nothing had happened.

Frustrated, I kicked at the dirt I'd displaced, which then blew up in a gust against the tree. A sneeze that I recognized came from somewhere deep within the elder's twisted trunk. A voice grumbled, as if recently awakened.

"Peter?" I whispered, incredulous.

"Maisie." It was his voice, wry, tinged with humor. "Forgive me, darling, I suppose I'd drifted off. It's fine to see you, though I fear we're in a spot."

I wanted to laugh, so familiar was his diction, so expected his response. Could he see me? If I looked straight on ahead, I saw the elder. And yet . . . If I turned to just the right angle, I could find my father, trapped within the trunk.

"Peter? Is that really you?"

"Maisie, my girl," said Peter, "I'm here."

And then I laughed aloud, startling Marlowe, and had to restrain myself from clinging to a tree branch. The weight of what was waiting in the wood fell away. The pressure of the past few months, my overwhelming emptiness and fear, all seemed to fade in Peter's presence.

"You don't know how much I've missed you." My words tumbled out, and in a rush I told him everything: the spiral paths, my double, falling into Rafe's trap and fighting out of it, the resurrected horses, Matthew's capture. Like a lapsed Catholic returning to confession, I named my sins—even the sparrow I'd let loose at age eleven—and knew my father could pardon them.

"I'm so sorry for all of it—the day I ran from Mrs. Blott's house, the cat. All those years when I was angry. You were right, and now it's my fault that you're in here, that it all—"

"Maisie," Peter stopped me, "don't apologize, my darling. There was no way to know. None of us could have known."

"Known what?" I frowned. "Known all this? That there really was a curse? That I came from it?"

"Any of it, darling. What had happened, what will happen." I climbed up on a root to see my father's eyes, strange and squinting without glasses, and was shocked to find that they were filled with tears.

"Well, I know what's going to happen," I said. I had found Peter quickly, and was confident the rest of my journey would fare equally well. Peter was here to protect me, and with his blessing, I knew I was invincible. "We'll get you out of this tree, go rescue Matthew, stop the shadow girl, and go home."

"No, my dear. We won't," said Peter, his voice softer than usual, tinged with regret.

"But we can! I know we can."

"*You* can, Maisie. And you will. But you'll do so without me."

I'd spent sixteen years obeying Peter's instructions, trusting his assertions. Even while I knew him flawed in myriad small ways, he had always stood heroic in his brilliance—both parent and deity at once as he plotted my life's course and steered me straight. Now he spoke with the same certainty he might when insisting it was long past my bedtime, that I could not join the villagers in celebration, that the soup I was about to slurp was far too hot.

"Don't be silly," I said, my tone optimistic, but brittle. "I'm sure we can get you out of here. I'll find an axe. Or touch the right spot on the tree trunk. It could be a matter of a pressure point, pulling the right branch. Certainly something in a book you've read can tell us what to do? I can run back to the library right now. I'll be so quick you'll hardly know I've gone. What should I bring you?"

"Maisie," said Peter, "all of the books would bring us to the same conclusion: I will stay here, and you will go help Matthew. You'll finish this, go back to live a full life at Urizon."

"But there is no life without you!" I could hear myself nearly shouting in frustration. This made no sense at all. We'd only just found one another, and now Peter was asking me to leave him. When was he ever so defeatist? How could he be so sure? "If you're staying here, I'll stay with you. Me and Marlowe. We'll stay, too."

"Nothing could sadden me more than to see you waste your potential."

"No."

"It would be worse than any death to see you sacrifice your future, have you end your journey here."

"No."

"I like to think I've taught you well, my dear. I trust you. You'll take up the Cothay mantle, and I know you'll do it proud."

"No."

"And what of Matthew? You're the only one who can save him."

He had me there. Must I choose between Matthew and Peter? I remembered standing in Mrs. Blott's kitchen all those months ago, looking from one to the other. I'd wanted neither, in that moment. Now I knew I needed both.

"I'll come back for you," I promised, "when it's over. When Matthew is safe and I've found my shadow double or whatever she is and—"

"Maisie," said Peter, "the wood requires a sacrifice to enter. Let that sacrifice be me."

"I can't. I can't do it. It's not fair. I need you."

"Are you afraid?" Peter asked the question simply, as if back home in the nursery-turned-lab, asking me how a sip of orange juice tasted on my tongue. As if I were five years old, with my tangly hair and my large, solemn eyes, fidgeting at the edge of my seat while he flipped through his notebook. *Tart, you say? And also sweet?*

Afraid? Of course I was afraid. But of what? Did I fear what waited for me, there in the shadows? More fearsome was the thought of continuing, of living on with no one to guide me, of being alone with my destruction, day after lengthening day.

"Don't be afraid, my girl," said Peter. "I am not afraid at all. You are a marvelous young woman, the best of my life's work."

These were the words that I had been waiting to hear all my life. I'd have given them up at once for his freedom.

The last words we had spoken at the cottage, I now barely remembered—that silly argument about Mrs. Blott's cat. Peter had come in from the drizzle and I'd handed him a towel, sighing while I watched him wipe his glasses. Such a common gesture, so easy to follow, a stepping-stone from one memory to the next: Peter letting me petition for a governess when I was eight or nine, his denial taking on the slow rhythm of his shirtsleeve as he polished each lens; Peter's laughter, coming inside from the cold, the glasses fogging; Peter telling me to fetch him his cleaning spray and cloth. *Maisie, have you come in with my tea?*

Already I felt these memories fading, as if each were a butterfly circling the glass garden of my mind, my every conscious recollection netting a specimen, setting it free into the greater world beyond. In ten years, what had once been a populous colony might boast only the shredded wing of scent, Peter's deodorant and mint toothpaste, the dried caterpillar timbre of his speech. Already I was scheming to keep him. To lock the greenhouse door to be reopened at some later, easier date. Or would there always be some window, busted open? Would the memories escape from me, regardless? Would I always be a child, grasping my beloved so tightly that he crumbled in my fist?

"It's time, Maisie," said Peter. He held out his hand, five fingers stretching from a gap within the bark.

"I can't do it." I shook my head.

"Maisie, my darling, I love you."

I almost echoed back: *I love you, too.* But I knew Peter—knew what he'd want from me—and so to show my love I followed his direction. Steeling myself, I reached out and took Peter's bare hand in mine. It was warm, calloused, his knuckles scraped dry, his wedding ring firm upon a finger. My father's hand—the pulse at the base of his thumb strong at first, and then nothing.

I closed my eyes.

30

The wood I found was not the shadow wood that I remembered. It was clear that we'd passed from one world to another, but no regiment of smooth-trunked trees greeted me, no sweet birdsong trilled. The smell of iron hung in the air. There was no daylight, though the temperature did suddenly shift warmer. Darkness here was heavier; no moon, no stars, broke through. When I took a step I tripped on an unexpected root, catching myself with both hands, yelping as my sore arm bore my weight. I crouched low, waiting for my eyes to adjust to the darkness, then checked the damage to myself and to the tree I'd just accosted. The edge of my bandage was muddied, but intact. The tree was still alive. Marlowe was still beside me, but I saw no sign of Peter.

Full fathom five thy father lies. Those are pearls that were his eyes. I could not remember the full verse, but I knew that it did not speak of a sorcerer—immortal—but the too-human traveler who'd been caught up in his storm. My father, too, had proven mere man. My entire body felt numb and cold and bloodless. I allowed myself a single shudder, then turned to Marlowe.

"If we wait until daylight," I said, swallowing, attempting to formulate a plan, "we might have an easier time. But I don't know if we have those hours to waste. I wonder what we should do . . ."

I did not have to wonder for long. Very faintly, from ahead of us, there came the sound of cracking branches, a slender figure moving through the trees. Marlowe nuzzled my hand, and moved to follow our mysterious companion. I stumbled after, almost running him over when he paused to try and catch the new direction of the sound. Even with my body stiff from recent abuse, my insides frozen from that final farewell to my father, I was more nimble than expected, my years of dodging furniture and avoiding plants having evolved into its own breed of grace. Able to touch what had long been forbidden, I used trees and rocks for balance, let my fingers brush past dangling branches, discovered the spongy softness of live moss. No heart beat in the tree trunks or crushed petals, but I felt a force fuse through them nonetheless, urging me on.

We followed the unknown figure quite some time, long enough for me to realize I was hungry, and berate myself for not bringing a snack. I thought of biscuits, hot soup. Mrs. Blott's raspberry jam baked into sugar cookies, the buttery crust of her cheese pie. Peter's forgotten dinner plates, greens limp and gravy congealing. Peter on my birthdays, eating cake with bright, fresh berries. Peter playing records. Peter lighting little candles, telling me to make a wish.

My only wish now was impossible: for things to return to what they had been. For us to all go back, to sit together in the library, cozy by the fire, and whisper about this very wood, this moment, as a distant, untold someday. A fairy tale. A dream.

"When you're older," Mrs. Blott and Peter had both told me, time and again, in response to my questions, my doubts, "you'll understand." So I'd willed myself older, barreling through the days I thought would stay the same forever. Now here I was, past them, no closer to wisdom, alone.

EVENTUALLY, THE DARKNESS around me dissolved into gray, misty morning. Marlowe and I emerged in a shallow clearing, large trees circling where we stood, the biggest one bent at the waist and reaching down to form an archway. The apparition I had followed stood in front of it: a girl in ragged cloth, blocking me from entering. She looked to be younger than me, maybe twelve or thirteen, though I knew she must be far older than Lucy, as old, perhaps, as the wood itself. Her eyes were very dark and round, like a beast's, and her teeth, when she revealed them, were unusually sharp. I could not see past her through the tree-arch, but felt certain it would lead me where I needed to be.

I hesitated before moving closer to her.

Still reeling from my encounter with Peter, I had not yet paused to reflect on my less obvious loss, the one shield I had been armed with even stripped in Rafe's prison: the power of my touch. Without the weapon of my body, at once my most loyal ally and most treacherous enemy, I was simply a girl, weak from injury, unprotected in a vast, enchanted wood. In my amazement at first touching unmarred tree bark, I'd forgotten my fallen defenses, how utterly normal I'd become. The thought struck me now in a full-bodied flood.

All my life I'd wanted to be normal. I'd thought that being normal would mean that I'd fit easily into the world. That might have been so were the world around me normal. However, in a twist of fate I'd swapped my own strangeness for this terrifying setting: a brambly pathway, a dark forest, my shadowed half, a creature even more macabre than me. It was the stuff of nightmares. I was never brave in my dreams: it always seemed more practical to will myself awake. That was not an option here. But some pragmatism in me knew that there was nothing to be gained from feeling frightened. My father's final words returned to me: *I love you.* I donned these words as my new shield.

"Hello," I said.

At this the girl came toward me, taking my chin in her small, dirty hand. I was taller than her, but the movement felt natural as she turned my face first one way, then the other, peering at my features like a buyer inspecting a horse. Her touch, though direct, held none of Matthew's tenderness. Her hands were cold as Lucy's, capable and firm. When she released me, I opened my mouth wide, as I'd done for Coulton during routine examinations, but she was not interested in dentistry, nor any other aspects of my body, not even the bandage that unraveled at my wrist. I waited a moment to see what she'd do before pulling it tighter and tucking the dangling bit back where it belonged. The girl stepped back.

"I've come for Matthew," I said. She said nothing. I felt my pulse cut by the bandage, imagined the flow of dammed blood that would follow its release. "Matthew Hareven," I repeated. "He's here somewhere, and he shouldn't be. Can you speak? Who are you? Do you know me?"

"I am Alys," the girl said. I squinted at her, waiting for an explanation that did not come.

"May I go to Matthew?" I asked finally.

"You can," said Alys. "She is waiting. She is everything you've cast aside, and you are everything she cannot be. You will come to an end, once together. The return to what once was, and what should be."

I frowned. "I don't understand."

"You will go in alone," said Alys, "and you will not both return."

"Both me and Matthew, you mean?" I paused. "Or me and . . . my other?"

Alys did not answer. I stared at her, and, sensing my frustration, she continued. "My cousin's prophecy has been fulfilled. Our family remembered. The fortress is finished. It is time."

"The fortress?"

"Urizon. The house that stands on what was once our home."

"What was *once* our home? My home, now, you must mean?" I saw how difficult it was for her to answer me, to cross the cavern of the thousands of years that fell between us so that I could understand. She was silent for a long moment. When she spoke again, her voice was soft.

"We should be free," she said. "The old land, that closed house. It is a cage. It confines us."

I nodded, trying to follow where she led me, trying to see. "But why now? Why is now the time? Why must it be me?"

"You were made to break the pattern. You were born of the wood but also of the world outside it. You are the connection between old and new, between death and life. Forever is too long. The forest knows. The forest needs you."

"Who is this girl I'm meant to find? Why does she look like me? Why do you think I can stop her?"

"She's your desires made flesh."

"I don't know what that means!"

Alys sighed. "She is your shadow. She indulges while you abstain. She takes while you give."

I closed my eyes. "And if I don't destroy her, this . . . shadow? If I don't go after Matthew? If I abandon this task? What then?"

"The wood stretches farther. Faster. She eats and she grows strong."

"And what of me?"

Alys did not answer.

I WOULD HAVE to go alone, I knew, into darkness. I'd leave Marlowe behind, and I would follow the dark forest path before me. I would find my other self. Though only now able to name her, I already understood her. I'd always known her: she'd been there in any urge I had not acted on, any temptation I'd pushed past. The Janus face of all the rules I'd followed, my precision and routines. I remembered Lucy's words at Urizon: *Peter Cothay? What a mess he's made. Hiding your true purpose.* Whatever awaited me under that archway was exactly what I'd hidden from, the darkness I had promised Peter that I would excise.

But none of my success in its avoidance had ever been my own. My good behavior was the result not of my self-restraint but of a forced extraction, a choice thrust upon me before I was born. I obeyed not because I possessed a preternatural self-control, some internal fortitude, but because my basic needs had been divided, my desires split in two. Mine was the poorer piece of girlhood, the forced smiles, the neatly crossed legs, the directives to sit straight, sit still, stop asking silly questions. As I'd acted through that sad charade of personhood, my other self had been in here, resisting. Allowing herself what she wanted.

To be whole again, to choose to give myself to death, desire, would irrevocably change me. No matter how she ended, if I walked through that archway, the girl I had been would be gone.

So, too, would she be if I did not go.

I knew it to be so but could not bring myself to speak, to step forward, to fully accept my fate. To join the women of the wood.

And then a cramp seized my gut, the dull pain of my womanhood churning, and with it I felt the weight of those who'd made me: my mother and her matriline, the Blakelys. The Cothays, the paternal line to whom I owed allegiance, though I knew so little of them, my many grandmothers and grandfathers, all lost so long ago. I was more than myself, and not just because the darkness I'd avoided had its own shape in the wood, or because I owed my powers to superstition or to science. However I had come to be, through prayer or spells or wishes, genetics or chemicals, deliberation or by chance, I was part of a long history that bound me to both endings and beginnings:

Mother Farrow, family by practice, if not blood, had led me cryptically, fancifully, to this knowledge. Those stories of girls in the wood, tales I'd assumed had been told to confine me, to warn me about life outside my cage, did not end at the close of their telling. Off went the naughty little girl to the forest, never to be seen again. Gone was the woodcutter's wife. Cast from the village the harlot.

But they were not gone, they had stayed within the wood. If their time here was tragic, if the tale that began after Mother Farrow's saw them equally frustrated, no freer than before, it was unfortunate, but not, I thought, proof that my failure was inevitable. They'd had no other options, and even the wood had not granted them a choice. They'd come to the wood desperate; I was here of my own volition. If I wanted to, I could easily turn back around and go. But I wanted to continue: it was my turn to know the forest, walk the path my tale would take.

Even the powerless can work to harness power. A forced hand can still clench into a fist. A girl commanded to marry, went an old story, had come to this wood, and with a rope around her neck snubbed both fiancé and father.

"I am ready," I told Alys. She nodded, stepped aside, and I passed through.

A Fruit in Its Fecundity

Laura, 1990

On the final morning of Laura Cothay's life, she boiled two dozen eggs for an egg salad. It was fitting, she thought, a clever way to tell her husband without telling him. Peter appreciated riddles, he'd made a career of deciphering them. The week before they'd played a game of walking through the portraits of old Blakelys that hung just outside the ballroom: "The suicide," she said, and Peter tried to guess the picture. The engineer, the poor old maid, the grandaunt accused of witchcraft. He'd done remarkably well, but Laura felt a bittersweetness at the ease of her reduction. Surely these relatives were more than their epithets; no person Laura'd ever met could easily be labeled just one thing. She and Peter had been married ten months. The year was 1990, and Laura was twenty-eight years old.

When Laura arrived from university eight years before, after choosing not to finish her degree, the villagers had said that she herself would likely end up as an old maid. Soon after her birth, Laura's father had shut up the great house and moved to the city, bringing his wife and small daughter to Coeurs Crossing some summers, but generally keeping far from the estate where he'd been raised. His death had coincided with what Laura would later consider her "unfortunate episode" at school. She'd packed her bags without a word to her roommate, withdrawn her registration, and taken refuge at Urizon, which had loomed throughout her childhood as a force of isolation, hidden behind the curse she'd been told soiled the family name. Just the place for a young woman seeking silence, hoping to relearn her body, call it her own.

"The villagers are frightened of your family," said Mr. Pepper, the sniffling solicitor still on retainer to handle her parents' wills, the affairs of the house. "Really, they are frightened of the women. There's little chance you'll meet Prince Charming here." He'd blown his large nose loudly with the handkerchief that Laura offered, afterward leaving it, crumpled and wet, on the carpet at the edge of the settee. Laura was middling pretty, but she had large breasts, yellow hair. "You'll waste yourself in Coeurs Crossing," said Mr. Pepper.

Laura wanted to waste herself, spend weeks without a shower, let the hair grow on her legs, under her armpits. She wanted to make a jungle of her pubis, a dank, dark wood that shouted *Keep away! This is mine, mine, mine, and here I will hide.* Urizon suited Laura's purpose perfectly.

So she read. She gardened. She took up oil painting, lugging her small easel to the village green, the forest, well aware she had no talent, but calmed by the ritual of brush against palette, against canvas, into water to rinse paint. She became a proficient baker, sending pies to the firehouse and cookies to the school. She played piano. The years went by, and she was happy.

Happiness, Laura had realized, was a matter of decision. If she told herself that rolling piecrust mattered, that the care with which she cut the phyllo flowers and stirred the fruit was more than herself in the kitchen, sweating in the heat, she could find pleasure in the simplest of actions. Weeding the lawn to let the shrubs breathe. Polishing the silver. If she slowed to watch the afternoon sun deluge the front parlor, closed her eyes while listening to an aria, smiled at the postman on his route, she could forget the self she might have been if she had not, that April night, gone to the party at the gallery, if she had not set down her small flute of champagne. That self departed was just one of so many selves lost. There was no need to mourn it.

By the time Peter Cothay came poking about the village, intent on proving the existence of a Blakely family curse, Laura had conquered her reclusion, resumed general hygiene. She was content, comfortable, missing only a companion to share in her comfort and contentment.

The owners of the souvenir shop in the village directed Peter's inquiries about the Blakelys to Urizon, and when Laura opened the front door to see him, wiping off his glasses, tucking in his shirt, fumbling through a speech about his research and his theory of her family, she knew that she would welcome him into her existence, that together they'd one day welcome a child.

THE AFTERNOON BEFORE her death, Laura had a headache. She lay down for half an hour in the library, shutting the blinds. Laura knew from her reading that early pregnancy was rife with headaches and nausea, swollen breasts. She thought herself twelve weeks along. In two days, she had a trip planned to the city for her first prenatal visit.

Of course it was too early to say, but Laura thought it was a girl. A little girl baby, fie on Peter's fears, the silly rumors. She would give all of herself to the child regardless. She did not fear a stretched stomach, sagging breasts, as she once might have. She did not fear her own end, now that this newness had begun.

Peter would like an egg salad with his tea. She'd slice the crusts from the bread, use extra spice, as he preferred it. She would bring him his sandwich with a wink, a little smile, tell him *Now you must interpret, here's your clue*. Laura imagined a fully formed child the size of a blueberry, wheedling for attention, sending a request for love up from the depths of her belly to her brain. Beaming, she shrugged off the headache.

To the kitchen, where the eggs had cooled, the teakettle whistled, where, through the thin-paned glass, she watched a robin make a meal of an earthworm, the oak leaves shiver with excitement, the tabby kitten mew.

Next, to the garden at the edge of the wood, to gather fresh parsley and dill.

Bending over, her knees sinking into the soil, Laura felt her vision double, then go dark. A deep pain, like forked lighting, pressed up through her pelvis. She felt a wetness at the back of her skirt, and took a long, deep breath, took a fistful of dirt. Were the trees moving, coming closer? When her sight returned, the edge of the wood seemed to waver, the trees stretching arms and gnarly fingers to grasp at her dress, their leaves whispering, *Finally*. Laura stood, unsteady, trying to remember the list of early symptoms she'd been told to expect. Maybe a bit of blood, but certainly not this much. She stumbled, herbs falling from her hand.

No! she thought. *I'm finally happy. Finally strong.* The wood rustled its agreement. It wanted its daughters to be happy. It had waited so long.

The forest seemed an open pair of arms, offering protection, offering to save the unborn child who even now she could feel being forced from her womb. Tears in her eyes, Laura accepted its embrace.

Strength comes from strength, Laura thought as she walked toward the tree line, her thighs slick with blood, offering her open palms.

THERE PETER FOUND her, at the edge of the wood. A lone root, wiry and thin, had curled into her abdomen, piercing her navel, and was ever so slowly pulling her closer to the boundary between estate and trees. Laura was smiling, not struggling, though Peter swore he'd heard her scream only moments before, a cry of pain that had sent him running from his office. He looked on a moment, frightened, and then grabbed his wife before the wood could take her, pulling her free of the forest, detaching her from the hungry vine. When he lifted her, a mass of black blood left an outline of her torso in the soil, frightening him further still. He couldn't know that the forest had already taken a part of his unborn daughter—had splintered off a piece of the girl's consciousness, and in the splitting left her with the curse of half life and half death. That, in doing so, the forest had saved her.

Peter cradled Laura, calling for help. He hoisted her onto his shoulders and into the house, bursting across the terrace, fumbling for the telephone once inside. Yet even then, he knew he was too late.

Too late in one sense, the forest understood. In another sense, all had been perfectly timed.

31

It is one thing to summon strength when in the company of others, quite another to maintain it alone. As soon as I passed under the bent tree, my body begged me not to continue: the air sucked out of me, each step forward warning *Death, you walk to death.* The forest itself was no consolation: rather than closing off the path behind me, the arched tree taunted me with a view of Marlowe and Alys framed beneath it when I paused, turned to look back. I decided that I would not look back.

I walked a long aisle, rows of trees on either side, until I reached the opening of what seemed to be a cave. Dark, deep, descending far under a hill of knotted roots and fallen branches. Teeming with a blackness that sucked up all sound, so that to enter would be to lose myself to the utmost. *Death.* I forced myself forward.

At first I thought that I had passed into the body of the forest, to its bloodstream. That somehow I had found my way into a woodland womb.

Peter had promised me that no one else remembered the time spent inside their mother either, those months of incubation, pulsing and warm. In those early days, we were all budding cells. So small, so nebulous, so utterly dependent, unscarred and unprepared for the bright, waiting world. I'd always thought myself disadvantaged to have had no such protection. I'd imagined others still carried the effects of their gestation, subconsciously attuned to what it meant to be alive in a way that I would never understand. I'd pitied myself. Was this what it was like to move through a living body?

Looking around, I was reminded of the images I'd seen in Peter's books, great churches with intricately tiled walls, swirling patterns of mosaic made in reverence to heaven. Perhaps I was, despite appearance, climbing up this twisting maze to some sort of empyrean. For a moment, I was consoled. Then, as the pathway steepened, as the walls around me narrowed and the little light there'd been began to fade, I saw the skulls arranged to make a doorframe. They were cavern-eyed and jawless—to pass under their gateway was to let them eat me whole. I turned back to examine the decorations I'd thought fungus and realized that they, too, were bones, stacked together like firewood, making up the walls of the tunnel, the blunted ends their only visible parts. Suddenly light-headed, I bent down with my hands on top of my knees to try to take in a good breath. I imagined the air in here to be rife with spirits, felt I'd sucked them all inside me.

These bowels of the forest were damp and dark, and gave off a fertile stink much like the scent that I'd noticed on the women at Urizon. The only light shone weak ahead of me, filtering through in divots, dappled as if breaking in through trees. The floor was made up of a sticky mud that sucked at the bottoms of my feet.

After several minutes of tromping, I came across a barrier made of smaller bones—little nibs of hands or feet—hanging as a beaded curtain might separate rooms of a house. From somewhere beyond came the overwhelming churning sound of the sea, the sort of noise heard listening to a seashell. I grimaced and pushed through the curtain, pretending I could not feel bones tickling my skin.

I arrived in a vast and echoing cavern, lit by a pale purple light. Its ceilings were patterned in bone, abstract, almost floral, each small piece of the body utilized with sweet precision and positioned in a keen and lovely way. A dais stood in the center, bone as well, I gathered. Six steps made of bones led to an osseous stage fused smooth. On it was a massive pile of wood and cartilage, a throne with arms of gnarled branches, bones braided through. It was flanked by great antlers.

And at the foot of the platform sat Matthew, cross-legged, his head bent in concentration, his brow furrowed and tight. He was fiddling with something in front of him, a puzzle-like contraption, propping it up and then letting out a frustrated huff when it collapsed. He did not respond to my arrival. Relieved, I went to him eager for our reunion, ready to demonstrate my newfound camaraderie with the trees, proud as a dog showing off a new trick. I'd almost reached him when a figure stepped out of the shadows, blocking my path. My shadowed double. Her eyes were whiteless dark.

Until she stood in front of me, I had not quite believed in her. Despite the many marvels I had witnessed, despite my own visions, Lucy's explanation, Alys's warning, despite telling myself, *Yes, I understand, I am prepared*, the sinking queerness in my stomach made it clear that I hadn't, I wasn't.

To look at her in front of me was like seeing Urizon shifted off of its foundation by ravenous trees, my father with flowers for eyes, my blood pooling onto the floor of Rafe's prison. All my life she had been waiting, growing stronger, of me and not me, given form and feeling by the urges I'd repressed. Each breath the doctors fed me through a plastic tube aroused her. Each blade of grass I twirled between my fingers lent a charge to the defibrillator that would start her heart. Each animal I encountered with Coulton, each creature I commanded, pushed her forward, gave her strength. This girl was my own black-eyed shadow, manifestation of my darkness, taking everything I wanted but denied myself, growing bold as I grew ruthless, sustained by each life that I touched. Her hair was richer than mine, shinier and thicker. Her skin was brighter, her figure more fit. It was as if she had absorbed all my vitality, as if I, not she, was the shadow. I was afraid to speak, had no idea what I could tell her, but when I looked again at Matthew, I knew I must say something.

There was a vacancy in his expression that I had never seen before. His eyes held none of their usual thoughtfulness. His hands made the same motions, again and again, though it was clear that such action would not work. He still had not acknowledged me. He scared me.

"Let Matthew go." I planted my voice low in my chest, hoping to sound older, more sure of myself. It came out as a croak. "Let him go and set him right. What have you done to him?"

My other self looked at me, her head cocked, mouth dancing to a grin.

"What have *I* done?" Her voice was velvety and rich. "You gave him to me, or don't you remember?"

"I what?"

"When you touched him. You gave all of them to me."

She was menacing in her stillness, as calm as Coulton, as sleek as a young fox. I felt lanky and awkward beside her. My skin itched. I scowled. As she spoke, she moved closer, shielding Matthew from my view.

"They are ours, really, both yours and mine," she said. "The gifts you gave them were a gift you gave yourself. But you already know this."

I shook my head, feigning denial. But I did know this. I did.

There was always, warned Peter, a price. Sometimes immediate, sometimes so long in its collection that we debtors might believe ourselves exempt. A princess promises her unconceived child to the fairy that frees her. A druidess curses a stolen tract of land. A little girl revives her father. And yet . . .

"You don't *own* him," I insisted. As I spoke, I considered my own trajectory, from my father to Matthew, to Coulton and Rafe. Even under their influence, I'd still been myself. "Even if you kill and bring him back, Matthew doesn't just *belong* to you."

"Yet here he is," the black-eyed girl said simply.

"Then where are the others?" I asked in frustration. "All of the other bodies, other lives?"

My black-eyed shadow smiled and pointed to the left side of her chest, raised her arms up to the ceiling and spun a slow circle. The implication, then, they were here, with us—Mr. Abbott's terrier a tinkling chandelier, Rafe a Corinthian column . . .

My shadow walked to where Matthew sat and placed a hand on his head. She licked her lips with a bloodless gray tongue, examining him as though he were a sort of barnyard pet, one she might raise and love and care for, and then eat without a second thought once suppertime arrived.

"I keep this one here because he is our favorite." My shadow stroked Matthew's temple. I felt the urge to lunge, push her hand off him, but held myself back.

"Then when he solves that puzzle, he can leave you?" I asked. I had in mind several old stories, other heroes given seemingly impossible tasks. There might be a trick to the game, the whole thing might be a riddle, and if we merely shifted angles, strategy would become clear.

My shadow laughed. "How silly," she said to me. "How quaint."

I walked over to Matthew and knelt down so I could see his puzzle's pieces, determine what they were and how they might remain erect. It was difficult to get a good look, as Matthew's hands moved fast about them, but when I finally did, I saw that they were merely little twigs, dried out and dirtied with stubborn bits of soil. There was no innate order to follow, no way to intuit their end goal. Still, Matthew's fingers were raw from them, from struggling, repetition. The tips of his fingernails were black.

"What are the rules, then?" I asked of my shadow. "What is it that he has to do?"

She smiled, ran her finger along the curve of Matthew's ear. "That he *has* to do?" she said to me. "Why, nothing." I saw in her my own attempted coyness, magnified and cruel. My throat tightened.

"Then what's the point? Why do you have him sit here? What does he think that he's doing?"

My black-eyed shadow stepped away from Matthew, cocked her head. Her chin jutted out, and she looked at me, eyes searching, in an attempt to understand. Did she not know me? Just as she seemed strange to me, did I to her? Were my true feelings, desires, incomprehensible? I knew more of the world than she possibly could, and I thought that my experience might give me some advantage in setting Matthew free. I could trap her, trick her, beat her at her own game. Perhaps all that I loved was not yet lost.

My shadow sighed, and the expression on her face became not wondering but weary, full of all I knew but could not bring myself to speak. And I knew she had seen to the core of me. She was me. She loved me. I knew what she'd say next before she spoke.

"Life is not some riddle to be solved. The things that matter most cannot be won, cannot be tricked. They won't be studied, never fully understood. There are no *rules* to things, you realize."

"Except they told me . . . Lucy, Alys . . . they explained . . ."

"You think because you name it and you tell it, it *becomes*? A story is a present, tied with ribbon and a wish. Real things aren't so easy. Choices not so black and white."

"You mean to say I cannot stop you?"

"Stop me?" Her black eyes were indecipherable. "Why ever would you want to stop me?"

"Because you hurt them, when you took over the wood. You hurt everything. They told me so, the women at the house."

"The house is gone."

"And so the wood will claim the village? The city? The world?" I struggled to make sense of what was happening, unable to fully comprehend the dissolution of the life that I had known. She spoke against my education, my faith in logic, in reason, in order. "You mean to say that we are bound by nothing? Breached by nothing?"

"Perhaps," said my shadow. I grasped at my last thread of hope.

"And my mother?"

"Gone." There was to be no reunion, no farewell. My mother was not waiting for me, chastened by belief, in any afterlife.

"My father?" Though the answer was clear, I had to ask the question.

"Gone."

I felt very tired.

"If you let Matthew go," I said softly to my shadow, "you can have me."

I imagined Matthew running, just ahead of the widening forest, ever eluding its grasp by a few steps. Perhaps when he reached the sea he might escape it. Perhaps he never could. Still, whatever happened seemed preferable to capture in this cave of death, his mind gone, fingers bleeding. I'd at least have given him a chance.

"You can have me," I whispered again. But you cannot give yourself to yourself, not as bargaining chip, not in sacrifice.

My black-eyed shadow smiled. "You've been taught," she said, "not to take what you want. Taught to ask. To be deferent. To bargain.

"Come," she said, "embrace me."

I wanted nothing more.

I closed my eyes, I went to her, forgetting Matthew, Peter, my journey, my fear. I put my arms around her, and hers came tight around me, and together we tangled and twined. I dove into her darkness as if she were water, inhaled her scent, felt the pressure of her breasts. I readied myself for oblivion, waited for death.

32

A breeze passed over me. I shivered. When I opened my eyes, I was clutching myself, my own hands crossed around my chest. The light was different, richer, more direct. What had been bones were only trees, and trees I recognized. That oak was carved with villagers' initials. That poplar had split years ago, its branches struck by lightning. The air was cool as it had been before I'd entered the strange forest. The sun was just cresting the canopy of trees.

I turned to look for Matthew, and found him standing beside me.

"Why, hello," he said.

I sat down in the clearing and cried.

My tears were thick and heavy, hot and salted. They splashed against my wrist, down onto the grass below, dry grass, littered with crinkling autumn leaves. I rubbed a blade between my fingers. I reached out to touch a thorn. Nothing changed.

What world was this, I wondered, that looked so like the one I'd known as real, yet proved itself so foreign? My tears came faster, wetter. When Matthew came to me, I could not stop my bawling. I reached down and picked up a leaf, papery and yellow. As I held it, it remained stagnant in form.

Matthew understood at once. He smiled, his own eyes bright with tears. He sat down beside me and held out his hand. I grasped it and squeezed.

WE LEFT THE wood, Matthew and I, carefully, together. Where Urizon had been, we found only two broken brick pillars, what had served as the entrance to the Blakely estate. No sign of Lucy, Imogen, or Mary. No naked newborn. Nothing of Alys or Marlowe. Nothing of Peter. The barricades of branches were gone from the main road, and a car rushed past at great speed, clouding us with its exhaust. I coughed, lifting my left arm to block it. My bandage was blood-soaked and dirty, but for a bit of white at my elbow, and I tugged, hoping to match the clean spot to the sorest part of my wound, however pointless it might be.

"Here," said Matthew, holding out his hands. I gave him my arm, and leaned against a pillar while he undid the bandage, gasping at the feeling of his fingers on my skin. Just a calloused thumb upon my dirty elbow. Such a small physical softness. So simple, so unremarkable. To me, it was everything.

Once the bandage was unraveled, Matthew wiped the dirt and dried blood from my arm. I cried, but not in pain: under the residue, we found my wound healed. In place of the raw muscle was a shining square scar, each side the length and width of two closed fingers.

Matthew raised my arm up tenderly, and kissed it.

When he was done, I looked him in the eyes and kissed his lips.

To Be Whole Again

The world works in circles. Stories repeat. There comes a tightening, a release; a gathering in, an exhalation. A ripening—wheat lengthening, wool thickening, a woman's body growing heavy—then a reaping.

Without its shadow, the forest feels the profound calm of abundance relieved: shorn fields, quiet skies, all set right and clean as a child's first breath. The daylilies return to the meadows. An elder tree stands tall, the rings on its bark forming two even eyeglass circles, a knot like a pair of lips ready to speak. Somewhere in the soil lies a shinbone. Somewhere in the forest hides a book.

Passersby wonder at the wildness of the landscape, when the trees will be cleared to make co-ops, the dirt roads turned to highway, the ore claimed from the earth. The locals shake their heads and smile.

And in the village of Coeurs Crossing a woman eases her old bones into a rocking chair: *Once there was a curious little girl, born from death with marvelous powers.* Children gather around her, listen rapt. Outside, a wood grows wild.

Acknowledgments

Thank you to the many wonderful people who helped bring this book into the world:

Stephanie Delman, agent extraordinaire, whose faith in this novel is unparalleled. Erin Wicks, the hardest worker I know, who poured heart and soul into every aspect of this project. All the folks at Harper and Sanford J. Greenburger Associates, who offered wisdom and support along the way.

Daniel Camponovo, Howard Simmons, Todd Summar, and Ken Gerleve, whose early feedback guided me. Brian Zimmerman, who convinced me that Maisie needed her own novel and then stuck with us. Sophie Brochu, whose late-night texts, editorial eye, and willingness to meet for pancakes at all hours have been vital to my writing process.

Jason Kalajainen, Mitch Kohl, and the rest of the team at the Luminarts Cultural Foundation and the Union League Club of Chicago Library.

My CCC mentors, Audrey Niffenegger, Joe Meno, Sam Park, and Nami Mun, for their wisdom and patience and care with my work.

Dick and Denise Berdelle, for love, support, and last-minute baby-sitting. Nora, Chrissy, Tom, and Pat—the best cheerleaders.

Phil and Barbara Fine, who taught me to love language. My brothers, Aaron and David, who show up every time. My parents, Michael and Susan Fine—all of my successes are due to your love and support.

To Rick, my rock, and Elliott, who grew alongside this book. I love you dearly.